A shot whistled through the air. Kendra and Ethan hunkered low for cover.

"Anyone else you know who might be shooting at you?" Ethan asked.

"Could be anyone," she said.

"You can play innocent with me, but I don't think the marines are gonna be as warm and fuzzy."

"If you think you're warm and fuzzy," she said, yanking the car's back door handle, "then you're pretty clueless."

"We have to move. Shooter is going to change locations to get a better bead now that we're pinned down."

Kendra lugged Titus's dog carrier out, and Ethan reached in to help. Another shot pinged the metal car roof, sending off sparks.

Dana Mentink
and
Maggie K. Black

Call of Bravery

Previously published as *Top Secret Target* and *Standing Fast*

Enjoy!
Dana
Mentink

LOVE INSPIRED
INSPIRATIONAL ROMANCE

LOVE INSPIRED®

INSPIRATIONAL ROMANCE

Recycling programs for this product may not exist in your area.

ISBN-13: 978-1-335-53298-5

Call of Bravery

Copyright © 2020 by Harlequin Books S.A.

Top Secret Target
First published in 2018. This edition published in 2020.
Copyright © 2018 by Harlequin Books S.A.

Standing Fast
First published in 2018. This edition published in 2020.
Copyright © 2018 by Harlequin Books S.A.

Special thanks and acknowledgment are given to Dana Mentink and Maggie K. Black for their contributions to the Military K-9 Unit miniseries.

This edition published by arrangement with Harlequin Books S.A.

For questions and comments about the quality of this book, please contact us at CustomerService@Harlequin.com.

Love Inspired
22 Adelaide St. West, 40th Floor
Toronto, Ontario M5H 4E3, Canada
www.Harlequin.com

Printed in U.S.A.

CONTENTS

Dana Mentink is a national bestselling author. She has been honored to win two Carol Awards, a HOLT Medallion and an RT Reviewers' Choice Best Book Award. She's authored more than thirty novels to date for Love Inspired Suspense and Harlequin Heartwarming. Dana loves feedback from her readers. Contact her at danamentink.com.

Visit the Author Profile page
at Harlequin.com for more titles.

TOP SECRET TARGET

Dana Mentink

There is therefore now no condemnation to them
which are in Christ Jesus, who walk
not after the flesh, but after the Spirit.
—*Romans* 8:1

To the men and women who serve bravely
and selflessly, and to the families left behind
who do the same.

ONE

First Lieutenant Ethan Webb of the Air Force Military Police brushed past the startled aide standing in Colonel Masters's outer office at Baylor Marine Corps Base.

"The colonel is—"

"Waiting for me," Ethan snapped. "I know." Lieutenant Colonel Terence Masters, Ethan's former father-in-law, was always a step ahead of him, it seemed. Ethan and Jillian's divorce had cemented the bad feelings. He led Titus, his German shorthaired pointer, into the office, found Masters seated in his leather chair behind the gleaming wood desk. Mahogany, he'd been told, nineteenth century. Hard lines, unyielding contours and pretentious, like the man who owned it.

"You're late," Masters said. "And I don't want your dog in here."

"With respect, sir, the dog goes where I go and I don't appreciate you pressuring my commanding officer to get me to do this harebrained job during my leave. I said I would consider it, didn't I?"

Masters gave him a smug smile. "A little extra insurance to help you make up your mind, Webb."

Ethan glared. "It's a bad idea, like I said before. Leave me alone to do my investigation with the team at Canyon, and we'll catch Sullivan." They were working around the clock to put away the serial killer who was targeting his air force brothers and sisters as well as a few select others, including Ethan's ex-wife, marine naval aviator Lieutenant Jillian Masters. Boyd Sullivan was a killer with a flair for the dramatic, leaving a red rose as his grisly calling card, along with a note. "I'm coming for you." He had earned his nickname, the Red Rose Killer.

"*Your* team," Masters said with a nasty inflection on the first word, "hasn't gotten the job done and this lunatic has threatened my daughter. There have been sightings near our base indicating he's zeroing in on her. You're going to work for me privately, protect Jillian from Sullivan, draw him out and catch him, as we've discussed. We're playing offense here, rather than defense. It's a Marines thing, son. Maybe you airmen can't understand, but we like to face our enemies head-on." He steepled his fingers on the desktop.

Ethan fought to keep the anger from balling his hands into fists. Masters loved his games. Now he held the stick and Ethan was the bear about to be poked. "So you think I'm going to pretend to be married to Jillian again and that's going to put us in the perfect position to catch Sullivan? A couple of sitting ducks waiting to be shot?"

Masters stared at him. "You're going to prevent that, remember?"

He shoved a hand through his crew cut hair, striving for control. "This is lunacy. I can't believe you're willing to use your daughter as bait."

"I'm not," he said. "I've decided it's too risky for Jillian and that's why I hired this girl. This is Kendra Bell." He gestured to someone in the doorway.

The civilian woman stepped into the office and Ethan could only stare at her. That creamy skin, that curtain of red hair skimming her face… Shock ripped through him like rifle fire.

"You're…" He shook himself slightly and tried again. "I mean… You look like…"

"Your ex-wife," she finished. "I know. That's the point."

He swallowed hard and peered closer and the truth assembled itself as the surprise ebbed away. They did resemble each other, this woman and Jillian—same build, same eye color, same tint of hair.

She shot a distrustful look at Titus, and raised an eyebrow in Ethan's direction. "If you're finished staring…?"

He gulped. His mama would have boxed his ears to know he'd been ogling, but honestly, the resemblance was mind-blowing. Heat climbed up his neck.

"People used to mistake us for each other in high school," she said. "Sullivan's going to make the same error, and that's how I'll catch him, without your interference."

"My *interference*?"

She ignored him, turning to Masters. "You neglected to tell me, when I agreed to the job, about this scheme to involve Lieutenant Webb."

"I sent you a follow-up email," Masters said.

"Uh-huh." She folded her arms across her body. "Anything else you failed to mention, Colonel?"

Ethan tore his gaze away and locked eyes with Masters. "This wasn't part of the plan I heard, either."

"Yes, it was. I just didn't tell either one of you all of the pertinent facts."

Ethan blew out a breath and shook his head. "No way. Working with Jillian would be bad enough, but at least she's a marine, not a civilian, and she knows how to protect herself."

"So can I," Kendra said. "I'm a licensed PI, with a real gun and everything."

He cast her a doubtful look and started to answer, but Masters cut him off. "You will pretend to be newly reconciled husband and wife."

"No one will believe that," Ethan said.

"Yes, they will. I've already started the gossip wheels turning here and at Canyon that you two are an item. Posted an old picture of you two on a few key military networking sites."

Ethan gaped. "You…"

"And when Sullivan comes for Kendra thinking she is my daughter, you will catch him before any harm comes to Jillian."

"And what about the harm that might come to her?" Ethan snapped, jerking a thumb in the civilian's direction.

Kendra glared at him. "Don't talk about me like I'm not here. Like I said, I can take care of myself. Before I was a PI I worked as a bounty hunter, and there's plenty of excitement in that job, let me tell you. I don't need, or want, your help on this case."

His cheeks went hot again. "That's A-OK by me, because I'm not offering it. We're not working together. I'm out of here." He stalked to the door, his dog at his heels.

"Lieutenant," Masters bellowed. "You will not walk out on me."

Ethan turned and fired a glance at Masters. "I'm not one of your marines, Colonel, nor am I your son-in-law anymore, so with all due respect to your rank…" He let the slam of the door fill in the rest.

Kendra felt the crackle of energy leave the room along with Ethan Webb and his dog. She had recognized him from the file Colonel Masters had sent, but in person he was more impressive. The guy could be on a recruiting poster. Dark hair, eyes like coffee with a hint of cream, six feet of muscle and barely concealed annoyance, and a Southern drawl that thickened in proportion with his anger. His arrival had thrown her off her game. Time to get the meeting back under control.

Calm, cool and collected, she told herself. *Nothing you can't handle.* But it was hard to brush off the unsettling scene she'd just been part of, and more important, the text message she'd gotten that morning just before she'd dumped her cell and gotten herself a new number.

You're dead.

No further explanation needed. Andy, her ex-boyfriend, recently released from prison, where she'd sent him, had wasted no time starting up the threats. She'd escaped his sick world, but not for long.

Deal with that issue later, Kendra, she told herself. Sullivan was her target, and Ethan's abrupt departure was an advantage. Now she had the chance to try to persuade the colonel that she did not need any help catching the Red Rose Killer before he murdered anyone else in this part of Texas. Temporarily leaving her tiny office in Colorado, the place she'd fled after her disastrous time in Texas with Andy, the job was an answer to her prayer, the only way she could both settle her debt to Jillian Masters. She would complete the mission much easier without a second party in the picture, especially Jillian's ex.

She expected the colonel to be furious at Ethan's disrespect, but to her great surprise, he chuckled, leaning back in his chair.

"Hasn't changed a bit. He'll cool off and come around."

"How do you figure?"

"He's one of those Southern gentlemen types. Don't let his lazy Tennessee drawl fool you. He's smart as a fox and he's proud and hotheaded, but he can't walk away from a lady in distress."

"I'm not in distress."

"Not yet." The colonel smiled—a cold, calculating smile—like a tiger sizing up its prey. Her stomach tensed. She did not need another ruthlessly determined man in her life, but she had the feeling she'd just been saddled with two of them.

Ethan headed to the parking lot with Titus. He yanked open the truck door for the dog and got in himself, clenching the steering wheel, wondering how he'd lost control of his life. There was absolutely no reason he should be doing the bidding of his devious former father-in-law, and now to find out he'd be partnered with a civilian of all things. Why had he accepted the request that bordered on a command? Ethan was a member of the Air Force Military Police, not property of the Marine Corps.

Masters's previous words echoed in his mind. *Jillian needs you.*

That was rich. His ex-wife didn't need him and never had. Sure, she was under threat from serial killer Boyd Sullivan along with a list of others who'd crossed him, but the investigative team Ethan was a part of would catch him. Besides, Jillian was a woman who could take care of herself—ruthless, determined and entirely self-absorbed. She'd been offered protection after Sullivan killed two K-9 handlers at Canyon Air Force Base, including Ethan's best friend, Airman Landon Martelli. He'd also murdered Chief Master Sergeant Clint Lockwood in the same killing spree. She'd declined the protection in spite of the risks. No surprise there.

Sullivan's not smart enough to hurt me, she'd said. Typical.

Yet all of a sudden Jillian had just gone along with her father hiring a look-alike as bait? Insane. He slammed a hand on the steering wheel. Titus regarded him from the passenger seat, head cocked, ears flopping as if to say, "What's going on?"

In the six years they'd trained, lived and served together, including their last deployment to Afghanistan, Titus could read Ethan better than any other living creature. And now that they shared a living space, the bond had grown stronger. Sullivan's break-in at Canyon Air Force Base had had other disastrous results besides the deaths of human personnel. Sullivan had let loose nearly two hundred dogs from the Military Working Dogs training center. Twenty-eight of them had yet to be found.

Ethan had been given special permission to keep Titus with him instead of at the kennel until the repairs could be done and security assured.

That was fine by Ethan, as he was cross-training Titus as a cadaver detection dog in addition to his patrol duties. The more time they spent together the better. Plus, military dogs were more than just animals, they were partners. And he had to be sure his partner was protected. Titus had his back and Ethan returned the favor.

"I've gotta talk this nutty lady out of standing in for Jillian before she gets herself killed," he muttered.

Titus flapped his ears and settled back into the seat.

Preparing his most convincing argument for Kendra, he waited for her to exit the office. He was surprised when she stepped out lugging some sort of small animal carrier. He started to exit the vehicle to talk to her, but she loaded the carrier and slid behind the wheel of her car so quickly he didn't have the chance. As she drove by, he caught her profile, her long red hair now captured in a tight twist at the nape of a graceful neck, a spray of freckles across the nose. His stomach dropped. So like Jillian. Anger choked him, and hurt speared through him as sharp as it had been the day he'd finally understood how his wife had betrayed him, repeatedly, and he'd been nothing but gullible and blind to it. What a sap. Dense as his aunt Millie's fruitcake.

"Let it go," he commanded himself. "You've been divorced for three years. She's not your problem anymore." He decided that with his current state of mind it was best not to head back to Canyon until he got his anger under control and then sorted out how to get Kendra Bell out of the picture.

He pulled out of the parking lot and took the back road off the Marine base, bathed in shadows from the trees that broke up the buttery June sunlight. Unseasonably hot, people were saying, which made him laugh. After returning from Afghanistan, where the temps could top 115 degrees before noon, he'd never complain about the Texas heat again.

Titus seemed to feel the same, stretched out to catch the sunshine, enjoying the moments free from enemy sniper fire and the constant tension born of living in a war zone. Titus was a top-notch patrol dog, sniffing out hidden insurgents and intruders at checkpoints, and he was taking easily to his new training in cadaver detection. The animal's incredible abilities never ceased to boggle Ethan's mind. God knew what He was doing when he made dogs.

The miles rolled by along with his thoughts until he was surprised to catch up to Kendra as she headed into a curvy, wooded section of road. A slow and careful driver, unlike the woman she resembled. The bumper of her car disappeared around a turn and gunfire ripped through the air, followed by the sound of breaking glass. Adrenaline exploded through his body as he floored the accelerator, stopping just in time to see Kendra's vehicle skid off the road and down the slope. He pulled the truck behind a pile of rocks and dialed both 911 and Masters's direct line. Titus went rigid, ears erect, nose twitching, waiting for a signal from

Ethan. Messages delivered, there was no more time
to spare. Kendra might be badly injured.

Clipping on Titus's lead, he unlocked the box from
under his seat and slipped the handgun in his belt.
Slamming the door, he sprinted toward the edge where
her car had gone over, praying the sniper's bullets had
not found their target.

Was Sullivan making his move already? Kendra
fought the bucking steering wheel after the last shot
had taken out the front tire. Then again, she had another enemy hot on her trail. She didn't know that
Andy was a good enough shot to take out a tire, but
he was skilled at many other means of inflicting pain.
Whether it was Sullivan or Andy didn't really matter
at the moment. She battled for control of her vehicle,
but there was no time. The car bumped and jolted,
skidding sideways toward the trees. "Hold on, Baby,"
she shouted to the elderly cat tucked in his back seat
carrier. Her words were lost in the jolt of the chassis
as it smacked against the rocky ground. Thick tree
trunks flashed past the windows as the car flew down
the slope, gravity overwhelming the brakes. The front
fender slammed into a pile of rocks so hard it snapped
her neck back and drove the breath out of her. For several seconds all she could do was cling to the steering
wheel, wondering why the airbag hadn't deployed.

"Baby?" she finally croaked. "Are you okay?"

With a painful effort, she unbuckled her seat belt,
grabbed her Glock and turned to peer over the head-
rest into the back seat. Her heart pounded at what she
might find in the cat carrier.

Please, God, don't let Baby be dead. I know I don't

deserve to ask You for anything, not one thing, but I'm asking anyway. The silence from the rear of the car galvanized her into action.

Shoving an elbow at the door, she forced it open, tumbling to her knees on the rocky ground. Pain in her ribs made her gasp but she pulled herself up and grabbed the rear door handle.

The crunch of footsteps made her draw back.

Sullivan or Andy?

Andy's last voice mail message echoed in her ears. *When I finally catch up to you, I am going to enjoy killing you slowly.*

She gritted her teeth. If he was going to kill her today, she'd make sure it would be the hardest thing he'd ever done.

The sounds drew nearer. Her mind sought options. Flag someone down? Ethan had been behind her for a while, she'd noticed, but she'd lost sight of him a few miles back. Incredibly, she heard no traffic at all on this back road out of the Baylor Marine Corps Base. She reached for her cell phone when she heard a whispered voice.

"Kendra?"

The voice didn't belong to Andy, that was certain. This voice was a low baritone, complete with a Tennessee drawl. Ethan. She let out a slow breath.

"I'm coming over to you," he continued, "so don't do anything crazy like shoot me."

She kept silent, gripping the Glock and training the gun toward the direction of the shots. Ethan rounded the corner with a dog at his side. The pointer immediately stiffened, ears erect.

"I don't like dogs," she snapped.

"That's okay. He probably doesn't like you, either. Cops and marines should be on their way."

"What are you doing here?" She shot a look at the animal still in alert position. A patrol or scout dog, she suspected.

He quirked an eyebrow. "Maybe we can do the pleasantries later? After the cavalry arrives?"

She would have retorted, but a shot whistled through the air and they hunkered low for cover.

"Sullivan doesn't usually do his dirty work in public," he said over his shoulder, peering in the direction of the shooter. "Anyone else you know who might shooting at you?"

"Could be anyone," she said, earning another exasperated look.

"You can play innocent with me, but I don't think the marines are gonna be as warm and fuzzy."

"If you think you're warm and fuzzy," she said, yanking the back door handle, "then you're pretty clueless."

He put out a hand to stop her. "Leave it. We have to move. Shooter is going to change locations to get a better bead now that we're pinned down."

She ignored him, pulling harder on the door, which opened with a reluctant groan.

He grabbed her forearm. "Didn't you hear me?"

"Hearing and listening are two different things."

A shot drilled the rear window, sending glass rocketing in all directions. They both ducked.

"You're really stubborn," he said, but she was already lugging the animal carrier out of the car, and he reached in to help.

Another shot pinged the metal car roof, sending off sparks.

"Come on," he said, taking her arm and propelling her toward the shrubbery.

It was all she could do to hold on to the carrier.

"I thought MPs were supposed to stand their ground," she huffed.

"We do, but this isn't my ground and I happen to be saddled with an irrational civilian."

So much for warm and fuzzy.

He pushed her ahead of him, and he and the dog took up position right behind her as another volley of shots bored into the tree just above their heads.

TWO

Ethan put as many sturdy tree trunks between them and the shooter as he could. His mind churned faster than his feet. Had Sullivan finally snapped and changed his tactics to include daylight ambushes? It was possible. Sullivan wasn't much of a shot, he happened to know, and this gunman was all over the place. Two more bullets whistled by, the last a wild one that lost itself in the tree branches. Sirens were converging from all directions. The marines would be responding, and the local police. With that many guns and that much adrenaline pumping, he figured their safest option was to stay still, very still. He put Titus into a sit.

"Stay put," he told the woman. "Marines are here."

The Jillian look-alike stood with her back to a tree, her arms curled around the animal carrier. Now that he got a close look without a couple of feet between them, he could see that her mouth was fuller than Jillian's, the hair more auburn than copper, the spray of freckles more subtle, but still…uncanny.

"Still staring?" she demanded.

He flushed. "How do you know Jillian?"

A flash of emotion crossed her face, indicating

that whatever her connection was to Jillian, it was a strong one. Then the expression disappeared and she shrugged. "Friends."

His instincts went berserk, as if he was inches from stepping into a trip wire, but he had to know. "You're a pretty good friend to paint a target on your back."

She flashed a smile this time as she pointed to several armed marines scurrying down the slope, geared up for battle. "I think that conversation is going to have to wait."

She was right. The marines were in no mood for chatting. Once they ascertained that Kendra and Ethan were not the bad guys, they searched the area until the police arrived, finding no sign of the shooter.

One marine approached them. "Hey, Airman. Heard you slammed the door on Colonel Masters an hour ago."

Ethan grinned at the marine police captain, friends from the time their deployments overlapped. "News travels fast, Hector."

MP Marine Captain Hector Sanchez squashed his smile and regarded the woman next to him intently. "Your name, ma'am?"

"Kendra. I had a meeting on base with Lieutenant Colonel Terence Masters."

He raised an eyebrow. "Pertaining to?"

"Ask him, if you want to know."

"Due respect, ma'am, but we're not in the mood for coy around here."

Ethan wasn't, either. He was in the mood for a little rest and recuperation before he threw himself back into the Red Rose Killer investigation. Now that he was working for Masters, the situation was changing from bad to atrocious. The good news was Kendra would have to come to her senses now and tell Masters she was quitting.

Hector greeted the arriving police officer and they launched into an intense conversation. The US Marines did not like having to relinquish any authority to the local cops, but the shooting was not technically on base property. The cop, whose name tag read Alonso Carpenter, drew Ethan and Kendra aside. He was a tall man, almost as tall as Ethan, with a narrow chin and skin tanned from the sun.

"We need to have a talk back at the station with you both, to document all the details," he said.

"It this really necessary?" Kendra's arms were still wrapped around the carrier as if she was holding on to a life preserver. "I'm sure Colonel Masters—"

"Masters," Carpenter said, with a certain something in his voice, "is not the boss on this side of the fence."

Ethan caught the grin on Hector's face. He realized he was sporting the same smug smile on his own. Masters always got what he wanted one way or another by whatever means necessary. It was nice to know the local police did not jump when he snapped his fingers.

He wanted nothing more than to head back to his apartment at Canyon Air Force Base and forget the whole nutty plan, but perhaps Masters's scheme would actually draw Boyd out. It was possible the shooting had been Sullivan's work. But something still didn't feel right. Sullivan was not the type to take shots from the bushes. His killings were up close and personal. Ethan's stomach tensed thinking of how Sullivan had snuffed out the life of his friend Landon Martelli. Landon hadn't even had a chance to defend himself.

If it wasn't Sullivan, then who else might want Kendra dead and why? He shook away the thought. *Not your problem, Webb.* He wasn't going to work with Kendra Bell only to see her become another victim of Sullivan's, and he intended to force her to see reality one way or another. The best thing for her would be to get away from this part of Texas, and especially from Masters.

Kendra walked by him and slid into a waiting police car. She did not flash him a glance, just bent her head and cooed to the bony white cat she'd removed from the carrier.

He could see that her profile wasn't exactly a match for Jillian's; her nose was smaller, the cheeks softer and there was more delicacy about this woman than his ex-wife. Her hair looked soft, as if it would be silky under his fingertips.

He brought those thoughts sharply to heel, calling to Titus, who had been nosing along at the tufts of grass. A moment later the cat caught sight of Titus and mewed in fright.

Startled, Titus barked loud enough to make Ethan's ears ring. The cat erupted from Kendra's arms and streaked away into the woods.

"Baby," Kendra screamed, leaping from the car. She fired an angry look at Ethan. "Can't you control your brute of a dog?" she said before she ran away in search of the cat.

"What?" he said dumbly to her back.

"She said, 'Can't you control your brute of a dog?'" Officer Carpenter said and Ethan detected a look of enjoyment in the man's eyes.

Ethan huffed out a breath and shot a glare at Titus.

The dog blinked and looked away as if to say, "Sorry, but it was a cat, after all." Then he noticed the officer was heading into the shrubbery.

"Aren't you taking her to the station?" Ethan called.

Carpenter chuckled. "Son, I've been married twice and I'd like to think I've learned a thing or two. I think I can safely say that Ms. Bell isn't going anywhere without that cat."

"Does that mean I can go and you'll call me when you're ready to talk to me?"

Carpenter raised an eyebrow. "No, that means you and Wonder Dog are going to comb every inch of this property until you locate the cat, Airman." He turned his back and left Ethan and Titus standing there.

Ethan turned to his dog. "This is your fault, you know."

Titus licked Ethan's hand.

"Don't try to act all cute now. Get into those bushes and find the cat you just bullied."

Titus put his nose to the ground and got to work.

Kendra's cheek was scratched from a low-lying branch and her feet were aching since she was wearing ballet flats instead of hiking boots. It didn't hold a candle to the pain inside her. Baby was gone. The sun was low in the sky and there was still no sign of the old cat.

The cop had trudged back to the car after she'd promised to follow in five more minutes. With each second her breathing grew more panicky, sweat making her palms clammy. Ethan and Titus continued to prowl through the bushes, but even the dog could not seem to catch a scent of Baby.

Ethan clumped out of the bushes, wiping sweat from his brow, and faced her. "Uh, I'm sorry your cat ran away," he said, not exactly looking her in the eye.

She rounded on him. "She didn't run away. Your dog scared her."

Now he turned eyes the color of melted chocolate in her direction. "Look, I'm really sorry, okay? I'll keep searching, or maybe I can get you another cat."

"Another cat?" she snapped, fury taking her breath away. "And if Titus there got lost, you'd just give up on him and get another dog?"

"No way, but Titus is a dog. I mean, uh, what I meant was, you know, cats can take care of themselves."

She stared at him, tears pricking her eyes. "For your information, Baby can't. She's sixteen and she's in poor health. She's been the only one…" She swallowed hard. There was no way she was going to unload all of her big fat messed-up life at the feet of this insensitive blockhead. "Never mind." She stalked past him, but he grasped her arm, his fingers strong but gentle.

"Hey, wait. I'm sorry. I was being a jerk. I've only been back a couple of months and I think I'm rusty at some things. I know the cat means a lot to you." His gaze was soft, or maybe it was a trick of the failing sunlight. Either way, she couldn't answer over the thick lump in her throat.

"I…" He sighed and shook his head, letting her go. "I lost a dog before Titus to a grenade. It hurts, no matter how you lose them. I, um, I'll keep looking. Give me your cell phone number and I'll text you if… I mean, when I find her, okay?"

Still unsure of her powers of speech, Kendra managed to give Ethan her cell number and programmed his into her phone.

"Ms. Bell?" Officer Carpenter called. "It's time to go."

She raised her chin and blinked hard, fighting for composure as she allowed the cop to usher her into his car.

Sitting next to the empty carrier, she was overwhelmed by the thoughts that she'd been blotting out the last few hours. Someone—maybe Andy, maybe the Red Rose Killer, maybe none of the above—had tried to kill her. That was not a new experience for a private investigator and a former bounty hunter, but this person had gotten very close to getting the job done. Muscles deep in her belly began to quiver.

And now Baby, the only creature in the world whom she loved and who loved her back, was gone, lost in the woods, an old cat, easy prey. She squeezed her hands together to stop the shaking.

You'll find her, she told herself savagely. *Right after the police interview you'll come back and you'll find her.* Baby had chosen somewhere to hide, that was all.

Lord, she prayed, *bring Baby back and help us both find a place like that.*

As they drove through the shadows, her newfound faith was not enough to screen out the memory of the bullets fracturing the windshield, boring into the trees.

She was just like the cat. Easy prey.

THREE

After hours of fruitless searching Ethan made it back to Canyon Air Force Base. He'd done his best, but there was simply no sign of the cat. Titus was ready for a cold drink of water and some grub and so was he. Maybe in the morning…

As he unloaded Titus from the truck, they both caught the sound of whimpering coming from the bushes in his front yard. Titus dashed toward the foliage, tail wagging. Ethan followed, getting down on his knees as the soft cries turned into full-blown yips.

Titus was nose to nose with a gangly puppy, a Malinois with pointy ears and a dark muzzle. The ears were erect and the tongue was out, busily bathing Titus.

"Hey, fella," Ethan said. "How did you get here?" He was close enough now to see that the puppy was wearing a filthy training center collar.

Ethan's throat constricted. It was one of the animals that had been let loose by Boyd Sullivan when he killed the two K-9 trainers and left his signature red rose calling card. With Titus's encouragement, he coaxed the dog to come out. It didn't take much, as the poor critter was clearly weak and terrified. The pup was skinny, his ribs protruding. He smelled of garbage, which was where he'd probably been scrounging for food to stay alive for so long. Ethan noted a long gash in the dog's side. His anger at Sullivan kindled fresh and hot. How could a guy who'd once wanted to become a K-9 trainer let hundreds of dogs loose to be injured or worse? But Sullivan's twisted sense of revenge didn't stop there. He'd killed a commissary cook a few miles from base, and some of those in his basic training flight group had received roses and threats... including Jillian.

Ethan poured some water from a bottle into his cupped palm and the dog lapped at it eagerly while Titus gave him a thorough sniffing. Wrapping the pup in his jacket, Ethan ignored the growling in his stomach and loaded both dogs into the truck.

In twenty minutes he was pulling up to the K-9 training center. He'd called Master Sergeant Westley James and his new wife, base photographer Staff Sergeant Felicity James, on the way. At the entrance to the training yard, Westley waited, a head taller than the petite Felicity, his face grave.

"Another one found," Felicity said, cooing to the puppy. "He's skin and bones. I'll get him to the clinic."

Westley shook his head. "If I could just get a lead on Sullivan..."

"You and everyone else," Ethan said. "We're all hoping to be the one that brings him down."

"And his accomplice," Felicity added. "He isn't doing all these things without help."

Someone was helping Sullivan certainly, but the list of suspects shifted constantly, and the team assembled to track down the killer was growing more and more frustrated.

Trainer Rusty Morton rushed over, tossing the rag he'd been using on the ground. "Oh, man. Is that Rocket? I heard he'd been sighted on and off in the woods and raiding garbage cans. I left out food and water where they said they'd spotted him." He leaned over to stroke the dog's ears tenderly. "I didn't think I'd ever see you again, buddy."

Puzzlement played across Felicity's face as she handed the dog into Rusty's arms. "Hang on to him for a minute while I alert the vet, okay?"

Ethan shared her uncertainty. Rusty was on the list of Sullivan's potential accomplices, under scrutiny from the investigation team as he'd been a friend of Boyd Sullivan's during their basic training days.

But Ethan saw tears shining in the guy's eyes. They weren't fake, he was certain. That contradicted Ethan's earlier suspicions. He made a note to mention it to the investigative team leader Captain Blackwood. Surely a guy who loved dogs as much as Rusty wouldn't have helped Sullivan let the animals loose, would he?

Ethan thought about his friend Landon. Man, he missed talking to him about anything and everything.

"You okay?" Felicity asked.

"Yeah." He shrugged. "Just thinking about Martelli."

"We miss him, too," she said quietly.

Ethan's phone rang and he moved away to answer it, Titus roaming the enclosed yard.

"Heard you got into some trouble near Baylor, Lieutenant," Justin Blackwood said. He was a captain in the Security Forces and a veteran of two tours of duty in Afghanistan, which gave him stellar credentials in Ethan's book, the perfect guy to be the leader of the team trying to hunt down Boyd Sullivan. "Was the shooting Sullivan's work?"

"Uncertain, sir. Doesn't seem like his MO." Ethan felt the tension crackling through the phone.

"I wouldn't rule it out completely. Sullivan was spotted near Baylor Marine Corps Base hours prior to your shooting incident."

Ethan's pulse ticked up a notch as Blackwood continued.

"A marine has been killed off base, his uniform and ID are gone."

Ethan's stomach dropped at the news of another murder. And now Sullivan had access to the base and Kendra. Perhaps the shooting really was a case of mistaken identity?

"We've got our hands full on this case," Blackwood said. "I know you'd rather be doing anything other than working with Jillian and Masters, but maybe you can find that lead we're all looking for."

"I'll do what I can, sir," he said.

"Fair enough. Keep me posted."

"Yes, sir," Ethan said, disconnecting.

His eyes landed on Rusty as he cooed to the pup, who looked half-starved in the training center lights. Immediately he thought about Kendra cradling the pet carrier, tears glistening in her eyes, knowing her cat was lost like Rocket had been.

Your fault, Ethan.

On impulse, he sent her a text.

Did you find your cat?

Should he add something like another apology? An "I hope so" or something to soften it?

"I'm glad to have Rocket returned," Westley said. "But there are still plenty of dogs on the loose as well as a serial killer." He looped a protective arm around Felicity's shoulders.

A text materialized on Ethan's cell phone screen.

No.

He imagined Kendra's lip caught between her teeth, a sheen of moisture in those brown eyes, the same brown as the glossy acorns that festooned the trees on his mother's property back home.

She's been the only one... Kendra had said of Baby, and he thought he had an inkling about the rest. The only one to understand, to listen to the painful things that could not be spoken to human listeners, the only one who did not judge, did not condemn. He got it. Titus had heard more about Ethan's life story than anyone, except for the One who'd seen him through it.

He nodded to Felicity and Westley. "Okay. Thanks for taking care of Rocket. I've got to get on the road."

"Where to?" Felicity asked him.

"Back to Baylor."

She quirked a look at him. "That's a three-hour drive. Didn't you just get back from there?"

"Yeah," he said, with a weary sigh. *But I've got to go find a cat.*

Kendra had finally returned to Jillian's rented home just outside base property somewhere after 7:00 p.m. It would be a short break to wolf down a granola bar and rehydrate. Then five minutes to change clothes and grab her pack and then she would search again for Baby. It was only another hour until sunset. Her stomach churned into nausea.

"Hang on, sweetie. I'm coming to get you."

A knock at the door startled her. She pulled the curtain aside a crack. Ethan Webb stood on the doorstep, arms crossed, expression stony.

What now? She had no time for another row with him. She yanked the door open, staring him down. "Come to apologize?"

He quirked a brow. "For what?"

"Disrespecting me in front of my boss. Scaring my cat."

"Disrespecting..." He rubbed a hand over his tanned face. "Whatever. We just have one piece of business left and then I'm hoping you'll see reason and quit this job."

She shook her head.

"You can't trust Masters," he said. "Get away from him as quick as you can. This situation is only going to get you hurt or killed."

"Thanks for your concern, but you didn't have to drive over here to tell me that. I've known Jillian for fifteen years so I'm well aware that her father is a manipulative man with no ethics."

He gaped. "Then why would you work for him?"

Because I owe his daughter my life. She shrugged. "Not your business, but thanks for dropping by."

"So you're still going to persist in acting as a decoy for Sullivan?"

"Yes."

His lips thinned, his nostrils flared and he started

to speak, stopped, then started again, folding his arms across his broad chest.

Amused, she folded her arms to mirror his. "Cat got your tongue?"

"Wait here," he snapped.

She was about to respond when he stalked to his car. Titus sat in the passenger seat, ears alert, snout poking through the open window. He reached into the back and returned with a blanket, pushing the bundle into her arms.

Her heart stopped at the sight of Baby, mewing plaintively. She could not hold back the tears that filled her eyes as she snuggled the cat under her chin. "You found her."

He shrugged. "Cost me a couple hours of searching and a million mosquito bites, but yeah. Baby's back. Titus was not thrilled about sharing his vehicle with a cat, but he's grounded so he doesn't get to complain about it."

She laughed. "Thank you, Lieutenant."

"You can call me Ethan," he said. "I guess we'll be stuck in this idiotic mission together if you won't listen to reason." With a sigh, he started to walk away.

"Wait." She put a hand on his shoulder, muscles hard under her touch, and he turned back halfway. "I'm sorry for my rudeness. I really do appreciate what you did, more than I can put into words. Baby is...so much more than just a cat to me."

She thought his cheeks might have pinked a bit, but she could not tell for certain. He blew out a breath and he turned to face her fully.

"I'm serious here. I know we got snarled up in the beginning, but Masters is trouble and so is his daughter. Neither of them cares who gets hurt, so long as they get what they want. You are expendable and so am I, do you get that?"

If she wasn't mistaken, she thought she saw a deep-down pain shimmer in his eyes before he cleared his throat. She nodded. "I understand."

His gaze lingered, poring over her face from under a thick fringe of lashes. "Okay, well, it's late," he said. "We can work out the nuts and bolts tomorrow. Call if you need…you know…anything."

He hesitated.

"Something else you wanted to say?" she said.

He held up his palms. "Now don't get a burr under your saddle about it, but did you check the house? Make sure the doors and windows are secure?"

She grimaced, wishing she could have answered yes. "Um, actually, I was in such a hurry to go searching for Baby, I didn't. I'm sure Jillian checked before she left." *Some PI you are, Kendra.*

"Want me to…?"

"No," she said firmly. "I can handle it, thank you."

"All right, then." He walked the few steps to his truck, where he leaned against the front fender. "Just wave at me when you get it done and I'll scoot."

"You always this pushy?"

"I'm as calm as clam shells on most days, but when there's a serial killer roaming around, I get a little testy."

Though his posture was relaxed, long legs stretched out, boots crossed at the ankles, she had a feeling he would stay there until she reported that the house was secure. Period.

"I'll just be a minute." Blowing out a breath she

made a quick check of the tiny front room and the kitchen, depositing Baby on the linoleum with a bowl of water and some kitty kibble. It warmed her insides to see Baby chowing down with gusto. She felt a deep surge of gratitude toward Ethan that, for the moment, outweighed her frustration with him.

Kendra moved onto a small bedroom being used as a study. The area was sparse, minimally decorated, as was in keeping with Jillian's unsentimental personality. Jillian hadn't said exactly where she was staying while Kendra lived at her place, only that she'd keep in touch by phone. Jillian was not touchy-feely about friendships, either. When Kendra paid back the debt she owed Jillian for saving her life that long-ago summer day when she'd helped her escape from Andy, she suspected there would be no further connection between them.

Kendra hastened to the back of the house to check the master bedroom. She reached out a hand to push open the door and something large and soft fell from above. A paper sack split as it hit the floor and suddenly the room was alive with enraged wasps streaming out of a fragment of wasp nest.

In her panic, Kendra stumbled and fell backward, screaming as the stinging insects swarmed over her.

FOUR

Ethan slammed through the front door at the first scream. He was down the hall and unexpectedly battling his way through angry wasps that thickened as he reached the bedroom. Kendra was on her hands and knees, crawling toward the threshold, insects enveloping her, trying to get her feet underneath her to escape. He caught hold of her arm and hauled her out of the room, slamming the door, which confined most of the vicious creatures. The remaining few continued to sting both of them, jabbing repeatedly. He killed as many as he could while they stumbled to the kitchen. Closing the swinging door, he grabbed the nearest weapon, a pot holder. With a startled mew, Baby scuttled under the nearest chair while he swatted the wasps that hovered over Kendra, trying not to hurt her.

Tears of pain streamed down her cheeks and red welts began to appear here and there along her arms.

"I think I got them," he said. He scanned feverishly until he realized there were more wasps tangled in her red hair.

"Quit wiggling," he commanded.

She twitched and flailed. "You try it sometime."

Commandeering her into a chair, he shooed the insects from the silky mass and squashed them.

Ethan and Kendra sat still, listening for more.

She breathed hard. "Somebody—" she swallowed "—somebody put the nest there, above the door."

Somebody? He filled a plastic bag with ice from the tiny freezer and gave it to her. "Hold this to the stings on your face. It was only some of the colony in that bag, fortunately. Looks like only half a dozen stings."

He filled another and grasped her forearm as gently as he could. He applied the cold to the worst of the welts. "Are you allergic to insect bites?"

"Guess we're about to find out," she said, a wry twist on her lips.

He grinned back. The lady had gumption. He'd known grown men so scared of wasps they ran at the first sight of one. "So who's the 'someone'?"

She looked at the floor. "What do you mean?"

"You know what I mean, so don't play clueless. This isn't the Red Rose Killer. This is personal, very personal, intended to shake you up, but probably not to kill you outright. So who's the someone who wants to torture you?"

Her swollen eyes weighed and measured him, like he had weighed and measured so many of the people he'd interrogated as a military cop. To trust, or not? It wouldn't surprise him if she decided not to, in light of their contentious relations to date. Her gaze shifted to Baby, who was lying flat on the linoleum, tracking a stray wasp that traversed the kitchen. He could read the emotions flickering across her face. He'd saved her cat, a creature who obviously meant everything to her. Decision made.

Kendra let out a breath that came out as a sigh. "My former boyfriend," she said. "Andy Bleakman."

He waited, silent, sensing there was more coming.

"He did prison time because of me."

"Why?"

Her cheeks blushed crimson to match her red welts. "I don't want to go into it now."

"No better time."

She yanked her arm from his grasp. "I've just been a wasp pin cushion and the bedroom is still full of angry insects, so I contend there is a better time. As a matter of fact, any time would be better than this time."

He liked the fire in her voice, the way she lifted that delicate chin and stared him down. It made his pulse kick up one notch.

Back off, Ethan. No more hotheaded women for you, especially one who is the spitting image of Jillian. He cleared his throat. "Just give me the critical points then. What was Andy in prison for?"

A beat of hesitation told him her trust only went so far. "Armed robbery."

"And he blames you."

"Yes. Jillian helped me get away from him, so now revenge on me is his mission in life."

Jillian helped? He considered that. Throughout their marriage Jillian had been busily helping herself, chasing after every adrenaline-fueled thrill she could get her hands on, but she also had a desperate need to be the hero. He could imagine her riding to the rescue of her helpless friend…and then discarding her like a used dishrag when she'd finished. Mouth open, he was just about to tell Kendra so, when it dawned on him that she looked plumb worn-out.

He went to the truck and let Titus into the backyard, filling a bowl of water for him and another with kibble. Returning to the kitchen, he palmed his phone.

"Who are you calling?"

"Pest control to come and retrieve your wasp nest." Ear to the phone, he strode to the refrigerator and opened it.

"Looking for something?" she said, brows quirked.

He poked around inside. "It'll do."

"Do for what?"

"Dinner. I'm hungry."

She gaped. "Are you expecting me to cook you dinner?"

"No, ma'am," he said. "I'm gonna do the cooking while you go wash your face and make sure you got all the wasps out of your clothes." He pointed to a door. "Laundry room?"

"Yes."

"There are no wasps in there and you probably have extra clothes there already."

She pursed her lips. "So…you can cook, Lieutenant?"

"Call me Ethan, and I happen to be an excellent cook thanks to my mama, who won so many blue ribbons at the fair I lost count." He gestured to the laundry room. "Get a move on."

"Are military cops always so bossy?"

"Only the good ones. Go. Pest control is on the way." He pulled the eggs from the fridge and began to prowl for a frying pan. Before she left, he'd located a spatula and brandished it like bayonet. "I'm armed and dangerous."

She smiled, as he'd hoped she would. "Okay. Be right back."

"Kendra?"

"Yes?"

"You said you're Andy's mission in life. What exactly does that mean?"

She rubbed at a welt on her cheek, eyes gone dark. "He's going to make sure that I suffer before he kills me." Shoulders bowed, she left.

So the man with a mission to hurt Kendra knew where she lived, and how to get into her house. Was he also the one who'd taken shots at her vehicle? Or could it be that Boyd Sullivan was changing things up, trying out new ways to torture his victims before he killed them?

The case was turning into a many-headed monster.

Monsters didn't scare Ethan one bit. There was no enemy that he and Titus couldn't put down.

Whistling, he set to work on the eggs.

She wouldn't admit it, but Kendra was thrilled to strip off her clothes and change into clean jeans and a T-shirt. The welts on her arms were red and angry, but they did not seem to be affecting her breathing. Her face was probably a mess, so she was grateful there wasn't a mirror in the laundry room. Part of her tensed at the thought of Ethan Webb clanging pots and pans in her kitchen. The last thing she wanted was a partner—a handsome, pushy, military partner with whom she'd already shared way more than she wanted to. The other part of her recalled the image of him dragging her away from the wasps with no concern for himself.

The minute she returned to the kitchen, Ethan gestured her into a chair and slid a plate with a perfectly golden wedge in front of her.

"Wow. That looks great."

"It is. Frittata without mushrooms 'cuz you didn't have any." His brash tone made her smile. "You should keep mushrooms on hand. Very versatile."

"I'll make a note of it. I only just arrived here last night, so I didn't have time for much shopping."

He sat across from her and to her surprise, he took her hand to give thanks.

"Lord, thanks for giving us this good food and another day to enjoy it."

After the "amen" he grinned. "Sorry. I shoulda asked if you wanted to say it."

"Is that your subtle way of asking if I'm a believer?"

"Are you?"

"Yes. A new one, I'm afraid."

He laughed. "Doesn't matter if you're new or got some miles behind you. Truth is truth, no matter when you arrive at it."

"Texas wisdom?"

He grimaced in mock affront. "Tennessee, ma'am. We got lots of wisdom there, way more than here in Texas."

She dug into the fritatta, redolent with red peppers and onions. "You really are a good cook."

"Yes, ma'am, I am," he said.

"And humble, too."

"Upon occasion."

Kendra laughed. A soft knock sounded on the

kitchen door and she was surprised to find a small woman, late thirties maybe, standing on the porch, her long brown hair caught in a ponytail. She held out a plastic bag of cherries. Her blue eyes were wide with alarm as she got a look at Kendra.

"Are you… I mean, are you okay, Jillian? Your face…is a little swollen."

Kendra snapped herself back into the role she should have been playing all along, thankful for her swollen face. "Oh, yes, I'm okay." She put a finger to her cheek. "I got tangled up with some wasps." She turned to Ethan. "Ethan, this is Mindy Zeppler, my next-door neighbor."

"We've only had a chance to say hi in passing," Mindy said. "You're so busy, Jillian."

Another blessing, Kendra realized. Jillian and Mindy hadn't spent time together, which made her more likely to accept Kendra as Jillian.

"I, uh, I heard you and Ethan were divorced. It's nice to see you still get along so well."

In one swift movement, Ethan stepped close to Kendra and looped an arm around her. "Reconciled, ma'am. We're both thrilled to be together again." He pressed a kiss to the temple free of stings and her blood raced right up to her face. "Can't believe we wasted so much time," he said as he leaned in closer, his breath warm on her neck.

Kendra's body prickled all over and chills raced up her spine. What was he doing?

Mindy smiled at Ethan. "Your dog is beautiful. Patrol dog?"

"And soon to be cadaver detector," he said proudly.

Mindy's mouth dropped open.

Titus's new skill was a real conversation stopper, Kendra realized.

"I was just bringing by some cherries. Nice to meet you, Ethan. I work for a real estate business in town. I can ask them about a good pest control guy." She shivered. "Wasps are the worst. They just keep stinging until they're dead."

Or their victim is, Kendra thought with a shudder. "We'll take care of it." She was not certain how much to tell Mindy, but in her experience as a private investigator, the less information she let spill the better. "Thanks, though, for bringing the cherries."

"Would you care for some frittata, ma'am?" Ethan was acting the perfect Southern gentleman.

Mindy waved a hand. "Oh, no, thank you, I just came to deliver a message with the cherries."

"A message?" Kendra felt an inexplicable chill.

"Yes, a man called me yesterday." She frowned. "I'm not sure how he got my number, now that I think about it. He said he was an old friend of yours and he was trying to find you."

"Did he leave his name?"

"No. I figured you were US Marine buddies."

"What made you think that, ma'am?" Ethan's voice as level and low, but intense.

"Well…" Mindy said, her mouth crimped as she thought about it. "I'm not sure. He was polite, like you, though no accent. Maybe I just imagined the marine thing because I know you're a pilot," she said to Kendra.

"Ma'am, would you happen to have that number on your phone?" Ethan asked her.

She shook her head. "It said, 'Unknown Caller.' I deleted it. I'm sorry. Is it important?"

Ethan shrugged. "It's okay."

"What was the message?" Kendra asked.

"He said to tell you he was looking forward to seeing you again soon and he was going to bring you some roses. I thought it was sweet."

Roses.

Sullivan.

Looking forward to seeing you again.

Soon.

FIVE

Kendra waited until Mindy was safely gone and pest control had cleaned up the nest before she drummed up the courage to face Ethan.

"Ethan, this isn't going to work."

"What isn't?" he said as he fastened a harness on Titus.

"This…pretend marriage thing."

He stopped and looked at her. "Oh. Did I freak you out?"

Was there a challenge in his voice? "No, you didn't. It's just that, I mean, it might be hard to convince people."

"Not for me. I'm—"

She rolled her eyes. "Let me guess, a great actor? In addition to being a good cook and a top-notch MP?"

His smile was warm and honey-sweet. "I was gonna say I'm not too proud to play the part of a love-struck fella if it will bag us Sullivan. Besides, you smell nice."

She blinked. "What?"

"You smell nice, like cinnamon or something. I noticed when I kissed you." He finished clasping on Titus's harness.

"You…you shouldn't be kissing me at all," she snapped out. *And I shouldn't be liking it!*

That got his attention. "You don't think we'd be kissing if we're gonna get remarried?"

"We're not going to get remarried, or date, or anything like that." Her face was now scarlet, she had no doubt.

He got to his feet. "All right, ma'am." He led Titus to the door, moving closer to her in order to edge around the chairs. "Have it your way, but for the record, you do smell nice."

Leaving her gaping, he led Titus outside. Thoughts zinging, she followed. *Be professional, Kendra. If he can focus on the job, so can you.* Obviously the kiss hadn't meant a thing to Ethan other than giving him a chance to sniff her, just like Titus. Maybe there was truth to the saying that men were dogs.

Ethan did a walk around the outside of the house. It gave her a small measure of comfort to be doing something, even as trivial as securing the yard. The knowledge that Sullivan was closing in sent her skin prickling. Or was it Andy? She didn't understand why Sullivan would have gone to the trouble to plant a wasp nest in her house, but it made perfect sense for Andy to have done so. She had calls in to check if he had reported for his mandated appointment with his parole officer in northern Texas. If he hadn't, then he might very well have come hunting for her. The air took on a sudden chill.

The ground around the outside of Jillian's small house gave up nothing of interest, no footprints, not so much as a blade of grass out of place. The only sign of an intruder was the bedroom window. Scratch marks and chipped paint indicated where the intruder had used a pry bar to force the old lock and gain entry. It must have been awkward, breaking and entering and transporting a wasp nest.

Titus paced around in Ethan's wake.

"Why is your dog whining?"

"He's a little off his game. Used to being kenneled at night, so now that he isn't, he has to be in close proximity to me when the sun goes down or he gets nervous."

"So you're a six-foot security blankie for your dog?"

"Six foot four."

She laughed. "You're a big baby, Titus."

The dog gave her a pitiful glance.

"That look usually results in people giving him ear rubs, if I allow it."

Kendra just shook her head. "Told you I'm not susceptible to canine manipulation."

"Just feline wiles?"

"Baby is too old to be sneaky. How exactly does this dog function in war conditions?"

"That's different. We sleep in the same cot when we're deployed."

The animal had to be seventy pounds, all legs and chest, wedged brown head and speckled all over with flecks of caramel that matched Ethan's eyes. "One cot for the two of you? Crowded much?"

"Nah, unless he's trying to hog the blanket."

Chuckling, she decided not to admit that Baby slept curled at the foot of her bed every night. Ethan's gaze went to the jimmied bedroom window and her humor vanished. Back to grim reality. Someone had been in her borrowed house. Someone who wanted to torture her.

Again her thoughts turned to Andy. Could he have violated his parole already? Somehow found her? He would have known from the trial of Jillian's involvement, perhaps figured Kendra would seek out her old friend. Andy was smart and as focused as a heat-seeking missile.

"Best to loop in the cops," Ethan said.

"I think it's better not to involve them at this point. They're looking into the shooting, that's enough. We don't need to bring them in for a bunch of wasps."

"I say you're wrong. If it's the Andy guy, cops can track him."

"If it's not," she countered, "too much cop involvement will scare away Sullivan."

He didn't answer and she knew she'd touched the right chord. He wanted Sullivan badly, and he wouldn't do anything to jeopardize the capture, even if it meant cozying up to a woman playing the part of his ex-wife.

Do your PI thing. Show him you're working through it, too. "This was elaborate, a lot of work for Andy, if it was him. How was it done?"

"Got to go at a wasp nest at night, when the insects are inactive. There's one hole at the bottom so you don't shine any lights or touch the nest in any way. Raise up a netted bag or something, with a cinch noose around the top, trap everything inside, knock the nest loose. Whoever it was botched the thing. Probably dropped it and retrieved only a small piece of it."

"Good thing for me," Kendra said with a shiver. "If it had to happen at night, it must have been harvested pretty recently or the wasps would be dead."

"Yes, ma'am."

"Probably from somewhere close by."

"Yes, ma'am."

"A lot of work just to freak me out."

"Yes, ma'am."

"Do you have anything else to contribute?"

"No, ma'am."

She huffed. "Will you *please* call me Kendra? If I promise not to tell anyone about your cowardly dog?"

He cocked his head. "I will consider it."

"It'll have to do."

He eyed the small outbuilding crowding one corner of the yard. "Okay to bunk there?"

She started. "What?"

"I should be on the property."

To be her personal bodyguard? "I could have handled the shooter and the wasps myself. I don't need you to—"

He cut her off with a look. "We're supposed to be reconciling, remember? So unless you want me to bunk inside the house…"

She went completely speechless, picturing the tiny home and him sprawled out on the sofa, long limbs draped over the ends, and her skin prickled all over again. It aggravated her that he appeared completely nonchalant, calmly discussing their fake marriage while she had a herd of elephants thundering around in her stomach. How could she send him packing without compromising the case? She realized the silence had gone on too long.

"Right. Of course. Yes."

He strode over to the little mother-in-law unit, Titus right at his heels. Pushing open the door, she peered over his shoulder at a minuscule kitchen that opened onto a cramped bedroom and living room. Ethan had to duck his head to enter. She stood on the doorstep as Titus pushed past her.

"It's kind of small," she said.

"Plenty bigger than a barrack's cot, and I'm not sharing it with a bunch of sweaty guys, so that's a plus."

She realized she was standing close, so close her shoulder grazed his arm. She edged away. "Do you need... I mean, stuff?" Why was her mouth going on without any consultation with her brain? "Uh, clothes and a toothbrush? I think there's a store close by."

He did not seem to notice her babbling.

"Got gear in my truck."

Of course he did. Her aggravation peaked. "Is that right? So you were planning to stay this whole time, even before you asked me? Isn't that a little presumptuous?"

He didn't exactly smile, but his lips quirked. "Always carry a pack, ma'am," he said. "Never know where you're going to be billeted. Guy's gotta have his creature comforts."

Mortified, her pulse pounding, she figured there was no possible way she could embarrass herself any further. Escape was the only answer. "Great. I guess you're all set then."

"One thing, though. Mind if I get myself some water and maybe a PB and J? I saw creamy peanut butter in the pantry. Not as good as crunchy, but I can make do. I'm tough that way."

"Still hungry?"

"Always hungry, ma'am. Mama says I was born

famished and it seems the condition has stuck." His caramel eyes were soft, sparkling with humor and sincerity. Ethan Webb was confounding, a mixture of cocky and kind, altruistic and chauvinistic, frivolous and ferocious, as if he would fit right on the screen of an old Western one moment and a military thriller the next. It was a heady mix. In short, Ethan Webb made her nervous.

"Help yourself," she managed.

"Okay. I'll fix my sandwich, then you can lock up behind me."

Titus sneaked around Ethan, and in one long jump he was settled in the bed, eyeing his partner as if to say, "I'm tired. Isn't it bedtime yet?"

"You better tell your dog it's not quite time for lights out."

"I could tell him," Ethan said, shaking his head at his hopeful companion, "but I don't think he's gonna believe me."

Ethan slept as he always did, like the proverbial log. He awoke at his customary 0500, ready for a sunrise run with Titus, the scent of cinnamon floating through his memory. He really had unsettled her and the thought made him smile for some reason.

A couple of miles would both allow him to stretch out his legs and familiarize himself with the neighborhood. He and Jillian had lived in a roomy apartment closer to Canyon when they'd been married. Somehow it made him feel better that Kendra wasn't staying in a house where he and Jillian had lived together, battled each other, and where his marriage had exploded into great big messy shrapnel.

The house was still dark and he didn't figure most civilian women would be up until sunrise. He set off on his run, Titus at his heels, past Mindy Zeppler's house just as the sky was shifting from black to gray. He was comforted to know there was a good deal of brush-filled space between her property and Jillian's rental, which meant she would not see Ethan coming and going from the mother-in-law unit. It'd be tough to explain that one.

The street was tree-lined and wide in the way of older developments, and the fresh morning air took him back to his boyhood in Tennessee. Long lazy summers when he and his brother, Luke, sneaked out to go fishing without waking his parents. He could practically taste the squashed sandwiches they'd thrown in their packs, which they'd wash down with warm water. The friendly competition between them led to good-natured wrestling and occasionally a few half-hearted punches. Man, how he missed his brother. Landon Martelli, the K-9 trainer at Canyon, had been the closest he'd ever come to someone besides Luke. He quickened his pace, feet pounding over the pavement.

Gonna get you justice, Landon. Gonna bring down Boyd Sullivan.

A car pulled up next to him.

"Did your dog sleep well?" Kendra wore a baseball cap, her hair peeking out from under it.

He stopped so quickly that Titus thunked into his shin and let out a bark of displeasure before he turned his nose toward the stopped car.

"What are you doing out by yourself?" Ethan snapped.

"I took a cab to the all-night rental car place and got

myself a loaner. Then I worked out at the gym before I did some internet business at the cafe."

So much for his theory that she'd been asleep. A bonehead move and a dangerous one, in his opinion. "That is not a good idea," he managed. "Going out on your own under the present circumstances."

She waved him off. "I was in public places the whole time."

"At this hour, how many people are around? Besides, it doesn't matter." He lowered his voice and forced a smile as a lone jogger neared. Keeping the smile plastered in place, he bent to her window. "Someone is trying to kill you and they're not missing by much." The man jogged closer. "Honey," he added.

"Well, darling," she said as she gave him a saccharine smile, "I have a job to do and you're not my boss, so don't talk to me like one."

"I wasn't," he said, waving at the runner who offered a friendly nod as he went past.

"Yes, you were." She was still smiling. "But I brought you some breakfast, pumpkin. A nice muffin."

Pumpkin? Glowering, he snatched the bag from her fingertips. "Thank you."

"No problem, pumpkin. See you back at the house."

She left him there on the sidewalk, holding the bag, grumbling to his dog.

"Pumpkin?" Was that payback for the kiss?

Titus flapped his ears.

Suddenly he did not feel quite so much like he had the upper hand anymore. "This situation is getting a mite tangled."

Titus sniffed the bag, swiped a tongue around his lips and turned back toward home.

Ethan walked behind, cooling down physically and mentally on the way back. In the kitchen, he found Kendra scribbling on a notepad, a phone pressed to her ear. A pot of coffee steamed on the counter. She waved to him to help himself while she finished her call. He was through his first cup of coffee and half the muffin when she disconnected.

"The dead marine—the one Sullivan killed. I was just getting some backstory on that. The man was assigned to the mess hall, custodial duty mostly. His uniform and ID were taken, of course."

She was suddenly all business. Okay, he would take his cue from her tone. "Sullivan's in the area, no doubt about it. Close. Could be your former boyfriend is, too. He made his last parole appointment, but that was Tuesday morning. Could have made it here in time to wrestle up the wasp nest."

She stared at him. "You've been investigating?"

"Affirmative. Need to know which threats are coming from where."

"We are working on catching Sullivan. Andy is my problem."

He put down his coffee cup. "Until the threats against you end, it's our problem."

Pink flushed her cheeks. "There is no 'our.' Andy is a separate investigation, mine only. When it comes to him, we're just…sharing air space."

He laughed, and slapped a hand on the table. "Good one."

"I wasn't trying to be funny."

He shook his head. She was so different than his ex wife, in spite of the resemblance. "Sorry, you have these really cute facial expressions when you're irate, but like it or not, we're partners until Sullivan is brought down and any baggage you bring to the case is relevant to that end."

"Baggage?" She stood suddenly, giving him her back and staring out the window.

He rubbed a hand across his brow and pushed away from the table. "I shouldn't have said that. You got a painful past with this guy, and I didn't mean to be callous about it." He reached out, her shoulder delicate to the touch. "Insert dumb foot into fat mouth."

She didn't react for a moment and he was about to take his hand away when she finally spoke.

"I deserved what I got with Andy," she murmured.

There was a river of anguish in that last statement. "You made mistakes."

"Big ones. Drinking too much, pills. Anything to make him—" She stopped.

Love me, Ethan finished silently. He knew what that was like, turning yourself into something you weren't in order to be loved. He could write a book on the subject. "You survived," he said softly, kneading her delicate shoulder. "You learned."

"God saved me from Andy by bringing Jillian into the picture at just the right moment. To this day it surprises me that I even sent her that text. She'd called me the day before to tell me she was in the area visiting a cousin and could we meet up. I blew her off. To be honest, I was ashamed for her to see me the way I was. I was so different in prep school when we were roomies." She sighed. "Fast-forward to age twenty-two and I'm up to my ears in alcohol and an abusive relationship. I didn't want anyone to see me like that, but when I finally figured out what Andy planned to do…"

"Hold up the convenience store?"

She turned and his hands fell away. Something like betrayal flickered through her eyes. "I forgot. You're a military cop. You already know all about my past, don't you? Why am I going on about it?"

"I know some of the facts, not the reasons behind them."

"What does that matter? I did terrible things and Jillian saved me from myself. That night, the night of the holdup, I called her and she came and got me while he was away, bundled up my stuff and drove me out of town. Andy went through with his plans anyway, got caught and he went to prison. I… I started going to church after that. But now I'm in deeper trouble than I ever was. Paying the price, I guess. I earned that."

"No condemnation, not anymore. God's forgiven you, if you've asked Him to."

She turned those eyes to him, warm and damp with suppressed tears. Then she looked down as if ashamed, but he crooked his finger under her chin and gently eased it up. "The past is in the rearview. It brought you where you are, but you can't drive if you're too busy looking backward."

A tiny sliver of a smile quirked the corner of her lips, his reward.

After a moment, she nodded and stepped away.

He found he wanted to do more, to show her with an embrace that he understood, that he could relate. There'd been plenty of shipwrecks in his own life, his marriage to Jillian being the worst. He prayed he would forget about her, but to date, he had not prayed he could forgive her. Maybe he never would.

So free with spiritual advice, aren't you, Ethan? his

conscience taunted. *Not lookin' at the mess with Jillian in your own rearview mirror?*

His phone buzzed with a reminder. "I have to go back to Canyon today to meet with the team about Sullivan."

"I'll stay here and keep digging."

"Uh-uh. You should be with me. Team should know what's going on."

She screwed up her mouth. "Want to tell the truth? You're afraid I'll do something reckless if left unattended, aren't you?"

"No, ma'am, but all the horses in this team need to be pulling in the same direction."

"More Tennessee wisdom?"

"If the saddle fits…" He drained his coffee. "I'm just…concerned about your safety. Sullivan murdered a cook and stole his ID to get onto base at Canyon, but someone's helped him."

"And now he's got a uniform and ID from the soldier he murdered at Baylor so he's got access to the US Marine base also. You're wondering if he's got an accomplice here, too."

Ethan nodded. "He always seems to be one step ahead of us."

"So maybe you've got a leak inside your investigation team."

Ethan washed his mug in the sink to avoid answering. He was not sure how much of the team's work to share with her. "Just keep your eyes peeled, okay?" His phone buzzed again. "And Marine battle dress will do. I assume Jillian left some for you."

She nodded and he checked his phone. A text from his pal Linc. You and Jillian patch things up?

Had the Canyon team heard of his undercover assignment so quickly? It was supposed to be kept on a need-to-know basis. He texted back. Where'd you hear that?

Before Tech Sergeant Linc Colson replied, he got a second message from a friend who rented the apartment next to him at Canyon.

Dude, madly in love with your ex?

Ethan was texting furiously when Linc sent him the source, a link to an anonymous blog that had cropped up recently and attracted dedicated followers on and off the base.

The first line made charges detonate all along his spine.

> *"Rumor has it that Ethan Webb is still madly in love with his ex-wife Jillian Masters and he's been making the long drive between Canyon and Baylor on a regular basis. Completely smitten, he's spending every moment with her, desperate to win her back. Will we hear wedding bells ringing out again for these two? Or is it all a ploy to help catch the Red Rose Killer?"*

He stopped reading, smacking the phone down on the table.

Kendra eyed him along with Titus. "Bad news?"

"When we get to Canyon, I'm going to have to make a side trip," he said through gritted teeth.

SIX

Kendra pulled on the baggy military pants, top and boots, gathering her hair into a tight twist and pinning it under the cap. Jillian was taller but no one would notice the extra length tucked into her boot tops. Baby sat on the bed and watched her.

"How'd I get to be a marine, Baby?" Kendra mused. "A naval aviator yet. I wouldn't have even survived boot camp." *And you might not survive this.* She tucked a small tape recorder in one pocket and locked her weapon in the gun safe Jillian had in the closet. There was no way she was getting through air force security with a Glock strapped to her side. Besides, a pilot would not carry a weapon unless on a mission. Was Sullivan hiding out on Canyon Air Force Base? Or was he right here near Baylor, enjoying toying with her until he was done playing?

She cuddled Baby, kissed her head and made sure the house was secure and the new lock Ethan had installed on the bedroom window firmly fastened before she went to meet Ethan and Titus at his truck.

If she wasn't mistaken, Ethan seemed to jump when he saw her, an involuntary jerk, before he looked down at his boots. His own airman battle uniform were of a darker palette than hers, the Security Forces blue beret snug on his head. Hastily, she scanned her uniform. "Did I get something wrong?"

"No, uh, you just..." He shook his head and gestured to the driver's-side door, which he had already opened. "Let's get rolling."

By the time the seat belt was buckled, she'd figured it out. Sometimes she forgot she was the spitting image of his ex-wife. He stared out the window, jaw tight, guiding the truck back to Canyon. What had Jillian done to him?

Best for you not to know. Just get the job done.

Titus whined from the space behind the driver's seat.

"Doesn't like riding in the back," Ethan explained.

"Sorry, dog," Kendra said. "Get over it. You're not the boss of me."

Ethan laughed, and she felt relieved to see the tension drain away. "Got two older sisters I wish I could convince of that. They live in Tennessee and every time I go home they have a bunch of women they want me to meet." He sighed. "They figure every man who isn't married surely should be working toward that end."

She chuckled. "I always wanted a sister. I guess Jillian was the closest I ever got."

"No siblings?"

"One brother. We're not close anymore."

"Why not?" He grimaced. "Oh, wait. Was that a nosy question?"

"Yes."

"That mean you aren't gonna answer it?"

Another back seat whine from Titus.

"When I started hanging around with Andy, my brother, Kevin, told me to break it off, that Andy was bad news. I didn't want to hear it. The deeper I got into trouble, the more I shut Kevin out until he washed his hands of me. I don't blame him really. My mother was an addict with mental problems, but Kev worked really hard not to repeat the pattern, to make a life for him and his wife and their baby." She cleared her throat. "I wouldn't have wanted me around them, either."

"Have you contacted them since?"

"Since I got clean? No. The farther away from them I am, the farther away Andy is." The remnant of the wasp sting on her cheek throbbed a reminder.

The long drive to Canyon Air Force Base finally ended. The road leading to the security gate was lined in barbed wire, until finally they got to an armed MP with a rottweiler tethered to his wrist. Ethan rolled down his window, and Titus issued a friendly bark, trying to jam his snout out the gap until Ethan backed him off. The rottweiler wagged his hind end in greeting.

"Ethan," the MP said after saluting. "Good to see you."

"Hey, Linc. Reporting for the meeting."

Linc's eyes shifted to the passenger seat. "Ma'am," he said bobbing his chin at her. His eyes were hard and flat, his mouth tight. Clearly he was no fan of Jillian Masters. She kept her cap pulled down.

Linc inspected the car and his dog sniffed every inch of the vehicle also.

"He's your friend?" Kendra whispered.

"Security's buttoned up since the killings. Linc's gonna do his job, whether we're pals or not."

When they were waved through, Kendra figured it was time to ask. "Who's on your list of suspects for Sullivan's accomplice?"

He hesitated. "That's a need-to-know basis."

"That's perfect, since I need to know." She could see him weighing it, measuring his trust in her.

He exhaled. "A few of the women he's dated. We've done initial interviews."

"No. I mean insiders, people on base or near it."

Again, silence.

"As you pointed out, I painted a target on my back."

More silence.

She grabbed his forearm, earning a growl from Titus. "Do you want to see my PI license? I'm not the enemy and I deserve to know. What's that you said about horses pulling in the same direction?"

He rubbed a hand over his face. "Man, I hate when my words are used against me."

She sat back with a victory smile. "So let's hear it."

Ethan fiddled with his beret. Fiddling? He wasn't a fiddler and he didn't want to tell her or anyone about the case. But he'd done a little checking on his own. She was a good PI, top-notch as a matter of fact, with plenty of cases solved and some with nasty connections to drug trafficking and murder. He figured she had a right to know.

"Three top the list at the moment. Rusty Morton, a buddy of Sullivan's, who works at the K-9 training center, but I'm having doubts. Second is Jim Ahern, flight mechanic."

"Who else?"

"A nurse on base here, Vanessa Gomez. She treated Sullivan after a fight, but she's gotten a rose so we initially struck her from the list."

"Initially?"

"Jillian was always jealous of Vanessa after she treated me for an injury. Accused her of flirting with me. Jillian always maintained Vanessa sent the rose to herself to throw us off the scent."

"But you don't believe it?"

"I don't believe anyone anymore. We got more suspects than Dole has pineapples. We did clear Zoe Sullivan, his half sister. Boyd's got a soft spot for her, but she's not assisting him. She's Linc's wife now and they're raising her son, Freddy, together." No need to go into the whole hair-raising story about Zoe's near-death experience from which Linc helped her escape. Linc, Zoe and Freddy were a family, and Ethan was pleased that at least one good thing had come out of the Sullivan mess.

"Anyone else?"

"Yvette Crenville, a nutritionist, dated him but they busted up pretty publicly when Sullivan was dishonorably discharged. That was the tip of the iceberg of course, since he was later imprisoned for a killing spree that left five people dead."

"Do you trust her?"

"Like I said…" He got out of the car in front of the base news office, and she did the same. Tension rolled off him like storm clouds. "It would be better if you stayed in the truck."

"Would Jillian meekly do what you ordered?"

"I…" His mouth snapped shut. "No."

She gestured. "After you, then." She added, low and soft, "Pumpkin."

Titus licked her hand as Ethan snapped on his leash before they strode into the office. Just before they entered, a man leaning against a trash can caught her eye. He wore clothes that matched hers—a marine, the markings indicating he was a combat pilot like Jillian. The brim of his cap shaded his face, but he was tall, strong, and she had a feeling he was staring right at her.

Muscles in her stomach tensed, deep down. She stared right back at him. Ethan noticed her look. He took a step toward her and the man turned away, heading in the opposite direction.

"Know him?" Ethan said.

"No. You?"

"No. We get marines in here all the time."

Or people who had stolen Marine uniforms and credentials?

Suppressing a shiver, she followed Ethan into the news office.

Ethan did not waste time approaching one particular desk, where a middle-aged soldier with horn-rimmed glasses was tapping away on his keyboard. The name placard on his desk read Captain John Robinson.

Ethan fired off a hasty salute. "The blog. Is it your handiwork, sir?" he said without preamble.

Robinson paused, fingers still on the keyboard until he returned the salute. "Hello, Ethan." He glanced at Kendra and quirked a smile. "Ma'am."

Ethan's shoulders lifted in a tense wall. "All this... drivel about love and whatnot."

Kendra felt her own cheeks heating up. Talk about

awkward. She'd not realized until then how difficult it would be for Ethan to pretend to be reconciled and back in love with a woman whom in reality he couldn't stand.

"What's the matter?" Robinson said. "Don't like having your love life splashed over cyberspace?"

Ethan went still, the anger radiating out of him like a solar flare. "Sir, this underground blog has been leaking info that only the investigation team should know. How is that happening? You're the base news reporter. Answer the question, please."

"Well," Robinson said, lacing his fingers together and cradling the back of his head with his outstretched arms. "The answer is… I have no answer, only a theory."

"What theory?" Ethan growled.

"That it's someone close." He turned slowly to the female lieutenant at the next desk, a blonde with blue eyes accentuated by dark-framed glasses. "Someone who felt slighted that he or she didn't get assigned the Red Rose Killer story. Someone who understands websites and is within earshot of all kinds of juicy tidbits both on base and off."

The woman whose placard read Lieutenant Heidi Jenks stood, chin up, and walked right to Robinson's desk. "At least do me the courtesy of not talking about me while I'm sitting five feet away." She squared off with Ethan. "I have nothing to do with that underground blog. Yes, I wanted the Sullivan story and yes," she added, her nostrils flared, "I could do a much better job on it than Robinson here, but I am a journalist, not a gossip columnist."

She fired a look at Kendra. "Personally, I'd be glad

if you and Ethan are back together. Marriage vows are supposed to be forever, right?" Her eyes narrowed. "No matter what?"

Time to act the part.

"That's right," Kendra said, keeping her voice even in that flat way Jillian kept hers, which she'd come to admire.

"Then again, some things are hard to forgive. You sure know how to humiliate a man," Heidi said in a low voice only Kendra could hear.

Kendra stared her down. "If you've got something to say, spill it."

"I was just thinking how you embarrassed Boyd Sullivan that day when you were observing the K-9 demonstration here on base and his dog wouldn't perform. It was right before he washed out, remember? You verbally annihilated him in front of everyone. The look on his face was painful to see."

"Are you sympathizing with Sullivan?" Kendra said. "Maybe you feel like he didn't deserve a prison term? Maybe you helped him out after he escaped?"

Heidi's eyes turned stone-hard, her silent pause taut as a steel wire. "No," she said after a moment. "Just wondering if you'd had any more threats against you."

Wasps. A shooting. A guy eyeing her like a mouse in the snake pit. Threats? "Nothing I can't handle, but thanks for your concern."

"Watch your back," Heidi said.

"Is that a warning or a threat?"

Heidi said nothing. She merely stalked from the room.

Kendra felt like she'd just made another enemy. Two minutes flat. A record, even for the woman she was impersonating.

* * *

Captain Justin Blackwood rubbed his tired eyes, waving Ethan and Kendra into chairs as he disconnected the phone. "Teenage daughters," he said with a sigh, "are more volatile than gasoline."

"Yes, sir," Ethan said. He'd heard the stories about the captain's daughter, Portia, and he sympathized with Blackwood.

Kendra sat next to him in a row of desks and Titus sprawled on the floor, soaking up the coolness of the tile. Since Linc was on gate duty and FBI Agent Oliver Davidson and Office of Special Investigations Agent Ian Steffan were absent, the team consisted of newlyweds Master Sergeant Westley James, along with his German shepherd, Dakota, his wife, Felicity, and Senior Airman Ava Esposito with her dog, Roscoe. They sat facing Blackwood, who perched on the edge of a table in front of an enormous white board.

Westley wriggled his eyebrows at Ethan. "You've been a busy boy." He shifted his gaze to Kendra. "Congratulations on your reunion, ma'am."

"So sweet," Felicity said, "only she's not Jillian."

Ethan started and Westley looked from his wife to Kendra. "What…?"

"She's shorter and Jillian doesn't have a dimple, not to mention the fact that Jillian would have already started chatting you up, Westley. She can't help flirting with handsome men, married or not."

Kendra sighed. "It's hard to fool a woman. I'm Kendra Bell." She explained her credentials and the plan with Colonel Masters.

"Harebrained scheme if you ask me," Felicity said. "Any progress?"

"I've been shot at, driven off the road and stung by a nest of wasps. Does that count as progress?"

Westley whistled. "Well, you've stirred someone up, that's for sure."

Captain Blackwood called the meeting to order then. After a brief preamble, he questioned his team. "Where are we in the investigation?"

"Nowhere," Esposito said. "Roscoe and I have been searching all over this area and I've seen no sign of Sullivan, or any more of the missing German shepherds, for that matter, though we did retrieve three other dogs in the last twenty-four hours."

"She's referring to the dogs that Sullivan let out the night he killed Landon Martelli," Ethan explained to Kendra. The knot in Ethan's gut tightened when he said his friend's name aloud. He cleared his throat. "The German shepherds are highly trained canines, the elite. I can't imagine them bolting, yet we still haven't found them."

"It's bizarre," Esposito said, "but that's a small point compared to finding Sullivan."

"Sullivan's accomplice is clever," Blackwood said. "Covering tracks as fast as the guy makes them."

"Linc's looking at the prison records again," Westley said. "Going over the visitor list. We must have missed something."

Blackwood stepped away to take a phone call. When he returned, his expression was hardened into the military mask that meant bad news was coming. The room went quiet.

"A witness who saw the killer leaving the scene of the Baylor marine murder gave police enough for a sketch." He turned his phone around to show them.

The air seemed to leak out of the room as they stared into the drawn face of Boyd Sullivan.

"He's been spotted at a corner store as well, this morning," Blackwood added.

He looked at Kendra. "So it's confirmed, then. Looks like Sullivan is in your neck of the woods now, at least for the moment."

How long would he stick around? Ethan mused.

Until "Jillian Masters," aka Kendra Bell, is dead, his gut told him.

Ethan ground his teeth in frustration as they hit the road back to Baylor. Now they had proof that Sullivan was zeroing in on Baylor and the woman he thought was Jillian.

Beside him, Kendra spoke. "Can you stop there?" She pointed to a gas station. "I have to use the bathroom."

He pulled in, letting Titus out to stretch his legs in the shade of some trees. A couple of kids eyed Titus as kids always did, but their mother pulled them back. Ethan was grateful. Military dogs were not pets, they were warriors, always poised for battle. Titus could be playful and loved kids, but now was not the time. The stakes were too high.

Titus stopped mid sniff, head cocked.

"What is it, boy?"

Ethan saw nothing that would upset the dog, but he knew that Titus had an arsenal of sensory detectors that far surpassed anything Ethan could muster. He moved closer, leaving Titus enough room to orient himself, and waited to see what the dog would show him.

Ethan's blood began to pound as Titus gave a little agitated shake of the head, a sign that meant there was trouble ahead.

SEVEN

Kendra stepped from the bathroom into the alley, heading toward the truck. A soft sound stopped her. The scuff of a shoe against the cement? The whisk of a shirtsleeve skimming the brick wall? Tiny hairs along the back of her neck prickled. She reached for the gun at her side that wasn't there.

Turning in a quick circle, she saw no one.

"Ninny," she told herself. Paranoia, pure and simple. *Don't let Andy and Sullivan inside your head.*

Continuing down the alley, she picked up her pace, passing a pile of stacked pallets. In a blur, a hand reached out and grabbed her arm, twisting it behind her, and she was shoved against the wall, her cheek jammed to the rough brick.

Heart thundering, she jabbed out an elbow, catching her assailant in the neck, but it set him back only long enough for her to whirl around and face him. His grip on her arm remained, tightened, and he forced her back until her head banged against the wall. It took a moment for her to place him. The tall man, the pilot, dressed in Marine fatigues, the one who'd been watching her at Canyon. His eyes flared with rage.

"I thought that was you. What are you playing at, Jillian?"

She struggled in his grip. "Let go of me."

He shook her until her teeth clacked together. "Not until you give me some answers. I've been trailing you since I saw you at Canyon."

"I'm not giving you anything," she gasped. The fingers of his other hand tightened the collar of her uniform into a ligature around her neck. She tried to claw at his eyes, but his grip prevented it.

He pressed close. "We were taking a break while you got your head together, remember? That's what you told me. Now I hear you're back with your ex? The happy couple?"

Her mind struggled to put it together. "Stop…"

He leaned close, his mouth to her ear. "You're not going to toss me out like a piece of garbage, do you understand me? We had a good thing going and you're not going to throw it away for that straight-laced hick of a dog trainer. Do you hear me, Jillian?"

He punctuated each word with a tightening of his grip. Her vision blurred and she knew she had to make a move to prevent him from choking her. Before he could track the movement, she shoved her free hand up through the circle of his arms and jabbed her rigid fingers into his neck near the throat. Gagging, he reeled back and she sagged against the brick, struggling to get her feet to cooperate to flee.

There was a sound of scrabbling paws, a thunderous growl that echoed in the alley as Titus exploded into view and leaped onto the man's back. Kendra panted in relief.

The man roared as the dog bit at his back, tearing sections of uniform away.

"Release," Ethan thundered.

Immediately the dog let go with a howl of displeasure, furry body still quivering.

Ethan trained his sidearm on the fallen man and eyed Kendra. "You okay?"

She nodded, breathless.

"Get up," Ethan ordered her assailant. "Hands behind your head."

The man climbed to his feet. He moved too quickly and Titus stood, teeth bared, barking so loud it made Kendra's ears ring. Ethan silenced the dog.

"Slowly," Ethan advised. "Just so you know, the only thing keeping this dog from tearing you to pieces is me, so I suggest you stand still, very still, and tell me what I want to know."

The man glared.

"Name?"

After a nervous glance at the dog, he said, "Captain Bill Madding."

"You a marine, or just playing dress up for the day?"

His mouth pinched. "I'm a naval aviator. I fly Cobra helicopters while you play around with dogs."

"Yeah? A hotshot pilot and you still got plenty of time to accost women?"

Madding shook his head, his arms dropping until Titus growled, when he raised them again. "I was mad. Hearing that she's back together with you. I mean…" He drilled her with his eyes again, searching, and she saw the moment realization dawned. He peered closer.

"Wait a minute," he said. "You're not Jillian. Who are you?"

Kendra pushed to her feet, willing her lungs back into a normal breathing pattern. "How do you know Jillian?"

He blinked. "I… We went to flight school together. We're colleagues."

"You're more than that," she said.

He pressed his lips together.

She brushed the grit off her arms. "If you don't want to be brought up on assault charges and lose your wings, you better start talking."

He swallowed. "Jillian and I are in a relationship, a serious one, have been for years. She wanted to ease off until after my divorce was drawn up, but when it was done, we got back on track."

Kendra sneaked a look at Ethan. Disgust shone on his face. "So you were having an affair with Jillian while you were still married?"

"My marriage had been over for a long time."

"You still had a piece of paper, didn't you?" Ethan snapped, his drawl thickening. "That's a vow before God, or doesn't that mean anything to you?" Titus stiffened, whining at Ethan's intensity, but Ethan holstered his gun and calmed the dog with a pat. "I guess it means about as much to you as it did to her." He shook his head. "Never mind. I'm calling your Marine cops. They can sort you out."

"No," he said. "Don't do that. Look, I'm sorry I went at you," he said to Kendra. "It was stupid and impulsive. I apologize. I'm set to deploy in a few days and I'll be gone for seven months. I won't be any trouble to you or Jillian."

Ethan's eyes blazed. "No way, Marine. You had your hands around her throat, hotshot. You need some prison time to consider the error of your ways."

Madding's expression went from desperate to something craftier. He arched an eyebrow at Kendra. "Okay.

Turn me in and I tell everyone who will listen that you're impersonating Jillian Masters. How's that going to help your investigation, huh?"

Ethan's shoulders tensed. "You're not gonna black-mail—"

"He's right," Kendra said. "Let him go."

"No," Ethan breathed, his ire now burning at her. "No way. He doesn't deserve it."

She walked to him, talking in a low voice. "Ethan, he can end this investigation by blabbing what he knows. Let him go. This isn't related to the Sullivan case."

Ethan looked at the ground and then blew out a long slow breath, his hands fisted on his hips.

"I guess I'll be on my way then." Madding straightened his rumpled uniform. "I don't know what you're working on, but Jillian Masters has stirred up plenty of hornet's nests around here."

Her breath caught. "Did you decide to teach her a lesson by leaving the wasp nest at her house?"

His expression was blank. "I don't know what you're talking about. I hate bugs and that would be a waste of time anyway. Jillian's not scared of anyone or anything on this planet."

But she'd agreed to go into hiding, Kendra thought, so Madding did not know Jillian Masters as well as he thought.

With a loud hiss of breath, Ethan about-faced and called to Titus to follow. The dog did as he was told. "If I ever see you assault a woman again," Ethan called over his shoulder to Madding, "the dog gets his way."

They escorted Madding to the parking lot and watched him get into his car. When they did the same Kendra took time to calm her still jittery nerves. Madding's rough hands brought back memories of Andy. She tugged at the collar of her uniform.

"Sure you're okay?" Ethan said.

"Yeah. I had it under control, but thanks for the assist."

Ethan glowered. "I should have spotted him tailing us. Rookie mistake. I won't make it again."

Back in the truck, Titus swabbed the back of her neck until she batted him away. "What's up with you, dog? I thought he didn't like me."

"You're growing on him."

And Titus was growing on her, too, the seventy-pound goofy bundle of ferociousness and loyalty. "Thanks," she whispered to the dog, "for having my back."

Ethan's brow furrowed and his grip on the steering wheel was unrelenting. He drove fast, too fast. She wanted to say something to break the awkward silence, but she couldn't come up with a single thing. She noticed for the first time a rolled-up scarf at her feet, with dark purple thread and fringe at the ends. "Spiffy scarf."

He shifted on the seat, running a palm over his crew cut. "Yeah, uh, my mom knits them for me. When I deploy I make sure to take a picture of me wearing it and send it to her. She thinks I'll be cold, even though I've tried to tell her it's 120 degrees on a daily basis in Afghanistan. Guys razzed me plenty when they found me taking that picture."

Kendra stifled a chuckle. Did he know how blessed he was to have a mother like that? She looked at his strong profile and decided that he did. After all, he was a man who risked his buddies' ridicule to please his mother. "You're a good son."

"She struggled when my brother died. Deserves a little extra TLC."

His brother. She wanted to ask, but now he was fiddling with the radio, rifling through static and stations. "Don't whine, Titus. Give me a minute. He's particular about his music, that dog. Turn on rap and he'll tear the car apart."

He settled on a slow country tune and Titus risked one more lick to the back of her neck before he settled down in the small space behind the driver's seat for a nap. The miles wound by and Ethan was silent. Okay, if she was going to get to know her enigmatic partner any deeper, it would be on her to make it happen.

"Ethan, does it…did it bother you to hear Madding talk about cheating on his wife with Jillian?"

He drummed on the steering wheel. "Reminded me of the betrayal. That hurt worse than a bullet for a long time."

"I get that. When you realize the person you loved isn't who you thought they were." Andy had been so charming when he wanted to be, but that wasn't who he really was.

"Yeah. Makes me some kind of crazy to have agreed to this charade with her father, huh?"

Not crazy, Kendra thought as she caught the pained twist of his mouth. Ferocious and loyal.

She reached out and grazed his forearm with her fingertips. "Thanks again for what you did back there."

He shrugged and shot her a cocky grin. "See? Told you we gotta be together on this investigation. And you thought I was only good for making frittatas."

She laughed. Just like his dog, Ethan was growing on her, too.

EIGHT

Ethan took Titus out into the woods behind Jillian's rented house that evening as the sun continued its descent. Kendra joined him, rolling her neck, relishing the cooler temperature and the sweet smell of sun-warmed grass, a welcome relief from the case that grew more puzzling with each passing day. "I've been on the phone with Colonel Masters. He wanted to know about our progress. He's anxious."

Ethan snapped a long lead on Titus. "He should be. He lost a marine and he's got people like Bill Madding working for him."

"Masters wants me to report to his office tomorrow for a briefing."

"We'll be ready." He shook his head. "Yeah, don't even bother with 'I don't need you to come along.' Sullivan's got access to Baylor now and Canyon. You're getting an MP and his dog along whether you like it or not."

She sighed. "Whoever's helping Sullivan is doing a bang-up job avoiding arrest. Maybe when your people review the list of prison visitors…"

"Already did that once, but it's possible we missed something."

He bent to Titus and ruffled his ears. "All right, boy, ready? Find it."

The dog took off, nose to the ground, tugging on the lead.

"I hope you're not expecting to find a real cadaver."

"Nah. I left a marker with Sigma Pseudo Corpse Scent earlier."

There was no hint of a smile so she figured he wasn't kidding. "There's a fake scent for corpses?"

"Yeah, comes in three kinds: recently dead, decomposed and drowned. Cool, huh?"

"You don't get invited to many parties, do you?"

He laughed. "Easier than getting real cadaver scents, let me tell you. You wouldn't believe the paperwork. I'm just happy the air force is allowing me to cross-train Titus as a cadaver sniffer."

"It was your idea?"

"Yes."

"Why? Don't have enough to do already?"

He stepped over a fallen log. "I want to help people find answers. If you don't, it can destroy their lives." He paused. "When my brother died, it took three weeks to find him. Those days nearly drove our family to madness."

They watched Titus zigzag from shrub to tree trunk.

Ethan scrubbed a hand over his chin, which showed the beginnings of a five o'clock shadow, and looked over at her. "You want to know, but you're too polite to ask, aren't you?"

She sighed. "Yes, Nosy, I suppose."

"Nah. Natural. I'd want to know, too. My brother,

Luke, loved backpacking. He was an outdoors fiend. We used to go all the time. The hard kind of traveling with only a backpack, water, a mat for sleeping, couple of protein bars and a fishing line and that's it."

"Sleeping under the stars, huh?"

"Yeah, we ate that stuff up. Anyway, one time he went by himself 'cuz I was in boot camp. Mama told him not to, of course, but Luke was never one to doubt his own abilities and he didn't take direction well." He held up a palm. "You aren't going to say it runs in the family, are you?"

She mimed locking her lips and throwing away the key.

"Luke was perfectly comfortable in every situation unless you put him in a suit and tie. Then he was like a trussed-up chicken." His grin was boyish. "Anyway, while out on this three-day adventure, he went and got himself hurt—busted femur and ribs, head trauma, the coroner told us later. No phone reception so he couldn't have called for help. Search and Rescue did their best, brought in a helicopter and the whole nine yards. I got leave to fly home to assist. It was twenty-two days before they found his body at the bottom of a ravine."

Her heart squeezed. "How terrible."

"We knew after a few days he was dead, Mama and me. He would have hiked out if he was able. But those days, the hours just stretched on and on. Our church family did their best and held us together, but the wait was agonizing, and the wondering was almost unbearable. At one point we had to wrestle with the knowledge that he might never be found. They can't keep searching forever. Resources have to be reassigned to newer cases. Soldiers' families have to wrestle with that, too, the fear that their son or daughter will never be found, especially if they're lost while deployed. I decided that someday, if I could, I would do something about that."

"It's a hard job to be the one who finds the body, isn't it?"

"Hard job, but a privilege. Finding the deceased is the end of hope, but it's also the start of closure and the beginning of healing." He shrugged. "So that's the story. I wanted to be part of that."

The dappled light from the setting sun teased the caramel streaks from his eyes, rich and vibrant. How could Jillian have betrayed him so brutally? "You are a good man, Ethan." She surprised herself by saying it aloud.

He made a funny face. "Aw, Titus is really the star of our operation, but I cook a better fritatta than him."

She laughed.

"Titus shows promise. When he's ready, he'll be able to detect decomposition of bone, body parts, blood and residue scents even if the body is no longer in place. I read about a case where a dog found a body buried twelve feet deep." He looked suddenly uneasy. "Was that more than you wanted to know?"

"No. Just reinforces that dogs are pretty amazing."

"Oh, yeah." Enthusiasm lit his face. "It's like when you walk into a room and smell chili cooking. Well, a dog walks in and smells each ingredient in the pot. They can discriminate odors individually. Awesome, huh?"

His smile was infectious. "Awesome," she agreed.

"We both have a long way to go. Titus isn't fully trained yet and we haven't even started water recovery work. He's not super enthusiastic about waves, which I tell him is pure cowardice on his part." He eyed the dog.

"Gonna have to get you some water wings, huh, boy? But like I said, all the other dogs are gonna laugh at you."

Titus stiffened, pulling to the left toward a wide pile of granite boulders.

Ethan groaned. "No, Titus. That's not where we're headed, buddy. He's still distracted by other things." He put the dog into a sit, earning a whine from the animal. "I know this is new for both of us but you gotta focus." He scratched Titus's muzzle. "Got it together? Okay. Let's do this. Find the package." He shot Kendra a look. "'Package' is nicer than—"

"A body," she finished.

Again Titus beelined to the left, and only Ethan's strength kept him from yanking the leash free.

"Titus," Ethan started to say when a high-pitched scream cut through the air.

Titus switched gears and bolted for the noise, Ethan and Kendra scrambling to catch up.

"Help," the voice called again. A woman's voice.

Kendra could not pinpoint the source as they crashed through the trees. The canopy of branches grew thicker as they pushed deeper into the woods, the shadows, distorting, disorienting.

"Please," came the cry again.

Kendra pushed faster, praying she would not trip over a tree root and break her ankle, but she dared not slow.

Someone was in the woods with them, someone who needed help.

Ethan followed a dirt trail, feet pounding on the earth before he skidded to a halt where the ground gave way to a creek bed some ten feet below them.

Titus would have scrambled down immediately if not restrained.

"Sit," Ethan commanded and Titus instantly obeyed, though he was probably chewing Ethan out in his doggy brain.

Kendra, he saw, was peering over the edge, but the water was screened by a thick tangle of shrubbery. "Who's there?" she bellowed.

A voice from below called out, "Please. I need help."

"Wait," he said, but Kendra did not hesitate, plunging down the steep slope, picking her way between the rocks. Biting back a complaint, he followed.

Branches slapped at both of them, the rocks shifting under his boots. As they cleared the bushes, he saw a bicycle lying on its side in the water, rear wheel spinning lazily. Jillian's neighbor, Mindy Zeppler, sat on a rock, wet and shivering, streaks of mud across her forehead and cheek.

Kendra splashed across the creek. "Are you hurt? What happened?"

Mindy pushed a clump of hair from her face, dirty water trailing down her cheek. "Jillian, I'm so grateful you found me. I forgot to bring my phone with me."

Kendra repeated her question.

Mindy took a breath. "I was riding. I love the woods at this time of day, except for the mosquitoes. I crashed and fell. I'm so glad you were here, too." She looked at Ethan. "Training your dog?"

"Yes, ma'am."

He did not see any visible bleeding on Mindy, no bruising apparent under the streaks of mud, but those would surface later. "Did you hit your head?"

"No. I don't think I broke anything, either." She examined her wrist. "I hope not anyway."

"I'll pull your bike out for you," Ethan said, eyeing it. "Doesn't look too badly damaged."

"We'll help you get home," Kendra said. "Do you want us to call an ambulance?"

Mindy shook her head. "I'm okay. I'm sort of a klutz, as my ex-husband would tell you, but this time I had a good excuse." Fear flickered across her face. "I crashed because…" She swallowed. "Because there was a man, here in the woods."

Ethan's gut tightened. "A man?"

She nodded. "I've only lived here for a couple of years and people are always coming and going, so I don't know everyone, but he was acting weird."

"How?" Ethan allowed Titus to poke his nose into the creek.

Mindy took a breath. "He had binoculars and he wore gloves. Way too hot for gloves, isn't it? He was watching something. I didn't know what at the time, but I think I do now."

Ethan's muscles bunched at the base of his spine. "I think I do also."

Kendra's expression told her she'd reached the same conclusion.

The man in the woods had been watching them.

NINE

Kendra swallowed hard. "Can you describe him?"

Mindy frowned. "It all happened so fast… About five-eight maybe? He wore a hat so I couldn't tell his hair color. I didn't get a good look at him because I was busy crashing my bike. But why would someone be watching you, Jillian?"

Kendra tried to rally her thoughts. She could not get into the Red Rose Killer details, but she had to give Mindy something. "I… I have a violent ex-boyfriend. His name is Andy."

Mindy's brows furrowed. "Boyfriend? I thought…" Her gaze traveled to Ethan. "I thought you two were back together."

"Yes, we are. Andy was ancient history."

"He must have a long memory, if he's still coming after you."

You don't know the half of it. "I'll call the police. They can help keep an eye out." Kendra wondered how she was going to explain the particulars to Officer Carpenter and still keep the investigation under wraps. There was no choice. They had to tell the cops about the current attack since it involved a civilian.

Andy couldn't be allowed to endanger anyone else but her, if it really was him.

"Can you stand?" Kendra asked her neighbor, offering her an arm.

Mindy took it, her fingers icy on Kendra's skin. "All your wasp stings are healed up," she said, her eyes wandering Kendra's face.

Kendra wished she had a cap to pull down. "Yes. Much better now."

"Do you think the guy with the binoculars was the one who called me looking for you? Maybe this Andy of yours?"

"I'm not sure," Kendra said. "I'll look into it."

With her support, Mindy seemed to gain strength and they crossed the creek. "Wait," she said. "When I rode up and saw him, he sort of jumped. I think he might have dropped his binoculars."

Kendra's spirit surged. Though he'd been wearing gloves, maybe an errant fingerprint survived, which would reveal exactly who was after her.

"On it," Ethan said. He and Titus began scouring the bushes while Kendra helped Mindy back up onto the trail. She heaved a breath and detached herself from Kendra.

"I'm okay, I think. Just banged up. I can make it back to the house."

"I'll go with you. The police will want to talk to all of us."

Mindy walked a few feet before she suddenly halted. "Here. Look."

Before Kendra could stop her, she reached under the shrubs and grabbed the binoculars, holding them triumphantly. "See? I told you he dropped them." She caught Kendra and Ethan's reaction. "What's wrong?"

"You've got your fingerprints on them now," Ethan told her.

Her face fell. "Oh. Sorry. I didn't think of that."

"It's okay," Ethan said. He pulled a plastic bag from his pocket and Mindy dropped the binoculars in, zipping it closed. "The guy probably didn't have time to search for them with you calling for help."

The three walked slowly from the woods, emerging some ten minutes later at the back gate to Mindy's property. Mindy let them into a small house similar to Jillian's, but decorated in light colors with framed photos covering the wall behind the sofa and a deerskin rug on the floor. A wedding picture showed a much younger Mindy, beaming and beribboned in a fluffy wedding dress, holding an elaborate bouquet.

Kendra touched the silver frame. "Pretty picture."

Mindy eased into a chair, holding an ice pack to her knee that Ethan had fetched from her freezer. "Yes. The marriage was a disaster, but I figured since the dress cost a mint I might as well keep that photo up. Are you…" She grimaced as she flexed her knee. "I mean, are you two going to have another ceremony?"

Kendra couldn't come up with a response.

"Sure we are," Ethan said, beaming. "Only this time it's gonna be a proper wedding on the beach with good food, country music and comfortable footwear. My uniform dress shoes were designed by the enemy to torture me, I'm pretty sure." He looked at Kendra. "This time we're gonna get it right, don'tcha think, Jillian?"

Somehow he had come up with the perfect response, as usual. Kendra heaved a silent sigh of relief. "Sure. Why not?"

Mindy giggled. "Sounds romantic."

Actually, it did to Kendra, too. She'd dreamed of a marriage like that, where things were easy and honest, with someone to encourage her in life and faith. She discovered Ethan was smiling at her. For some reason it brought warmth to her cheeks.

After a thirty-minute wait, Officer Carpenter arrived to take their statements. Kendra met him at the curb.

"Ms. Bell?" he said, eyebrow arched.

"There are a few things I need to tell you before you go in there."

"You don't say?"

"Yes, sir."

"Is it possible that you have not been forthcoming with the police?"

"You know who I really am, sir, but I need to tell you who I'm pretending to be and why I need you to keep the pretense going."

He folded his arms across his chest. "You may talk, Ms. Bell, and I will decide what I will or will not do with your information."

"Yes, sir," she said. Blowing out a breath, she plunged in.

Ethan stayed mostly silent as Carpenter finished scribbling down the information, took the binoculars and said good-night to Mindy Zeppler. Ethan, Titus and Kendra walked him to the car. Kendra had told him everything, and apparently he was going to keep her cover intact since he had not revealed Kendra's true identity in front of Mindy.

"I will check on the whereabouts of Andy Bleakman," Officer Carpenter said. "As far as Sullivan goes, I've only got the barebones information that your task force has been willing to share." His tone was bitter, as Ethan's would be if he was being shut out of an investigation.

Ethan had already been forced to share more than he wanted to in the first place. Sullivan was discharged from the air force, and it was their duty, their responsibility, to put him away. "Got anything from the shooting yet?"

The officer shrugged. "Gun wasn't military issue. Rifle, standard Ruger. Plenty of folks around here have them for hunting. Shooter didn't recover his brass at the scene so we've got shell casings. Not the best marksman, in my humble opinion. How about Sullivan? He any good with a rifle?"

"Enough to pass basic training, but he was no sniper, that's for sure."

"What about accomplices?"

Ethan stiffened, watching the officer's body language. "What are you thinking?"

Carpenter shrugged. "Just wondering if he's got a lady friend."

Ethan stared at the cop, assessing him now. "We've got females on the suspect list. Why?" Carpenter was enjoying making them wait, payback for being shut out of the investigation to date.

He thumbed his mustache. "We picked up a partial footprint in the soft dirt near the shell casings. Real small. Looks to be from a woman's shoe."

"You took—"

"Impressions, of course, and when we're good and finished examining them I'll send them along to your people at Canyon."

Ethan didn't argue. It was the best they could do. "Thank you, Officer."

"Don't thank me," he said. "Footprint isn't gonna help much. Likely the binoculars aren't, either, but we'll scan for prints anyway."

They walked back to Jillian's house in silence. The air was thick with the promise of a storm, Texas style. In the kitchen he supplied fresh water for Titus and let him out in the yard before the rain arrived. Baby crept out from under the sofa, where she'd streaked the moment they returned. He leaned on the counter, details pinging rapid-fire through his mind. Finally he went to the fridge and opened it, staring inside as if there might be an answer somewhere in there. He sighed. "You want a Coke?"

"Sure."

"What kind?"

She quirked an eyebrow. "Coke is a kind."

"Nah, that's a category. What kind do you want?"

She laughed. "That's a Southern thing, isn't it?"

He returned the smile and handed her a root beer, taking one for himself, too. He had a need to hear her talk, to soak in the way her face showed her feelings. "Where you from then where they don't speak properly?"

"I grew up in Colorado. My brother's still there with his family, but I haven't been to see him since I left for prep school, only texted a few times. I have a small office clear across the state, closer to where I went to prep school."

"Where you met Jillian."

"Yeah. I met Jillian on my first day when I transferred in as a sophomore. I was a charity case. Scholarships paid for everything. I was surprised that Jillian wanted anything to do with me. I certainly wasn't part of her circle, her being the daughter of a high-ranking marine. She had all the money and clothes she wanted while I was wearing a secondhand uniform and working at the gas station at night. Jillian was what I wanted to be—smart, confident, popular. She never had a Saturday night without a guy by her side." She broke off. "Oh, I'm sorry if that was insensitive."

"Nah. I admired her confidence, too. I was just dumb enough to think that when we got married, she'd give up all the other men." He sipped the cold soda, gesturing for her to continue.

"I met Andy when I was eighteen and all my good sense went out the window. I thought he was made for me, the glue for all my broken parts. I never knew my father. My mom had me when she was sixteen, and she had mental problems as far back as I can recall, so I guess I didn't know what real love was supposed to look like."

"It can be tricky to spot," he said. "I'm not sure I know what it would look like, either."

A look, both gentle and poignant, washed over her and he watched, dazzled by it.

"Real love would be two people putting God at the top of the list," she said. "That's all I know. Man and wife are going to disappoint each other at times, but

He won't and He's got to be the glue that holds it all together."

He examined the rich mahogany of her eyes, the light dusting of freckles across her nose. In the small circle of overhead light, with her hair loose, swimming in her baggy ABUs, she did not look much like his ex-wife. Certainly not the sincerity that made her so very vulnerable, the honest desire to start over again and start fresh with God at the center. He wanted to keep right on staring at her, memorizing the details of her face, her long fingers, the tiny scar next to her eyebrow, but something achy and tight took hold of his heart and he got up to knock it loose. "I'm going to check the perimeter again, be sure no one tampered with any locks while we were gone."

She nodded. "If that was Sullivan in the woods, he's close."

"Too close."

"Carpenter believes the accomplice is a woman," she said. "Your suspect list included Vanessa Gomez, Zoe Sullivan, Yvette Crenville and the two women Sullivan dated."

"Linc interviewed one again just recently. I'll call and pick his brain and schedule an interview with the others."

"And you've ruled out Zoe. Vanessa got a rose, though it might have been a diversion." She paused. "There's one more name I was thinking of."

"Spill it."

"The woman at the base news office."

"Heidi Jenks? What would her motive be?"

"I can't imagine, but she has access to information, and you suspect her of being the underground blogger. I think she suspected I wasn't Jillian, the way she looked at me."

"I've learned by now not to toss any theories aside. I'll look into it."

"Me, too. Good night."

Ethan paused at the door. "Storm coming in."

She sighed. "Seems like there's always a storm coming in."

He smiled and put on a hick accent. "Lessen it's a frog strangler, I reckon we'll be okay."

She laughed. "Tell that to your chicken of a dog."

Smiling, Ethan let himself out and waited until she locked the door, the light silhouetting her in gold. Titus wandered over and the two made their way back to the in-law unit. As he pulled off his boots for the night he found his eyes traveling to the window, to the tree-tops visible just over the fence, shadowed by ominous clouds.

If you're out there, Sullivan, I'm going to find you.

There'd be no more victims.

Especially not Kendra.

TEN

They arrived at Colonel Masters's office and waited outside the door until they were summoned. Ethan looked about as happy as he had the last time they'd been to see Masters. When the aide ushered them in, he brought Titus with them and let him up on one of the chairs.

Kendra gave him a questioning look.

"Masters hates dogs," he whispered.

She smothered a grin at the mischievous gleam in his eye. They entered, and Ethan fired off the obligatory salute.

The colonel did not offer them a seat. "I want to know everything about the hostile in the woods."

"All we know," Kendra said, "is that it was a male that matches Sullivan's description. The police have the binoculars for printing."

"I didn't want police in the picture," he snapped.

"We had no choice," Kendra said. "There was a civilian involved. She could have been hurt."

"We reported all this over the phone," Ethan said. "Why are we here?"

Masters didn't raise his voice, but his tone turned to

steel. "Because I sent for you, and you're both work-ing for me."

Ethan's cheeks went scarlet. "You don't—"

"He brought you here because of me," said a voice from the file room. Kendra gasped as Jillian stepped out wearing jeans and a T-shirt. She almost didn't rec-ognize her with her hair dyed a dark brown and her eye color changed to green with the help of some tinted lenses.

Jillian smiled and the women hugged. She nodded at Ethan who was breathing hard, staring at Masters. "You're nuts, bringing her here. If anyone who knows her happens to—"

"You worry too much, Ethan," Jillian said. "Al-ways have."

His eyes sparked fire. "You must be plenty wor-ried, too, to go into hiding and let someone else fight your battles."

Jillian's face settled into an angry mask and she started to retort, but the colonel stopped her with a raised palm.

"Enough. Jillian's here because she wanted an up-date and she's impatient for results."

"Can you blame me? I want my life back."

"We ran into a friend of yours who wants the same thing," Ethan said. "Bill Madding."

Her lips thinned. "We're over."

Ethan glared. "Funny, he doesn't seem to think so."

"That's personal."

"You were in a relationship with a married guy. He attacked Kendra. That makes it our business."

Jillian folded her arms. "He's divorced now, but he has a wandering eye. I dumped him when I saw the text on his cell phone from someone named Lizzie with all the kissing emojis."

Ethan's tight jaw telegraphed his feelings. Kendra understood. How could Jillian stand there and criticize someone for being unfaithful? It was a case of the plank in the eye blocking out the speck in another's.

Kendra took a subtle step between Jillian and Ethan. "What can you tell us about Madding?"

Jillian sniffed impatiently. "Nothing to tell. He thinks he's a macho man's man, hunts, fishes. It gets old after a while." She waved her hand, as if to push aside that line of questioning. "That's a dead end. Where are we with Sullivan's accomplices?"

"The police suspect it might be a woman," Kendra replied.

"That's not a new theory."

"What do you think about Heidi Jenks?" Kendra asked.

Jillian's eyes narrowed as she considered. "I've always thought she was the one behind the underground blog. She'd be in a good position to help Sullivan, since the press has access to plenty of places on base and off." She tugged on a strand of brown hair. "Motive?"

"Could be she had a secret relationship with him."

Masters raised his voice. "This is all well and good about the accomplice, but I want Sullivan, so we've got to force his hand."

"We're working on it," Ethan said. "We'll keep you apprised of our progress so there's no need to drag us in here again." He took a step toward the door, Titus beside him.

"You're not leaving yet," Masters said.

Kendra's stomach tightened. "Why not?"

"Jillian needs to be seen around the base. I've pulled strings to cover her duties, but she can't simply disappear. To that end, I've scheduled you for an overnight SERE training refresher course."

Jillian started to explain. "SERE is—"

"Survival, Evasion, Resistance and Escape training, I know," Kendra said. "I did my homework before I agreed to impersonate a marine."

"No way," Ethan barked. "She'll be out there in the rough, unprotected."

"Not unprotected. You will go with her," the colonel said smoothly. "I'll set the wheels in motion. It's just one overnight, twelve hours max."

Kendra noticed that Jillian did not look at all surprised by Masters's announcement. She blew out a breath. "You are here to prep me for what to expect at the SERE training so I don't blow my cover, aren't you?"

Jillian didn't respond.

"And you're hoping Sullivan will make a move to kill me during the exercise."

Ethan glared at Jillian and her father. "That's exactly what they're both hoping for."

Jillian took Kendra's hand and squeezed, her smile wide, a pained twist to her brows. "I don't want you to get hurt, Kendra. I just need this to be over. I have to get my life back."

By putting mine at risk? Kendra realized in that moment that Ethan had been correct. Jillian really would be content sacrificing Kendra to save herself. She detached herself from Jillian's grip. "I took the case and I'll see it through. You'll get your life back." *And I will have repaid my debt.* She turned to Masters. "When and where do I report?"

* * *

Ethan and Kendra were given the standard gear, except for the substitution of blanks for live ammo, and one hour to return home. Just long enough for Kendra to leave Baby with Mindy.

"I would leave her alone for one night, but she needs medicines," Kendra explained to the neighbor.

"Don't you worry about a thing." Mindy cooed into Baby's neck. "I'll take good care of her. Have fun traipsing with your training, now, you hear?"

"We won't go too far. It's just a twelve-hour trek through the wilderness," Kendra said. Ethan wondered if she was trying more to calm herself or Mindy. She was a tough lady, he knew that for sure, but she had no idea what to expect from SERE training. It was going to be a long night.

"In the woods?" As Mindy stroked Baby, a worried frown appeared on her face. "Where the man was?"

"Farther south," Kendra soothed. "It will be okay. I'll be back in the morning. Shall I wait until a decent hour to retrieve Baby?"

"I'm not an early riser, so that would be good." She gave Ethan a sly look. "You two sure know how to go on some pretty wild dates."

Ethan was annoyed to find himself blushing. Survival training was the furthest thing from fun, he wanted to say, and an even further thing from a date.

Besides, if he was going to take Kendra on a date, he would take her to the best BBQ place in Texas and then maybe for a walk under the stars. He'd show her the constellations and buy her the nicest box of chocolates he could find and a big bunch of tulips. His mama always drummed into him that a classy woman must have chocolates and flowers, fine quality chocolates in shiny boxes, preferably soft centers, for some mysterious reason he'd never understood. Nuts and chews would not do. Deployed or not, every year on Mother's Day that was exactly what he got her, too, his mama, the finest woman he knew.

He imagined handing Kendra a bouquet of tulips, maybe pink, the color her cheeks turned when he teased her. That soft, silky pink of sunsets and shells tossed up on the sand.

He blinked. *Where is your mind?* he chided himself. Planning imaginary dates with Kendra when there was a killer at large? "Time to get going."

The training would begin at Baylor with a refresher, and then they'd move out, traversing the course, which would take them off base and deep into the surrounding woods. Twelve hours in which the twenty some odd soldiers would spread out, conceivably on their own, but he fully intended to break that rule, until they rendezvoused back at base at precisely 0600 hours. Normally he'd relish the situation, the challenge of relying on his wits and savvy, but now he had Kendra to think about. Open spaces and sitting ducks came to mind, and the delicate pink of her cheeks that kept popping into his mind to his dismay.

They reported to the classroom first, where an instructor gave Titus a stern eye but made no remark about Ethan's presence. He'd been given his marching orders from Masters but it didn't mean he had to like them.

"Your job, soldiers, is to survive, evade, resist and escape. If you fail at these endeavors, you will face your enemy armed only with the articles from the Code of Conduct."

He slapped a hand on the poster on the wall and they read the articles aloud.

"I am an American fighting in the forces which guard my country and our way of life. I am prepared to give my life in their defense," Ethan recited.

He sneaked a look at Kendra, small and determined, her chin high and proud in a way that made his stomach tighten. She recited, "I will never surrender of my own free will. If in command, I will never surrender the members of my command while they still have the means to resist."

The room swelled with the words of the dozen men and women. He felt the ripple of pride, as he always did, the privilege of serving shoulder to shoulder with people who meant every word they spoke.

When they reached the last article on the poster, their volume rose together, each syllable crisp and precise.

"I will never forget that I am an American, fighting for freedom, responsible for my actions and dedicated to the principles which made my country free. I will trust in my God and in the United States of America."

Kendra looked at him then. She didn't smile but the courage in her eyes got right inside him.

"Soldiers," the instructor said, sweeping the room and lighting for a moment on Kendra. "Don't get caught."

She won't, Ethan promised silently.

They assembled outside and prepared to load up in the back of a truck.

"Be back here at oh six hundred or you flunk the course," the instructor said.

Kendra crawled up into the truck and Ethan followed, hoisting Titus up behind him.

"Since when are dogs allowed, man?" a young marine said from the corner, a touch of resentment in his tone.

Ethan shot him a grin. "Don't worry. He's not much of an advantage since he's scared of the dark."

That got the chuckles he was looking for.

"How long has it been since your last SERE training, Jillian?"

Ethan's head jerked toward the familiar voice.

Lieutenant Heidi Jenks sat against the truck wall, wearing the same woodland fatigues, notebook in her hand. The plastic cover was torn, held together with duct tape.

Kendra gaped. "What are you doing here?"

"I was talking to the Baylor base reporter to get some intel on the murder and I heard about this class. I thought it would make for an interesting article," she said as she eyed Ethan, "since one of our own is participating for some reason."

"Planning on putting this up on the underground blog?"

Jenks smiled. "I told you, that isn't me."

"I don't believe you," Ethan said.

She lifted a shoulder. "I'm having trouble believing a few things myself." Her eyes locked on Kendra. "So when exactly was your last SERE training?"

Ethan had to get her off that line of questioning. "So you're going to complete the SERE training with us?"

"Just until sundown when the hunting starts," Jenks said.

"And who gave you permission?"

"Colonel Masters himself."

Ethan bit back a groan.

"Weird, huh?" Jenks lowered her voice to a whisper. "I mean, why would Masters have his daughter participate in SERE when she's got a serial killer gunning for her?"

And why would he let a nosy base reporter tag along?

Same reason.

He wanted to make it easy.

If Heidi Jenks was Sullivan's accomplice, Masters had just invited her to take the kill shot.

ELEVEN

Kendra repeated the instructions to herself.

"Find water. Move toward the rendezvous point while avoiding capture." And Heidi Jenks, she told herself. They had a two-hour grace period before the marines began to hunt them down.

Ethan and Titus were somewhere close by, she knew, but they could not join her with so many other soldiers around. Participants were supposed to go it alone. She suspected Ethan would be breaking that rule early on. She started hiking up river, grateful that her brother, Kevin, had repeatedly dragged her out camping in the mountains. She had a basic idea of how to stay alive, at least for one night. First order of the day was to obtain safe water and fill the empty container in her pack.

Jenks appeared at her elbow. "So you didn't answer my question. How long has it been since you completed your last SERE training?"

The reporter was as determined as a dog on the scent, Kendra thought. She squared off with her. "My sole job right now is to survive and not get captured, so with all due respect, I won't be able to answer your questions. As a matter of fact, I'd like you to leave me alone, period."

To her surprise, the woman laughed. "That's more polite than I would have thought from you, Jillian. You've changed. Is that why you and Ethan are back together? You've turned over a new leaf?"

Kendra's pulse kicked up a notch. This reporter knew Jillian well enough to know that Kendra wasn't acting quite the part. "That's another question I'm not answering," she said, marching purposefully. "Go find someone else to badger, why don't you?"

"I'm used to reluctant subjects. They warm up eventually."

"Not this one."

To her dismay, Jenks trekked right along with her until they were about a mile upstream. Once she collected her supply of water she intended to move to deeper cover to find shelter until she could decide on the best way to evade the marines assigned to capture her. Sullivan, if he was nearby, would most likely not make a move during the daylight with soldiers in the vicinity. Then again, maybe Jenks would attempt to act for him.

She glanced at the reporter. No visible weapon. But that didn't mean she wasn't carrying a gun in her small pack. Keeping Jenks in her line of sight as best she could, she scooped water into the small bowl from her pack and carried it to a flat spot under a thick canopy of trees. The ground was wet but she managed to find some relatively dry twigs. Removing the faro fire starter from her pack, she knelt and began to rub the striker against the block, a trick Ethan had tried to explain during their drive back to Baylor after leaving Baby with Mindy.

A spark dropped into the tinder, eliciting a wisp of smoke. Elated, she blew gently on the pile, but instead of igniting a flame she promptly extinguished it. She slapped a hand to her thigh.

"A little rusty?" Jenks said.

"Everything's too wet," she muttered.

"I'll see if I can find something drier."

Kendra stared. "You're helping?"

"Yeah, 'cuz you're going to share the water with me, right?"

Mutual cooperation, or an excuse to stay close? Kendra kept at the fire starter until her hands were cramped. The stiff breeze left over from the storm both chilled and frustrated her.

Jenks returned. "Nothing much drier than what you've got."

Kendra fastened a hand on Jenks's notebook. "I need that tape."

"What?"

"The tape that's holding your book together. Let's have it."

"But I—"

"You want the water or not?"

Jenks reluctantly peeled away the tape and handed it over. Kendra made a loose ball of it and nestled it on top of the tinder. This time, the spark caught the tape and sent up a respectable flame that ignited the tinder. Fire. Awesome.

Jenks nodded. "I have to admit, I wouldn't have thought of that."

The fire boiled the water and after it cooled, Ken-

dra filled both their bottles. Never had she appreciated clean water more.

"Thank you," Jenks said. She checked her phone.
"Uh-oh. I have to go."

"Where?"

She raised an eyebrow. "You think you're the only
one with a duty here?"

"What's your duty exactly?"

"Sniffing out a story, just like I said. I have great
instincts and something tells me you've got *newswor-
thy* written all over you."

"I'm just a soldier trying to get through training."

Her eyes narrowed. "Somehow, I doubt that." A few
drops of rain began to fall. "Oh, boy. Another storm.
Looks like you're in for long night."

Kendra shrugged. "I've had plenty of long nights."

The shadows shifted, painting Jenks's face in eerie
stripes of light and dark. "Some nights are longer than
others."

Was that a threat? A promise of trouble to come?

Jenks opened her pack and Kendra bolted to her
feet. No sense reaching for her weapon as they were
not allowed to use live ammo.

She calmed down when Jenks merely stowed the
water bottle in her pack and fastened it closed.

The reporter wasted no time. She shouldered the
pack and went on her way. "Hope the morning comes
quickly."

Kendra waited until Jenks vanished into the trees
before she struck out into the woods. The more tree
trunks between her and Jenks the better. Wind rattled
the leaves, teased prickles on her skin, but it dampened

the heat of the day. She kept within earshot of the river to maintain her sense of direction.

As she hiked the clammy ground she thought she heard someone behind her. She stopped and turned. No one. A few yards off a bird shot from the bushes, startled by something. Ethan and Titus were out there somewhere but for the moment, Kendra was totally and completely alone.

Unless there was someone in the shadows, watching and waiting for their moment to strike.

Kendra followed the river and Ethan and Titus trailed her. There was no imminent danger, yet his instincts were poking him like a kid with a sharp stick as he trailed her.Sullivan was at large; he'd murdered a marine not fifteen miles from here. And now Jenks was cozying up?

Titus managed the hike with his typical enthusiasm, finally flopping down in the shade to rest while Ethan boiled water for both of them when Heidi and Kendra stopped to rest. They'd been hiking for a few hours. Technically, they were not allowed cell phones, but since this wasn't official training for him, he'd taken it along. Unfortunately, the farther he delved into the woods, the worse his signal became. Anticipating the problem, he'd strapped on the trusty Timex he'd bought when he delivered pizza as a sixteen-year-old kid to track the time. The thing had seen him through two deployments, not to mention the adventure when he'd tumbled off a mountain bike back home. It was almost five o'clock. His stomach grumbled. Food was the last item on the agenda. A person could live for weeks without anything to eat, but drinking was another matter entirely.

The canopy of branches squeezed out the light, stripping away the warmth. A branch caught his ankle and he tumbled down a steep incline, the breath driven out of him. Titus looked down from the ridge as if to say, "What did you do that for?" He wagged his tail and barked.

Muttering, Ethan climbed laboriously out. "You could have come and helped," he grumbled to Titus. He huffed out a breath when he realized he was no longer within sight of Kendra. She'd moved out during his tumble.

Quickly, he drank again, refilled the bottle for him and Titus and shouldered his pack.

"Time to find Kendra, boy." He pulled her sweater from his pack. Titus sniffed and tongued the fabric before trotting confidently off between the tangles of spiky branches. Titus wasn't a scent dog, but he'd never failed to blow Ethan away with his skills. Trusting his dog, he followed. He wished he had a good scent article for Sullivan. He'd feel a lot safer knowing Titus had Sullivan's essence stored in that amazing nose of his.

But the woods were full of invisible aromas, and Titus took off after one. Ethan prayed it would lead to Kendra.

As the sun set completely, the rain started to come down in sheets. Kendra figured there was no point in putting up the shelter since there would be an "enemy" soldier combing the woods for her in a matter of moments.

She pulled on the dark-patterned poncho that billowed over her with enough room left over to cover her backpack. Sitting in the scant shelter of a rock formation, she tried to pick out a path. The rising darkness cloaked everything in odd shadows, and a wall of clouds obliterated the moon. The only sound she could discern above the crashing rain was the pounding of her own heart. She'd always avoided the darkness, ever since those long-ago nights when Andy would pace in manic circles deep into the night, smoking and drinking with his friends after she'd crawled away to her own room, addled by drugs, filled with self-loathing. Now, she and Baby slept with a small lamp on so when the nightmares came, bringing the self-recrimination, she would sit up and read the little plaque set on the night table.

There is therefore now no condemnation...

She'd been forgiven, washed clean, but sometimes, especially on moonless rainy nights, she still felt the vicious bite of fear. She wondered why Ethan hadn't tried to make contact.

"Get moving," she ordered herself. "You know which way the river is, so follow it." She forced her cold limbs into motion. As she picked her way over slick logs, past dripping trees, something stirred in the brush. She took cover behind a tree, crouching as small as she could manage, her pulse thundering.

A flicker of light shone, small, the soft glow of a cell phone screen. Phones weren't allowed by the SERE participants, but Kendra had one anyway. Useless without a signal. Those playing the enemy had satellite phones, which worked in spite of the terrain. The glow could be a soldier enacting the enemy role. They had privileges the hunted did not.

Someone moved through the bushes five feet to her right, a man in cammies, walking soft-footed with his rifle raised, water dripping from the brim of his hat. He was tall, like every soldier, it seemed. Like Sullivan. Fright roared through her.

Who are you hunting? her mind screamed. If it was Sullivan, it would be a relief to confront him, to finally face the man she'd been hired to capture. But she could not see clearly through the pounding rain.

When he'd moved a safe distance away, she eased up from her hiding place, intending to follow at a safe distance. If it was a marine tracking her, she'd have to head in the other direction and loop around when the coast was clear. Easing each booted foot along as quietly as she could, she kept her eyes on the ground, scanning for twigs that might snap and give her away, or rocks that might result in a noisy fall. She'd made it several yards when a rough palm clamped over her mouth, holding in her scream.

TWELVE

Ethan felt Kendra tense under his palm.

"It's me," he whispered, but not before she drove an elbow into his stomach. He lurched back, doubled over, and Titus shoved a wet nose in his face. "I'm okay," he assured the dog.

Kendra whirled, hands on hips, glaring at him. "What were you thinking?" she whispered in a tone just south of furious.

"I was thinking," he muttered back, "that you might cry out and give away our location."

She was breathing hard. "You scared me."

He managed an upright posture and a half-hearted breath. "I'm sorry." Titus stood on hind legs and licked Ethan's face, double-checking his handler. "Okay, down, you big galoot." He pressed a hand to his throbbing gut. "I saw the sentry. He's twenty yards to the north."

"I saw him, too," she said. "I was busy avoiding him when you decided to scare the wits out of me with your ninja skills."

"Seems like you still have your wits to me," he said. "I think you might have damaged my spleen."

"Serves you right for that bonehead move." She shook her head, disgusted, then her expression shifted into concern. "Did I really hurt you?"

He smiled. "No, ma'am. I was just looking for some sympathy."

She exhaled. "Okay. Sorry about the elbow." She offered a small pat to his shoulder. "If your spleen is fully functional, we'd better move."

"Yes, ma'am." They continued looping around away from the river, making their mucky way over the forest detritus.

"Did you recognize the soldier?" Kendra asked.

"Tall, dark and deadly, that's all I got."

"Me, too. Probably a marine."

"Probably." He picked up the pace. In spite of the doggy raincoat Ethan had put on him, Titus kept stopping to shake the moisture from his ears. "He's more used to dry conditions than rain."

"Me, too," she said. They continued on, the irregular slope requiring all their mental and physical energies. The night ticked away and fatigue began to prey on Ethan, but Kendra did not complain nor slow, so they pushed on, Titus as tireless as ever.

After an arduous uphill climb, Ethan signaled a stop. They'd arrived at a mad jumble of rocks, some piled as high as fifty feet. "Good lookout point." He ordered Titus to sit at Kendra's side under the shelter of a rock overhang. He began to climb, the footholds easy to find but slippery. When he reached a smooth section of stone, he lay down and peered through his night-vision binocs. He located one soldier easily enough, probably a newbie to the SERE training or cold enough to risk a fire where he thought he wouldn't be seen.

He'd be captured quickly. Nothing else moved that he could detect. To the east lay the road they would take to Baylor before sunup in order to reach the base by the appointed hour.

His watch read 2:00 a.m., still three hours to evade capture. At that point, the evasion portion would be complete and all they would have to do was get back to base. Best to hole up. He figured this was the optimal location and time to do it. Good view, plenty of hiding spots, shelter from the rain.

He returned to ground level and found Kendra and Titus gone. His stomach dropped to his boots. For a moment he second-guessed himself, but it was precisely the spot he'd left them with strict orders not to leave.

Frantically he examined the ground for any signs of attack. Why hadn't Titus barked? He plunged into the shrubs, wildly scanning, calling as loud as he dared. A gleam of movement, a subtle shifting in the darkness burned into his vision. He drew his weapon, figuring blanks were better than nothing as he raced forward, keeping low under an overgrown thicket with razor-sharp thorns. He must have misjudged their safety, missed a sentry or missed Sullivan. Nerves kicked up all over his body.

Titus darted out from behind a bush, running at Ethan, blood showing on his mouth. Ethan's breath crystallized in his lungs. Where was Kendra? The dog bounded up, and Ethan inhaled the smell of berries.

Not blood. Juice.

"You rotten dog…"

"Quiet," Kendra said, stepping out of the shrubs.

"You're making enough noise to bring in the marines for sure."

"Where…where did you go?" he sputtered.

"I got us some dinner."

He couldn't believe his ears. "What?" he finally managed.

She held out a handkerchief full of glistening black-berries. "There's a whole thicket of them."

He goggled, fear crystallizing into anger. "You shouldn't have moved. I thought something happened to you."

She raised an eyebrow. "Did I scare you?"

If the light had been better, he figured he'd have seen a glint of satisfaction on her face. "Dumb move."

"I weighed the risks."

"You didn't have the right to take my dog off his assignment."

"He shouldn't have let me, right?"

Ethan glowered at Titus. "Right, and we're going to have to do some retraining."

The dog snaked a tongue over his lips. Kendra laughed. "He doesn't look the least bit sorry."

"Well, you should be," he snapped. "This isn't a game, Kendra."

She went still. "It's never been a game for me, Ethan."

"Then stop treating it like one. One bullet and you're dead, don't you understand that?" One bullet, like Martelli, like the others. One shot you didn't see coming, from an enemy you'd let stray from your mind for one second.

Even in the darkness he could see her eyes glimmer. "I know what it's like to be hunted."

Hunted. The word disintegrated his anger. Hunted, by a man she thought she'd loved. Stung, shot at, terrorized. She'd lived her own kind of war for longer than he had. *Yeah, dumb comment, Webb.*

"Let's get to shelter," he said before anything else came out of his mouth.

Titus trotted to his side. "I mean it, dog. You need retraining," he said. "Since when do you take orders from her?"

Ethan scouted the area until he located the crevice he'd spotted earlier, a depression punched into the rock wall. It was not high enough for them to stand up, but it was comfortable for two sitting adults and a sprawling dog. The floor was mostly dry and clean after he kicked the debris away. By the time they entered, Kendra was shivering, her teeth chattering together.

"Sorry, we can't risk a fire."

"It's okay. At least we have dinner." She laid the berries out between them. Perfectly ripe, thumb-sized, succulent.

He ate a handful. "Best berries I've ever had," he declared, "but it still doesn't make it okay what you did wandering off."

"So Titus and I are still in the doghouse?"

"He's definitely in the doghouse." He rubbed his sticky hands clean on his wet pant leg. "But, uh, what I said back there, that wasn't cool."

She wiped her fingers on her pants. "It's okay. In a way there's some truth to it. I think Andy thought of our relationship as a game. How far could he string me along, how much could he push." She leaned against the rock, her gaze drifting to the rain falling outside the cave. "He was raised by a single parent, too, an alcoholic." Her smile was rueful. "We had a lot in common."

"Not the right stuff, though."

She shrugged. "I didn't think I was worth too much when I met him and he agreed. Just strung me along, like I said, and I was dumb enough to let him."

"What was the turning point?"

She didn't answer for a moment, and then she rolled up her right sleeve to show a long narrow scar. "I found a stray cat starving under our apartment step. I took her in and Andy grumbled, but he didn't resist too much until she used his guitar case as a scratching post."

He saw the play of emotion as the memory unfolded itself.

"He went after her with a kitchen knife. I fended him off with a chair, but he cut me." Her fingers stroked the edge of her sleeve, as if she was comforting the terrified cat. "The cat was able to hide, though."

"Baby?" he said.

She nodded. "I realized that we weren't alike, Andy and me, not fundamentally, not deep down, but I wasn't sure how to get out of the mess I'd made. A few days later he told me we were going to rob a mini mart and if I didn't go along with the plan, he would kill me and the cat. That's when I decided to call Jillian." She looked at him then, tears glistening in her eyes. "See why Baby means so much to me?"

He took her hand and pulled her into the circle of his arm. "Yeah, I sure do."

She snuggled next to him, leaning against his chest as if they'd known each other forever. The scent of the woods clung to her wet hair, as alluring as the silk of her cheek brushing his chin. He kissed her temple, pressed her close as if he could blast away her terrible past.

Not possible.

And not the right thing anyway. Her past was what made her who she was, turned her to God. The fact that she'd shared it with him, her worst moment, made something inside him crack open. He wanted to kiss her as she turned her face to his. She was so beautiful, like an angel painted on the wall of stone behind her. He cupped her face, bent close and fitted her mouth to his. A current of electricity jolted through him, the completion of a circuit he hadn't known about. She kissed him back, warm, giving, tender.

Nothing ever felt quite like this. Comfort, belonging, wholeness, peace.

But something wriggled in his memory. He flashed back to Jillian, how he'd bared his soul to her, how she'd stripped him of his dignity and his pride. Pain and humiliation and shame all roared back in a split second.

Not again, not ever.

He eased Kendra to his side and they leaned against the cold rock, breathing unsteadily.

"I, uh, sorry," he mumbled. "Got caught up. Won't happen again."

He thought he heard her sigh. From disappointment? Or relief?

"It's okay," she whispered and he couldn't decipher the emotion in it.

Get her through it and don't let yourself want anything more. Wanting led to yearning, to trusting, to a heart flayed wide-open. His mind remained stone-cold logical, but his heart hungered in a way that scared him silly.

Cold seeped inside him, wrestling with a warmth that she kindled in the dark places. In agonizing slow motion, the minutes crept by.

It felt like morning would never come.

The hours wore on and they took turns keeping watch. While Ethan hunkered down somewhere outside with his binoculars in hand, she lay on the ground with Titus snuggled against her back. The unaccustomed freedom that she had finally shared her burden with Ethan gave way to grief.

Got caught up. Won't happen again.

His words were a harsh reminder. Ethan wasn't interested. He'd said so from the beginning. Her feelings had changed, his had not. *Wake up and smell the coffee, Kendra.* Besides, why would she have wanted more kisses in the middle of SERE training with threats coming at them from all sides? Was she losing her mind?

It was her turn to take over the watch, so she sat up. Though it was still dark, she figured it had to be sometime near the end of the evasion portion of the drill. Sullivan wasn't going to make a move, or so it seemed, but at least they'd survived the SERE refresher, satisfied Masters's whim and could move on with their investigation.

She heaved herself up, muscles complaining, back aching from her time on the hard ground. Rejoicing to see that the rain had stopped, she stepped out, and that's when horror fired her nerves into flame.

Ethan lay stomach down on the ground, a soldier standing over him with a gun aimed at his skull.

"Time to die," the soldier said.

Kendra didn't hesitate, she swung her rifle like a club, smashing the soldier in the back of the knees. He went down like a felled tree. Titus was out of the cave in a flash of fur, diving on the man and nearly ripping off his uniform.

Ethan leaped to his feet.

"Get him off, Ethan," the marine hollered, rolling into a ball to protect his face.

Ethan hollered at Titus, who promptly returned to Ethan's side and sat, staring down his enemy.

The soldier sat up and Kendra thought he looked vaguely familiar.

"Hector," Ethan said with a smile. "Fancy meeting you here. Out for a stroll?"

Hector was the marine who'd investigated when she'd been shot at. He was not smiling. He got to his feet. "Not cool to bring your dog along to save your bacon."

"He didn't save me," Ethan said. "She did."

Kendra wriggled her fingers. "Hey, Hector. Sorry about that."

He eyed her name patch. "Thought your name was Kendra. How come you're Jillian Masters all of a sudden?"

Ethan shook his head. "Long story, but for now, she's Jillian. You can confirm that with Colonel Masters."

"Jillian, as in your ex-wife Jillian?"

He nodded.

"Man," Hector said, "you airmen sure know how to get yourself into a pile of trouble, don't you?"

"That's an affirmative," Ethan said.

"Well, anyway, you're dead 'cuz I got you down on the ground before ole slugger and Fido here saved you."

"No, sir," Ethan said, holding his ancient Timex. "It's zero five ten hours, Marine. You're ten minutes past the deadline. We won."

Hector laughed. "All right. Leave it to Webb to land on his feet." His smile vanished. "Lieutenant Masters, I am charged with delivering a message to you."

Kendra stiffened.

"Yes?" she said.

Hector brushed off his uniform, jammed a hand into his pack and pulled out a piece of paper. He held it out to Kendra, who took it. "Safe travels back to base."

Ethan waved and Hector began to clamber down the rocky trail.

Kendra opened the note.

I need to speak with you both immediately. Urgent.
—*Officer Alonso Carpenter.*

THIRTEEN

Kendra puzzled over the message as they hiked back to the road. She desperately wished her cell phone signal would kick in.

"We'll be back in less than an hour. We can call from base or when our cell phones are operation. Whichever comes first," Ethan said.

In spite of the adrenaline, Kendra found her legs were leaden as she tried her best to keep up with Ethan and Titus. Muscles screamed for attention, made worse by the cold infiltrating her limbs via her damp clothing. After stopping twice to remove stickers from Titus's paws, they finally made it to the frontage road that would take them to base. A smooth surface. She felt like cheering.

Behind them, barely discernible in the gloom, were two other soldiers dragging themselves back to base, tired, hungry, no doubt as relieved as she was that it was all over. Somewhere sprinkled along the road were the rest of the trainees.

She scratched at a row of mosquito bites on her neck, a new series of welts to replace the wasp stings that had died away. What had the whole exercise gained them? Not much. Sullivan had not showed his hand. Heidi Jenks had proved just as much of an enigma. Kendra had bared her soul to Ethan in the cave, only to have him back away. Now every muscle was screaming for her to stop, but they had a generous three miles to go back to base. She had a whole new admiration for the men and women of the US military.

A hot shower, she told herself. She'd have a hot shower and a cheeseburger and then call Officer Carpenter. That mantra echoed in her mind as she forced one soggy boot in front of the other. The trail funneled toward a ten-foot bridge that spanned a narrow section of river. Below, the water roared, swollen from the spring rains. Still wet and clammy, she'd had quite enough water for one day.

She'd moved a couple of feet onto the bridge, Ethan a few feet ahead of her, when a shout cut through the gray morning.

She stopped, whirled and then she heard it.

One shot, followed by three more.

A soldier raced up the road, awkward in his heavy pack and muddy boots. "Incoming," he hollered. "Guy's driving crazy. I tried to fire some warning shots."

"What?" Kendra yelled.

Tires squealed and a car with no lights careened past the soldier, who futilely fired another blank round at the tires.

Kendra froze, staring as the car hurtled toward her.

"Run," Ethan shouted. He was beside her now, Titus barking wildly. "Get across the bridge to the woods on the other side." He took up a position dead center in the road and began firing blank rounds at the car.

"Ethan, no," she yelled. "They'll run you down."

"Go," he snarled. "Now."

She ran farther onto the bridge, tossing aside her heavy pack. The car edged closer. Had Ethan got out of the way?

Her boots weighed her feet down, but she ran as fast as she could, her pulse thundering, lungs straining, gasping for breath. Now the car was so close it kicked up gravel that struck the back of her neck. She turned to look, horrified to see the bumper inches away, the shadow of a figure in the driver's seat cloaked in darkness, its gloved fingers gripping the wheel. She couldn't see the driver's face but he emitted the same kind of crazy she'd seen in Andy.

Crazy, mixed with hatred and a need for vengeance that would only be satisfied with her death.

With every ounce of energy she could muster, she sprinted for the other side, for the safety of the trees, but the end of the bridge might as well have been miles away.

Despair hit hard and heavy as she realized she was not going to make it. She would be crushed under the wheels, the life expunged from her in a violent punch of metal on bone.

No. God, give me strength. Just a little more.

But she did not have the stamina to escape the car. There was only one way to survive…if she had the courage.

In one explosive leap, she vaulted onto the bridge railing, sprawling across the rail, folded in half by the force. Time slowed down as she teetered there. The car scraped the side of the bridge, sending sparks, tremors that shook her body as she heaved herself over and plummeted down into the water.

* * *

Ethan scrambled up from the spot where he'd dived with Titus as the car roared past him. "Kendra!" His shout was lost in the grind of metal on metal as the vehicle scraped the rail, crossed the bridge and disappeared.

His heart hammering and his stomach knotted, he ran. He pounded onto the bridge, scanning, searching, dreading what he would find.

Where was Kendra?

He found the impact site where the car had skimmed the side of the bridge. No Kendra. Titus put his paws up over the railing and barked. Ethan threw himself against the rail, staring down into the oil-black eddies.

"Kendra!" he shouted as loud as he could. Forget the investigation, forget her cover. His heart burned, his soul ached with one thought only.

He had to find her.

Reversing course, he met the other soldier and Hector tearing up the road.

"Sit rep, Airman," Hector barked.

"Vehicle headed north on Pine Hill Road," Ethan told him. "Front and rear plates obscured. She... Jillian Masters is in the water. We need a rescue crew."

Hector pulled a radio from his belt and relayed the information. "Water's moving fast," he said to Ethan.

He understood. By the time the rescue crew was in place, she might very well be dead. He got the flashlight from his pack and called Titus.

Hector reached out a hand to stop him. "Ethan—"

"I'm going to find her. You and the police get the car."

Several soldiers had gathered around.

"That driver was nuts," one said. "Like he was gunning right for her."

"How'd they pick her out?" his partner said. "We all look like filthy, dirty grunts."

Ethan's gut clenched. The driver knew Kendra was with Ethan and the dog. Titus had been a neon sign. *Come and get her.*

"Sir, permission to aid in the search for the victim," one of the soldiers said.

Hector considered. "You up to it, Soldier?"

"Sir, yes, sir."

His compatriot chimed in as well. "Me, too, sir."

Hector nodded. "Report in every fifteen."

"Yes, sir," the men said.

Ethan felt a swell of gratitude for his brothers in arms.

They shoved flashlights in their pockets and Hector handed one a first-aid kit along with a coil of rope and a radio.

"We'll take the north bank, Lieutenant," one of the soldiers said.

"I've got the south," Ethan confirmed.

"Good hunting, Marines." Hector said. "You, too, Airman."

Ethan and Titus raced in the direction the current must have taken her. He prayed the water under the bridge was deep enough to absorb her fall without causing broken arms and legs or worse. The roar was intense along the shore. He and Titus pushed through the tall grasses. He was not sure Titus was a good enough tracker to detect Kendra's scent in the water and the specialty they'd been training for recently wasn't finding the living. Nonetheless, Titus stuck his nose to every muck-filled pocket and rock, wriggling his way along. *Trust your dog.*

Under the dense shadows of the trees, Ethan shone the flashlight and shouted her name with every few feet. He heard the echo of the soldiers on the far bank doing the same. He shouted again and stopped to listen. No answer but the roar of water.

His flashlight picked out a massive tree trunk, flipped on its side in the water, a mad tangle of roots protruding in every direction. The beam danced over the wet wood, and he was about to pass by when the light caught a flick of white in the darkness. He splashed in up to his knees, fighting the current, rubbing his eyes to be sure. This time he knew he was not mistaken. Curled around an exposed root was a tightly clenched fist.

Kendra was dizzy from her tumultuous journey, numb both from the icy water and her vicious impact into the river. She'd swallowed a lot of water and the cold was beginning to ice over her limbs, loosen her precarious grip on the root or branch or whatever it was that she had tumbled into. She had to hold on, recover enough to make it to shore, or call for help in case Ethan was within earshot.

She remembered his defiant stance as he faced the car head on, firing shots into the front windshield. What if…?

Stop thinking and start moving, she ordered herself, but her fingers were frozen into a desperate claw and she found she was shivering too much to even fill her lungs with air to call out.

Cold.

It was all she could think of.

So cold.

When something landed in the water near her she was too chilled to look.

"I've got you," a voice said.

Ethan. Where had he come from? She wanted to fall into his arms but she could not move, could not let go. Her body would simply not obey.

Titus grabbed hold of her uniform sleeve and began to tug.

"Stop," she whispered. "I'll drown."

Ethan's face swam into view through the spray. "Let go, honey. I've got you now."

Can't. Cold. Scared.

He put his face closer and kissed her. His lips were soft on hers, and she wanted to disappear inside the tenderness, the comfort, the warmth. The kiss was all she could feel. It was everything.

"It's okay," he said, his eyes riveted to hers. "Trust me. I'm going to get you out of here."

Out of here. Trust me.

He pried gently at her grip. "Put your hands around my neck. Here. Like this." He prized her fingers from the wet wood and she almost screamed, but he placed them around his shoulders. She clung to him, his body strong and steady against the current.

Trust me.

She pressed her face to his, her lips against his stubbled jaw as he yelled to someone on shore. A rope splashed down in the water and Ethan fastened it around them. After a tug, a lurch that made her want to cry out again, they were in the thick of the current, being pummeled by the raging water.

Sensing her rising panic, he pressed her head to his neck. "It's okay. You're okay. They're pulling us out."

Ethan called to Titus, and when the dog did not follow quickly enough, he grabbed him with the arm that wasn't fastened around her. Inch by inch, they were loosened from the iron grip of the water until she heard the mud squishing under Ethan's boots.

The others, soldiers, too, she realized, took her arms and moved her away from the water onto a flat rock outcropping. She felt rather than heard the man next to her snap to attention. "He's gone back in."

She jackknifed to a sitting position.

"Ethan? Why?" She thought she screamed the words but only a whisper came out.

The soldier raced back to the water's edge, running alongside the riverbed, shouting something she could not hear. She tried to crawl, but the other soldier held her back.

"Stay here, ma'am. They'll handle it."

"Handle it?" she gasped. "The water is a roller coaster and he's wearing boots and gear. You have to help him. He'll drown. Why would he go back in? Why?"

"The dog, ma'am."

"Titus?"

"He couldn't make it out. Got loose and the water sucked him back in. The lieutenant went after him."

She stared. He'd risked his life for her and now he was doing the same thing for a dog. Not just a dog, a fellow soldier, a brother.

"I want to help," she said, trying to get her wobbling legs to cooperate as he unfolded a metallic blanket and draped it over her. She pushed it away.

"Ma'am, stay here. You're nearing hypothermic."

"I'll warm up."

"No, ma'am." He unclipped the radio from his belt. "Medic will be here shortly."

"I have to help Ethan. Titus…" She pictured the big goofy dog, stained with blackberry juice, trying to persuade Ethan that it was bedtime. Ethan's best friend.

She made it to her knees when the radio squawked.

"Is he… Did they find him?"

A funny look came over his face and he pointed upriver. She sank back to the ground, fear thick as the night air.

Ethan clomped over the rocks, the other soldier at his side, Titus draped over his shoulders, a still, dark shadow. Her heart twisted into a knot until Titus raised his head and barked, a throaty, beautiful, raucous sound.

She blinked back tears.

Ethan knelt and eased Titus to the ground.

"Nutty dog thinks he's an Olympic swimmer. I told you to get out of the water. Didn't you hear me?" He pressed his nose to the dog's wet head. Titus slurped a lick over Ethan's forehead. Ethan ordered him to a sit next to Kendra. She reached out a tentative arm. Ethan did not correct the dog, so he snuggled up next to her, shivering. She wrapped the silver blanket around them both, cuddling as much as she could of the wet animal.

Ethan crouched next to her. "How are you?" he asked gently.

"I'm f-f-fine," she said, teeth chattering.

He pulled the blanket around her tighter. "It's okay not to be."

No, it's not, she thought. *You could have died. Titus*

could have died, all to help me. It was not tolerable even to think it.

The medics arrived carrying a stretcher between them since there was no way to get a vehicle close enough. They checked her vitals after Ethan coaxed Titus away and bundled him in his own blanket.

"I'm not going to the base clinic," Kendra said. "I'm going home."

The medic arched an eyebrow. "Ma'am, you need to be checked out by a doctor."

"No, I don't." *I need to get home, lock the doors and take the hottest shower I can manage.*

The medic looked at Ethan. "Lieutenant?"

Ethan nodded and came to her side. "Jillian," he said, "I'm not gonna argue with you about this."

"Good."

"And I know I'm in for it later."

"What—" Before she could say another word, he scooped her up and laid her on the stretcher. If her body wasn't trembling like a leaf in the storm, she would have leaped off immediately and given him a sock in the shoulder. As it was, all she could do was lie there and glare at him as the medics strapped her to a board and hoisted her between them like a sack of laundry.

"Ethan," she snapped.

"I know, you're gonna make me pay. I get it." He turned to the medics. "I'll follow you."

They nodded and carried her away, helpless, miserable and furious.

FOURTEEN

Ethan refused to debrief one word of the incident with Hector and his security team until they summoned a local veterinarian to come and check Titus over. Unsettled and on edge, Titus wasn't having any of it until Ethan forced the growling dog to cooperate. Still, the veterinarian was a shade paler by the time he completed his work. Ethan didn't blame him. With a bite strength of more than two hundred pounds of pressure, Titus wasn't to be trifled with and he hadn't even gotten his man. Ethan felt like growling, too.

The vet wiped his brow. "I gave him some antibiotics just in case he swallowed something nasty, and treated the abrasion on his paw. He's earned a cheeseburger or something for not eating me."

"Aww, he wouldn't have eaten you," Ethan said with a smile, "not unless I told him to. Might have taken a little bite, just to taste."

"Good to know," said the vet as he left.

The doctor was still with Kendra when Ethan settled in the waiting room where Hector stood leaning against the wall. He'd been more than patient...for a marine. Titus sprawled out on a sofa and promptly started snoring.

"I looped Officer Carpenter in," Hector said. "He's on his way."

"Even though you didn't want to?"

He lifted a shoulder. "Just like last time, the incident wasn't on base property so it's out of my hands, which irritates me." Hector drilled him with a look. "Ethan, what's the real story here?"

"What do you mean?"

"Someone's trying real hard to kill Jillian Masters. First the gunshots, now the car. We've been briefed on your Red Rose Killer, at least what the air force has been willing to share. Is this who we're dealing with here?"

"I don't know."

Hector's dark eyes shifted. "Can I tell you what I think, bro?"

"I would like to hear it."

"I think this isn't the work of Boyd Sullivan."

Ethan blew out a breath. "Okay. How'd you get there?"

"Because when he wanted to kill here at Baylor and at Canyon, he did. Our marine was shot through the head, up close and personal. Your trainers were, too."

"We figured that also, but it could be he's had to get more creative now, since both the US Air Force and the Marines are after him."

"Could be." Hector clicked his pen.

Again, Ethan waited. *Click, click.*

He would only get what Hector was willing to share with him and that would have to be enough, since

Ethan was not at liberty to tell his friend the whole story.

After two more clicks, Hector started talking. "I heard one of the guys he killed over at Canyon was your buddy," he said slowly. "You two close?"

Ethan gazed at his boots. "Yeah. Landon was a quality person. Gentle with the dogs and respectful to everyone, you know?"

Hector nodded.

Ethan let his mind wander back to the past. "He was going to propose to his girl and he was driving us all crazy trying to figure out the perfect romantic gesture. He was planning to wait until winter and build a snowman holding the box with the ring." Hector laughed. "I told him he was crazy and we teased him that she'd dump him way before the snow fell." Ethan shook his head. "Didn't dampen his spirit one bit. Asked me to be his best man."

Best man, who wasn't even there when he was killed in cold blood. "He was an excellent soldier and a good man."

"Yeah, our marine was a good guy, too. Married, with a baby on the way." More pen clicks. "How's his wife gonna explain Daddy's murder to the kid someday?"

Ethan felt the bile rose in his throat. "I'm sorry."

"Me, too." Hector gave it another moment of thought. "Okay. We're going after Sullivan with both barrels then, but you better keep your eyes peeled for a different enemy, 'cuz like I said, I got another reason to believe this ain't him."

"What's that?"

"One of my marines got a funny impression."

Ethan's instincts prickled. "Funny how?"

"That the driver of the car was a female."

Ethan stared at Hector.

"Just an impression, mind you, nothing concrete. Something about the face… A glimpse really. I had to badger him into telling me since he wasn't certain."

Hector's radio chattered. "Gotta go make a phone call."

"Thanks, Hector."

"Watch your back, man, and you'd better watch hers, too."

The doctor appeared at the door and crooked a finger at Ethan. Titus awakened and followed him into a nearby room. Kendra was sitting up on the exam table, a hospital gown pulled around her. Though her face was pale under the freckles and her hair curling in dirty spirals, her look was determined. She was telegraphing him a message.

Heads up.

"Jillian tells me you two are going to get remarried."

He swallowed. "Yes, sir."

"Not to be rude, but I've heard talk that your breakup was rather…nasty."

"We're putting all that behind us, Doc." He went for a polite smile. "What's her prognosis?"

"Bumps, bruises and a mysterious condition which I can't explain."

His heart thumped. "What?"

"We're a big base here at Baylor, so I've never treated Lieutenant Masters before personally, but we're pretty good at keeping records. Know what my records show, Airman?"

"What's that, sir?"

"That Jillian Masters is five foot eleven."

"Is that right?"

"Yes, it is, and I can't help noticing that this woman is not that tall. In addition, the blood types don't match. Shall I go on?"

"No, sir," Ethan said.

Kendra sucked in a breath. "There is a good explanation, Doctor."

"Great." He picked up the phone. "You'll be able to explain that to the cops when they arrive."

There was a rap on the door frame and Alonso Carpenter stuck his head in.

"No need to call, Doctor," he said. "I'm already here."

Kendra wasn't sure how to feel at Carpenter's arrival. Relieved? Frightened? At the moment she was fighting the numbness that crept into her when she'd hurtled over the rail into the river. She knew for certain whatever Carpenter had to say was going to be big and she did not want to be sitting wrapped in a clinic gown while he said it.

"I'd like to change, please," she announced.

All three men stared at her as if she'd just spoken in Latin. She gestured to the Marine sweat suit on the chair. "They loaned me clothes. I'd like to change before this discussion goes any further."

"All right," the doctor said. "We'll wait in my office next door."

The men and the dog shuffled out and Kendra stripped quickly, pulling on the heavyweight sweats, her muscles complaining as she did so. The dry cloth felt luxurious on her skin but it did not quell the ire beginning to kindle in her belly.

"Didn't I tell Ethan not to bring me here?" she muttered. How exactly was she supposed to explain things to the doctor? There was no way but to reveal the truth and hope he was discreet enough to keep the secret and in no way connected to Boyd Sullivan. Then she'd have to explain to Colonel Masters how her cover had been blown.

Her skin crawled as she pulled on her wet boots, but there was no help for it. She wasn't about to confront the doctor and Carpenter in bare feet.

She snagged a rubber band from one of the neat jars on the doctor's cabinet and twisted her filthy hair into a ponytail. Not good, but at least she didn't look like a bedraggled child just pulled out of the kiddie pool.

She tried to force her brain back into investigator mode. The person who had run her down was familiar with the area and knew what road the soldiers would be taking back to base when the drill was completed. Someone local? Or someone who had asked questions, ferreted out the information? Someone like Heidi Jenks? Or Andy?

Her brain addled, but shoulders straight, she ignored the squeaking of her boots and made her way with as much dignity as she could muster into the adjoining office.

The doctor was gone.

"He got a call from Colonel Masters," Ethan said.

Kendra sighed. "Well, that's a relief. Masters is gifted in twisting the truth to suit his needs."

"So's his daughter." He looked as though he wished he hadn't said it. She examined him further and real-

ized he appeared as though he'd been through a combat zone. His face was scratched, one eye swollen,
his uniform still muddy and damp. Guilt licked her
insides and her anger that he'd delivered her onto the
stretcher melted away.

*He's been through this because of you, Kendra, not
because of Masters.* For her it was a job. For him…
duty to his ex-wife? That Southern gentlemen complex? An order? And why did his bruised mouth look
so inviting at that moment when she knew full well
he regretted their earlier kiss? She hugged herself to
cage in the feelings. "I don't suppose there was any
success finding the driver."

"No." Carpenter patted his pockets for the pen that
was shoved behind his ear.

She pointed.

He smiled. "Thanks. Marines say the plates were
concealed. Someone was being careful. They lost the
tracks when the dirt road rejoined the highway. My
cops couldn't do any better."

Ethan blew out a breath. "There was a wrinkle
here," he told her. "One of the soldiers said he thought
the driver was female."

Kendra's mouth dropped open. "You're kidding."

"No. Not a total surprise, I guess." Ethan eyed Carpenter. "We figured Sullivan has a female accomplice, if
this is even Sullivan's work to begin with." He scrubbed
a hand over his forehead. "I'm not sure anymore."

Ethan was obviously exhausted. It had taken every
ounce of his energy to wrestle her from the river and
then do the same for Titus. Even the dog seemed tired,
sprawled on the tile floor. There was nothing more to
be gained until they both got some sleep.

"We need to get some rest," she said. She turned to Carpenter as she remembered. "You left a message for me. You said it was urgent."

"Yes. I thought you should know that Andy Bleakman did not check in with his parole officer two days ago."

Fear punched her in the gut.

"And the thing is," Carpenter said, "I'm not sure he really did last week, either."

"What do you mean?" Ethan demanded. "We were told he checked in. If not, he should have been tracked down and arrested immediately."

"Should have been, yes. There's been some confusion in the parole department. Overworked, underpaid and…"

"And?" She stared hard at the cop.

"And possible corruption."

"Oh, that's perfect." She groaned. "He paid off his parole officer, didn't he?"

Carpenter nodded. "It appears that way. The officer in question has been suspended pending an investigation, which means—"

"That Andy's been free since the moment he stepped out of prison," Kendra said with only a small tremor in her voice.

Free.

Mindy's words about the stranger who called her house echoed in her mind. *Looking forward to seeing you soon.* Andy had tracked Jillian down because he figured she'd be staying with her, the faithful friend who'd helped double-cross him.

Free to come and kill me.

FIFTEEN

Ethan didn't like the silence. Kendra sat in the passenger seat of his truck, nonreactive, even when Titus rolled a tongue down the back of her neck. He'd gotten her to drink some water, but she'd refused any of the snacks he'd kept in the car. Titus was not so picky, wolfing down a handful of dog treats before they'd started for home.

"Later we'll interview the women Sullivan had contact with besides the ones we've already investigated in depth, in case the marine was right and it was a woman who tried to run you down. One's on base at Canyon, an ammo specialist, the other's just outside Canyon and Linc will talk to her."

She offered no answer, except for a faint nod. They passed Mindy's house, quiet and still. He could tell by the crimp of her mouth and the laced fingers that she longed to go collect Baby, but Kendra was not herself.

"And Heidi Jenks," he continued. "I'll find out what Linc got from her. He's already going over the prison visitor list again, to see if we missed something."

Kendra sighed. "Ethan, you and I both know this isn't Sullivan."

"No, we don't. That's an assumption, one we can't afford to make."

She shook her head as he pulled the truck into the driveway of Jillian's house. "It's Andy. I can feel it." She sniffed, pulling the sleeve of her borrowed sweatshirt across her teary eyes.

"Hey," he said, catching her hand. "We'll get him. We'll get them both."

There was another long pause, and she removed her hand from his. "Ethan, we can't do this together. I want you to stay away from me."

He cocked his head. "Are you dumping me as a partner? It's the dog, isn't it? He's so bad for my mojo."

She didn't even crack a smile. "I'm going to continue the Sullivan investigation, but I'm Andy's target and if you're near me, you're his target, too. That's not what you were ordered to do."

"News flash, but I don't always follow orders and I'm not afraid of Andy. As a matter of fact, I hope he is coming, because we're going to have ourselves a set before I arrest him."

"It's not your battle."

"Yes, it is."

"I don't need you."

"Yes, you do."

First he saw a spark of anger in her eyes, then a flush of vulnerability. Then she asked the question that brought his own vulnerability front and center.

"Why? Why would you put your life at risk for mine?"

He tried for flippant. "Dog handlers' motto. We find what you fear. You fear Andy, so I'm gonna find him and sort him out. Simple as that."

"Duty?" There was a current of emotion in her eyes, running deep and swift as the river. Her lips parted, gleaming soft in the darkness. "That's the only reason?"

He didn't want to, his mind screamed against it, but he reached out, trailing fingers over the satin of her cheek, her chin. And then he was moving toward her, his mouth seeking hers. For a moment, she was reaching out, too, her hands pulling him closer, until he stopped himself. He pressed his forehead against hers and tried for a steady breath. He held her there, forcing himself with every ounce of self-control to forgo kissing his ex-wife's double.

What is wrong with you, Webb?

The trauma of the last twenty-four hours had pressed his emotions into overdrive, overriding all common sense and logic. There would be no more determined women in his life, no more access to his already wrecked heart. No more Jillians.

He felt her move away and he did the same. Clearing his throat, he sought the safety of the driver's side. Though they still tingled from the feel of her, he put his hands on the wheel. "Kendra, I…"

But she was already out of the car and striding toward the house. He remembered his brother's favorite saying.

Smooth as sandpaper, Ethan.

He looked at Titus. "I didn't handle that right, did I?"

Titus gave him a weary expression that probably meant, "So what's new?"

Heaving himself from the car, he waited until Kendra was safely inside before he went to seek the solace of a hot shower, a heartfelt prayer to thank God for their survival.

* * *

Though his body hollered for a couple hours of sleep, Ethan's stomach willed him into the kitchen in midmorning. He left Titus snoring in a pile of blankets and went into the main house. The dog had earned some extra downtime.

Rounding up eggs, cheese and mushrooms, Ethan started an omelet in one pan and a mess of bacon in the other. Since he could not love her or any other woman with his present state of brokenness, he would jolly well fix her problems, the first one being her unsated appetite. The aroma of bacon and eggs had the desired effect, Kendra appeared in a fresh Marine battle dress uniform, her hair neatly caught up low on her neck. He'd hoped she would not bring up their near kiss and she didn't, though he thought he saw a faint pink blush underneath the bruise on her cheek when she encountered him.

"Feel okay?"

"Hungry," she said.

"I can fix that."

She poured herself a cup of coffee from the machine, sighing as she sipped the brew. "Did you talk to your people at Canyon?"

"Yeah. I have the interview scheduled. You game to come with?" He feared she would say no, and wondered what kind of plan he'd need to come up with if she did. There was no way he was leaving her alone, whether she liked it or not.

She ate a mouthful of eggs. "I'm in. I worked this morning on tracking Andy's movements, but I didn't get very far. He's not using his old credit cards, nor the same car."

"We'll get him." He sat across from her. The click of utensils and the sipping of coffee wasn't enough to break up the silence. He wished he could undo his bonehead behavior in the cave and then the truck, close the unprofessional gap he'd created between them. He had the uneasy feeling he'd led her on somehow, made her care about him in a way that just wouldn't do.

"Kendra, I'm sorry about—"

"Nothing to apologize for," she said quickly. "You saved my life. I don't want you to be in danger again, but I can see that you're not going to budge until Sullivan is caught."

"And Andy is in prison."

"That's not your problem."

"But like you said, I'm not going to budge."

She held up a hand. "Ethan, I'm too tired to go through this at the moment. For now, we'll follow the trail we have on Sullivan and see where it goes."

And I'll work my own leads to find Andy. He'd already put in calls while Kendra showered to the contacts Hector had given him, locals in town who would recognize Andy from the mug shot he'd gotten from Carpenter, and emailed them. The coffee shop owner, the gas station attendant, a couple of bartenders.

"Fair enough," he said. They finished their breakfast on somewhat neutral ground. "Let's go get your cat before I wake up the beast."

"Some beast," Kendra said with a snort. "I can practically hear him snoring from here."

He was so glad to see her smile, he grinned back like a fool. "He worked overtime."

"You're right," she said. "He went into the river

right along with you to save my life, so I owe him a steak dinner." She eyed him. "And you, too."

"Ooooh, dangerous offer," he said. "Titus and I can eat our body weight in beef."

She laughed, even better than the smile. "I'll start saving my pennies."

They washed the dishes together, shoulder to shoulder, and things were easy again between them. Once the kitchen was clean and bottles of water and kibble packed into the truck, at 10:00, she tapped on Mindy's door.

Mindy pulled it open, wearing a pink robe, curlers bristling all over her head. Baby snuggled in her arms, mewing when she saw Kendra. Kendra took the bony cat, murmuring baby talk against her small head.

"Thank you for taking care of her." She smoothed the cat's fur.

"Oh, she wasn't much trouble," Mindy said. "We watched silly television and ate ice cream until we fell asleep. Well, I ate the ice cream," she said with a laugh.

Ethan inhaled. "Wow. That smells great. What's cooking?"

Mindy looked pleased. "It's minestrone. Kind of a ritual. Every time before my ex deployed, I'd make a big batch. I heard through the grapevine that he's shipping out." She shrugged a shoulder and sighed. "I guess it's harder for me to let go than it was for Billy. He'll never be lonely. Women swarm to combat pilots like moths to porch lights. Anyway, do you want some soup? I've made a big batch because I don't know how to cook a small pot."

"We're on our way out now, but thank you for the kind offer."

Mindy nodded. "I heard sirens during the night. I wondered if there was an accident at the training."

It was no accident, he wanted to say. "Everyone is okay, but, ma'am, I have a favor to ask."

Mindy shook her head. "I'm no good with dogs."

"Don't worry. I wasn't going to ask you to dog-sit. I was going to ask if you get any more calls asking about Jillian, would you mind writing down the caller's number and letting us know?" He handed her a card. "And if you see anyone, any strangers hanging around, especially this guy, call me right away." He showed her Andy's mug shot on his phone.

A frown creased her brow. "Uh, sure. Are you thinking it's the guy from the woods that made me fall off my bike? Is he stalking Jillian?"

Ethan smiled. "We have reason to believe that he wants to hurt Jillian, but we can't prove he was in the woods. Just being cautious. Thank you, ma'am."

"You're welcome," she said. She was still frowning as she closed the door.

As soon as the bolt slid into place, Kendra turned to him.

"You've been busy. You got Andy's mug shot?"

He shrugged. "I'm not military police for nothing, you know."

"If Andy was the stranger in the woods, he won't bother calling anymore. He knows where I am. All he needs to do is wait for the right moment."

"He's not going to get the right moment, and it always pays to have a friendly neighbor watching out for you, the nosier the better."

"I'm not sure Mindy's going to be much help."

"We'll take every little bit we can get."

* * *

Kendra's cell phone rang as they returned to the kitchen. Recognizing the caller, she punched the speaker button.

"Hi, Jillian. I'm here with Ethan."

"Did you recognize the driver?" Jillian asked without preamble.

Kendra gripped the phone tighter. "No. And the plates were obscured, too."

"Yeah, I got that from Dad, but I figured maybe your memory kicked in with some other details."

"No, I couldn't see the driver's face well enough."

"She didn't drown, though," Ethan snapped. "That's a plus."

Kendra heard Jillian blow out a breath.

"I'm glad you're okay," Jillian said. "I should have started with that."

"Yeah, you should have," Ethan said under his breath. Kendra hoped Jillian hadn't heard. Then, in a louder voice, he informed Jillian, "Andy Bleakman's out of prison and skipped out on his parole officer."

There was silence on the other end of the phone for a few seconds. "Yeah? So this might be Andy going after you, not Sullivan?"

"I wish I knew," Kendra replied.

Jillian heaved a sigh. "If that creep messes up this investigation, I'll wreck him myself."

"That's good to know," Kendra said. "In the meantime, we're proceeding with the Sullivan case."

"Good. What is your next move?"

She looked at Ethan. A scowl crept over his face.

"Well…" she started.

Ethan shook his head. Should she keep things from

Jillian? She wasn't sure, but Ethan was insistent. He shook his head again.

"We're chasing down a lead," she said.

"What lead?"

"I'll fill you in later."

"You'll fill me in now," Jillian said, her voice shrill. "Sullivan wants me, Kendra. I should know everything."

Ethan stepped closer to the phone. "And Kendra's standing between you and him, so you'll get the info when we have something concrete to tell you."

"My father—"

"Jillian," Ethan said, blowing out a breath and sounding suddenly weary. "Don't pull the father rank card here, okay? We are both doing everything in our power to bring Sullivan down. We want you safe, just as much as your father does."

Jillian laughed. "I thought you'd be the first one to celebrate if he took me out."

Ethan looked stricken. "No, Jillian, I wouldn't. Things were bad between us but I don't want to see you hurt. We'll call you when we've got something."

Jillian disconnected without another word.

Ethan stood, arms braced on the table, staring at the phone.

"You okay?" Kendra said, putting a hand on his shoulder. Tension made his muscles tight as steel.

"Yeah. I just… I mean… How bad did I let things get if she thinks I want her dead?"

"I'm sure she doesn't really believe that."

He closed his eyes and sighed. "She hurt me bad, yeah, but hating her is hurting me worse."

She squeezed his shoulder. "Is it time to forgive?"

He opened his eyes. "It's time to start praying for God to help me do that. I don't think I'm gonna make it on my own. Too much damage and I'm too shallow."

"I'll pray, too."

His eyes brightened like a sunlit autumn leaf and his smile touched a tender place inside her. He gazed at her until she felt she could not tear herself away.

"Thanks," he said after a moment. "I don't think I've ever had a woman pray for me besides my mother."

"I'm a newbie, like I said, but I'm making up for lost time."

He bowed his head so his lips grazed her fingers, sending sparks tripping up her arm. *No, Kendra. He doesn't want this and he doesn't want you.* She pulled away, missing the connection immediately. "Ready to go wake up your slowpoke dog?"

"Sure. Did you finish fussing over your spoiled cat?"

She huffed. "Not that it's any of your business, but I'm going to fix her a special breakfast to enjoy before we leave."

"I would expect nothing less," he said, grinning as he went to wake up Titus.

SIXTEEN

He'd arranged to meet ammo specialist Lara Dennis in an empty classroom at Canyon. They arrived with plenty of time to spare. Ethan settled Titus in the room and Kendra took a chair at the table.

Linc Colson strolled in, his rottweiler, Star, brightening when she saw Titus. He greeted Kendra politely and declined the chair Ethan offered.

"I'm on my way to a meeting but I wanted to brief you on my interview with the other suspect, Jolie Potter." He glanced at Kendra. "She's a—"

"Scientist in a biomed lab," Kendra finished.

Ethan raised an eyebrow at her.

Kendra filled them in. "I did my homework."

Ethan fought a grin. The woman had skills. "What'd you get from her, Linc?"

"Nothing substantial. They dated casually, looks like Sullivan dumped her for being too much of a brainiac."

Ethan rolled his eyes. "That figures. What a chump."

"Yeah, so most likely a dead end there. Let me know if you get anything new from Dennis."

"Will do."

Linc called to Star. "I forwarded you Sullivan's prison visitation list." His frown said it all.

"What's up?"

"There's a name on it that wasn't there before."

Ethan didn't bother to hide his shock. "How can that be?"

"You tell me."

"Name?"

"Senior Airman Chase McLear."

"No way."

Linc lifted a shoulder. "It shocked me, too. I'm just telling you what I know."

Ethan explained it to Kendra. "McLear's former Security Forces. Now he's at Canyon, raising a toddler on his own, almost done training to be a K-9 handler. He wasn't on the list when we did our initial investigation."

"Is this an official list from the prison we're talking about?" Kendra asked.

"Yes, ma'am."

She looked from Ethan to Linc. "How could McLear's name suddenly appear?"

"Question of the hour," Linc said. "This document says he visited a week before Sullivan's escape."

Frustration kicked at Ethan. "Every time I think we're making progress…"

Linc sighed. "I hear you."

"I'll arrange to meet with McLear before we leave today."

"All right." Linc left with Star.

Ethan began to pace. He didn't want to believe Chase had anything to do with Sullivan. He liked him personally, and from what he'd seen, the guy was doing a great job raising a little girl all by himself, which had to be harder than anything either of them had done on the battlefield.

Kendra eyed him. "The pacing's not going to help, you know."

"It might."

"It just makes Titus go bug-eyed trying to watch your every move."

He stopped. It was probably agitating Titus as she said, and the dog had been through enough. Besides, fatigue from Ethan's wrestling match with the river bogged him down, too. "Gonna get coffee. May I get you some?"

She lit up like a string of Christmas lights and his stomach got a weird flutter. "I would adore a cup of coffee, you wonderful man."

He laughed. "And I thought you admired my killer MP skills. Turns out I could have just impressed you with a cup of coffee."

"I'm already impressed, but the coffee gets you extra points."

"Coming right up." He went to the vending machine, whistling as he went. Already impressed? It felt good, he could not deny it, to have Kendra think well of him. That thought both thrilled and scared him. *You care too much what she thinks. Just get the coffee and do your job, Webb.*

At the vending machine, he found former combat pilot Isaac Goddard collecting his own cup of joe. Shadows smudged Isaac's eyes. Clearly, combat did not come without a price and Isaac had paid it many times over. Getting help for his PTSD was the first step. Bringing home the dog who saved his life was the second. Beacon had kept him alive, though his handler, Isaac's good friend Jake Burke, did not survive. Ethan wondered what would happen to Isaac if bringing Beacon home proved impossible.

"Hey, Isaac."

He looked up, his green eyes hazy for a moment. "Hey, Ethan. I heard you found one of the missing dogs."

"Yeah. Little Malinois pup."

"Gonna be okay?"

"He's improving daily from what I hear from Westley." He considered whether or not to bring up Beacon, but one thing he'd despised about his return after combat was people treating him like an egg, as if he might crack at any moment. So he asked the question.

"Any word on Beacon?"

Isaac frowned. "He's been spotted in enemy territory. Guy from my outfit's been trying to lure him over, but no success yet."

"I'll keep up the prayers."

Isaac blew out a breath. "Yeah. Thanks."

Ethan imagined for a moment what it would be like to lose Titus. He'd lost a dog before, and it burned like wildfire, but at least he knew what had happened. There was grieving and closure. Thinking about Titus running loose, scared, injured…? He shook the thought away and returned to the conference room. He handed Kendra the coffee just as a small woman with her long hair pulled back into a tight bun entered the room. Her hands were fisted before she snapped off a salute.

Ethan returned the salute. "Thank you for coming. Specialist Lara Dennis, right?"

"Yes, Lieutenant," she said, shooting a quick glance at Kendra.

"I'm Jillian Masters," Kendra said. "I'm helping Ethan with the investigation."

Dennis's eyes shifted between them. "Isn't he your ex-husband?"

Kendra nodded. "Yes, but we're getting remarried soon."

The word *married* jolted him. It had taken him countless painful days to accept the label of "ex-husband," a title that reminded him just how gullible he had been.

After a blink he said, "Please sit down." He offered a smile that she did not return.

"All due respect, I'd prefer to stand, Lieutenant."

Was she sending him a defiant message or just nervous? "All right. Just a few quick questions and we'll get you on the road. Tell me again about your relationship with Boyd Sullivan."

She didn't react. She'd been expecting the question, of course. Why else would she be summoned? Still he caught the tightening of her mouth.

"I've already told the investigation team everything. I… I was attracted to Sullivan when we were going through basic. We had lunch together, we talked. That's it."

"I don't think so," Kendra said.

Dennis stared. "Yes, it is."

Kendra didn't say anything, only stared. Ethan knew the tactic and he remained silent also. If Kendra sensed there was something deeper, he'd go with her instincts.

Dennis's gaze fell to her boots. "I… It took me a while to realize what kind of guy he was. He wanted more, another date, I didn't. I declined any further contact with him and he was horrible about it. End of story."

"Why didn't you like him?" Kendra said.

Dennis started, "I… He was the center of his own universe, ma'am. I liked the confidence at first, or I thought I did, but there's a difference between confidence you earn and confidence you have no business with. You get the difference, ma'am?"

Kendra nodded.

"How was he horrible when you brushed him off, exactly?" Ethan said.

Her lips thinned. "Phoning me all the time, sending flowers, alternately begging and then calling me names and then apologizing. He wasn't…stable."

"Yet you didn't complain to your CO?"

Her gaze dropped to her lap. "No, sir."

"Why not? That's protocol for harassment."

Dennis remained quiet, her hands clenched.

"I think I can answer that," Kendra said. "Tell me if I get anything wrong. You didn't tell your CO because you worked hard to get where you are, a woman in a man's profession. You're raising a child, a son, by yourself, and you put yourself through high school at nights, working days, passed all the basic training and Airmen's Week plus the National Agency Check and Local Agency checks. You've worked harder for this than anything else in your life and you didn't want the possible stigma attached to a messy relationship with a guy you could kick yourself for even giving a second look." Kendra raised an eyebrow. "Am I close?"

Kendra had done her homework on Lara Dennis.

Dennis swallowed. "Yes, ma'am. I just want it to

be over and get on with my life, take care of my boy
and make him proud of me. I messed up a lot as a teen
and this is the first time I've made something good for
both of us. I can't jeopardize that, not for Sullivan or
anyone else." The look she gave Kendra was pleading.
"Do you understand, ma'am?"

"Yes," Kendra said quietly. "I understand completely."

A guy she could kick herself for even giving a second look.

Unstable.

Yes, he realized. Kendra did understand.

Ethan stood outside the moment, watching two
strong women who'd never met make a connection because of the lives they'd chosen and the consequences
they hadn't. The strength of it stopped him, the grace
of it.

He forced himself back to the task. "Have you had
any further contact with Boyd Sullivan since?"

"No, sir, and that is the honest truth."

He looked at Kendra who gave him a slight nod.
"All right. Thank you for coming in. We appreciate
your time." They exchanged salutes.

Dennis walked to the door, stopping before she
crossed the threshold.

"Ma'am, if I may," she said, looking at Kendra.

Kendra nodded at her to continue.

"Ma'am, Sullivan used to talk about people who
crossed him. He said that no one would get away with
humiliating him." She twisted her cap in her hands.
"Uh, I've heard talk and all, that you cut him down
pretty good in front of his friends."

"Say what you need to say, Dennis," Ethan said.

One final wring of her cap and she plunged in. "He's not going to forget, ma'am. He's that kind of person and he'll be carrying that grudge until the day he dies."

"Or until we put him in prison again," Ethan said.

"Just saying, ma'am," Dennis said. "He won't forget."

Again a look passed between them, something that spoke of the instant bond they'd formed. "Thank you, Dennis."

"You're welcome, sir, ma'am. I hope you get him."

"We will," Ethan said, eyes on Kendra. "We will."

SEVENTEEN

Private eyes and MPs had a lot of duties in common, Kendra thought. Limited glamour but plenty of leg-work and reports to complete. After four phone calls, Ethan discovered that Chase McLear was off base for the day, but he managed to get him to agree to meet at a coffee shop in a town a couple hours outside of Canyon. They walked to the truck, the sun blazing at just before noon.

More coffee was fine by Kendra. Her body felt like it had been put through a violent wash cycle and chucked against some sharp rocks to dry. She was physically wrung out, but worse was the emotional upheaval that churned below the surface. The tasks of the day were all that was keeping her from reliving every terrible moment of her plunge into the creek. On top of that, their lack of progress chafed.

Had they accomplished anything at all with their most recent visit to Canyon? Lara Dennis was a dead end, she was sure of it, and the scientist, no more promising. Yvette Crenville, the base nutritionist, had been interviewed several times to no avail. Kendra was straining to muster further possibilities when Heidi Jenks caught up to them.

Ethan stood taller, tension visible in the set of his jaw.

"Jillian," she said. "I heard about what happened after I left the drill. Are you all right?"

"Yes. Thanks."

She waited for the inevitable and the reporter did not disappoint her.

"Would you be interested in talking a bit about your experience?"

"No."

"It might help the investigation, you know, to get more information out there about Sullivan's accomplice." She lowered her voice. "I heard it might be a woman who tried to run you down."

"How'd you hear that exactly, Jenks?" Ethan demanded.

She glared at him. "I have contacts, Ethan, that's my job. People are always willing to talk eventually."

"Not me," Kendra said. "I have no comment now or ever."

Jenks sighed. "Okay. If you change your mind, let me know."

"I'm sure none of the details will wind up on the underground blog, right?" Ethan's tone was acid.

Jenks stared right back at him. "I wouldn't know, Ethan. I told you, that isn't me. Whoever's leaking information isn't reporting, they're gossiping."

He snorted. "And you don't do that?"

"No," she said. "No matter what you think about me, I'm a reporter and I take my duty seriously. I have a job to do, just like the two of you, and I'm going to do it with or without your cooperation." Turning on her heel, she stalked away.

"You trust her?" Ethan said.

"I don't know. She was there at the drill, she knew the details of the exercise. She had plenty of time to leave and make plans to run me down, but she has no connection to Boyd Sullivan."

"That we know of," he said darkly.

They got in the car and drove off. With the air conditioner cranked to high, the truck gradually cooled and Kendra logged on to her email to check for any new info.

"Andy's still not using his car or his credit cards, as far as I can tell," she said.

A movement behind them caught both their attention. Ethan stared into the rearview mirror. "Black car, tinted windows at our six o'clock."

"I see it," she said, staring into the side-view mirror.

"Changed lanes to stay with us, two cars back."

"I saw that, too."

"Can you get plates?"

She squinted into the side mirror, making a note in her phone. "Got it."

He handed her his phone. "Text it to Linc. Have him run the plate numbers."

She did. "He said to give him a minute."

Ethan continued on, keeping pace with the flow of traffic. Kendra could not get a good look at the driver. Goose bumps prickled her skin and she could recall the roaring of the engine as the driver came at her on the bridge, aiming for a kill. Possible suspects clicked through her mind. Sullivan? His female accomplice? Andy? Her palms were slick as she gripped the phone, the minutes stretching along with the miles until she thought she would scream. *It's like a combat zone, with potential enemies around every corner.*

The phone buzzed. She read the details from Linc's message aloud to Ethan.

"The car belongs to a real estate agent, Louis Bickford. No ties to Baylor or Canyon that Linc can see." Kendra deflated, sagging against the seat. Frustration edged out over relief.

Ethan groaned. "Do you think we're getting paranoid?"

Was she? The familiar tightness squeezed her belly. She bit her lip, staring out the window as the black car gradually eased back into the flow of traffic.

"Hey," Ethan said, startling her by taking her hand. "You drifted away there for a minute. Did I say something wrong?"

"No." She swallowed. "It's just…my mom had severe paranoia, exacerbated by her addiction, before she was hospitalized full-time. It…hurt, when she turned that paranoia on me." She could still hear her mother's screams from her hospital bed. *Get her away from me. She hates me. She wants to kill me.* Her mother's rejection had ripped open such a gaping hole, leaving Kendra vulnerable to Andy, and seeking alcohol and drugs to fill it.

"Aw, man," he said. "I'm sorry. Let me just try to pry my boot out of my big mouth."

She squeezed his fingers. "There's no way you could have known." Her eyes drifted to the scarf still rolled up on the floor. "I think Mom tried her best, but she was sick and addicted. It was hard not to take it personally, though, especially when I was younger, but I've grown. I understand now. People have flaws, big ones."

"But it still hurts."

She heaved a sigh. "Yeah, it hurts, but I think God's going to make something good out of it."

"How?" His brown eyes were so warm and sincere, she found herself articulating it aloud.

"It came to me as we talked to Lara Dennis about her son. For a long while, I thought I would never have kids because I didn't want to risk breaking their hearts like my mother broke mine, but you know what?" A spark of new hope danced inside her. "I think I'm going to be a better mother because I know how hard that job is, and how incredibly important, like Lara Dennis does."

He looked as though she'd slapped him. "Ethan? I think it's my turn for a boot in the mouth. What did I say?"

"Ah, it was a bone of contention between me and Jillian." His face flushed. "I really wanted kids and she told me she did, too, so every month after I thought we'd started trying, I'd get my hopes up." He shrugged. "She just gave it lip service, never intended to have children, not with me anyway."

"Then she's crazy." She couldn't stop blurting out the words.

He didn't seem to hear. "I decided a guy who couldn't tell that his own wife was lying to him probably wasn't good father material. I'm not going to have a family." He forced a smile that didn't reach his eyes. "Gonna stick to dogs."

She clasped his hand between hers. "Like I said, He uses that stuff for good. Jillian's betrayal and my enormous mess-ups and everything. Don't focus on the rearview, right?"

For a moment, he looked at her, eyes shimmering, as if he was probing in search of some answer he keenly wanted. Then he squeezed her fingers again and pulled his hands away, his face expressionless behind the handsome mask.

"I learned my lesson," he mumbled. "I'll leave it at that."

She'd made him uncomfortable by mentioning children. Yes, he was working on letting go of the hatred for his ex-wife, but the damage would take a long time, maybe a lifetime, to overcome. It dragged her heart down and she ached for him. As the miles silently wore on, she lost herself in the beat of the country music.

Bless the broken road.

That led me to you.

Thank You, God, for the broken road that led me to Ethan Webb, she prayed inside. The prayer was automatic and she knew in the deep places that they would not travel that road together much longer. But for now, for the moment. with the warm sun and the snoring dog and Ethan's strong profile and the purple scarf at her feet, she thanked Him.

Ethan gripped the wheel, pulling into the parking lot of a coffee shop, and parked in the shade.

From the back seat the dog gave a might yawn.

"Titus is coffee shop approved?"

"He goes where I go. End of story." He scoped out the outdoor seating area. "I'm gonna sit him in the shade, grab a table away from everyone else. Want to get us some coffee?" He reached for his wallet.

"You have to ask? Don't worry. It's on me. A stall tactic until I buy you and Titus that steak dinner."

He chuckled. "You make me laugh, and that's a rare gift in this world."

She smiled, realizing that it had been a long time since she'd shared laughter with a good man. A rare gift, for sure. Sullivan would be caught, and she would track down Andy Bleakman on her own. Once the case was closed, their time together would end. The laughter would be only a memory. So be it. She'd savor each chuckle and smile, storing them carefully away in her memory.

The twinge of sadness remained as she pushed past the coffee shop door.

Ethan faced Chase McLear. McLear's green eyes took in every detail, the space, exits, entrances, everything a former Security Forces guy would notice. He gave Kendra a long look.

"She's not leaving my side until Sullivan is caught," Ethan said, by way of explanation. "You've heard about the threats."

McLear played with his coffee cup. "I can't believe we're even having this conversation. You know I had nothing to do with Sullivan. I'm minding my own business, training my dog. This is crazy and you know it."

Ethan thought so, too. McLear and Queenie, his beagle, were almost through their sessions and Queenie would be one of the first dogs ever to be qualified as an electronic sniffer at Canyon. McLear was also the single father to young Allie after her mother had abandoned the child.

But he needed to keep his emotions out of this investigation.

"I don't want to be here any more than you do, but your name is on the prison list. You visited Sullivan."

Chase put the cup down hard, splashing coffee over the edge, each word sharp as a blade. "I did not."

"Can you explain why your name's on the list?"

"I can't." He grimaced. "But one Security Forces guy to another, if I were you, I'd be coming to two possible conclusions."

Ethan watched for any sign that McLear was lying, a change in the timbre of his voice, a sideways glance, an unusual gesture. He saw only confusion and mounting frustration. "Do my work for me then, Chase. What are my two theories?"

McLear rolled his coffee cup between his palms. "First theory. I did visit Sullivan because I'm his accomplice. Maybe I paid off a prison staffer to keep my name off the list, but I refused to keep paying off said staffer and he or she corrected the record."

"Good theory," Ethan said. "What's the second?"

"That someone is trying to frame me, to throw suspicion off themselves."

"And to which theory do you ascribe?"

McLear scowled. "What do you think?"

Kendra stood and walked to the trash can to throw her paper napkin away.

"Ethan, this isn't some adventure story here. This is my life," McLear said. "And my kid's life."

"You don't have to tell me that," Ethan snapped. "There are a lot of lives at stake."

Kendra's for one. He glanced her way again, noticing the way the sun burnished her hair into copper fire. She brushed a flyaway strand back, her attention drawn by something.

McLear smacked the table, claiming his attention. "Ethan, someone is manipulating the evidence and this investigation. I'm not guilty of anything and you know it."

"I don't know anything right now, Chase, but I'm gonna find out, I promise."

McLear started to answer when Kendra called Ethan. He turned to her and when he saw her expression, he hurried to her side. Titus scrambled after him. The patrons gave the dog a wide berth.

"Isn't that the car?" she whispered, craning her neck toward the parking lot.

He followed her gaze to the black car, the one that he'd thought had been following them earlier. Coincidence? There weren't very many coffee shops convenient to the freeway here. Maybe the Realtor had stopped, too. But Ethan knew there were not too many coincidences in combat zones, either, only missed clues that got a person dead.

"Kendra, stay here, I'm going to—"

His words were drowned out by the crash of breaking glass.

EIGHTEEN

In a blur, Kendra saw Ethan catapult down the landing into the parking lot, Titus keeping pace at his heels. The sound came from under the trees where Ethan's truck was parked next to an older model Mercedes. Across from the two vehicles was the black sedan they'd had Linc trace earlier, empty, as far as Kendra could tell.

She heard the sound of more shattering glass, then the thwack of a blunt object against metal.

Racing after Ethan, hand on her gun, she yelled at a patron to call the cops and hit the blacktop, sprinting. Zeroing in on the noise, she saw bits of broken glass sparkling through the air as a man—Caucasian, medium height, wearing a baseball cap pulled low on his brow—brought a tire iron down on the windshield of Ethan's truck.

Ethan shouted as he closed in and the man flung down the tire iron and hurtled into the driver's seat of the Mercedes, the engine already running.

She caught up just as Ethan leaped at the door of the Mercedes, which the driver had not had time to close fully. Titus jumped up at the back windows, scratching and clawing as the driver gunned the engine, headed for the parking lot exit. Kendra's fingers itched to fire at the rear tires, but with Ethan and Titus so close, she didn't dare.

With a grunt of frustration, Titus bounced off the car, rolling once and springing to all fours again. Undeterred, he again started to chase after the car and Ethan, his legs churning into blurs of brown fur. Ethan managed to wrench the door open and reach in to grab the driver.

Her heart soared. Finally. They would have something tangible, someone to interrogate. A fist struck out and punched Ethan in the jaw, sending him flying onto the pavement, where he tumbled over twice, coming to rest on his back. The car roared away onto the main street, out of sight in a matter of moments.

A patron raced up, a phone to his ear, blinking incredulously. "That's my Mercedes. That guy just stole my car."

"Hot-wired it," another said. "Had it running the whole time while he bashed in some guy's windows. What a looney."

Kendra holstered her weapon and ran to Ethan, stopping a few feet away to avoid Titus's frenzy. The dog pranced around him, darting licks and whining, barking savagely at anyone who got close to Ethan. She tried speaking calmly to the dog, but her voice did not penetrate. He was all teeth and claws, determined that no one was going to approach his fallen partner.

At last Ethan propped himself on his elbows, breathing hard. "It's all right," he panted. "At ease, boy." Titus was unconvinced until he all but sat in Ethan's lap, slathering him with a wet tongue and poking a nose into his face. Gradually, after more soothing from Ethan, the dog calmed enough that Kendra could get near.

"Are you all right?"

"Yeah," he said, sitting up and rubbing his jaw. "I would have got him if I had better leverage." He caressed the dog, massaging his quivering sides. "I know, boy. I should have let you go first. You'd have gotten him." Ethan's forehead was scratched, his chin smudged with dirt, but he wasn't hurt, not badly, and Titus was in a state of bliss, legs sprawled in every direction as he did his best to be a lapdog.

Tousling the dog's floppy ears, Ethan ordered him to a sit, which he reluctantly obeyed, never taking his eyes off his handler.

Kendra helped Ethan to a standing position. He leaned on her, his chin brushing the top of her head. She circled his waist, holding him close, secretly grateful that there had been no shots fired. They hadn't gotten their man, but for the moment, she couldn't care too much about that. She held on tight, willing herself not to think, just to feel Ethan's solid presence in her arms, the steady beat of his heart, the Southern drawl echoing in her ears.

"I'm okay," he said.

And it was truly all that mattered in that moment.

"Cops are on their way," McLear said, trotting up. "You okay, man?"

They stepped back from each other. "Just bounced around is all. The black car must have been recently stolen. That's why Linc's earlier search didn't trigger the info. Owner probably doesn't even realize it's missing yet."

"He's got a new set of wheels now, since he just stole the Mercedes. I relayed the plate info to the cops," McLear said. "Looks like you're going to need a new vehicle, too."

Ethan sucked in a breath. The front windshield was bashed to pieces, a hole punched through the safety glass and the driver's window shattered.

Kendra clamped her lips together when she saw the rest. Sprayed in orange paint across the hood of his truck was a phone number.

The dripping numbers made her skin crawl. A taunt, from a man so angry or so desperate that he'd risk everything to deliver his message in broad daylight in a very public place. Who was that kind of desperate? Sullivan? She cast a glance at McLear. He could have tipped off Sullivan about their meeting place. All the concern on his face might just be acting, pure and simple. Suspicions whirled around in her mind, dizzying. Too many suspects. Too few solid leads.

With a look of unadulterated fury, Ethan yanked his phone from his pocket and dialed the number sprayed on his truck, stepping away from the bystanders into the shade of the trees. She followed and he put the phone on speaker.

"Let's talk," Ethan growled when someone picked up. "Who is this?"

"Hello, G.I. Joe. Too bad about your truck," a man said.

Kendra's heart stuttered to a stop. It was a voice she

would never forget, a voice rooted deep in her memories and nightmares.

You'll do what I say because you love me.

You'll do what I say.

Or you'll die.

From the corner of her memory she heard Baby's terrified mewing, her own harsh breathing, the sound of a knife yanked from its leather sheath, the muffled slam of a terrified heart beating against quaking ribs.

"Identify yourself," Ethan said. "Or aren't you man enough?"

He laughed. "Why don't you ask Kendra? I know she's there with you. I've been watching her play soldier. Working on a case now that you're a fancy PI and all, Kendra?"

Ethan looked at Kendra. Her mouth went dry and she could not produce one single syllable.

I've been watching.

Every nerve, every atom was slowly icing over, freezing her from the inside out.

"Come on, baby," Andy crooned. "It's been a while and I'm dying to hear your voice. I know you're looking forward to seeing me again, aren't you?"

Her brain had known he was close, circling like a shark, but hearing his voice was a nightmare come to life, as if she could feel the nip of razor-sharp teeth as they prepared to rip into her, severing her body, devouring her a piece at a time.

"Andy…" she whispered.

"There you are, Kendra," Andy said. "I knew I'd find you. Piece of cake after I figured out where Jillian lived."

Find you.

She wanted to scream. It could not be real. She could not be powerless again.

"Time to settle some things, don't you think?" Andy said.

One cell at a time her body turned to ice.

Well past time, she thought.

Ethan held the phone in a death grip. "Bleakman," he grunted through his teeth. "Why are we talking on the phone? Not man enough to stand up to me in person? You smash up my truck and run away like a scared rabbit?"

"Listen, G.I. Joe. This isn't your business. This is between me and Kendra."

"I'm making it my business. Drive on back here right now and we'll settle it."

There was a pause, a long one, long enough for Ethan to feel the stampeding blood in his veins, the bone-cracking tension in his muscles, the overwhelming need to punish Andy Bleakman, to grind him under his boot like a poisonous scorpion.

"So it's like that, huh, Kendra?" Bleakman said. "You left me to rot in jail while you moved on with G.I. Joe here?"

"No," Kendra said. "That's not it."

"Doesn't matter," Ethan barked. "You're not gonna terrorize her, not gonna lay one finger on her, you hear me?"

"Kendra needs to pay her debt, G.I. Joe. Everyone has to pay." The background traffic noise revealed him to be on the freeway. He mouthed the info to Kendra, watched her text the info to Linc, who would funnel it to the police. He didn't trust that McLear would do it, didn't trust anyone at the moment.

"And you know what?" Bleakman said. "Anyone who gets in my way is going to pay the price, too."

"Easy to spout threats on the phone," Ethan told him. "Be a man. Come and face me."

"What a good soldier, just like my old man. Sheep, all of you. Follow orders and do what you're told, a grunt to the end."

Ethan breathed hard. "Where are you, Bleakman? Stop running, coward."

Another laugh, low and slow. "I'm done talking to you, Soldier. You're dismissed, so toddle along like a good little grunt and take your dog for a walk. Kendra," he said and Ethan could hear a smile in the tone. "I'll see you soon. Very soon."

The connection went dead.

He pocketed the phone, noting the color fade out of Kendra's cheeks. The rapid rise and fall of her chest made him reach for her.

"Maybe you should…" He was going to say "sit down" but she was already turning away, wrestling a phone from her pocket.

"Who are you calling?"

"First the tow company," she said, no quiver in the voice.

"Second?"

"I need to tell Jillian that Andy's definitely in town." She hesitated, her troubled eyes locked on his. "Andy will hurt anyone who gets between me and him. Including Jillian…and you."

He edged in front of her, fighting the urge to crush

her to his chest. "I hope he does make a move, Kendra, because I'm going to take him down."

Now he saw her tears sparkling like morning dew before the sun, and her body shook all over. "I don't want anybody hurt," she whispered. "Especially you."

He went to her then and she let the phone drop to her side. For a while he held her, wrapped in his arms, and murmured comforting words into her ear.

"We're going to get him, Kendra."

She jerked and tried to back away but he held on.

"No. No more 'we,'" she whispered, her eyes feverish. "I can't allow it."

He cupped her chin in his hand, preventing her from escaping, willing her to listen. "I know what you're thinking and stop it right now. We're going to get him together, just like Sullivan. No lone wolf here, no John Wayne action."

A flicker of a smile. "Says the guy with the accent and the rifle."

He kissed her, on the corner of her mouth, drinking in the soft scent of her, the strength and delicacy, the marvel. For a moment he was swept into another place where he could love again, a place where his heart was not in pieces.

"Kendra," he started. The luscious brown of her eyes drew him, beckoned him to trust. What would happen if he did?

While he wrestled with the question, she answered it by moving away. The inches between them spoke volumes. She was ready for kids, a healthy relationship built with a man who could trust and love and forgive. He'd shown her he was not that man.

"We have a job to do," she said.

He stared, tried to absorb the unspoken.

"The cops," she continued. "They're here."

"Okay." He swallowed hard. He understood what she wasn't saying. She didn't want to go to that place with him. Maybe she might have earlier. He thought he'd felt that in her embrace after she'd nearly drowned, and again the moment at the kitchen table over omelets. But he'd let the moments pass out of fear and now she'd put up a wall, invisible but impenetrable. She was right anyway. It wasn't the time nor the place.

He watched her go to the cop. "You let that chance slip away," he told himself. Only the job stood before him now, duty, purpose, meaning.

Get Sullivan. Get Andy and get on with your life, Ethan.

NINETEEN

Kendra forced her fears into a tight ball and shoved it down deep. Uncertainty clawed at her. She was not sure how to proceed, how to both escape Andy and capture Sullivan, but she knew one thing for certain: she could not allow Ethan to get hurt because of her sordid past. And he would.

Andy wasn't bluffing when he said he would destroy anyone who got in his way. He'd beaten senseless a man in prison who'd bumped his lunch tray. A savage, with a hair-trigger temper. How stupid she'd been not to see it sooner. She deserved to pay the price for getting tangled up with him, but Ethan did not.

They finished with the police and waited for a tow truck. Ethan's look was mournful as he surveyed the damage. He ran his hand over the hood. "Aw, Big Mac. Just look at you."

She smothered a giggle.

He gave her a sheepish look. "Don't you name your cars?"

"Well, no."

"This truck is special. Bought it when I was seventeen." He gave it one final pat. "Don't you worry, Big Mac. Gonna get you all fixed up."

It would take a chunk out of his salary, depending what the insurance supplied, to have the glass and body work done and the repainting on the old truck. All because of Andy. Her fingernails bit into her palms.

Ethan stopped the driver just before he drove away with the wrecked truck. He retrieved the scarf his mother made for him, quickly shaking out the glass and shoving it in his pocket, probably hoping no one was looking. She pretended not to notice but it stirred her inside. Ethan Webb was a good man. He'd make someone an excellent husband someday if he could accept who he was and forgive himself and Jillian. She fought a sudden lump in her throat.

They rented an SUV with room for Titus in the back, and as they drove, both of them constantly checked the rearview mirror to be sure Andy wasn't following. Every black vehicle made her breath quicken until she considered that Andy might have already stolen another car, since he knew the police had the plate number of the Mercedes.

They finally pulled up at Jillian's house. It was evening now, the heat giving way to a wind that blew in the clouds and promised another storm. Kendra's legs felt like they were made of cement as she dragged herself to the front porch.

"Stay here a minute," Ethan ordered.

Too tired to protest his bossiness, she waited on the mat until he and Titus had checked every square inch of the house.

"All clear," he said as his phone pinged. Kendra

could hear the colonel's anger clearly as Ethan held the phone slightly away from his ear.

"Yes, Colonel Masters, I can confirm it was Andy Bleakman." Ethan shot a look at her. "It's a…situation from her past."

More angry ranting from the colonel.

"We're both tired, and we need to discuss strategy tonight. We'll brief you on base tomorrow afternoon."

Ethan winced and she heard the accent creep deeper into his conversation along with a dark stain on his cheeks. "That will have to do, Colonel. I don't work for you, remember? So if you wanna demote me, take it up with the air force."

He disconnected.

"He has a right to be angry," she said as they entered the house. "I didn't tell him about Andy when I took the Sullivan case."

"He's always angry whether he has a right to be or not. Your past is your business, not his."

"You shouldn't jeopardize your career."

"Like I said, Masters is not my boss."

"But he can make trouble for you."

He gave her a cocky grin. "I can handle it. Trouble is my middle name. Ethan William Trouble Webb."

"Rolls right off the tongue."

"You got that right, ma'am."

That charm, the sincerity, inched their way into her heart again. She heard his stomach growl.

"Up for some early dinner?" he said. "I can make a mean spaghetti."

Her heart said yes, but the fear still circled down deep and her conscience pricked her. *You need a plan to keep Ethan away from Andy.* "I want to be alone for a while, to think." She scooped Baby from the floor and stroked her.

"All right. As long as that doesn't mean planning to go after Andy without me."

His eyes bored into her, but she kept her attention on Baby. "I'm doing nothing until the morning. That's the best I can promise."

He huffed and folded his arms across his middle. "You're not doing this alone, Kendra. Not anymore."

"I made the mess. I have to clean it up." *Because I would never forgive myself if something happened to you.*

"It's my job to help you."

My job. She wondered why the words hurt. He'd never said anything, never even hinted that he wanted something else from her, no false promises, just a pledge to do his duty. As a matter of fact, he'd fought hard against working together in the first place. His job. She would leave him to his duty, and she would do hers. It was easier, better for both of them.

"I'm tired, Ethan. I want to lie down for a while. Can we talk more in later?"

He held her gaze for a moment more. "All right. I'll check the yard one more time before I go to my unit. Your phone charged?"

"I'll make sure."

"Titus and I are going to do a few patrols throughout the night."

"You don't—" She realized the futility of what she was about to argue. Duty.

"Gotta keep the skills up," he said with a grin.

She pointed to Titus. "His or yours?"

Ethan huffed. "My skills are sharp as a good cheddar."

"I feel safer already."

He laughed. "Should have come up with something better than a cheese analogy, but I'm tired, too."

She carried Baby to the bedroom and took a shower, pulled on some fatigues and tried to read, with no success. She knew she should be resting, but hearing Andy's voice had stripped all her normal senses away, leaving only the naked pulse of fear.

She went to the window, looking out into the yard now filling up with shadows. A light shone in Ethan's unit, a pinprick of gold against the gloom. Wind riffled through the branches of the trees in the woods that bordered the property. Was Andy out there now? Watching? Biding his time?

Forcing away the notion, she pulled the curtains closed tight and checked that her weapon was loaded and ready.

Ethan didn't have to work hard to wake Titus for their first check at midnight. The dog seemed to be sleeping as fitfully as his owner. "Patrol," he said and Titus offered the little wiggly rump dance while Ethan zipped on his harness.

He let them out quietly. The smell of rain hung heavy in the air, which would not pose a problem for Titus unless it came down in buckets. Light rain would actually refresh any human scent and he felt confident that Titus would alert if he got a trail on a stranger hiding anywhere near the house. He let the dog have his lead and followed him around the perimeter, flashlight on to pick up any broken foliage or footprints.

When Titus whined and sat, he drew his weapon,

until he realized it was Kendra watching him from the bedroom window.

"Goofball," he said to his dog. Titus flapped his ears.

Kendra slid open the window.

"Can't sleep?" he said.

"No. Want company?"

He wanted her company, craved it to be truthful, though he told himself it was foolish. "Better for you to stay in the house."

"I need fresh air."

"But—"

She'd already vanished from the window. He sighed. "She doesn't listen any better than her cat," he told Titus.

The dog offered a wide yawn.

Kendra joined them in a few minutes wearing fatigues and armed, he was glad to see. She trailed along behind Ethan and Titus, careful to stay out of their way. She smelled of some fruity shampoo. He felt something inside slide into place, some jagged piece that seemed to find a spot to belong, and he realized it was because she was near him. He sped up, but the thoughts kept pace. He did not want a relationship, not now, so why did his emotions refuse to get the message? The clouds obscured the moon, and the porch light that they'd left on cast a glow that accentuated her resemblance to Jillian.

Remember that, Ethan? You thought Jillian was your missing piece, too. You were an idiot then, giving your heart away without the consent of your brain. And what had it cost him? Everything, his pride, his self-confidence, his future. He wasn't ready for a re-lationship with Kendra, or anyone else. Period.

Titus completed his perimeter check and they moved onto the yard. There were very few places a person might hide, but Titus checked every inch any-way, behind the shed, along the fence line, stopping at the back gate. He whined, pawing at the metal gate. Ethan's adrenaline went through the roof.

"Go back in the house, Kendra. Wait for my text. If you don't hear from me in twenty, call the cops." He pushed the gate open, Titus barreling through.

"I'm coming."

"No, you're not."

"You're not facing Andy alone if he's out there."

"Kendra," he snapped.

She lifted her chin, eyes blazing. "Unless you're going to handcuff me to the fence, get moving, Lieu-tenant."

Smothering an angry retort, he pushed out into the woods, fuming. If Titus was alerting to Andy, he would take care of it without risking Kendra's life. He was an MP, after all. Did she think he needed her to back him up? Think him a pushover like Jillian had?

Titus yanked and pulled and Ethan worked to keep up and not trip over any fallen branches or rocks. Ken-dra shadowed them easily.

Ethan was puzzled. Titus did not seem to be latch-ing onto a scent and following it to a potential in-truder's hiding place, as he did in his patrol duties. Something about the dog's erratic behavior was atypi-cal. He thought about stopping him and resetting, but Titus was wired, filled with frantic energy. *Trust your dog*, his gut told him.

"What is it, boy?" Titus did not acknowledge Ethan, his nose glued to the ground, the hair on his back raised.

"What's he after?" Kendra whispered.

"I don't know," he whispered back. "Titus, if you're dragging me around these woods looking for a squirrel, you're grounded forever."

The dog whined, swiveling from one side of a grassy basin to another. The area was clear of trees, a jumble of rocks off to one side, glittering with moisture. Titus beelined to the rocks. He pawed, sniffed, pawed again. To Ethan's utter shock, the dog turned a circle and lay down, head on his paws.

Ethan gaped.

"What?" Kendra said. "What is he alerting on? Nobody's here."

The words seemed to come from far away. "Nobody alive," Ethan said.

Her eyes widened. "Are you saying…"

"That's the signal he's supposed to use to tell me he's discovered human remains." Her shock mirrored his own.

Almost imperceptibly at first, the rain began to fall, cold droplets that he did not feel. Titus put his head on his paws and let out a long, mournful whine.

TWENTY

The morning finally dawned, poking feebly through the rain clouds. Kendra was chilled, both inside and out, from the night in the woods as Carpenter led his team to clear the rocks to reveal whatever Titus had detected.

Ethan's words circled in her memory. *Nobody alive.*

She prayed the dog was mistaken, but deep down she knew he wasn't.

The county coroner was leading the proceedings, a yellow slicker keeping the rain off. She and Ethan watched from under the cover of pine trees, Titus whining and bumping Ethan's leg.

"Easy, boy," Ethan said. "He's never alerted on a cadaver before except for our drills. I'm not sure why he's so agitated."

It wasn't a stretch for Kendra. Her nerves were strung to the breaking point, too, as the police dug, photographed, dug some more, brushed the debris away and repeated the process. It was time-consuming and laborious but Kendra was touched at the respect the officers showed to the victim.

When the remains were finally exhumed from the hole, Kendra gasped.

"It isn't… I mean, that didn't happen recently."

Ethan looped an arm around her. "No. Looks like the body has been there for a while, a couple of months at least."

"More than eight months, I would speculate," the coroner piped up. He talked into a tape recorder as he took samples and made measurements. Using the tip of a pen, he lifted something off the female victim and held it to the light. A filigree earring that glittered in the beam.

"I… I thought it was Andy's work," Kendra said, "but he was in prison. But it couldn't be Sullivan either could it? He was in jail too until his escape two months ago."

Ethan grimaced. "Right."

"What is going on?"

They turned to find Mindy, dressed in jeans and a sweatshirt, one curler still clinging to her hair, an umbrella over her head. "I heard all the noise." Her gaze went to the grisly bundle. "Is that…?"

"A body," said Officer Carpenter. "And we need to keep this area clear, okay? Ms. Zeppler, isn't it? I'll be asking you some questions later, but for now, I'd like to ask you to return to your house and not alert anyone. We need to finish our work here."

Mindy took a faltering step back, her palm pressed to her heart. When Ethan reached out to steady her, Titus yanked the leash from his grip and bolted.

"Titus," Ethan roared, but the dog flew over the carpet of pine needles.

"Dog, you're in such bad trouble I can't even begin to describe it," Ethan hollered as he ran.

"Where's he going?" Mindy blurted. "Is someone out there? A killer?"

Kendra reassured her neighbor. "Everything's okay, Mindy. The police have it all under control. Go straight home, like they said, okay?"

"I'll send an officer to escort you," Carpenter said.

Her mouth pinched, Mindy hugged herself and walked quickly back in the direction of her house with an officer. As soon as Kendra was sure Mindy was headed away from the horrible scene, she took off in pursuit of Ethan and Titus.

The woods seemed to close around her, shutting off the sound of the police activity. Dripping leaves and rustling branches played havoc with her nerves. How long had the woods kept the secret of the dead woman? Who was she? There must have been someone looking for her, wondering and mourning, praying each day that she would be discovered. Bile rose in her throat.

Forcing in some air to combat the nausea, she took a path up, pushing by shrubs that reached out to snag at her.

"Ethan?" she called.

The chilled air held no reply. Branches snapped to her left and her hand went to her gun. She backed against a tree trunk, heart pounding, until she caught Titus's bark. Blowing out a breath, she followed the sound. Slipping on the debris, she lost them for a moment until she heard another shout from Ethan to her right.

She scooted down a hillock, mostly on her bottom due to the thick layer of wet leaves. In a crevice sheltered by a cluster of tall pines, she found Ethan standing over yet another pile of rocks. Ethan's expression was unreadable. To her horror, she saw Titus lying down, staring intently at Ethan, a posture that said everything.

Surely it could not be. Her eyes must be deceiving her. Titus must be confused about his new training. "That isn't…"

Ethan bent slightly, as if he'd been punched in the gut. "He beelined right here, no question about it. Circled three times and lay down, just like I trained him." He crouched by the dog, absently praising him and rubbing his ears. "I… I think he alerted earlier. Remember when we were training before with the fake scent? But I pulled him off to go help Mindy after she fell off her bike." He grimaced. "I should have let him do his thing then. He was trying to do his job and I got in his way."

The moan of the wind accelerated, driving rain into her face with stinging lashes. She forced the question out. "So there's another body?"

The shock rippled across his face. "Yes," he said. "A second one."

Cold forced its way down deep inside her, past the disbelief. "Ethan, what is going on here? We know it wasn't Andy, and it couldn't have been Sullivan. Who has been killing people and burying them in the woods?"

"Right behind Jillian's house," he finished.

She stared at him. It had not occurred to her. Two bodies buried virtually in Jillian's backyard.

"Get her on the phone, will you?" Ethan said,

standing. "I want to talk to her before the police come calling."

She thought as she dialed, *What could Jillian possibly know about two dead bodies?*

In his office, Colonel Masters paced in front of his wall of photos, Ethan, Titus and Kendra squeezed into the corner chairs.

"Why do you have to bring that hound in here?" Masters snapped.

"K-9 training, Sir. We're a team, all the time, not just when we're at Canyon."

Masters appeared too agitated to note the smile on Ethan's face, so Ethan sent Kendra a sly wink. She didn't exactly smile, but he thought she might have relaxed a fraction.

Jillian joined them and this time he did not feel a jolt at the sight of her. But he did notice the worry lines carved around her mouth.

"These bodies," she said, hands on hips. "I can't believe it. Right behind my house."

"Two women," Ethan said, "and according to the coroner's unofficial findings, buried within days or weeks of each other."

"I've got more unofficial intel," Masters barked. "The first body you found looks to be a twenty-year-old female named Elizabeth Carver. She was a local, worked at a bar across town called Oasis."

"How'd they get the ID so quickly?" Kendra asked.

"She was buried along with her purse and wallet. And some money and gold jewelry, so the motive wasn't robbery. She didn't show up for work about eight months ago, but the bartender assumed she skipped out. No family came looking or filed a report. As I said, this is all unofficial until the coroner does a complete analysis, but it's probably Elizabeth Carver." He looked at Jillian. "That name mean anything to you?"

Jillian folded her arms. "No, and in answer to your next question, I'm not a 'hang out in a bar' kind of woman. I've never been to Oasis. I mean, since I started renting that house two years ago, I've barely been home at all. When I'm not deployed, I'm training and when I'm not training..." She shrugged.

You have plenty of other places to stay, Ethan thought ruefully.

"The other body is also a female of similar age. No ID so that's going to take longer. These are complications, slowing our progress." Masters glowered at Ethan and Kendra. "You two. What have you accomplished on the Sullivan case?"

Ethan related their findings about Lara Dennis. "We're also looking again at the list of prison visitors." He did not care to share specifics about the Chase McLear investigation. Until he had evidence on the guy besides a name suddenly appearing where it hadn't been, he wasn't going to smear McLear's reputation.

"So in other words, you have nothing, only some vague idea that he's got a female accomplice but no further proof about whom. And now," Masters said, his face purpling as he looked at Kendra, "you've brought in another complication. Andy Bleakman and your twisted love life."

As Kendra tensed beside him, Ethan stood. "Don't talk to her like that. She didn't bring anyone in. Bleakman tracked her here after he was released from prison."

"I know the details," Masters snapped, "because I ran them down, since neither of you bothered to brief me. Kendra, I've half a mind to fire you."

Kendra stood and gazed calmly at Masters, though Ethan saw her cheeks blossom with color. "If that is what you feel is best, go ahead. I am still going to continue tracking Sullivan until Jillian is safe whether I'm employed by you or not."

"With a stalker at your heels?" Masters asked.

"I will deal with that, too."

The colonel's nostrils flared. "Bleakman is your problem and these bodies are the cops' burden to handle. All I care about is Sullivan. He, or his accomplice, has taken a couple of whacks at killing you, so we're close."

Ethan's hands fisted at the cavalier way he tossed Kendra's safety around, but Kendra only smiled.

"There's a sunny point," she said, and he could not help but chuckle at her droll humor. What spirit she had.

"But we need to speed things up, force his hand," Masters continued.

Ethan's gut tightened. "How?"

"I've made some calls. Jillian's going to deploy to Afghanistan."

Ethan shot a look at Jillian. She did not show surprise. "You okay with that?"

She brushed the hair from her eyes. "Yeah. I think it's for the best. You know how I love the rush."

He did, but he also knew she did not like the feeling that she was running away from a threat. It wasn't in her makeup. Then again, noting the uncertainty he saw in her eyes, perhaps she was changing.

Maybe he was, too. He found that though he'd never love her again, he could hope good things for her. "When do you leave?"

"This afternoon," Jillian said. "Vans depart at sixteen hundred hours for Fort Levine, where we get final briefings."

Ethan remembered an earlier conversation. "So you're flying out with Bill Madding's unit?"

Her face sparked some emotion. "Yes, but I told you. We're over."

Ethan waited for the rush of anger or suspicion, but it did not come. "Good," Ethan found himself saying. "You can do better than Madding."

Her mouth quirked in surprise. "Thanks."

Masters continued, "We'll make Jillian's deployment very public. Sullivan will want to take her out here before she leaves the base so you'll be standing in, Kendra. Jillian will secretly take an earlier flight to Fort Levine, right after she leaves this meeting." He handed Kendra a garment bag. "Here's your flight suit and a duffel so you look the part. You're dismissed."

Jillian followed them into the hallway. "I don't like to be leaving it like this. Be careful, you two."

"We will," Kendra nodded, hugging her.

Ethan shook her hand. "Watch your back, Lieutenant."

"I will. And you do the same." Her mouth crimped in thought. "You two make a good team," she said. "Better than we ever did, Ethan."

There was no malice there, no caustic undertone to the remark. He accepted it with a semi-puzzled nod.

She walked down the hallway without a backward glance.

Ethan touched Kendra on the shoulder as they walked to his truck. "You don't have to do this. You can quit."

She fired a plucky smile. "What? And miss the exciting finale?"

"Figured you'd had enough excitement to last you a lifetime."

"To be honest, I think you're right, but I made a promise and I'm going to see it through."

"Duty to Masters?"

"No, to Jillian."

"She doesn't realize what kind of a friend she has in you."

"No matter what she's done, she saved my life. Besides, I think she's changed just a bit, don't you?"

Ethan took a deep breath. "Yes, and maybe I have, too."

"Not drinking your own poison?"

He knew it was true, finally. *Thank You, God. And thank you, Kendra.* She'd given him the gift of listening, understanding and a loyal friendship he'd never known with a woman before. "Yes, ma'am," he said, awed. "I believe you might be correct."

"Aren't I always?" she said, poking him with an elbow.

"You're beginning to sound like me."

She put on her best Southern accent. "Then let's get busy, partner."

With a massive eye roll, he led the way outside.

TWENTY-ONE

Kendra felt even more like an impostor in her flight suit when they reported to the assigned area on the base. The number of people crowding around the assembled military vans made her nervous. Wives stood close to their husbands, cradling children. Girlfriends clung to their young pilots, trying to keep from crying. Though no one said it, they all felt the dangerous reality of deploying to a war zone.

But at the moment, civilian life was a deadly game as well.

Kendra thought about the two twentysomethings buried and forgotten in the woods. Had they dated marines? Likely, in a town set smack up next to Baylor. Her heart throbbed thinking of the people who would mourn them when they were officially identified. So many lives destroyed and they hadn't a single clue as to why. No answers, only more and more questions.

Ethan touched her hand. "You all right?"

She nodded. "Head in the game, right?"

He glanced at the gathering. "Best case would be to spot and apprehend Sullivan before he makes his move."

Everyone within her line of sight had the appropriate visitor tags on, or base identification. But Boyd Sullivan had his own ID, acquired from the marine he'd murdered. In spite of the heightened security, with a uniform and an ID he could probably sneak into a lot of places on base without a second look.

Ethan's expression was pleasant, but his eyes were intense, scanning everyone who got close, Titus tethered to him by a short lead. Ethan was in ABUs, no rifle, only a handgun tucked under his top, since he was supposed to be playing the part of her soon-to-be spouse, an airman on a Marine Corps base.

A couple strolled by, the uniformed man's arm wrapped around the woman's waist, murmuring something into her ear that made her giggle.

Ethan suddenly pulled her into an embrace that sent her heart racing.

"What are you doing?" she gasped.

His chin grazed her neck. "Preparing to miss you when you deploy," he said. "We gotta blend. Awesome acting. It's one of my skills."

But the kiss he brushed over her neck and temple did not feel like the work of an actor. *Oh, stop it, Kendra. He's pretending, remember that.*

Still, the kisses kicked up her pulse and sparked a ridiculous longing that she could be his partner, his confidante, his woman. If things were different…if she was not a dead ringer for his ex, if Andy was not a permanent threat hovering over her, if he was not too soured on marriage…

Head in the game, she reprimanded herself.

Ethan scrutinized the crowd from over her shoulder and she tried to do the same, but his proximity made the task difficult. Finally he let her ease out of his arms and she recovered enough to study someone she'd noticed in passing.

Behind the refreshment table covered by a dark linen tablecloth, a marine tended to the coffeepot. There was nothing outwardly different about him and she wondered why he'd caught her attention.

Kendra listened with half an ear to the talk around her.

...when you come back.

...I'll miss you so much.

...email every day if you can.

She noticed Bill Madding approach. She tensed as the pilot, who had accosted her outside the gas station believing she was Jillian, looked closely at her, forcing her back a step. "Another impersonation gig? You're more in demand than Elvis."

"Keep your voice down," Ethan snapped.

Madding huffed. "Don't give me orders."

Ethan shot him a forced smile. "I'm doing my job. Why don't you focus on doing yours? Fly your plane, protect your country and stay away from Jillian."

"The real one?" His eyes darkened. "We're deploying together. How is my behavior with her any of your business? You're not back together with her for real."

"Because I don't want to see any woman get mixed up with a low-down snake like you."

Anger flashed over Madding's face. For a moment, Kendra thought he was going to let loose with a punch, but instead he scowled and walked away.

She blew out a breath. "I wonder what Jillian ever saw in him."

"All ego and limited charm, which doesn't speak

well to her tastes." He sighed. "Of course, she chose me, too, so..."

Kendra's attention again drifted to the marine fiddling with the coffeepot. He had dark blond hair, a small mouth and his lips were thinned in concentration, but there was something about him... His posture, the way he looked out of the corner of his eye every so often, the sheen of perspiration on his brow. "Ethan?"

"Yeah?"

She saw the guy reflected in the silver surface of the coffee machine, a dark shadow followed by a glint of metal, as he pulled a weapon from under his shirt. "Gun," she shouted, going for her own.

The man at the coffeepot turned and aimed his weapon at her, center mass. It was as if time stood still and at long last she was face-to-face with Boyd Sullivan. Both Ethan and Titus charged at the same moment, leaping between Kendra and Sullivan. The roar of a shot cut across her senses as Sullivan fired. Ethan jerked back a step.

Sullivan overturned the coffee cart, sending a river of hot liquid and mugs crashing to the ground. Soldiers scrambled after Sullivan, civilians pushed children behind them and ran for the safety of buildings. Someone near her shouted into a radio.

Sullivan raced around the end of the last military van. She bolted after him, catching up as he edged around the van. Bringing her gun up, she turned the corner of the vehicle and plunged in, finding herself looking down the barrel of his gun.

"Drop your weapon, Sullivan," she said.

"I was just about to say the same thing."

Kendra noted a shadow creeping over the hood of the van. A marine, gun drawn, was inching closer.

"It's over," she said. "You won't get out of here alive."

"You'd be surprised what I can do," he said. As he fingered the trigger, she braced herself and aimed for his heart, just as the marine edged closer. Sullivan caught the movement, fired one shot at the marine and a second at her. Both shots missed. She wheeled back behind the van. Risking a quick look, she bent down and saw the marine searching under the vans, a furious look on his face and her heart sank when he did not find his quarry. They'd lost him. Again.

She got to her feet.

And suddenly, there Sullivan was, across the quad. He aimed a mocking salute at her.

She did not have a clear shot and he knew it. "There," Kendra shouted, alerting the marine and his cohorts.

Sullivan's smile was tight and filled with hate as he disappeared into the darkness, the marines shouting orders hot on his trail.

His smugness baffled her. He could not possibly escape this time, not from a Marine Corps base. Then her brain processed the shot, Ethan's reaction as Sullivan's bullet caught him. *No. It can't be...*

Fear pumping her legs, she ran.

Ethan was already getting to his feet, blood darkening the shoulder of his fatigues where the bullet had grazed his bicep. Titus stayed close by, whining, but this time he let Kendra in.

"Are you...?"

"Oh, yeah," he said. "Just a nick. I told you Sullivan couldn't hit the broad side of a barn."

She was crushed by both relief and frustration. "I almost had him, but he got away again."

"Marines will get him." Ethan grimaced as he grabbed Titus's lead. "I'll help. Titus can track him."

She stilled him with a hand on his arm. "No, you're going to see the doctor."

"But I'm—"

"Not going to argue, just like the time you plopped me on the stretcher and wouldn't listen to a single world I said."

"That was different."

"Why? And if you say 'because you're a girl' you'll get a sock in the jaw, bullet wound or no."

He was spared from answering when two Marine medics hustled over to assist. They gave Titus a wary look.

"Sorry, guys," Ethan said. "If you want me, you get him, too."

Grumbling, they checked Ethan's vitals, applied a bandage and loaded him into a vehicle with Titus in the back. Another vehicle pulled up and the driver motioned for Kendra. Before she left him, Ethan handed her his pack and phone. "Can you hold on to these for me? Don't wanna bleed on them." He quirked an eyebrow at her. "It's okay. We messed up Sullivan's plans. He didn't hurt you. He might even give up, since Jillian... I mean, since you're going away for seven months."

She took comfort in that. At least for now, Jillian Masters was safe. But she'd never be completely in the clear until Sullivan was captured. It still felt as though she'd failed. All she could do was hope and pray that the marines would track him down and make sure

Ethan would get proper medical treatment in spite of his stubbornness.

After a quick drive, she sat as patiently as she could at the base hospital waiting room, checking in with Officer Carpenter by phone. "Do you have anything further on the two bodies in the woods?"

"I told you I'd let you know when we had more info. You can't rush our coroner, and believe me, I've tried," Carpenter said.

She was going to press harder when she felt Ethan's phone vibrate in her pocket. She fished it out in time to see the message appear on the screen.

G.I. Joe. I'm driving to your girl's house. Tell her to come out or I'm coming in to get her. No cops, or things will get bloody.

Adrenaline exploded in her veins. Andy was waiting, laying a trap for Ethan in order to get to her. She'd had her showdown with Sullivan.

Now it was time for another, and this one was personal.

Ethan endured the wound cleaning and the obligatory patient care instructions. He stopped listening to the doctor when Hector Sanchez pushed into the room.

"Give us a minute, Doc?" Hector said.

"You can have all the minutes you want," the doctor said. "He's free to go."

When they were alone, Hector sat heavily in a vinyl-covered chair.

Ethan's heart sank. "You didn't get him."

"No, we didn't."

Ethan slammed a palm on the exam table. "How is that possible? How could Sullivan get away from your security guys on a fenced Marine Corps base?"

Hector huffed. "We think he may have climbed underneath a fuel truck leaving through the gate."

"And your people didn't check?"

"They did, but they must have missed him."

"Titus wouldn't have."

Hector exhaled and glared right back at Ethan. "Yeah? Well, we didn't have Titus on duty, now did we, hotshot? And you didn't fill me in on the 'let's trap Sullivan' plan so I was going in blind, wasn't I? You tied my hands and I don't appreciate it."

Ethan ground his teeth together. It wasn't the time for blame. They hadn't done any better at Canyon. "Right. Sorry."

Hector sighed. "We found his stolen Marine uniform a mile away from the base. He's not getting back onto Baylor that way."

"My guess is he's not planning on returning at all since as far as he knows his target is going overseas for seven months."

"You sure about that?"

"Let's call it a hunch," Ethan said. "Sullivan has plenty of other targets on his list and he's not a particularly patient man. He can't afford to be with the US Marines and Air Force hunting him. If he wants to get his kills in, he knows he's gonna have to make his moves elsewhere."

Hector let that sink in, and Ethan could almost see the wheels turning.

"What is it you want to ask, Hector?"

"Jillian Masters, or the girl whose impersonating her."

He sat up straighter. "What about her?"

"If she's supposed to be pretending to deploy with her squadron, why did my guys tell me that she checked out the front gate?"

He froze. "When?"

"'Bout fifteen minutes ago."

He reached for his phone, groaning when he remembered. Kendra had it, and for some reason, she'd made the insane decision to leave base without him.

He could think of only one reason she might have done that. One very deadly reason.

TWENTY-TWO

Kendra thanked the driver for giving her a ride when he dropped her at the curb a block from her house. She stood in the shadows of some dripping oak trees. Andy's text to Ethan was a trap, of course, one she could not let Ethan walk into. And he would, willingly, delivering himself to Andy to save her. He would believe he could win, but no one won against Andy Bleakman. Until now.

There was no option but for her to face Andy before Ethan did. If it was not now, it would be another day, another place, but it would come, their showdown. She would do her best to win, to end it, finally, but at least she would know that Ethan had not been devoured by Andy's voracious need for revenge. Hopefully the whole nightmare would be over and done with before Ethan was discharged from the clinic.

Her throat was dry, her hands ice-cold as she observed the house. A strange car was parked in Jillian's driveway. Another one Andy had stolen, probably. She took a picture and texted it to Carpenter, whom she had already called. He would be arriving in ten minutes, no lights, no sirens. Her job would be to draw Andy out and he would be arrested. Clean and neat. But nothing with Andy was ever clean, nor neat.

She'd taken a moment before she left Baylor to change into jeans, a T-shirt and a windbreaker, taking the 9mm Beretta from Jillian's survival vest and stowing it in a holster she'd strapped on her ankle, one round chambered, safety off. She'd rather have had her Glock strapped to her side, but he would detect that in a moment. The Beretta would do and she prayed she wouldn't have to use it.

A cold drizzle fell steadily, dampening her hair. Just over the top of the fence she saw the light shining in Ethan's unit behind the house. Andy knew Ethan would not deliver Kendra. He intended to get Ethan and Titus out of the picture first. What surprise had he prepared in the mother-in-law unit? The house? Was he right now crouching behind a curtain with a gun in hand?

She remembered the sound of the wasps swarming over her, the pain of their stingers plunging into her skin, the whir of bullets whistling over her head and the crash of her car hitting a tree. And her headlong hurtle into the icy waters of the river.

Andy's text replayed in her mind. *You're dead.*

Fear suddenly turned to anger that such a man could have power over her life and Ethan's. Yes, she'd made mistakes, craved love too much, trusted blindly and stupidly, but God had saved her from her grievous errors. He'd forgiven her, allowed her to move on, to experience what a decent man was like. More than decent.

Her heart beat the truth with every pulse. She loved Ethan. He'd become the light in her darkness, the God-loving, joke-cracking embodiment of what a man, a real man, a partner, should be like. But he was not open for a relationship, not now, and not with her. As much as it hurt, she knew it was reality. Shoving the pain down, she wiped rain and tears from her face and straightened. If all she could do was ensure Ethan's safety by handling things with Andy, so be it. It would be her gift to him and to herself.

There was no movement from the house, nor the mother-in-law unit. She checked her watch. Another five minutes max until Carpenter arrived.

Baby, she thought suddenly, her stomach clenching into a fist. If Andy had gotten into the main house, what would he do to Baby? She thought of the time long ago when he'd tried to kill the cat, the fury in his eyes, the desire to maim, to inflict maximum pain. Panic nearly forced her feet into motion.

Calm down, she ordered herself. Baby was an expert at hiding and she didn't like Andy one bit. The first sign of him and she'd have scooted to the nearest hidey-hole. *It's fine. Baby is okay and you're not going to do something dumb like go in there without backup.*

A car approached and she tensed, ready to take cover. Mindy Zeppler rolled down her window. "Jillian? What in the world are you doing standing there in the rain? I almost didn't see you."

"I, uh, I just needed some air."

"I heard in town this morning that you were deploying, but you didn't say anything about it to me." There was a flash of hurt in her eyes, betrayal.

"I'm going to catch a ride to Fort Levine later, but yes, I'm deploying." And there'd be no need to continue to impersonate Jillian Masters, no need to stay in this part of Texas. No reason to be around Ethan. She swallowed. "It came up suddenly. I'm sorry I didn't tell you."

Mindy shrugged. "That's the military for you. My ex deploys today, too, but he never minded the short notice. Billy was always chomping at the bit to leave home."

How sad. Kendra felt in that moment that if God blessed her with a spouse, a home, she'd never, ever want to leave it.

"But aren't you sad to be leaving your hubby?" Mindy asked her. "What about the wedding?"

Kendra forced a smile. "We'll have that beach wedding when I get back."

"Ethan's a good man to wait for you."

"Yes, he is," she said.

"Do you need a ride somewhere? You're getting soaked."

"No." Kendra felt desperate to get Mindy safely away before the cops arrived and the situation went critical. "No, I'm just going to, um, drive to the corner store and buy more cat food. I'll see you later."

Before Mindy could question her, Kendra jogged across the street to her car and slid into the driver's seat. She watched with a sigh of relief as Mindy drove by with a bemused smile and a wave.

The woman thought she was crazy, but at least she would be safely inside before anything happened. Kendra checked her watch again. It was time. Where were the cops?

An arm wrapped around her throat from the back seat.

"I figured you might get in sooner or later. Patience is a virtue, isn't it, Kendra?" Andy said into her ear.

* * *

Ethan borrowed a phone and slammed the SUV into gear. Titus braced himself in the back. They flew off the base and along the road toward Jillian's house. His nerves screamed with tension, louder than they had in a combat zone. On the fourth ring Carpenter finally answered his phone.

"I'm en route there right now," he said when Ethan told him to meet at Jillian's house. "Just pulling up on the street."

"It's a trap," Ethan practically shouted. "Andy figured I'd show up and he'd take me and Titus out first. He's in position already, I know it."

"Not my first rodeo, kid," Carpenter growled. "Let us handle securing the scene. You stand down, do you hear me?"

"Yes, sir," Ethan said, ending the connection with a stab of his finger. But hearing and listening were two different things, as Kendra said. He practically throttled the steering wheel, picturing her taking off without him to handle Andy, the psycho. What was she thinking?

But he knew. She'd told him.

I made the mess. I have to clean it up.

Her determination alternately awakened his admiration and his flat-out exasperation. She was actually planning to face down Andy Bleakman alone in order to keep him out of the picture. It was ludicrous. He careened down the highway and the thought floored him. He'd never been with a woman who put his needs ahead of hers. It was stunning, breathtaking and utterly infuriating. He pressed the accelerator harder and nearly missed the turn to her street, pulling up a block away behind Carpenter's car. Fear knotted his stomach when he noticed that Kendra's car was missing. The MP in him imagined the scenario. Kendra had surprised Andy. He'd rendered her unconscious, or worse, and taken her car to escape. Or he'd forced her into the vehicle and taken her somewhere.

Fear accelerated his breathing. *Work the scene*, he told himself savagely.

"I told you to stand down," Carpenter barked, a radio in one hand, as he and Titus hurtled from the truck. "I've got an APB out on her vehicle. My people are inside checking."

"Titus can check faster." He didn't wait for an answer, clipping Titus to the leash and pulling his sidearm. "Tell your cops I'm coming in."

"You're gonna get yourself killed."

"Tell them," he snapped.

Carpenter relayed the message. "I ordered them all to the yard. Clear the house and if you find him, don't be a hero."

Ethan didn't answer as he and Titus ran to the front door and pushed their way inside.

Kendra drove slowly, her mind searching for escape possibilities. Andy kept a firm hold on her throat, his nails cutting into her skin, and a handgun at her temple.

"Cozy, huh? Our reunion? Just the two of us without G.I. Joe and his dog."

"You don't want to do this," she said.

"Oh, yes, I do. I really, really do." His breath was hot and sour on her cheek. "You betrayed me and I got sent to prison while you went off and had your jolly life as a PI. That's why you're playing at being G.I. Jane, isn't it? Undercover work? Made it harder to find you, but I'm a good investigator, too."

She battled back the fear. "They'll come after you. They know you ducked your parole."

"That's my problem to deal with, but judging from the level of cop expertise around here, I'll be fine. You called them, I assume. They're probably out in front of your house now. They'll look for your car soon, but they won't find it in time."

In time.

"They'll be busy for a while, cleaning up the mess."

Her heart stopped. "What mess?"

He laughed. "G.I. Joe's going to have an accident."

"No," she said, twisting. He pressed the gun harder until it ground against her skull.

"Drive the car," he grated out through clenched teeth.

Tears of pain and fear blurred her vision as she drove slowly around the block. There were no houses along the stretch, just a cement-covered culvert that funneled water back out to the river and the woods beyond.

"Here," he said. "Turn here."

"There's no road. I can't—"

He tightened his hold and she coughed.

"Drive over the culvert, Kendra."

No, her mind screamed.

"We're going to take a walk in the woods, just you and me."

"I won't do it," she whispered.

His fingernails sliced into her neck. "You will do

what I want," he said as he squeezed harder, "or I'll knock you out, but that wouldn't be as much fun."

Hardly able to breathe, she guided the car over the culvert and onto a flat section of ground that paralleled the back of the fenced properties. Why didn't he want them to drive away from the house? To put some distance between him and the police? Fingers clutching the wheel, she kept the car creeping forward until he commanded her to stop.

He peered past her at the fence next to the car. A fresh eruption of goose bumps swallowed her up as she realized they were parked behind Jillian Masters's property.

"Do you know who killed those girls, Andy?"

"What girls?"

He would give away nothing and she would never know the truth.

"This is the perfect spot," he said. "Park the car."

With quaking hands she turned off the engine.

Andy laughed. "So easy. One quick stop at the hardware store. Cell phone, pressure cooker bomb, little camera to let me know when they make entry. Too easy."

A bomb. Her mind struggled to process the information. It could not be true. He was bluffing. "Andy, no," she started.

Not loosening his grip, he kicked open the door and dragged her from the car, walking her to the nearest tree.

"Sit," he ordered.

"I don't want to."

With a kick he swiped the legs out from under her

and she collapsed to the wet pine needles, falling onto her knees.

"You've got to watch this, Kendra."

He shoved the cell phone in front of her face. "Would you look at that? G.I. Joe has just pushed the door open. Let's see what happens next."

She saw Ethan there on the screen, crouched low, Titus nosing forward past him through the hallway, checking for intruders, looking for her. Everything inside her screamed in terror. "No," she said. "No, please don't, Andy. Please."

Andy just smiled, madness glinting in his eyes. "Watch, Kendra. You won't want to miss a minute."

Ethan's face, raised to the camera, was grainy, indistinct, but her mind filled in the fine details, eyes tender and filled with humor, strong shoulders that had helped carry her burdens, a heart that beat for others.

"Please," she said to Andy one more time. "Hurt me, don't hurt him."

"Oh, I will, Kendra. Don't worry about that." He stepped back and pulled the phone away from her. She bent into a tight ball, her fingers finding the gun in her ankle holster. Her skin was slick with sweat, hands trembling. One shot, one chance. In one fluid movement she stood and drew her weapon.

"Stop, Andy."

He tipped his head back and laughed. Her finger pulled the trigger as his tapped the cell phone.

Ethan kept low as they breached the door of the mother-in-law unit. Titus did not alert on any intruders but still he kept the dog close. Andy wouldn't hesitate to target the dog. The lights were on in the small kitchen, and he cleared the small place quickly. Nothing. So sign that Andy had ever been there.

Final stop was the kitchen. That was where his eyes latched onto the device on the counter.

Pressure cooker bomb.

Adrenaline flashed through him.

He grabbed Titus and hurtled for the back door, ripping it open as the bomb exploded. He felt a massive force of air pick them both up, heard a sound that detonated inside his head with such percussive force that everything went quiet. As if in slow motion, he saw himself tumbling over and over, blown into the wet yard, saw Titus landing several feet to his right. Still.

TWENTY-THREE

Kendra realized the scream that split the air was her own. There were voices, shouts from behind her that she finally understood came from Jillian's backyard. On limbs that refused to cooperate, she scrambled to Andy, who was sprawled backward on the ground, and kicked the cell phone away from where he'd dropped it, pocketing his gun. His eyes were closed, blood staining his windbreaker. With fingers that seemed to belong to someone else, she checked his neck for a pulse.

A tiny beat thrummed. He was alive. Her bullet had caught him right of center, missing his heart. His eyes flicked open and he stared at her.

"Didn't think you'd have the guts, Kendra."

She was too frantic to answer, too crazed to get to Ethan, yet terrified of what she'd find. The gate opened and Officer Carpenter ran toward her with another officer, both with weapons drawn.

"Andy Bleakman?" he asked, eyes on the moaning man.

She nodded.

"Ambulance is rolling."

"Thanks," Andy said, his mouth pulled into a grimace. "Nice to know I'll be well cared for."

"Oh, we don't care much at all," Carpenter said. "We just want you well enough to stand trial so we can send you to prison for good this time."

Kendra was staring at the gate, willing her legs to carry her into the yard so she could see. She had to see. But her body would simply not respond to the commands of her brain. Legs gone rubbery, she could only stand there, gaping, fearing, mourning, afraid to know, afraid to not.

The seconds ticked by. She looked at Carpenter, her expression somber.

"Is…?" she started, then stopped when she caught movement out of the corner of her eye.

Ethan stumbled through the gate, his eyes latching on hers and then flicking to Andy on the ground. Blood dripped from his forehead and his expression was dazed. Nerves firing and spirit soaring, she ran to him and he crushed her in an embrace. He pressed a kiss to her mouth that brought praises welling into her soul, a comfort so sweet she thought she might die of it. Then he wrapped her in a tight hug that smelled of smoke and sweat and she clung to him.

"Ethan," she murmured. "Ethan, I love you. I love you so much."

He did not react, simply squeezed her tighter. Then he seemed to sag and she pulled away. "Ethan?"

He watched her mouth and pointed to his ear. "I can't hear."

The explosion. He hadn't heard her profession of love, not one word.

"I…" She was going to repeat it, but instead she touched her fingers to his face, to his trembling mouth.

Tears welled in the brown depths, grief that robbed the light from his eyes. Grief for…?

She jolted as she realized Titus was not with them.

"Oh, Ethan…" The lump in her throat squeezed off the sound.

His head sagged, his forehead pressed to hers.

"No, no," she whispered.

He heaved in a ragged breath, pressed close for one final moment, then turned and limped back into the yard. Heart pounding, she followed. The backyard was abuzz with activity. A fire engine had arrived, pouring water through the broken front window of the mother-in-law unit, where a small fire licked at the kitchen curtains. Three police officers were directing neighbors away. Kendra saw Mindy in the distance, offering a tentative wave, her face white as paper in the darkness.

Kendra could not lift her hand to return the gesture.

An officer beckoned Ethan, who knelt next to a dark heap on the grass. Titus. *No*, her mind screamed. *God, please let it not be Titus.*

But it was and the dog did not move, even when Ethan knelt over him, cradling the still form as if it was a child. His shoulders were shaking, and then he stood quickly when the cop finished his radio message.

"We're ready," the cop informed him. "We called your people at the number you gave us and asked them to meet us at the nearest animal hospital. I've got you a ride out front."

Ethan couldn't hear and the officer gestured toward the squad car that awaited. Tears streaming down his face, he lifted Titus in his arms and turned one anguished look at Kendra.

"I'm sorry," she said. "I'm so sorry."

She knew he could not hear her as he turned and carried his dog out of the yard.

Hours later, Kendra could not sleep. There had been no word from Ethan about Titus's condition and she suspected the worst. Her heart broke a little with each passing moment. What had she done to him? What had she cost him by bringing Andy into his world like some horrible pestilence? Worst of all, she'd thought she could handle it herself, deal with Andy alone, and her arrogance had seemingly cost the life of a noble animal, Ethan's closest friend. Her arrogance, like Jillian's, had cut him down.

She remembered how Ethan and Titus had hunted for Baby, scoured the bushes and shrubs for hours to rescue a bony cat for a stranger, and one who was impersonating his ex-wife to boot. They'd come so many miles since then, sharing little bits of themselves, the slivers of pain and joy and mistakes and triumphs, and best of all, laughter. She smiled through her tears thinking about his wild story about marrying her on the beach.

Just a story, but sweet enough to last her for a lifetime. She would try to see him once more, to say goodbye and thank you and… How could she express the terrible regret she felt at what she now expected had happened to Titus? She'd have to try before she left town. She owed him that at least. The doorbell chimed. Ethan? Heart soaring she ran to the door and threw it open.

Mindy stood there holding a container of soup, startled. "I…um… It seemed like a good time for soup."

Kendra sighed. "You're very kind. Thank you." She stood aside to let Mindy into the kitchen.

She set the container on the counter. "What happened, Jillian? The police said there was an explosion, but they wouldn't tell why."

"Someone set a bomb in the mother-in-law unit."

Her eyes rounded. "Who would do that?"

"The ex-boyfriend I told you about."

Mindy shook her head. "What did you do to upset him that much?"

Kendra kept her flare of temper in check. "Mindy, it's late and I'm not going to get into it. He's in custody, that's all that matters."

"Is Ethan okay?"

"Yes, but Titus…" She swallowed hard. "He's at the vet with him."

"Oh." Mindy shoved her hands into her pockets. "You must feel terrible."

"I do. The bomb could have killed them both."

"I meant, how you've treated Ethan."

"How I've…?" She'd almost forgotten. She was Jillian, not Kendra. She could go ahead and explain it, but until she was officially dismissed by the colonel, she was still Jillian Masters, and she owned her friend's mistakes as well as her own. "I'm tired, Mindy."

She ignored the remark. "I mean you cheated on him. Repeatedly." A bright sheen crept into her eyes. "And he took you back, even though you didn't deserve it, and now you've cost him his dog. I hope he doesn't forgive you for that."

Kendra jerked back. "I know you were hurt, Mindy, but you don't have the right—"

"Sure I do," she said. "My husband cheated on me with two other women, you see. He wasn't just sleeping with you."

Her mouth fell open. "Your ex is…"

"Billy Madding, the man you're going to deploy with." She glared. "Isn't that nice? You'll have all the time in the world to rekindle your tawdry affair."

"Mindy, this isn't what you think."

"No? That's what the other two said before they died."

Chills erupted along Kendra's spine. "The other two?"

Mindy cocked her head. "Elizabeth and Jackie. The two young bimbos he was having affairs with. I killed them," she said. "And buried them in the woods."

Jillian's words came back to her.

I dumped him when I saw the text on his cell phone from someone named Lizzie with all the kissing emojis. Lizzie… Elizabeth. The truth crashed home with a vengeance. The woman accomplice wasn't an accomplice at all. They'd been so focused on the trees they hadn't seen the forest.

"That's why I moved to this house, next to you, with the woods behind. It's taken a long time to work it all out." She sighed. "Titus almost ruined everything prematurely when he sniffed out one of the bodies a few days ago, but I pretended to see a stranger and rode down into the creek, threw the binoculars under a shrub. Clever, huh? It worked so well. You two were completely freaked. Totally distracted you from the bodies."

"Mindy…"

"It was a matter of time until Titus found the dead girls, of course, but I was having trouble getting close to you. Shooting your tires out would have put anyone else out of commission, but not you. No, not you. The wasps were fun, but that was pure theater. Running you down after your wilderness survival drill didn't work, either."

"All those attempts, they were your doing, to punish me?" Not Sullivan? Not Andy? Her brain struggled to process it all.

"Surprised, aren't you? Who would expect the mousy neighbor? So easy to ignore. Billy certainly ignored me on a regular basis. Well, I'm not as dumb as you all think I am. I made those girls pay for cheating with Billy. I buried them deep, but you know what?" She stepped closer. "I left a spot for you." Madness, like in Andy, like in Sullivan, shone in Mindy bright as a neon sign.

"I'm not Jillian," she blurted. "My name is…"

"Nice try," Mindy said, cutting her off.

Kendra fumbled for the drawer behind her. If she could get a knife, a rolling pin, something to defend herself…

Mindy took a Taser from her pocket and fired.

Kendra's scream was locked inside as ribbons of fire coursed through her and she fell to the floor.

Bleary-eyed, Kendra swam back to consciousness. Images of Andy, an explosion, Ethan's tears, jumbled through her mind as she gradually resurfaced. It took her several moments to figure out that she was in the driver's seat of Mindy's car, the same car that had nearly run her down on the bridge, parked in Jillian's garage. Her wrists were duct-taped together around the bottom of the steering wheel and there was another strip of tape across her mouth. Her whole body pulsed with one message…terror.

"You're a bad person," Mindy was saying matter-of-factly. "I mean, you have a stalker ex-boyfriend trying to kill you, and me. Plus I heard rumors that you're a target of this Red Rose Killer who the air force is hunting. Three people want you dead. That should tell you something right there."

Kendra tried to flex her wrists, breathing hard through her nose.

Mindy leaned in the open window. "I had an even better idea than burying you in the woods, one that will draw less attention from the cops," she said with a girlish giggle. "Here's how it goes. You borrowed my car, see, since yours was impounded for evidence, and unbeknownst to me, you were so overcome with remorse about being such a tawdry home wrecker and killing Ethan's dog, that you decided to kill yourself. Tragic, huh?" She patted Kendra's hand.

Kendra recoiled from the touch.

"Don't worry. After you're dead, I'll take off the duct tape so it looks real official and I'll be sure to tell Ethan that you were so sorry for treating him like you did so he will think you had a shred of remorse. That will help him heal. He'll be better off without you. So much better."

She reached over and started the ignition. "'Night, Jillian."

Kendra fought the panic. It could not end like this. She'd hurt Ethan in the most grievous way, taking away Titus because she'd insisted on doing things on her own…like Jillian, she thought. And worse, he would take responsibility in his heart that he had not seen through Mindy. Kendra had destroyed Ethan Webb and he hadn't even heard her say she loved him. Maybe that was kinder. Despair darkened her vision.

She slammed back and forth against the seat, trying to loosen the duct tape, begging Mindy with her eyes. *Don't do this. Please.*

Mindy leaned close. "You don't deserve a future with a good man like him. Think about that while you die."

Kendra screamed through the tape as Mindy let herself out the side garage door and closed it behind her.

TWENTY-FOUR

Ethan still felt as if he'd been run over by a Humvee, but at least the roar in his ears had subsided to a dull ringing. He paced the floor of the local emergency room where they'd all but forced him after he'd taken Titus to the closest animal hospital. They didn't have to tell him how close he'd come to death. He knew. A second more and he would have been killed and if Kendra hadn't been able to draw her gun in time…

A chill gripped him, the kind that gets you after the battle has been fought, when the full impact comes home to roost on your psyche. But she was alive. His vision blurred as he thought of the other victim, Titus. Dogs could not talk, of course, but Titus had told him in so many ways, "I would give my life for yours without hesitation." There was no greater love than that. He'd been blessed, pure and simple. *Please, Lord, let Titus make it*. Swallowing hard, he texted Kendra again in spite of the late hour.

She didn't answer. Again. Something niggled deep down in his gut.

Was she sleeping?

He should leave her alone to rest, but he burned

to talk to her, to hear her voice if only for a moment. The explosion had changed him somehow, though he didn't fully understand how. It was as if the blast had bulldozed away the stubborn barriers he'd constructed to keep him from his own happiness. The past regrets, fears, had vanished and in their place was one echoing desire overriding his senses. *Find Kendra and make her yours, no matter what it takes.*

He dialed again.

The phone rang and rang before it went to voice mail.

The niggle of unease expanded to a quiver.

He texted again and called.

Maybe she doesn't want to talk to you. The thought stopped him. He'd given her enough reasons to cut him out by pushing her away, comparing her to Jillian, hanging on to his own failings. Besides, she had her life back. Andy was in custody and her role as Jillian had come to an end. Maybe she'd packed up and gone. Still, she would have said goodbye, wouldn't she?

Unless he'd misjudged her.

Misread feelings.

Believed she felt affection for him when it was really only circumstantial need. Like his ex-wife.

Doubt. He'd let it in and now he felt paralyzed by it. He looked at the screen again and felt a twitch that sent him pacing afresh. Facts and emotions twirled themselves together but one thread kept coming to the top.

The bodies in the woods. They did not fit in either investigation. It wasn't Andy, and it wasn't Sullivan. The coroner said both women were likely stabbed in the back, not especially deep thrusts, but deep enough to kill. It made him think the perpetrator wasn't a man.

Then there was the proximity of the graves to Jillian's house. With acres of woods, why choose somewhere so close, where discovery would be much more likely? The location was a message of some sort, by someone who hated Jillian, perhaps. Someone who could go in and out of the woods without being noticed.

He picked up the phone and called Officer Carpenter.

"Stop yelling," Carpenter said.

"Sorry, my ears are still ringing. Did you find any connection between those victims in the woods?"

"No connection to each other, but we did some interviews with some frequent fliers at the bar. Got one interesting tidbit."

"Yeah?"

"Both women were seen drinking at Oasis, and both with a local guy."

"Who?"

"Captain Bill Madding. Trouble is, he was out of the area at training around the time the coroner figures the first victim was killed. We're looking into his family connections. There's an ex-wife." An ex-wife. Ethan suddenly remembered a moment from their visit to Mindy Zeppler's house. *I guess it's harder for me to let go than it was for Billy. He'll never be lonely. Women swarm to combat pilots...* All Ethan's suspicions cleared up in his mind, and he knew. His heart slammed into his ribs. "It's not Madding," he said. "It's Mindy Zeppler."

Carpenter frowned and looked at his notebook. "We've turned up nothing substantial on her yet."

"It's her. Madding cheated on her repeatedly. She

discovered he was having an affair with Jillian and those other women." He forced the words over his dry tongue. "Kendra's not answering her phone or texts."

"I'm rolling now. We'll take care of it. Stay—"

Ethan didn't wait for the cop's orders. He was already pulling on his dirty ABUs, tossing the hospital clothes on the floor. He raced past the startled nurse and the security guard at the door.

As he sprinted into the parking lot, he felt keenly the absence of Titus by his side. This mission he would have to complete alone. Once in the truck, he sped to Jillian's house, praying with each twist and turn that he would not be too late. His pulse hammered home the truth.

Kendra was everything he longed for. Everything he needed. He was a better man when she was with him and he wasn't going to lose her.

Yanking the truck to the curb and hurtling from the car, Ethan ran straight to Kendra's front door, pounding hard and yelling her name. Carpenter rolled up a moment later.

Ethan slammed his palm on the wood again. "No response."

"I'll check the rear door," Carpenter said.

Then Ethan heard it, a soft low rumble, the sound of an engine.

"The garage." The main door was closed and he did not know the code to override it. The gate to the yard was locked. He took a running start and climbed over, splinters sinking deep into his flesh, his breath raging in his lungs. He made it over the gate and landed hard on the other side, scrambling to his feet and throwing himself at the side door to the garage. He flung it open, and his senses were assaulted by the smell of car exhaust. Slamming a hand on the garage button, he opened the big door, releasing the cloud of noxious carbon monoxide that had built up in the enclosed space. He ran to the driver's side, nerves on fire as he saw Kendra slumped behind the wheel.

"Kendra, I'm here, I'm here," he shouted. Was he too late? No, he would not allow his mind to think so. He cut the ignition, pulled a knife from his pocket and began to saw her wrists free of the duct tape. He thought he noticed her eyes flicker open, a slit, only a crack that ignited a firestorm of hope in him.

"I'll get you outside to some fresh air. You're gonna be okay."

Her eyes widened a crack more and he saw the warning spark in them.

He whirled just in time to avoid Mindy Zeppler's stun gun. She stumbled against the car, losing her grip on the weapon, and he snaked a boot around her ankle, sending her to the floor where she thrashed and screamed.

Carpenter sprinted up, quickly turned Mindy on her stomach and pulled her hands behind her back. "Get her out of here," he said, coughing.

Ethan didn't need the direction. He finished slicing through the tape and dragged Kendra from the car, carrying her out onto the grass. Inside the garage, Carpenter was handcuffing Mindy Zeppler.

"Jillian's a tramp, Ethan," she screamed. "She fooled around with Bill, just like those other girls. She deserves to die."

No, he thought, looking into Mindy's hate-filled eyes. No matter what Jillian had done, she didn't deserve to die. And Kendra… She had been hurt many times over, by her family and by a man, just like Mindy, but she'd chosen another way, the only way.

He turned away from Mindy and peeled away the tape from Kendra's mouth as gently as he could. He began chafing her hands. "Come back to me, honey," he said. "I'm right here waiting for you."

He stroked her hair and her face, his fingers tracing the contours of her cheeks, her brows. This woman, his woman, with a broken past and a golden future.

Their future.

"Come back," he whispered, one more time.

An agonizing headache, nausea, confusion. That was all Kendra could identify. She felt as though she was underwater, surfacing only long enough to see the doctor's face and watch Ethan speak words she could not hear, his expression grave. There was a vague sense of time passing, minutes turning into hours. Somehow, she finally emerged from the water, awake enough to discover it was the next morning.

The doctor said she was recovered sufficiently to be discharged from the local hospital. She wasn't sure. Her body was well enough, but her spirit would not lie easy. As the noxious chemicals left her body, she still felt keenly how much she'd cost Ethan, Mindy's words working their way into her flesh like a spiked thorn.

You don't deserve a future with a good man like him.

Maybe Mindy was right. He didn't promise her anything anyway. *He saved your life, isn't that enough?*

But it wasn't, not nearly enough to salve the ache in her soul as she ran through the plans in her mind.

Pack up. Reengage in her PI business. On to the next case, the next part of her life without him.

As soon as the doctor finished her discharge papers, she pulled on clothes that somebody had brought for her, Ethan perhaps. Blindly she punched the elevator button and made her way to the parking lot, blinking against the onslaught of sunshine, looking for a cab.

"Going my way?"

She jumped, spotting Ethan's newly repaired truck at the curb, him standing at the passenger side, beckoning. She allowed her feet to carry her to him and he folded her into a hug.

"I step out to get some coffee and come back to find that you've been discharged. How are you feeling?"

"Headachy, but alive."

"Yes, ma'am." He grinned. "I thought we could celebrate your operational status with a little lunch back at my place, if you're up to it. Got something I want to show you."

The brown eyes, so warm, the strong arms, not meant for her, created an unbearable level of pain. "Oh, I'm not sure. I should be packing up, giving my final report to Colonel Masters."

"He can wait," Ethan said. "The investigation team at Canyon needs a face-to-face report anyway, so we might as well knock two things off the to-do list."

How could she resist that smile, the crinkle under his eyes, the almost dimple on his cheek? She must be still groggy from the carbon monoxide, but she found herself unable to do anything but acquiesce. A few more hours, and she meant to savor each precious moment of them. "Okay. I guess packing can wait."

"Yes, ma'am," he said. Once they were in the car,

he tuned the radio to the country station as they made the drive back toward Canyon. His fingers drummed a sultry rhythm on the steering wheel and the warmth of the June morning seeped inside her, lulling and comforting her. If only she could stay in the moment, live in it…

To her mortification, she awoke a little while later, just as they were entering the base.

"I slept. I can't believe it. I'm sorry."

"You should be. You missed some amazing music." He stroked her hand. "Anyway, you've been through a lot. You've earned a rest."

"A lot" didn't nearly cover it. She wondered how long it would be before she could rid herself of memories of Andy and his bomb, Mindy and her Taser. She shivered and he gripped her fingers.

"Allow yourself to feel and remember," he said softly. "And then try to let it go."

Let it go. How would he ever let go of losing Titus? she wondered. She yearned to tell him again that she was sorry, to ease the burden she knew he must be feeling, but the words stuck in her throat, sharp edged like glass.

"Okay to make a stop?" he said.

She nodded. He checked in with security at Canyon and drove to the K-9 training center. Her heart sank as they got out. Was it time to place Ethan with a new dog? Already?

Master Sergeant Westley James poked his head out the front door. "Thought I heard you. Ready? Because he is."

Ethan chuckled. "Might want to stand behind me, Kendra."

The door opened and Kendra's mouth dropped open as Titus shot through the gap, running full tilt at Ethan. The dog slowed only a moment before leaping up and knocking Ethan to the ground. Titus tongued Ethan's face until Ethan pushed him back a piece.

"Oh, all right. I get it. You didn't want me to leave you here, but these docs had to check you out for themselves." Titus finished licking Ethan and raced to Kendra, wriggling his rump and slurping up the tears that dripped from her face.

"I thought… I thought he was…" she mumbled.

"Nah. Titus is stubborn, just like his handler. He's tougher than an overcooked brisket." His face softened. "I told you in the hospital, but you must have been a little fuzzy still."

She laughed and rubbed Titus down until the dog returned to Ethan for some more licking. *He's alive*, she kept saying to herself. *Thank You, God.*

They loaded Titus into the truck and went to Ethan's base apartment. He picked up a wicker picnic basket from the counter. "Not too hot yet. Figured we'd hit the beach."

"What? There's no beach around here."

He waggled his eyebrows. "That is where you are mistaken, Ms. Bell. Come along. Close your eyes please." Laughing, she complied, took his hand and he led her to the backyard, where they stood on the porch, bathed in June warmth.

"All right. Eyes open."

She blinked against the sunlight, as an unbelievable scene came slowly into focus. Sand glittered on top of a big blue tarp, an inflatable palm tree sticking out of the gritty pile. There were a couple of shells tossed onto the sand and a beach ball nearby, which Titus promptly went after, his paws batting it ahead of his snapping teeth.

Ethan had spread a blanket in the middle of the sand and there he placed the picnic basket and handed her a pair of pink sparkly flip-flops.

"Gotta have the proper footwear. I guessed at the size."

Laughing so hard she almost could not breathe, she took off her shoes and put on the flip-flops, while he donned a ridiculous multicolored bucket hat patterned with flamingos.

"Are you feeling all beachy now?" he said, eyebrows wiggling.

She stopped her laughing long enough to answer. "Yes, but you didn't have to go to all this trouble just for me."

His face grew serious. "Yes, I did. We need to start planning."

"Planning what?"

His shoulders rose and fell with the force of a deep breath. "Our wedding."

Wedding. She'd imagined him saying it, surely.

"It's gonna be at the beach, remember?" he said.

Kendra froze. She'd heard wrong. It was her heart overriding her ears. But there he was, sinking down on one knee in the sand, doffing his flamingo print hat as he fished a ring from his front pocket.

"Kendra Bell, I love you. I want you to marry me."

She gaped. "But… I…" She closed her mouth, her throat suddenly too thick to speak, just as her mind was unable to process what she was hearing. *I love you.* It must be her own desire confusing her, tricking her senses.

He took her hand and kissed it. "I love you, and let me tell you that was a God thing considering that you look just like my ex-wife. But I think He arranged all that so I could go face-to-face with myself, what I really believed, about forgiveness and trust. Typical of God to do that kind of thing to a poor unsuspecting clod, isn't it?" He smiled.

"Ethan," she whispered. "I hurt you and Titus. You almost died because of me."

He shook his head. "No. We both almost died because of three twisted individuals, two of whom are already in custody. Now, back to what I was saying…"

"My past is a mess."

He laughed. "Mine, too."

"You don't want children."

"I've been stubborn there, too, but now that I've met you, I've reconsidered. Let's start with a few and see where it goes. I'd say we should cap it at a dozen, for sure." His grin grew even wider.

"But—"

"Kendra, we're going to get married and it's going to last forever. You know how I know that?"

She could only shake her head.

"Because I'm not your number one."

She frowned until he pointed a finger at the sky, his expression both soft and serious. "He is. We have Him and He will join us together and keep us together if we always put Him first. He's the best at sorting out messes, the absolute best."

"Yes, He is," she whispered. He'd kept her alive, taught her what love was supposed to look like, helped her to forgive herself. She brushed a finger over Ethan's cheek. And this man had helped.

"I've never felt this way about anyone," he said. "Not Jillian, or anyone. I want a life with you, every day, month, year and decade that I can get. What do you say, Kendra?"

She fought for composure, to make real with words the love that had revived her soul. "I never thought I'd find a man as amazing as you, Ethan. I love you. I'll always love you, every single day of my life."

He rested his cheek in her open hand for a moment, and she thought she heard his breath catch.

"Then you're saying yes?" he asked as he raised his gaze to her.

She could only nod, more tears trickling down her face.

Ethan slipped the ring on her finger and stood, stroking her hair, soaking in every square inch of her face. Kendra's face, not Jillian's.

"I want to take you to meet my mom," he said. "She's my hero and she's going to absolutely adore you."

"Are you sure?" Kendra felt the twist of doubt. "I've not exactly lived a model life."

"Yes, I'm sure. She's going to pull out her girlie yarn and start knitting you a scarf and trying to feed you at every opportunity."

"I'd love that."

His expression suddenly went serious again. "And I'm not going to stop until Sullivan's behind bars for life."

"I happen to know a good private investigator who will be happy to help you in any way she can."

He gazed at her, his heart brimming over into his eyes, and she saw the love there, pure and gentle, a forever promise nestled deep down.

Then he pulled her close and kissed her. She wrapped her arms around him and kissed him back, the sun embracing them both.

Titus, having succeeded in flattening the beach ball, began to dig, spraying them all over with sand. They held their hands up to shield themselves, laughing.

"'Course, it may be a little tough with our blended family," Ethan said. "Cats and dogs, you know."

She laughed. "I think He'll help us with that, too."

He gathered her close again. "You know it, pumpkin," he said, going in for another kiss.

* * * * *

Maggie K. Black is an award-winning journalist and romantic suspense author with an insatiable love of traveling the world. She has lived in the American South, Europe and the Middle East. She now makes her home in Canada with her history-teacher husband, their two beautiful girls and a small but mighty dog. Maggie enjoys connecting with her readers at maggiekblack.com.

Books by Maggie K. Black

Love Inspired Suspense

Protected Identities

Christmas Witness Protection

True North Heroes

Undercover Holiday Fiancée
The Littlest Target
Rescuing His Secret Child
Cold Case Secrets

Amish Witness Protection

Amish Hideout

Military K-9 Unit

Standing Fast

True North Bodyguards

Kidnapped at Christmas
Rescue at Cedar Lake
Protective Measures

Visit the Author Profile page
at Harlequin.com for more titles.

STANDING FAST

Maggie K. Black

Wherefore take unto you the whole armor of God,
that ye may be able to withstand in the evil day,
and having done all, to stand.
—*Ephesians* 6:13

Thank you to my wonderful editor, Emily Rodmell, for including me in this, my first continuity series. Thanks as always to my agent, Melissa Jeglinski, who discussed series writing with me over chicken Parmesan.

Also, huge amounts of gratitude to Lynette Eason, Valerie Hansen, Shirlee McCoy, Dana Mentink, Terri Reed, Laura Scott and Lenora Worth for your support, guidance and friendship as I was crafting this book. I'm honored to write alongside you.

ONE

The scream was high-pitched and terrified, shattering the muggy darkness of predawn July and sending Senior Airman Chase McLear shooting straight out of bed like a bullet from a gun before he'd even fully woken up. Furious howls from his K-9 beagle, Queenie, sounded the alarm that danger was near. Chase's long legs propelled him across the floor, clad in gray track pant civvies. He felt the muscles in his arms tense for an unknown battle, as the faces of the brave men and women who'd been viciously killed by Boyd Sullivan, the notorious Red Rose Killer, flickered like a slideshow through his mind.

Help me catch him, Lord, and end the fear that's gripped the base!

Sudden pain shot through his sole as his bare foot landed hard on one of the wooden building blocks his daughter, Allie, had left scattered across the floor. He grabbed the door frame and blinked hard. His eyes struggled to focus on shapes in the darkness as his throbbing foot yanked him back to consciousness.

He was standing in the bedroom doorway of his modest Canyon Air Force Base bungalow. A humid breeze slipped in through the thick screen at the very bottom of his bedroom window where he'd left it ajar just a couple of inches to save using electricity on air-conditioning. The clock read twenty after five in the morning. His three-year-old daughter was crying out in her sleep from her bedroom down the hall.

Seemed they were both having nightmares tonight.

He started down the hall toward her, ignoring the stinging pain in his foot. The beagle's howls faded to a low warning growl, which he suspected meant in Queenie's mind the danger had passed. Had she just been howling because of Allie's cries?

"No!" His daughter's tiny panicked voice filled the darkened air. "Bad man! Hurt man! No!"

His brow creased. "Bad man" and "hurt man" were common themes in his daughter's nightmares these days. He wasn't sure why. Her preschool teacher, Maisy Lockwood, had assured him that many parents on base had told her their children had been having nightmares since Boyd had broken out of prison, killed several people and released hundreds of dogs from the K-9 kennels back in April.

But he'd done everything in his power to protect Allie from hearing anything about it—including the fact that because someone had apparently used his name when they visited Boyd before he escaped prison, Chase had been recently questioned as a suspect. It had been a little over three weeks since Air Force Investigations had first put him through the ringer, questioning his alibi for the night Boyd had broken onto the base. They seemed determined to pick a hole in Chase's story that he'd been on a video call with a buddy he'd worked with in Afghanistan at the time. Even he had to admit the fact that he couldn't provide the investigators with the video logs didn't exactly make him look innocent. But his laptop had been stolen from his truck early the next morning, along with his toolbox and gym bag. He just had to hope the investigators would corroborate his alibi soon and realize they'd targeted the wrong man. He'd been doing a whole lot of praying in the meantime.

"It's okay, Allie! Everything's going to be okay. Daddy's coming!" He reached her room. There in the gentle glow of a night-light was his daughter's tiny form tossing and turning on top of her blankets. Her eyes were still scrunched tightly in sleep. His heart swelled with love for the little girl who'd brought such unexpected joy into his life. His voice dropped softly. "Hey, it's okay. Daddy's here. You're safe."

As he took a step toward her, his toes brushed something warm and soft in the darkness. A wet tongue licked his heel. He crouched down and felt Queenie's small furry head under his fingertips. It had been just a few months since he and the electronic-sniffing dog had started training together, and already Queenie had attached herself to him and Allie as if she'd always been a member of their small, fractured family.

"Good dog," he whispered, wondering how it would look to someone from the outside world to see a man who stood almost six foot four crouched down in a purple room with his arms spread between two such tiny beings, both of whom, in their own way, tugged on his heartstrings. Allie had been the one person who had given his life meaning and purpose after her mother, Liz, had shattered his heart, falling for another man and then filing for divorce while he was deployed in Afghanistan. And the small beagle at his feet represented the fresh start the K-9 unit would bring to his Security Forces career. He'd had enough of shipping off overseas to guard weapons transfers and depots in Afghanistan. It had been time to take on a different type of air force law enforcement work and become the kind of father his daughter needed him to be.

But now, it could all be snatched away. Someone who'd been accused of helping Boyd terrorize the K-9 unit, endanger the dogs and kill two trainers had no place in the kennels. So just three weeks before he and Queenie were due to graduate, their training had been put on hold while investigators decided whether to charge him or clear his name. He was just thankful Master Sergeant Caleb Streeter had allowed him to continue training with Queenie at home. The bond between trainer and dog was at a vital stage, and if they'd broken it now, Queenie might have had to have been retrained again from the start. Maybe she'd have even been reassigned to a different partner.

A loud crack outside yanked his attention to the window at his right. He leaped to his feet and started for the glass just in time to see the blur of a figure rush away through the bushes. His heart pounded like a war drum in his rib cage as he threw open the window. The screen had been slit with what looked like a knife and peeled back, as if someone had tried to get inside. He mentally kicked himself for assuming Queenie had been howling about Allie's nightmares and for not doing a sweep of the room when he ran in earlier. But his focus had been on one thing—his little girl.

Lord, please help me be the man she needs to protect her!

He closed the window firmly, locking it in place, and cast another glance at where his daughter lay sleeping peacefully. Then he looked down at Queenie. "Stay here. Protect Allie."

He left the dog curled up beside his daughter, ran back down the hall to his bedroom, pulled his Beretta M9 pistol from his bedside safe and slid a pair of running shoes on over his bare feet. Then he stepped out the back door, locking it behind him. The sky was dark, with only a sliver of pink brushing the horizon. He moved slowly and carefully around the side of the house toward his daughter's window. There was no one there. But the footprints that scuffed the ground made it clear that somebody had been. Jagged edges of the screen ran from one side of Allie's window to the other, like an ugly wound. Presumably, the dog's howls had scared the prowler away. A prayer of thanksgiving for the small dog filled his heart.

As he moved away, something crunched under his feet. He bent down.

Half of the cherished macaroni-and-cardboard framed picture of Allie with her teacher, Maisy, was lying in the dirt. The picture that had been on his daughter's dresser just hours ago. Whoever had slit the screen had reached in, grabbed the picture and torn it in half, ripping off the part of the photo with Allie on it and leaving just the preschool teacher's image behind. Horror poured down his spine like ice. Someone had grabbed a picture of his daughter. But why? Who would possibly target his little girl? Boyd Sullivan, the Red Rose Killer, killed only those who he'd felt had wronged him in some way. Chase's precious daughter was an innocent.

He held the damaged picture up to the glow of his back porch light. Maisy's blue eyes sparkled up at him, filled with a happiness and energy that had only been matched by that of the little girl whom she'd held tightly in her arms. Petite and bubbly, with a spunky blond pixie haircut, Maisy had first caught his eye several years before he'd met Liz, when he'd been suffering through basic training under her notoriously tough father, who had been head of basic military training. At the time, so much as saying a quick "Howdy" to Chief Master Sergeant Clint Lockwood's daughter would've gotten him more laps around the track than he'd been willing to risk. He thought he'd gotten over his foolish attraction to Maisy when he'd been deployed overseas, met Liz and settled into the rut of their unhappy marriage. Still, he couldn't deny the fact that ever since coming back to Texas, the sight of Maisy's smile still made those tattered corners of his good-for-nothing heart flutter something fierce.

The fact that his motherless little girl clearly adored her made that all the stronger.

He recalled the panicked news that had filtered through the base the morning of April 1, when Boyd had broken out of jail and continued his terrifying crusade against those he felt had wronged him. In addition to taking the lives of two trainers, he'd murdered Maisy's father in apparent revenge for having once washed him out of basic training. That night, something had unexpectedly pounded so hard in Chase's chest that he'd wanted to run through the base to find Maisy, scoop her up into his arms and promise he'd do anything in his power to avenge her father's death. Instead, a nod and an "I'm sorry for your loss" at the Sunny Seeds Preschool gate had had to do.

Sudden footsteps sounded in the darkness. Bright light shone in his eyes. Voices shouted so loudly they seemed to be coming from all directions at once. "Hands up! Hands up! Get down! Down on the ground!"

Six members of the Air Force Emergency Services team swarmed his yard in full flak gear. Someone must have seen either him or the prowler in the bushes and called the police. Instinctively, he dropped to his knees and put his hands up as instructed, with his gun in one hand and the picture in the other.

"Hey, guys! It's okay! This is my house. There was a prowler, but they're gone!"

"Hands where we can see them, Airman!" The voice was brusque and male.

Chase complied. What was going on? True, he'd only been stationed back at the base for a little over a year, and before starting K-9 training, most of his Security Forces work had involved things like guarding gates and patrolling secure facilities. But that didn't change the fact that these men and women in uniform were still his colleagues. He searched past the barrels of M4 carbine rifles and Berretta M9 pistols for a familiar face. From inside the house, he could hear Queenie barking. Allie's wails rose. Cops rushed past him, kicking down his front door to get inside and fanning out around his small home.

"Clear!" voices echoed from inside his home.

"Clear!" came another.

What was this? What were they searching for?

"Let me explain," he said, in the calmest voice he could muster. "There was a prowler. But they're gone."

No response. His teeth clenched. His heartbeat roared. Enough was enough! They were terrifying Allie, and for what? "Please! Let me go get my daughter!"

A sigh of relief filled Chase's lungs as the tall form of Captain Justin Blackwood, head of the Boyd Sullivan investigation, stepped around the corner. Blackwood's reputation as a stellar cop was beyond reproach.

"Sir!" Chase said, instinctively feeling his shoulders straighten and his fingers flinch, wanting to salute. "What's going on?"

But any relief he'd felt melted away as he saw the grim frown on the captain's face. "Airman Chase McLear. We have a warrant to search your premises. We have reason to believe you're harboring Boyd Sullivan."

Faint hues of crimson and burnt orange sky brushed along the edges of the horizon as Maisy Lockwood jogged down the sidewalk and through the residential neighborhoods of Canyon Air Force Base. Water sloshed back and forth in her metal water bottle as it knocked around inside the backpack that sat heavy on her slender shoulders. The sun had just started its climb into the morning sky, but already she could smell the humidity in the air. Today was going to be another scorcher.

The whole base is on high alert and you're out jogging alone? The voice of her close friend and newlywed Staff Sergeant Felicity James filled her mind.

At least I'm not wearing headphones, she mentally

argued back. As much as she missed pounding her sneakers down the pavement in time to the music, running without it was one of the many changes she'd made since Boyd Sullivan had escaped prison and broken onto the base to kill those his twisted mind thought had somehow wronged him. But giving up jogging around the base before heading into work at Sunny Seeds Preschool each morning, just like she had with her father every day for years before he was murdered, had been one thing she'd refused to let that demented killer take from her.

Something inside her needed that time to pray, and sometimes even cry, before opening the classroom doors each morning and welcoming the shining, hopeful little faces who counted on her to be the caring one who doled out hugs, wiped away tears and blew air kisses over bumped foreheads and scraped knees. They needed her to be at her best. So she mourned for the father whose approval she'd never quite managed to earn, knowing with each step that maybe if she'd gotten there just a few minutes earlier on the morning he was murdered by Boyd, he'd still be alive.

She blinked back a tear and tightened the pink bandanna that held back her hair. Her father's basic training officer voice thundered through her ears. *I'm not here to baby anybody's feelings or hold anybody's hand. There are two types of people in the world, the weak and the strong. Which one are you?*

Weak. That was his implication. Just like her beautiful and delicate mother who'd died from a drug overdose when Maisy was thirteen, leaving her in the care of a man who didn't do hugs and definitely wasn't about to blow an air kiss over any of life's wounds.

At barely five feet tall, with two left feet, Clint Lockwood's only child hadn't even tried to take the air force's physical test, much to his disappointment. A sudden lump formed in her throat. Their relationship hadn't been perfect, true, but when Boyd had murdered him, he'd taken not only his life but Maisy's hope that their relationship could ever be better. She swallowed hard. Her father had considered Boyd weak too. And the angry and disturbed young man had returned the day he'd escaped prison to get his revenge.

Red-and-blue lights flashed ahead. The sound of sirens mingled with the fierce sound of fearless K-9 dogs barking. Security Forces cops in combat gear swarmed a small bungalow. Her breath caught. Had police finally caught Boyd or the accomplice who'd been sneaking him on and off the base?

Please, Lord, may the nightmare finally be over. Help them catch Boyd before anybody else gets hurt!

As she approached the police operation, her footsteps faltered. There was someone ahead of her, crouched low in the bushes, watching the police operation.

They had their back to her and their features were obscured by an oversize hoodie and a black baseball cap. The figure seemed too slender to be Boyd. Could it be Boyd's accomplice? Was it the anonymous blogger who'd been making people's lives miserable with a steady stream of salacious gossip? Or even some paranoid Canyon resident who thought they needed to skulk in the shadows and disguise themselves to avoid the Red Rose Killer?

Maisy's pulse quickened. She reached into her pocket, feeling for her cell phone.

The figure turned. A bandanna covered the lower half of their face. A knife flashed in their gloved hand.

Save me, Lord!

Instantly, she whipped her backpack off her shoulders and spun it around in front of her like a defensive shield. A heavy metal water bottle wasn't much against a knife, but one way or another she'd go down fighting. Her eyes searched in vain for a glimpse of the figure's eyes or anything solid to identify who they were.

"Stop right there!" she yelled, wincing at the way her own voice quaked. "Drop the knife! Right now! I mean it!"

The figure hesitated. Maisy's limbs shook.

Help me, Lord! What do I do?

She wasn't authorized to carry a weapon on base and the backpack wouldn't do much. But there were large rocks encircling a nearby garden and she had a whistle on her key chain. Whatever it took, no daughter of Clint Lockwood was going down without a fight. The barking of Canyon's K-9 dogs seemed to be growing louder, followed by the sound of even more sirens.

The figure lurched forward a step. Hot tears rushed to Maisy's eyes as she steadied herself to fight. Then the figure turned and sprinted away through the base.

Relief washed over Maisy's body and tension fled her limbs so suddenly she felt her knees go weak, nearly pitching her to the ground. Who was that? Had that knife been for protection or violence? She propelled her wobbly legs toward the cops, as her heart beat so hard in her slender frame. In the three and a half months since the Red Rose Killer had broken out of prison, it was like a deep fog of uncertainty and fear had descended over the base. Neighbors suspected neighbors. Colleagues viewed each other with suspicion. Stamping out gossip among her students was a daily task, and when parents arrived at the school, they hugged their children closer and were slower to let them go. Two of her friends, Felicity and Zoe, had quickly married the men of their dreams, rather than waiting a moment longer to start their happily-ever-afters. It was like everyone was a little more aware of how precious life could be.

Something crunched under her feet. She bent down. Her fingers reached for the glittering shapes, cupping them into her palms. They were seashells. No. Wait. They were dried pasta. Bright pink with gold paint splotches and coated in purple glitter, they were the same kind of pasta she used for craft time at Sunny Seeds, and unless she was very wrong, she'd helped one of her own students paint these very shells herself before painstakingly placing them on a cardboard picture frame—*Allie McLear*.

What would remnants of little Allie's treasured frame be doing out here on the ground? Confusion gripped her heart again as the bright-eyed toddler's face swam unbidden into her mind, along with that of her handsome, broad-shouldered father, Chase McLear. The students had made the frames and taken them home as a Valentine's Day present for their parents and caregivers. She could still remember the sweet and chagrined look on Chase's face the next day as he'd stood with his lanky form half leaning against the door frame to the entrance of Sunny Seeds and explained that Allie would like a picture of herself and Maisy to put in it, if she'd be okay with him taking one. She hadn't been about to say no.

She'd always tried her best not to have favorites, but she had to admit that Allie had burrowed a meaningful place in Maisy's heart. There was something special about the tiny blonde, motherless bundle of sunshine with vulnerable eyes and an eager smile. And if she was honest, she suspected Allie's father was something special too.

While he'd told her that he was one of thousands of airmen who'd been trained by her father, she hadn't actually met Chase before he'd been deployed to Afghanistan many years ago or spoken to him until he moved back to Texas and enrolled his daughter in Sunny Seeds. She'd vowed long ago that she'd never fall for a man in uniform. It was a promise she'd stuck to for all twenty-five years of her life. But she couldn't deny that over the past few months she'd developed a bit of a crush on Allie's father. Probably ever since the day the single father had first dropped Allie off in her care.

Her steps quickened as she recognized the house number and street from the Sunny Seeds's attendance records. Police encircled Chase and Allie's house. Were they in some kind of trouble? Had they been targeted by the Red Rose Killer? *Please, no!*

She started running toward the house. A small crowd of people had formed on the sidewalk. She pushed past them, her heart stuttering a beat as she caught sight of the tall and strong form of her friend Captain Justin Blackwood standing among the cops. What was the head of the Red Rose Killer investigation doing at Allie and Chase's house? She ran for him. She had to tell him about the knife-wielding figure.

A hand in the crowd caught her arm. She turned

back. It was the tall, blonde form of Yvette Crenville, the base nutritionist and someone else who she knew had been targeted and threatened by Boyd Sullivan thanks to a failed past romance.

"We've got to stay back," Yvette said. She let go of Maisy's arm. "They're making an arrest. It might be Boyd's accomplice."

"Thanks for the warning," Maisy said. She prayed Chase and Allie were all right. "I just saw a prowler in the bushes. I have to report it while there might still be a chance to catch them."

"Could it be Boyd?" Yvette's beautiful eyes went wide. "Someone reported that he was seen going in and out of that house."

Chase and Allie's house? "No, that's not possible. One of my students lives there. Her father seems like a really great guy. There's no way…"

Her voice trailed off, unable to find the words to finish the sentence. After all, Yvette had never expected that the man she'd once loved would turn out to be a serial killer. She ran toward Justin, even as she felt her gaze pull toward the house. Two cops flanked a tall and broad-shouldered man in soft gray track pants and a simple white T-shirt who knelt by the back door of the bungalow. His head was bowed and his hands were linked on top of his head.

Chase looked up, and his eyes widened as his gaze met hers through the chaos, and the previous stutter she'd felt in her chest turned into a jolt so painful it seemed to shock her heart's ability to even beat.

No, no it couldn't be. Her secret crush, and the single father of her favorite student, was being arrested for harboring her father's killer.

TWO

Maisy watched, her head swimming in confusion and disbelief, as Chase stayed kneeling between the uniformed cops. Prayer filled her aching chest.

Lord, what's happening? Did Chase really have something to do with Dad's murder?

"Justin!"

The tall cop turned toward her, his lips set in a grim line. "Morning, Maisy. I've got to ask you to step back."

Justin Blackwood was a tough and reliable captain, but even then, she'd never seen his face so serious.

"I just saw a prowler in the bushes with a knife!" she said, forcing herself to leave the question of Chase's arrest for now. If there was even a possibility it was Boyd Sullivan, that was all that mattered for now. She pointed. "Over there. I couldn't tell if it was a man or a woman. But they were thin. I don't think it was Boyd Sullivan, but he's been living in the woods for months, so who knows how much weight he's lost. They had a hoodie and a bandanna over their face. They pulled a knife, but when I yelled they ran away. I think they had part of a picture frame Allie and I made."

She held out her hand to show him the pieces she'd

picked up. Justin's face paled. In an instant he'd summoned two K-9 officers to his side and quickly took a
detailed description of the suspect's appearance from
Maisy and the direction he'd gone. The cops and
their canine partners took off after the suspect. Justin turned to Maisy.

"Are you okay?" Concern reverberated through his voice.

She nodded as something about the sincerity of her
friend's caring question made her voice catch. The single father of a teenaged girl, Justin had been someone
Maisy had considered a friend for years. If she was honest, she suspected her father had been disappointed that
no romantic spark had ever bloomed between her and
the military police captain. She'd definitely noticed how
the cut of Justin's jaw and the intensity of his gaze had a
certain attractiveness, which had turned more than one
female head on base. But the fact that his obvious good
looks had never had any impact on her personally had
been one of the reasons she figured she was immune
to the charms of any man in uniform—a thought that
had promptly evaporated the moment Chase McLear
had brought little Allie into Sunny Seeds and sent a
thousand butterfly wings flapping in Maisy's chest.

"I'm okay," she said. "They didn't threaten me or
come anywhere near touching me. They just pulled
a knife and then ran. Whoever they were, I wasn't
their target."

Justin nodded slowly. She had a pretty good guess
what he was thinking. In the several sightings of the
Red Rose Killer since he'd escaped prison, one constant that remained was that he only killed people
he thought deserved it—*like her father*—or that he
needed something from to achieve that aim.

"What's going on?" she demanded. "Why are you arresting Chase McLear? Yvette said Boyd had been seen going in and out of his house. That can't be true."

He paused and his eyes rose to the sky as if he was trying to decide what to tell her.

"I know that different members of the investigative team have been chasing down a lot of different leads," she added quickly. "I don't expect to be kept in the loop about all of them and I know there's a lot you can't tell me. But Chase is the father of one of my students."

Justin's brows furrowed and for a moment, it looked like he was weighing his words before deciding what to say. "I can confirm that the investigative team received an anonymous tip that Chase McLear was harboring the Red Rose Killer—"

"But that's impossible!" Maisy felt her hand rise to her lips. "Chase... I mean, Senior Airman McLear is a good man and a devoted father."

A single eyebrow rose. "I assume this is your subjective personal opinion of the man from your interactions with him and not based on any specific evidence as to his relationship with Boyd Sullivan?"

Heat rose to her face. If she was honest, she wasn't even sure why she was defending Chase so quickly and eagerly. There was just something about him that got to her. She'd always believed in Jesus's teaching from "The Sermon on the Mount" that the true character of a person's heart was known by the things he did. Despite his reserved exterior, she was convinced Chase truly loved his daughter. It was obvious every time she'd watched Allie barrel into his waiting arms at the end of the day. And sometimes when he met her gaze over his daughter's blond curls, it was almost like she caught a glimpse of something lost and broken behind his deep green eyes.

"Senior Airman McLear says it was all a misunderstanding and that there was a prowler on his property—"

"And I saw a prowler with a knife," Maisy interjected again. The slight narrowing of her friend's eyes suddenly reminded her that as a friend and civilian she was being treated with far more latitude than anyone serving under the strict captain would have ever received for such an outburst. "I'm sorry. That was rude. I'm just really shaken by this."

"I understand," he said, but the firm timber of his voice let her know just how little impact her passionate defense of Chase would have on his investigation. "Senior Airman McLear has maintained his innocence. We will of course be taking his claims of a prowler seriously and hopefully my officers will be able to track down and catch the person you saw. I'm trusting you to respect the fact that there is additional information about this investigation that I'm not at liberty to tell you. But I do feel a responsibility to let you know this is not the first time this suspect has come to our attention. Now, I have to ask you, do you know if he had any kind of relationship or interaction with your father?"

"No." She shook her head, feeling her sweat-soaked hair dance and fly around her head. "My dad was his basic training officer, but that was years ago."

"Do you know if your father was particularly hard on him?" the captain pressed.

"My father was hard on a lot of people." Especially her. Again, her eyes flicked to where Chase was kneeling, flanked by officers. Anger burned in his eyes, mixed with a quiet desperation bordering on panic, like a wounded animal desperately scanning the snare that had just trapped him. "Look, Chase can't be working with Boyd Sullivan. I'm almost certain of it."

The lines of Justin's brow furrowed deeper. "Again, do you have any evidence to back that up?"

"No." Her chest fell. She had a hunch and nothing more.

Was her blind faith of Chase's true nature any different than Yvette's had been about Boyd?

A frightened and furious wail seemed to break through the early morning air and rise above the chaos. A cop in flak gear was carrying a squirming and pajama-clad Allie out of the house. She recognized him. Lieutenant Preston Flannigan was the slightly pushy single father of one of the boys in her preschool.

"No!" Allie squirmed, fighting against the firm arms holding her. "Stop! No! I want Daddy!"

Sudden tears rushed to Maisy's eyes. "What's going to happen to Allie?"

"That's up to Chase. We'll be taking him in for questioning. Hopefully, he has someone who can take her. If not, we'll arrange for a base social worker."

A stranger? She knew the social workers on base were wonderful people who did a difficult job, but still, she couldn't imagine how hard it would be on little Allie to understand where she was going and what was happening to her. She glanced at Chase. His face had paled with an agony that seemed to rip her own heart in half. No, she couldn't just stand there and watch this happen. She took a step toward the little girl. "Allie, it's going to be okay."

Allie's tearstained face turned toward her. "Maisy! I want Miss Maisy!"

Her little arms shot out, and Maisy felt her arms instinctively wrap around the child.

"Justin, I'll take her to the preschool with me, if Chase is okay with that. She's one of my students and watching her the extra hour before school starts is no trouble at all. I know her and she knows me."

Concern rumbled in the captain's voice. "Are you sure?"

Maisy's eyes glanced from father to daughter. "Absolutely."

"All right." He led her through the crowd until they reached Chase. "Maisy has offered to take care of your daughter while you come in for questioning. Is that acceptable to you?"

Chase turned toward them and gratitude filled his gaze. "Yes, thank you. Please, don't let her out of your sight. There was a prowler outside of my home this morning. They cut the screen on her bedroom window."

Was that the same person she'd seen skulking in the bushes? She wanted to ask him more and tell him what she'd seen, but with Security Forces all around and little frightened Allie in her arms it would have to wait. "I'll keep her safe, Chase. I promise."

"Thanks," he said again. "She'll need to get dressed and changed. Plus, I haven't fed her breakfast yet. She's recently been refusing to eat cereal if milk touches it, but she's okay with fruit…" His voice trailed off, as if his mind was struggling to figure out what else he should tell her.

"Don't worry," she said quickly. "I've got a change of clothes for her in her cubby at the preschool. I bought some fresh fruit yesterday and I have frozen waffles and yogurt on hand for breakfast."

The number of students who'd been having problems both eating and sleeping had increased since the
Red Rose Killer had broken onto the base. She heard
Allie's babbling voice at her ear, and the toddler took
Maisy's face in both of her hands, turning the preschool teacher's gaze away from Chase. Allie looked
at her seriously. "Police broke my house, Maisy."

"The police are just searching your house to make
sure that you and your daddy are okay," Maisy said,
softly. "Like Queenie searches your house for things.
Now, your daddy is going to help the police and you
are going to come to school with me. We'll have special strawberries and waffles for breakfast. Would you
like that?"

Allie stuck her lip out. "Queenie comes too?"

Maisy looked down. A young beagle sat by her ankle.
It looked up protectively at Allie in a way that told her
that she wouldn't be able to shake the dog, even if she
wanted to. "Yes, of course. Queenie can come too."

"Queenie likes waffles." Allie tucked her head
against Maisy's chest and she felt the young girl shudder in the safety of her arms.

Chase met her eyes over Allie's head again. "Thank
you."

"No problem. We'll see you later."

The pink-and-orange glow of a Texas dawn had
deepened over the horizon. The first parents would be
at the preschool ready to drop their kids off in a little
over an hour. She started to turn away when she heard
Justin calling her name. She looked back. The captain
was striding toward them. Something glittered in his
gloved hand. It was a sturdy gold cross, dangling on
the end of a chain.

He stretched the pendant toward her. "Before you go, one of our officers just found this buried under the floorboards in Chase's house. I was wondering if you could identify it?"

Her blood ran cold as suddenly as if she'd just plunged into ice. She nodded. Her mouth opened, but for a moment, no words came out. Justin Blackwood turned the cross over and the early morning light fell on the engraved words she'd so carefully chosen as a teenager years ago. *I love you, Dad—Maisy.*

Her heart sank to a place that was worse than disappointment or even sadness. "Yes, that's the cross I gave my father for Christmas when I was thirteen, a few months after my mother died. Despite our differences, he wore it under his uniform and never took it off. When the Red Rose Killer murdered him, somebody stole it from his body."

She could almost feel Chase's gaze on her face, but she forced herself to turn away without meeting his eye. She didn't even begin to know what to think. But the fact that it had now shown up in Chase McLear's home made it a lot harder to hold on to the faint hope that the father of the little girl she now held in her arms wasn't somehow linked to his murder.

"Stephen Butler, commissary cook!" Preston slapped the glossy photo of the corpse of one of the Red Rose Killer's most recent victims down on the interrogation table in front of Chase. "Found dead behind a restaurant off base. Boyd Sullivan used his uniform and ID to sneak onto base after escaping prison. Did you lure him to the woods for Boyd? Are you responsible for this man's murder?"

"No, sir." Chase's jaw ached and his lower back twinged with the reminder that he hadn't stood or stretched in hours. But he wasn't about to let his bearing relax. They'd brought him in for questioning in the same track pants and T-shirt he'd been wearing when they'd arrested him. Being challenged by uniformed men while in his civvies made the humiliation he felt even worse. But he wasn't about to give in to the temptation to slouch.

An airman was an airman, even out of uniform.

His eyes roamed over the glossy picture of the dead young man. The Red Rose Killer's first set of victims before his arrest had been linked by a common thread—they were all people who'd treated him worse than he felt he'd deserved. A homecoming queen who'd broken his heart, a high school bully and a gas station attendant who'd fired him had been the first three people he had killed. A woman he'd once dated and her new boyfriend rounded out the five murders that he'd gone to prison for. But since breaking out of prison, his targets had been more mixed. Some seemed to be revenge killings, complete with a red rose and a note left on the body. Others, like poor Stephen Butler, seemed to have been killed for practical reasons, like gaining access to the base or the kennels. Preston had already covered the first set of victims and had now moved onto crimes committed since Boyd had broken out of prison.

Captain Justin Blackwood stood stone-faced and impassive by the door, apparently content to watch as Preston conducted the questioning with the volume and aggression of an angry terrier that had cornered a rat. Chase wasn't sure what that meant. Was the captain not as convinced of his guilt as the lieutenant was? He could only hope that the forensic team was taking the cut in Allie's window screen, the torn picture and the footsteps in the dirt as seriously as Security Forces were taking their investigation into him.

When Lieutenant Ethan Webb had met him in a coffee shop three and a half weeks ago and told him his name had shown up on Boyd Sullivan's prison visitor list, Chase had been both shocked and indignant; his frustration at just how ludicrous the whole situation was had shown in both his tone of voice and his body language. He still kicked himself for that. Growing up, his grandfather, Senior Master Sergeant Donald McLear, had drilled into him that a man and a hero always kept his chin high and his emotions in check. But the idea that he'd do anything to help Boyd Sullivan had been both insulting and laughable. How could anyone think he'd want to spend one minute in the presence of that monster? He'd expected his name would be cleared immediately and that whoever had used his name to cover their tracks had picked him at random. Even the fact that his laptop had been stolen from his truck, along with his gym bag and toolbox, had seemed like a cruel coincidence.

But any hope that he wasn't being personally targeted, which had remained flickering in his heart, was completely snuffed out the second Captain Blackwood had held the late Chief Master Sergeant Clint Lockwood's gold cross in Maisy's startled face. The thought that it had been found under his living room floorboards chilled him to the bone. He'd been set up, no doubt about it, by someone who'd both been inside his home and had eyes on his truck. He didn't know who and he didn't know why. But one thing was certain—for the sake of his little girl, he had to clear his name.

"Landon Martelli and Tamara Peterson," Preston barked, as he slammed the pictures of two more of Sullivan's victims down on the table. "Both were K-9 trainers and murdered by someone who opened the kennel doors, letting about two hundred dogs go free. You don't have an alibi for the morning this happened, do you?"

Chase fought the urge to cross his arms. "As I've stated before, I was on a video chat with a military contractor named Ajay Joseph, who I used to work with in Afghanistan, from four fifteen in the morning until my cell phone rang shortly after oh five hundred with an alert that Boyd Sullivan had escaped prison and let dogs loose on base. I paused the video call and went into the bedroom to answer my cell phone and spoke to Master Sergeant Westley James. When I returned to the living room, approximately eight minutes later, my daughter, Allie, was up and playing with Queenie and the video call had ended."

"But you have no way to corroborate that story," Preston interjected.

"That I was at home and on a video call when Sullivan broke onto base? No, I don't. Because my laptop was stolen, along with my gym bag and toolbox, from my truck when I was off base and I haven't been able to reach my contact."

Preston smirked. Yeah, Chase knew how weak his alibi sounded. It didn't help that he hadn't been able to reach Ajay since then. But he was an Afghan, an independent contractor and a coordinator between locals and the United States Air Force. Ajay wasn't stationed on base, and off-base communication in his part of Afghanistan had been unstable.

"Two dozen of the dogs Boyd let out of the kennels still haven't been found, Airman," Preston said. "Many of them had PTSD from serving their country and saving the lives of service members overseas. You recently transferred to the K-9 unit, didn't you?"

Was it his imagination or did Chase pick up a hint of resentment in the lieutenant's voice. It was no secret that Preston had done basic K-9 training as well but had yet to be paired with a canine partner. Did he resent that Chase had been partnered first? He hadn't thought so. He'd have expected a man like Preston to be focused on getting a fierce and dangerous animal, who specialized in something like suspect apprehension, rather than a sweet little search dog like Queenie.

"Yes, sir, I did request a transfer to the K-9 unit," Chase said. "Though, as I'm sure you know, completion of my training with the team is currently on hold until this mix-up can be resolved. I have the utmost respect for what the dogs in the unit and their trainers do to serve our great country. I hope the missing dogs are found soon."

"I spoke to your old boss, Captain Reardon," Preston said, "and she described you as a quiet man who kept to himself."

Chase didn't answer. He hadn't been asked a question and didn't like Preston's insinuation that being private and quiet was somehow a crime.

"Why did you request a transfer?" Justin's voice snapped his attention to the doorway. Chase blinked. He couldn't remember the lead investigator asking any other questions since the interrogation had started.

"Your previous career was security, correct? You guarded missiles, weapons transfers and installations in Afghanistan?"

"And personnel, yes, sir," Chase said. "I requested a transfer because as fulfilling as it was to be overseas, serving my country on the front line, I couldn't neglect my duty to my own daughter. Seeing the difference we were making in the lives of Afghan children made me miss my own. I figured my daughter deserved better in life than a daddy who she knew only through a video-chat screen, sir."

Justin's eyebrows rose. His mouth opened, like he was about to ask a follow-up question, and Chase suddenly remembered that Justin himself was the single father of a teenaged daughter.

The sound of another picture smacking the table yanked Chase's attention back to Preston. He looked down and his heart ached. It was Maisy's father, Chief Master Sergeant Clint Lockwood, lying on the floor in a navy blue PT uniform. A red rose was tucked under his arm. A dark pool of blood stained his crisp white shirt.

Maisy thinks I had something to do with this? Anger and sadness crashed over Chase like competing waves battling on the shore. The look of disbelief and doubt in her eyes when she'd looked at the gold cross was seared in his mind. It reminded him all too much of the look of defeat that had greeted him when he'd answered the overseas video call from his then pregnant wife, telling him that she'd given up on their marriage and fallen in love with another man who was "emotionally available" for her in a way Chase could never be. Liz had filed for divorce almost immediately. Thankfully a DNA test after Allie was born had proven she was Chase's little girl. Even before Allie was born, Liz had decided to restart her life without them.

"Chief Master Sergeant Lockwood was my basic training officer," Chase said, quickly, snapping his errant mind back to attention and filling in the information before Preston could try to hit him with another question. "It's well-known by everyone who trained under him how tough he could be. He didn't give me a rougher time than anybody else, and I certainly didn't hold a grudge."

Before Preston could speak, Justin asked another question. "What's your relationship like with his daughter, Maisy Lockwood?"

"Much the same as I imagine Lieutenant Flannigan's is, sir," Chase said. "Polite and courteous, but not personal. My daughter is in her preschool, as his son is."

Was it Chase's imagination or did irritation flicker in Preston's eyes?

"Then why were you holding a picture of her when you were arrested?" Preston snapped.

"I've already answered that question. There was a prowler outside my daughter's window. I went outside to investigate and found the picture in the dirt. They cut the screen on Allie's bedroom window, pulled the picture from her dresser and ripped my daughter's face from the frame. My baby daughter's picture is now in this person's hands."

He fought the urge to drop his head into his hands. Instead, his eyes rose to the ceiling as he prayed. Did they believe he'd cut the screen and scuffed the ground himself to cover his tracks in case someone saw Boyd near his home and called the police? Didn't they get how ridiculous that would be?

"My name was used by someone visiting the Red Rose Killer in prison," he added. "My truck was broken into. I was robbed. My home was invaded by someone who planted evidence under my floorboards. My daughter is in danger. I need to protect her. What you should be investigating is who is so intent on framing me."

A quick, curt knock sounded on the door, interrupting wherever Justin was going with his next question. Justin excused himself and slipped out into the hallway.

"I don't care what sack of lies you try to sell, I know you're helping Boyd Sullivan," Preston said. His lip curled. "A few scuffed footprints in the dirt and a hole in a window screen doesn't prove anything. You've been sneaking him on and off base. You helped him kill these people and I will prove it."

Chase felt his jaw clench. How could anyone possibly think he'd allow a man like Boyd in his home or near his daughter? He held his tongue and stared straight ahead as if Preston was nothing but a window and he was looking through him. Still, he couldn't miss the dangerous glint in the lieutenant's eyes. A lifetime in the Security Forces had taught him to spot a hostile element.

The door handle began to turn and Preston leaned forward so suddenly the table lurched.

"You better stay far away from Maisy Lockwood," he hissed. "Take your little brat out of her school and never bother her again. Or I will make sure you pay."

THREE

The lead investigator walked back into the room, giving Chase barely a moment to process Preston's words before rising to his feet and saluting. Preston rose as well.

Justin's eyes scanned their faces. "Everything all right, men?"

"Yes, sir," Preston said.

Chase did his best to keep his face impassive. Preston's determination to nail him was immaterial. Chase knew he was innocent.

As if he read Chase's thoughts, Justin turned to him. "You're free to go."

So he wasn't being charged? Did that mean they didn't have enough evidence? Or did they think that if they let him go and trailed him, he'd eventually lead them to the Red Rose Killer?

"You are not being charged with any crime at the moment," Justin went on, his face so steady he might as well have been carved out of marble. "We may wish you to come in for future questioning and appreciate your continued voluntary cooperation with our investigation. JAG can inform you of your legal rights going forward, including your right to cease cooperation and retain legal counsel. Don't leave base without letting my office know. I believe the team has finished processing your home as well. You can collect your cell phone later this afternoon."

"Thank you, sir." Chase saluted sharply.

The other man returned the salute, and Chase was escorted from the building. But it wasn't until he stepped inside the front door of his own Canyon bungalow that he let his shoulders slump and his bearing relax. Twenty minutes later he was showered, shaved and dressed in his crisp dark blue uniform, with its pale blue shirt, navy tie and laces tight on the leather shoes that were so well shined he could almost see the mess of the house that surrounded him reflected in them. He'd need to have the front door replaced before Allie came home. It still opened and closed all right, but the visible dent and damaged hinges would upset her. His bedroom and the living room had both been tossed, but nothing seemed broken—he was thankful for that—and his daughter's room would only take a minute to set back to rights. Even the window screen would be easy enough to replace. He'd change the locks on the doors as well. A bigger problem would be repairing the baseboards and floor tiles. He'd carefully peeled back half a dozen of each to create little hiding places for electronic SD cards and thumb drives, as part of Queenie's training, and this had no doubt seemed suspicious enough for deeper investigation. Now, patches of his floor looked like a sloppy and haphazard contractor had quit partway through the job. He took another deep breath, let it out slowly and reminded himself that the investigators had only been doing their job. They'd done it with the utmost of respect and professionalism too—for the most part. He ran his hand over the back of his neck.

God, what do I do? Who's out to get me? How do I find them?

The red light on his answering machine was blinking. He pressed the button. The light and airy sound of Maisy's voice filled his wrecked and damaged living room, as sweet and as comforting as a chilled glass of sweet iced tea.

"Hey, Chase? It's Maisy. Not sure when you'll get this message, but Justin…uh, Captain Blackwood said you wouldn't have your cell phone. Allie wanted to give you a call to let you know we were having a good morning…" There was the sound of whispering and the scuffle of the phone changing hands.

Then he heard the voice of his daughter, Allie, sounding so tiny and little, and a sudden lump formed in his throat. "Hi, Daddy! Maisy let me have a special pink hair bow! And I had berries. And waffles. Queenie is here too. Say woof, Queenie! Queenie! Say woof, woof! Queenie doesn't want to say hi. Bye!"

There was the thump of the phone falling, another scuffling sound and a pause that lasted so long he wondered if they'd forgotten to hang up. Then he heard Maisy's voice again. There was an unmistakable strain of worry pressing through her light and cheerful tone. "Allie ate a lot of breakfast. She's good. Felicity gave me a scoop of dog food for Queenie. We're just going to hang out here and have a fun day. Give me a shout when you—"

The phone message cut off in a long beep. He sat down on the couch, feeling his heart beat hard against his rib cage. Then he played the message again, finding comfort in the sound of his daughter's voice and Maisy's reassurance. Did Maisy have any idea how much her act of kindness meant to him? His daughter had been screaming, his world had been falling apart and she'd been there for him, stepping into the chaos, reaching out her hands to his little girl, like a heroine plucking his daughter out of the rubble and into safety.

He'd never met a more beautiful, kind and generous woman.

Real men don't whimper and they don't complain. Nobody ever solved a problem by sitting around feeling sorry for themselves. Unexpectedly, his grandfather's voice echoed through the back of his mind. The Senior Master Sergeant had been in military intelligence long before Chase had been born and was proud of having gone to his grave never breathing a word of what his work had entailed. He'd been widowed when Chase was a baby, moved in with Chase and his parents and stepped into the role as head of the household, filling the void that was left behind by the hectic nature of his mother's long and exhausting overnight shifts as an ER nurse and his father's lengthy deployments overseas. He'd instilled in Chase at a young age that real men didn't lose control of their emotions, ever, even if they were four years old and had broken their leg jumping off the garage roof.

Chase gritted his teeth and stood up. This was no time for self-pity. Someone was out to get him, and he had to find out who. That was never going to happen while he was sitting around thinking about some pretty preschool teacher.

If Security Forces wasn't going to track down his alibi for the morning of the Red Rose Killer's murders, he was going to have to do it himself. The fact that Preston had brought up his former boss, Captain Jennifer Reardon, in the interrogation had reminded him that there might be more than one way to track Ajay down. He dialed Captain Reardon's office number. She answered on the first ring. "Morning, ma'am."

"Morning, Airman." The captain's voice was clipped and her words precise. He often thought she spoke the way a sniper fired. "What can I do for you?"

He imagined word of his early morning arrest had already made it to her ears.

"I'm trying to track someone down," he said, "and I'm hoping you could help. When I was in Afghanistan, I became friends with a local contractor named Ajay Joseph…"

"I can't say I remember him," she said briskly.

That didn't surprise him. There had been hundreds of American servicemen and -women on the base, as well as hundreds of local contractors. She hadn't been wrong when she'd told investigators that he'd been a quiet man who kept to himself, though he seriously doubted she'd put the kind of negative spin on it that Preston had implied. A certain inner calm was important in the kind of Security Forces work that involved protecting high priority targets for long and potentially boring periods of time, when nothing was happening and there was empty desert spread in all directions. He hadn't socialized much with the broader team. Not because he hadn't liked them, but because he was the kind of guy who'd always preferred just having a couple of close friendships.

"He was an Afghan contractor who helped as a local liaison to get our weapons into the hands of the right people on the ground," he said, "and keep them out of the wrong ones. It's very important that I speak with him as soon as possible, but I haven't been able to reach him in weeks. I considered contacting your counterpart on the ground, Captain Teddy Dennis, but I don't know him personally and never served under him directly."

"May I ask what this is regarding?" Her voice was guarded and cautious, even clipped. Under the circumstances, he wasn't surprised.

Lord, I hate asking anyone for help. But I don't have the resources to track Ajay down on my own.

"I need him to confirm a video communication we had on the morning of April 1," he said, knowing the date would probably trigger the same shudder of familiarity down her spine as it did his. "Ajay and I used to be in a small Bible study together, and consider each other friends. He had been dealing with a tricky situation and was looking for my advice."

Specifically, the young Afghan had been noticing some slight discrepancies in some of the weapons shipments and wondered if a fellow contractor was skimming off a few items to sell on the black market. Considering the desperate poverty some of his men were coming from, Ajay had been tempted to look the other way. But his new and growing Christian faith had been nudging him toward making a full report to Captain Dennis. He'd asked Chase to pray with him and had also promised to send through some supply records to get Chase's second opinion. He didn't want to ruin another man's life until he was positive theft

was actually happening. The supply record emails had
arrived encrypted. In the chaos of Boyd's breakout and
the release of the K-9 dogs, Chase hadn't managed to
unencrypt them before his laptop had been stolen from
his truck. When Chase had gotten a new machine and
asked Ajay to resend the files, Ajay had emailed back
saying the matter had been resolved. It had been nothing but an accounting error. He'd also said that his father was ill, so he was going to visit his family in the
mountains. Chase had wished his father a speedy recovery. That was the last Chase had heard from him.

He was thankful Captain Reardon hadn't pressed
him for more information about the call. If Ajay had
been right, and it had been nothing but an accounting
error, he didn't want the notoriously aggressive Captain Dennis firing Ajay's crew over it.

"While we were talking, a phone call came in about
the Red Rose Killer breaking onto base and releasing
K-9 dogs," he said. "We'd been on the call from four
fifteen onward, which proves I wasn't helping Boyd
Sullivan on base that morning and was not involved in
any of the crimes that took place. I got an email from
him a few weeks ago telling me he was going to visit
his family in the mountains and I haven't heard from
him since. But, as you can imagine, I'm quite eager
to talk to him now."

"While I don't recognize his name, Captain Dennis did recently mention his main liaison with one of
the Afghan independent contractors had recently left,"
she said. "I assume we're talking about the same man.
Communication lines in the mountains are virtually
nonexistent."

"Did Captain Dennis have any idea when he'd be

returning or how I could contact him?" Chase asked. "Do you know if Ajay's company has anyone who'd be heading up into the mountains who could try to pass along a message for me?"

He ran his hand over his face. Maybe he should have gone to Captain Dennis directly.

There was a heavy pause, which he knew meant Captain Reardon was choosing her words carefully. "Airman, I know you're frustrated. But you know that things don't work in Afghanistan the way they do here. It's the middle of the summer. The heat is extreme and we can't expect one of our partners on the ground to send someone wandering through a war zone to find one man who might not even remember a conversation he had with you three months ago."

He blew out a long breath. She was right and he should probably be thankful she was agreeing to talk to him at all under the circumstances.

"I understand, ma'am," he said. "I apologize for putting you in this situation. I realize I'm grasping at straws. But my laptop was stolen from my truck and along with it any evidence of the video call. Someone threatened my daughter's life this morning. There was a prowler outside her window who tried to cut the screen with a knife."

She took in a sharp breath.

"Oh, Chase, I'm so sorry." Her voice softened. "As I hope you can understand, my hands are fairly tied and there's very little I can do. But I will speak to Captain Dennis directly today and ask if there's any way he can speak to the man's organization and access his computer logs. If he was using a base computer, Captain Dennis might be able to access the records himself and confirm when you spoke and for how long. I can also ask him if he knows of any way to contact him directly. Although, I would've assumed Security Forces would've already sought to access that information."

So would he. But the almost gleefully vindictive look that had glinted in Preston's eyes was now making him wonder. Was it possible Captain Dennis had already provided that information and investigators were so eager to see him hang that they'd discounted it? "Do you think I should contact Captain Dennis directly?"

"May I be blunt?" she asked.

"Of course."

"You're suspected of helping a serial killer who murdered several fine servicemen and -women." Her voice sharpened. "You know what Boyd Sullivan has done to our community. His crimes and the fact that he's still on the loose is tearing Canyon apart. Everyone you speak to is going to be under a cloud of suspicion and it could have an extremely unwelcome impact on anyone serving overseas if you start making calls on secured lines about accessing old video logs. I'm talking about how it will look, Airman, regardless of how innocent your intentions are. Let me talk to Captain Dennis. I'll impress on him the importance of the situation and tell him to pass everything he can find directly onto investigators. You and I have served together. I have broad shoulders and can take a bit of heat. I've already been questioned about you once and I won't be surprised if I face some additional questioning over this conversation."

He hadn't even considered how talking to Captain Reardon or Captain Dennis would impact their careers, their work or their teams. Suspicion was like a toxin. It had been spreading through Canyon Air Force Base for weeks now, poisoning hearts and infecting relationships. He prayed that neither of the captains would face any trouble for helping him.

"Let me assure you that nobody you've served with believes for a moment you have anything to do with Boyd Sullivan," she added. "Hopefully, this will all be cleared up quickly. But, in my opinion, the best thing you can do right now is to lay low and let the investigators do their job."

"Thank you, ma'am, and thank you for the help. I really appreciate it."

"No problem, Airman."

They ended the call and he set the phone back in its cradle. Relaxing was the last thing on his mind. He'd been framed for murder, his life was falling apart and he wasn't about to sit around and wait for someone else to sort it. The uncharacteristic silence of his empty house surrounded him. He knelt in the mess and closed his eyes to pray. He couldn't remember the last time he'd been truly alone in his bungalow without his daughter and dog running around. He wasn't sure he liked it. Questions tumbled through his mind like Ping-Pong balls in a dryer. His daughter's frightened face filled his mind.

Help me, God. I'm in really deep trouble and You're my only hope.

He opened his eyes and set out for Sunny Seeds Preschool.

"Doggy, Doggy, go find the phone!"

Maisy sat cross-legged on the brightly colored carpet in Sunny Seeds Preschool's large open classroom and chanted along with her students and classroom assistant, Esther Hall, as little Allie whispered the search command in Queenie's ear. Then Maisy let Queenie climb off her lap and into the circle. The children giggled as Queenie walked over to each one and sniffed them in turn. Then the small dog trotted off in the direction of the dress-up corner. Eleven small shining faces watched her go.

"Queenie finds phones!" Allie had explained to Maisy when they'd first gotten to the preschool. The toddler had then whispered something in the dog's ear and then Queenie had walked over and sat neatly in front of where Maisy's phone was on the table, and refused to move until Allie had patted her head. "I gave her a command just like Daddy. Queenie finds computers too."

Maisy hadn't even heard of an electronic-sniffing dog, let alone expected to find one in such a small and adorable size. All the K-9 dogs she'd met had been large, majestic and formidable breeds, like rottweilers, German shepherds and Doberman pinschers. But when Felicity and her newlywed husband, Westley, had dropped by with some dog food, she'd told Maisy that Chase and Queenie had done the electronic search of her home back in April and found two listening devices. Westley had then explained that while ESDs were relatively new in law enforcement, they had incredible abilities to sniff out the smallest electronic devices on command, as small as tiny thumb drives and picture storage cards, no matter where a criminal hid them. A beagle's small size and excellent nose made it the perfect breed for that kind of work. He said it seemed that while little Allie had been watching her father train Queenie at home she'd picked up how to give the dog the search command with the exact same tone of voice, intonation and gestures her father used. Ultimately, Chase would have to train the dog to ignore Allie's instructions. At least, thankfully, it only seemed to be Allie that the dog responded to that way.

Even then, Maisy had been a bit skeptical until Allie got Queenie to sniff out each arriving parent who came to drop off their child and then reported back whether or not they were carrying any electronic devices on their person. If they weren't carrying any, she moved on. If they were, she howled once, sat directly in front of their feet and stared.

She hadn't gotten it wrong once.

So now, on top of the general excitement of having a small dog as a very special visitor at the preschool, the regular circle time had turned into a game. Maisy, with Allie's help, held Queenie and theatrically covered the small dog's eyes while her assistant, Esther, helped one of the students hide the phone, and then Allie would give Queenie the command to find it.

The coat hooks, book nook and building blocks hadn't proven to be a challenge. This time Queenie sniffed around the costume trunk, then dove under the dress-up rack and disappeared in the costumes and uniforms for a second. Then her tiny furry head reappeared through the flowing fabric. She barked and sat. Maisy laughed. "Good dog."

She got up from the circle, went over and stroked the small dog's head. Queenie licked her fingers.

There was a short, polite rap on the glass window separating the classroom from the front hallway. She glanced back. Her breath caught in her throat. There stood Chase, dressed in his crisp, clean uniform blues, looking every bit like a hero as he had the day she'd first laid eyes on him. Unexpected heat rose to her cheeks. Whether he was guilty or innocent of the crimes he was being suspected of, Chase's life was in serious danger. Her crushing on him like a schoolgirl was the last thing either of them needed.

Maisy broke his gaze and nodded toward where Allie now rolled on the carpet, giggling with Zoe's son, Freddy. The little girl hadn't noticed her father yet. Something softened in Chase's eyes as he glanced at his daughter, but he shook his head slightly and pointed to Maisy. Then he stepped back away from the window and out of sight. Seemed he wanted to talk to her alone for a moment before he greeted his daughter. She wasn't sure why, but once Allie caught sight of her daddy, Maisy suspected she wouldn't be in a hurry to let him go. Maisy wanted to talk to him alone too, more than she'd realized. She needed to look him straight in the eyes, ask him if he was guilty and demand the truth about why he had her father's cross.

Maisy turned back to the classroom. The other pre-school teacher, Bella Martinez, who taught the class next door, and her classroom assistant, Vance Jones, had taken their students outside to the playground. No doubt, her students would enjoy the opportunity to play with the other kids.

"That was fun, wasn't it?" she said, keeping her voice light and cheerful. "Now I think it's time for outside playtime. Everybody follow Miss Esther outside."

She waited and supervised, keeping a watchful eye as the slender and dark-haired newly qualified teacher

led the herd of children out to the shady fenced playground behind the preschool. Two years younger than
Maisy and very ambitious, Esther was the granddaugh-
ter of base commander Lieutenant General Nathan
Hall and never tried to hide that she was eager to run
her own class and not be anyone's assistant. But she
was good with the students.

Maisy turned back to where she knew Chase would
be waiting. She took a deep breath and prayed as she
exhaled. *Lord, is this man guilty of the crimes he's
been accused of? Help me be wise. Help me see the
truth.* Then she raised her chin and pushed through the
door into the small entranceway. "Hello, Chase. Allie's outside in the back playground. It's fully fenced
in and supervised."

Although, since paranoia and suspicion had spread
across the base, a handful of the more overprotec-
tive parents had argued a locked five-foot-tall fence
wasn't enough to protect their children from intruders.
The preschool director, Imogene Wilson, had installed
extra security cameras and keypad locks on the playground doors, but still some parents were demanding
the school take down the beautiful and colorful picket
fence that Maisy herself had painted and replace it
with a much taller chain-link fence with barbed wire
on top. One or two other parents wanted to cancel re-
cess and field trips altogether. Thankfully, so far the
preschool director hadn't given in.

Chase stepped back, nearly bumping into a cheerful
hand-painted wooden sign of smiling fruit proclaim-
ing Hugs Happen Here! He was so tall the top of her
head barely came up to his chin, and not for the first

time, she felt her eyes lingering on the strength of his arms and the breadth of his chest.

"Maisy, hi." His voice was oddly husky, as if there was something caught in his throat. Sad eyes searched her face, looking even more lost and alone than when he'd first walked into her preschool. "I... Honestly... Well..." Then Chase closed his mouth again and shook his head as his words failed him. If she'd ever seen someone in need of a hug, it was him. He swallowed hard. "How's Allie?"

"She's fine," she said, crossing her arms. "She was pretty confused and upset at first, as is to be expected. But she's a strong kid and very resilient. I let her take a pink hair bow out of the birthday box, which calmed her down a bit. She helped me make toaster waffles and fruit for breakfast and showed me how to get Queenie to hunt for cell phones."

He chuckled. "Did she now?"

"When Felicity and Westley brought over some dog food, Westley said to mention that before you integrate Queenie to the K-9 unit you'll have to train Queenie not to take commands from anyone else," she said, "including Allie. Although, he suspects Allie's only able to do it because she's done a really good job figuring out how to mimic you. She's a really smart kid."

His Adam's apple bobbed as if it stung to be reminded of his training with the K-9 unit that Westley had also told her was on hold while he was under suspicion.

"I don't know how to begin to thank you," he admitted. "Everything I can think of to say seems so inadequate considering what you did for us."

"How about giving me a straight and truthful answer? Did you have anything at all to do with the death of my father?"

He blinked as if something about her bluntness surprised him. But then he looked down at her again, his gaze strong and unflinching. "No, ma'am."

"Then how did my father's cross end up in your home?"

"I have no idea."

Her gut said he was telling the truth, but her brain was a whole different matter. She'd placed a lot of faith in the team investigating the Red Rose Killer in the past few months. The only thing that allowed her to sleep at night was the knowledge that some of the very best people she'd ever known were working around the clock to find Boyd and put him back behind bars where he belonged. But if Chase was innocent, then was her faith in the team misplaced? Or was she wrong to believe the man now standing in front of her?

Neither option was a comforting one.

"Did you ever have anything to do with Boyd Sullivan?" she pressed. Instinctively, her hand reached for his arm. She didn't know why. But somehow she found her fingers brushing the fabric of his uniform, as if trying to hold him in place. "Anything at all? Anything that could explain why the police think you would be helping him or hiding him in your home?"

Chase shook his head. Then he looked down at her hand like it had been a really long time since he'd seen a woman's fingers on his arm. His hand slid over hers, as if he was about to lead her into a party on his arm, or he was double-checking she was really there. The warmth of his touch spread through her skin. Then his clear and flawless eyes met hers again.

They were the same shade of green as a deep cool pond on a hot Texas summer day.

"No, ma'am," he said. "I give you my word. I would never put Allie in danger like that. She is my entire world."

She believed that, right? That no matter what else she knew or didn't know, Chase loved his little girl too much to sneak a man like Boyd Sullivan around the base and into their lives?

A chorus of panicked shouts erupted from the playground. Queenie barked and her students screamed. Maisy pushed through the door and pelted through the classroom and toward the back door, feeling Chase just one step behind her.

What was happening?

Then one child's voice rose above them all—"No! Stop! You're hurting me!"—and Maisy knew in an instant which student the voice belonged to.

It was Allie.

FOUR

Chase ran past her. She watched as his long legs sprinted through the classroom's maze of cushions, books and toys. He reached the door to the playground and yanked hard. His big hands struggled with the child safety lock.

"Wait, let me get it!" Maisy slid her slender body under the crook of his arm and in between him and the door. Her small hand brushed his large one out of the way. For a moment, his chest brushed against her back and her own fingers seemed to fumble with the same latch she'd done more times than she could count. Then it slid back and she slipped to the side as Chase yanked the door open and burst through.

"Allie? Allie!" His eyes scanned the fenced-in playground. Plastic toys, balls and trikes littered the ground. Bella was calling her students to line up against the wall for a head count. Bella's classroom assistant, Vance, was nowhere to be seen. Some of Maisy's students huddled around Esther. Others ran for Maisy, as she instinctively opened her arms to comfort them.

"Help me, Lord," Chase prayed aloud. "Help me find her!"

Maisy turned to Bella. "What happened?"

"I was getting my class to line up to come back inside when some kids started screaming about a stranger at the fence." Bella's dark eyes met Maisy's. The other teacher's face was pale. "I sent Vance to alert Imogene to initiate a lockdown and call police. Thankfully, all my students are accounted for."

But what about hers?

Maisy turned to Esther. "We have to get our class lined up and inside. Is anybody missing?"

"I don't know!" Esther's hand rose to her lips, suddenly looking years younger than twenty-three. She was breathing so fast she was almost hyperventilating. "It all happened so fast. Everyone was screaming. Kids were pointing at the fence. It was chaos." It still was. Esther gulped a breath. "I saw him. He was tall with a black hoodie and baseball cap. He had a bandanna over his face."

Like the figure she'd seen outside Chase and Allie's home. "Where?"

"I don't know. He ran, but I didn't see which direction." Esther's eyes grew wide. "Maisy, I think it was Boyd Sullivan."

It couldn't be! Could it? The world swam. A prayer for help moved through her. Bella's classroom assistant and the preschool director burst out the preschool back door and started helping a stunned Esther get students inside.

"Chase!" Maisy called. "There was someone at the fence! In a hoodie, hat and bandanna. Esther thinks it was Boyd Sullivan."

"Allie's gone." Chase spun toward her. Allie's bright pink bow was clutched in his hand. His eyes met hers, and it was like she could see through them to the pain piercing his chest. "I can't see her anywhere."

"We'll find her," she said, but he'd already run for the fence. His strong voice shouted his daughter's name.

She watched as Imogene helped Esther usher the last of her students through the door.

"Police have been called," Imogene told her. The gray-haired preschool director's face was grim. "Every teacher has their class on lockdown. All students were accounted for but one. Allie."

Maisy's gaze rose desperately to the fence that had given her such a false sense of security. *Oh, Lord, how can this be happening? How can a child disappear from my preschool in broad daylight? Had she been snatched over the fence?*

Maisy nodded numbly. She heard the sound of Bella locking her classroom door, the muffled children's cries from within the preschool and Chase's desperate calls for his daughter. Then one noise rose above it all—Queenie was howling.

"Let me go help Chase look for his daughter, Imogene, please," Maisy begged the preschool director. "I think I have an idea of how to find Allie."

Her boss paused. Maisy prayed the older woman would trust her on this. School policy was all hands on deck during a lockdown. But if Maisy could help Allie before it was too late…

"Okay," Imogene said. "I'll get someone to help Esther watch your class. When you come back, go to the front door and buzz in."

"Thank you."

The preschool director closed the classroom door and locked it behind her. Maisy ran for Chase.

"Chase, can Queenie track Allie?" Maisy asked. "I know that's not her K-9 specialty. But my grandmother used to say her beagle could find every one of her eight kids by just hearing their name. She said that breed had the best nose of any dog for finding her pack. And Allie's part of Queenie's pack. Right?"

Doubt flickered in Chase's gaze. He dropped to one knee. The tiny dog ran to him instantly. Her ears perked. Her unwavering brown eyes fixed on his face. He held out the pink bow.

"Queenie. Where's Allie?" His stern voice hid any hint of the doubt she'd seen on his face. "Go search. Go find Allie."

Queenie barked. Then the tiny dog pelted in a blur of brown, black and white fur toward the farthest corner of the fence. Chase matched her pace, scooping the dog up into his arms just steps before she reached the perimeter and held her to his chest as his long legs leaped over the fence. Then he set the dog down and they kept running over the grassy lot behind the preschool. Maisy cast one glance behind her at the closed door and then ran after Chase and the small dog.

Then she heard it, a faint voice sending hope surging through her veins. "Daddy! Help!"

"Allie!" Chase shouted his daughter's name and fresh strength seemed to course through him. "Hold on! Daddy's coming."

Maisy reached the top of the small hill and paused. The grass spread down to a parking lot below her. A slender figure, tall and shrouded in an oversize hoodie far too warm for the blazing sun was half carrying and half dragging a tiny squirming bundle of rage and fight toward the trunk of a car. Allie thrashed. Chase pelted toward his child, the dog howling at his heels. "Let. My. Daughter. Go!"

The black clad figure stopped, as if startled, turned back. Questions clashed hard and sudden, all within a fraction of a second, inside Maisy's frightened mind. If the person she'd seen had been trying to abduct Allie, why weren't they still struggling to get her into the car? Had everything happened more quickly than Maisy had realized? Had they hesitated? Or been unprepared and underestimated how hard it would be to make an upset toddler do anything they didn't want to?

"Daddy!" Allied wrenched her body from the kidnapper's grasp. She hit the pavement. Chase and Maisy kept running toward them. The figure fled, leaping into their vehicle and peeling off, without even stopping to close the trunk. Chase reached his daughter and scooped her up into his arms. He cradled her to his chest and kissed the top of her tiny blond head with such tenderness and fierce protection that Maisy felt tears rush to her eyes.

A fatherly love that deep had to be real, right? A man who loved his daughter that deeply just wouldn't invite a serial killer into his home. Would he?

Allie was babbling, something about a bad person and a picture, but her words seemed to run together in a stream of sounds. Then Allie's small tear-filled eyes met hers. "Maisy need hug too, Daddy."

Chase's eyes met hers in a split-second glance that seemed to last a lifetime. Then he nodded and slowly opened his arms for Maisy to take Allie. She reached out her arms and felt Chase slide the most precious thing in his world into her hands, just moments after coming within a hairbreadth of losing her.

"Thank you, Allie." She hugged the little girl close as her voice barely rose above a whisper. "You're right. I would really like a hug right now."

Chase closed his eyes and she watched as silent prayers poured from his lips.

"I get down now, Maisy," Allie said.

Maisy chuckled. She dropped to her knees on the soft ground.

"Are you okay?" She searched the toddler's tear-stained face. "Are you hurt?"

"No." The little girl shook her head. Her gaze dropped to the ground. "I bit, Maisy. I bit. I… I did bad…"

Tears filled her voice. *Oh, precious girl!* Maisy cuddled her closely.

"You're a good girl, you hear me?" Maisy said fiercely. "You did very good to bite the bad person trying to hurt you. You're right that we don't hurt or bite friends. But bad people aren't friends. You are important, Allie. Do you know what important means? It means you're special and I don't want to lose you. So if somebody bad hurts you, I want you to fight back and do whatever it takes to be safe, okay?"

Allie's eyes grew wide and Maisy's heart hurt having to tell her that.

"Because I'm im-por-tant," Allie said solemnly.

"Yes." Maisy hugged her. "Because you're important."

Allie took Maisy's face in her hands and made sure she was looking her in the eyes.

"Bad man hurt man, Maisy," Allie said.

Maisy rocked back on her heels and looked up at Chase. He looked as puzzled as she was. "Was the person who hurt you a bad man?"

Considering the slender build, Maisy had suspected it could be a woman.

Sirens rose in the air. Police were on their way. Within seconds, Security Forces would be surrounding her tiny preschool, followed almost immediately by parents and others as the news of what had happened would spread like wildfire through the base— especially if Esther stuck to her guns that the figure she'd seen was Boyd Sullivan.

"Bad man!" Allie said. Her voice rose with a tinge of panic. "Bad man hurt man!"

"She's been calling that out in her sleep," Chase said. He bent down and reached for Allie. "Come on, let's go."

The little girl's chin rose. "I wanna walk."

"Would it be okay if Daddy carried you?" Chase asked.

Allie shook her head stubbornly, sending her curls flying. Chase paused and Maisy could tell for a moment that he wanted to argue. She could only imagine how badly her father would've reacted if she'd insisted on walking instead of being carried at Allie's age after what had just happened. Allie's stubborn lip jutted out farther and quivered slightly.

"I wanna walk." Allie's voice shook. Her tiny hand grabbed Queenie's harness and squeezed it tightly. "Please, I walk with Queenie. Please, Daddy."

Maisy watched Chase's face, waiting and half expecting him to sweep her up into his arms and carry the squirming toddler back over his shoulder as her father would've. Instead, he nodded. "Okay, Allie. If it's important to you, you can walk with Queenie. Maisy and I will walk right behind you."

Allie nodded. "Thank you."

Maisy felt an odd longing for something she'd never had move through her heart as father and daughter shared a look. Then Allie turned and led Queenie back toward Sunny Seeds. Chase and Maisy followed, walking side by side, two steps behind her. She watched as his long legs and large feet took tiny little steps to keep from catching up with his daughter.

"That was very kind of you," she said softly, "to let her take the lead like that."

"It seemed to matter to her and what matters to me is that she feels safe."

"Esther thought the man at the fence was Boyd Sullivan," she said. "But he seemed too slender to me. I would've guessed it was a woman, if Allie hadn't kept saying 'bad man.' Do you think it was the same person who was outside your house this morning?"

His back stiffened, as if every molecule suddenly drew itself to attention. "Who informed you of that?"

"Nobody informed me. I saw someone in the bushes outside your home in the early hours of the morning—"

"You what?" He stopped walking and turned toward her. His hand reached out, his fingertips coming within just an inch of brushing her shoulder. "When was this? What did you see? Why am I just hearing about this now?"

She stopped too and turned to face him. "This morning I was jogging near your home and saw a figure in the bushes." His mouth opened like he wanted to say something, but she didn't pause. "They were slender with a black hoodie, bandanna and baseball hat. I couldn't see their face and I couldn't tell if it was a man or a woman. I'm guessing they were about five foot eight or nine. Not that I'm the best at judging heights, but definitely taller than me and shorter than you. They drew a knife, I challenged them and they ran away. I then found some dried pink and purple pasta that I thought might've belonged to Allie's picture frame and turned it over to Captain Blackwood. I also made a full report."

His head shook. "Why didn't he tell me?"

"You'll have to ask him that yourself," she said. Allie was about five feet ahead of them now. Maisy started walking again. She was surprised and impressed that Queenie had the discipline to walk that slowly. "But I trust Justin and I know that whatever decisions he's making about this investigation he's doing it for the right reasons."

He matched her pace. "Why didn't you tell me?"

"Because we haven't exactly had much time to talk!" At the sound of her raised voice, Allie glanced back. Maisy smiled reassuringly. Allie smiled, turned back and continued walking. "We hardly had time to talk when you were being arrested, and I didn't want to say anything in front of Allie when she was already very upset. And then we'd barely been talking five minutes at Sunny Seeds before someone tried to abduct her."

His jaw clenched and she could see his facial muscles tighten under the skin. "I still don't understand how that could've happened. How could someone just show up at the back fence and kidnap a kid?"

It was a fair question, but it burned harsh in her ears. Did he have any idea how sick her stomach felt and how long the knowledge of how she'd failed one of her students so catastrophically would burn in her brain?

"I don't know," she said. "There were three teachers outside. The area was fenced. The Texas Education Agency and the Department of Family and Protective Services recommended a student-teacher ratio of eleven to one—"

"I don't care what the guidelines are," he said tersely. "There is no excuse. It shouldn't have happened."

His voice was sharp, like she was a subordinate who'd messed up, or an airman whose mistake could've gotten people killed. Or like he was her father telling her yet again how disappointed he was in her.

"You're right," she said. "It shouldn't have happened."

He nodded curtly and turned to face the horizon. She watched as his spine straightened and a look filled his face, so determined and fierce that it made her breath catch. It was the kind of look that would have been as attractive and compelling as the sun itself in the eyes of a man who was her protector and defender. And downright terrifying in the face of an adversary.

Was it possible this man was as innocent as he'd seemed just minutes ago when he held his daughter in his arms? If so, why would anyone try to kidnap his daughter? Or be lurking outside his house? Or have planted her father's cross at his home, as he claimed?

The memory of her father's cross sitting in Justin's gloved hand filled her mind, unbidden.

Lord, am I foolish to believe he had nothing to do

*with my father's death? My father always said I wanted
to bring home every stray dog and wild animal I spotted, not realizing my big old naive heart wouldn't stop
them from hurting me. Is that what's happening here?
Am I foolish for believing Chase's love for his daughter is so strong he'd never let the Red Rose Killer
near her?*

She turned back and was struck by his expression. It
was a look that was silently asking her for something,
like he was a desperately thirsty man and she had the
only pitcher of cold water. And suddenly she realized
what a foolish, narrow tightrope she was walking in
her mind—not fully accepting he was innocent, but
not believing he was guilty, either.

His footsteps stopped again and he swallowed hard
as if making a decision he didn't want to make. "In
light of everything that's happened, I think it's for the
best if I keep Allie home, and she leaves your class
and stops coming to Sunny Seeds."

Her blue eyes widened with such acute pain that
for a moment he was tempted to take back his words.
Instead, he planted his feet beneath him. Maisy didn't
get what was happening here. How could she, when
he barely got it himself? She seemed to have so much
faith that Blackwood and the Security Forces would
get to the bottom of everything. She'd trusted that her
assistant teacher would keep a criminal from kidnapping his child.

She had a good heart, a better heart than anyone
he knew, and he could tell that all she wanted to do
was help. And yes, something inside him craved that,
in a deeper way than he knew how to express. He

wanted to feel like there was someone on his side. He
wanted someone to make Allie smile and to hold his
hand and tell him everything was going to be okay.
But as much as he wanted to rely on Maisy like that,
he couldn't. She was a sweet woman who meant well,
but she deserved better than the mess and chaos he'd
bring to her life.

"I'm sorry," she said. But this time her voice wasn't
soft. Instead, it was firm. It was what he thought of
as her "teacher voice," the one that demanded respect.
"I'd obviously be sorry to see Allie leave my class, but
you have to do what you feel is best for your child."

Lights danced ahead of them now, sirens blared
loudly and Security Forces swarmed the preschool.

"You should've told me about the prowler outside
my home earlier," he said, but even as the words left
his mouth, he wasn't sure why he was bringing it up
again. All he knew was there'd been a certain joy in
his heart earlier as he'd jogged to Sunny Seeds. That
joy was now gone.

Her chin rose. "I thought it was more important to
ask why you had my dead father's cross in your pos-
session."

Her words struck him in the chest and knocked
him back an inch.

"Maisy!" a loud male voice called from within the
chaos ahead. Preston was striding toward them.

"I've got to go," she said quickly. "If I don't see you
later, Esther can help you gather up Allie's things."
Then, before he could answer, she quickened her step
until she reached Allie, leaned over and ruffled Allie's hair. "I'll see you later, Buttercup."

Then she ran toward Preston. Chase was about to

follow when he felt a tiny hand brush his. "Pick me up, Daddy?"

"Of course, Sweet Pea." He bent down, swept her up into his arms and watched as Maisy disappeared into a sea of uniformed Security Forces officers.

He took Allie and Queenie home after making his statement to Justin Blackwood. The captain took his statement so professionally it was hard to imagine he'd been the same man who'd stood in the doorway while Preston had hammered Chase earlier. Then Justin questioned Allie gently, caringly even, letting her sit on Chase's lap while he softly tried to coax her side of the story from her stubborn lips. But all they'd gotten from Allie was a babbled mixture of words about "bad man" and "hurt man"—who Chase was beginning to think of as some character in a story he was never going to understand. They'd been left no closer to figuring out who had grabbed her or why the abductor had moved slowly enough that Chase had been able to catch up with them.

He didn't spot Maisy again before leaving, not that he didn't search her out in the crowd. He couldn't shake the feeling he'd been harder on her than he'd meant to be. Liz had often accused him of being unfeeling. It hadn't been true. It had been more like his feelings were locked somewhere inside a hidden heart, and he didn't know what to do about it.

He took Allie home, where the afternoon dragged out, long and endless, as he tried to juggle setting his home back to rights and replacing both the front door and Allie's window screen, while keeping her distracted and happy. To make matters worse, she was unusually fussy, wanting to stay close to him while he worked and bursting into tantrums whenever he tried to set up cartoons on his new laptop for her to watch.

That evening fell hot and deep, with a sun that seemed to grow redder as it sank into the sky. Sweat clung to his skin. Grime streaked his clothes. He dropped onto the couch.

"Daddy, I'm hungry." Allie crawled up onto his lap. "I need dinner."

He wasn't surprised. He'd made Allie her favorite peanut butter and banana sandwiches hours ago and she'd barely touched them. His eyes glanced at the clock. It was after nine. He should've put Allie to bed well over an hour ago, but every time he'd tried, she'd whined and clung to him, and he'd been too thankful just to have her there, alive and real and in his arms, to fight her. After all, it wasn't like either of them had anywhere to be in the morning. "What would you like for dinner, Sweet Pea?"

She looked up at him, sleepy and hopeful. "Carmen's pizza?"

He smiled at the cheekiness of the question. Carmen's Italian Restaurant was his favorite eatery on the base and somewhere he'd only taken Allie on very special occasions. They'd had someone there making balloon animals on her last birthday and they'd made Allie a hat with a bear on it. It seemed so very long ago. Would people stare at him now? Would they whisper among themselves as the man accused of helping Boyd Sullivan walked in the door? Would he ever feel comfortable sitting in a place like that again?

His stomach rumbled. On the other hand, Carmen's

did a decent takeout. He could use a walk, and special pizza might help a terrible day end on a better note.

"How about we go for a walk to Carmen's and pick up pizza?" he suggested. "You could ride in the wagon? We could make it a special treat? Just for tonight?"

Her eyes grew wide. She nodded. "Queenie comes too. Queenie likes pizza."

"Right." He smiled. He wasn't sure Queenie had ever tried pizza. As a K-9 dog, her diet was supposed to be strict and limited. But he wouldn't have been surprised if Allie had been sneaking her all kinds of treats under the table when he hadn't been looking. "Good idea. If we walk, then Queenie can come too."

He loaded Allie up in the wagon with extra blankets for cushioning. Then he slipped the leash on Queenie and they stepped out into the night.

The evening surrounded them, warm and welcoming. Cicadas thrummed an invisible chorus from the trees. The thick scent of lavender and Texas lilacs filled the air, mingled with the smell of hot dogs and hamburgers from backyard barbecues. Laughter seemed to spill from behind every fence. It was like the whole base was out enjoying the July night. And he felt like an outcast or a phantom, moving through the shadows, with the rhythmic sound of the wagon wheels bumping over the evenly spaced cracks in the sidewalk like they were marching in lockstep with his feet.

The questions he'd been asked about Maisy's father filled his mind. He'd told Preston and Justin that Clint Lockwood was a hard man to train under. What he'd left out was that he'd appreciated that the Chief Master Sergeant was hard on him. There'd been something comforting about knowing there were standards and that those standards were high. When he'd marched in formation, he knew where he belonged and what needed to be done. He'd blended in, which was hard to do for someone of his height who'd gone through school as the tallest kid in his class. There'd been something about being in that uniform for the first time, and going through the same drills and exercises as every other new recruit, that made a person stop noticing the height, weight, age, gender or background of the person marching alongside him. Because they were a unit. A family. They were in it together. And he'd been just another part of that whole, doing his part and doing what needed to be done.

Liz had always questioned why he didn't strive harder to stand out and get more prestigious assignments. She hadn't understood. He'd always done the very best to serve his country, even on those days when all he was doing was directing traffic or guarding depots. But he'd never cared about being distinguished or important. He'd never minded less glamorous work. All that had mattered was being the best possible cog he could be, serving in whatever role he was assigned, in the amazing, glorious machine that was the United States Air Force.

His grandfather, despite his faults, had instilled that much in him—that it was better to quietly do your part to serve others than to claim fame and attention for oneself the way that Boyd Sullivan had. When Chase had been first deployed overseas, his grandfather had sent him a postcard. On it was a poem entitled "When I Consider How My Light is Spent" by John

Milton, which ended with the reminder that standing and waiting was also a form of serving. That line had kept him focused on many long patrol nights. But what was he now? A random cog that had busted loose from the machine and fallen to the floor? A cog that the larger glorious machine was apparently willing to run without?

His eyes shot to the red-and-pink jet contrails crossing the sky and prayed for help without even knowing how to find the words.

"Look, it's Maisy!" Allie's voice made him stop. "Look, Daddy! It's Maisy! Hi, Maisy!"

He turned back. Allie was sitting up in her wagon, waving happily, but for a moment he couldn't figure out where she was looking. He crouched down to her level. "Where?"

"There! It's Maisy!" Her little hand pointed toward a fence to his right, with that odd laser-sharp focus that toddlers and K-9 dogs seemed to share. His eyes followed her gaze. At first he saw nothing but indistinct figures in fatigues. Then the scene shifted and he caught a glimpse of a smiling blonde with a pixie haircut and peach sundress.

"See, Daddy?" Allie asked, her eyes serious with the clarity of innocence. "Can we go say hi?"

"No, honey, Miss Maisy is busy with friends," he said as the glimpse of Maisy's smile sent unexpected feelings through his chest. He looked away. One of his shoelaces was hanging long. He knelt and tied it sharply, pulling on the laces so tightly he could feel the pinch at the top of his foot. He'd been curt with Maisy and had brought danger to the door of her preschool. Regret washed over him with a million words he wished that he could say.

He wondered what his life would've been like if he'd had the courage to speak to her when he was a much younger man. If he hadn't become romantically involved with Liz. If he'd waited instead to earn Clint Lockwood's approval to date his daughter. He wondered what it would be like to be the man standing beside Maisy, protecting her from harm, instead of being suspected of aiding the man who'd ripped her father from her life.

A hand landed heavily on his shoulder, its grasp firm. A low and deep warning growl sounded to his right. Then he heard a voice, male and with unrelenting authority. "Stop right there. Don't move."

FIVE

Chase turned slowly and looked up at the tall and muscular form of dark-haired Technical Sergeant Linc Colson. His huge attack-trained rottweiler, Star, stood alert by Linc's side. Instinctively, Chase felt his body stand to attention. He saluted. "Evening, Sergeant."

"Evening, Airman." Linc returned the salute. Suspicious eyes glanced down at Allie and Queenie, and then scanned Chase's face. Chase found himself oddly impressed that the sergeant didn't drop his guard because Chase was with his daughter. "Care to tell me what you're doing crouching behind the fence outside my new home?"

"It wasn't intentional," he said. He clasped his hands behind his back. "I was out walking with Allie and she was excited to spot her preschool teacher, Maisy Lockwood, through the fence. I stopped and laced up my boot."

It was the truth and he said it without a flicker of a muscle on his face. But that didn't seem to damper the wary look in Linc's eyes. Was this how it was going to be from now on? Would he never be able to so much as stop and tie his boot without rousing suspicion?

Chase met his gaze and held it firm like a man who had nothing to hide.

"Hi, Star!" Allie chirped. He looked down. Despite the fact that his presence lurking at the other side of the fence had set Star growling protectively, the dog's tail was now wagging. Allie waved her hand happily at the huge dog, keeping her fingers just far enough away from the canine's fur to let Chase know that his instruction to never touch a dog without permission had sunk in. "Daddy, Star is Freddy's new dog!" Allie said cheerfully. Then she pointed at Linc. "That's Freddy's new daddy."

The two men paused. Allie's bright eyes looked from Linc to Chase. She pointed to each man in turn with that tone of voice he knew meant she was trying to be helpful. "You're Freddy's daddy and you're my daddy! You're both daddies!"

She said the word *daddy* with both a force and an innocence that made an emotion catch in his throat. She said it like *daddy* was a special word and like she expected everything should be all right between him and Linc because they were both daddies. And the fact that the word meant something so important to her small, innocent mind filled his heart with thanksgiving.

He prayed he'd never give her any reason to think any other way.

"Linc, is everything okay?" An unfamiliar woman's voice dragged his attention to the fence. While he didn't know the voice, he definitely recognized the face of the woman now opening the side gate and stepping through. Zoe Sullivan, a petite woman with flowing brown hair, was a flight instructor and Boyd

Sullivan's estranged half sister. She was also the single mother of a three-year-old boy named Freddy from Allie's school. As Zoe reached for Linc, he saw a tasteful gold band on her left hand, and the final pieces of the puzzle clicked into place. Looked like she was Zoe Colson now. He'd vaguely heard the single mother had recently gotten married and moved into a new house with her husband. But he'd never been much for standing around gossiping, let alone reading the anonymous blog that some mysterious person at Canyon had set up to spread rumors about the Red Rose Killer's crimes, his possible accomplices and the state of the investigation. At least now he understood better why Linc was so protective of his home and wary of anyone lurking outside. He wondered how it was for them, always wondering where her half brother was, who he'd target next and how soon he'd be caught.

"Hello, Sergeant." Chase saluted her. "Sorry to cause a disruption to your evening. I was just passing by. Congratulations on your recent nuptials."

"Thank you." She smiled and returned the salute, but she also looked slightly confused. He suddenly wondered if anyone said nuptials anymore. "It's Chase, right? You're Allie's dad?"

"Yes, ma'am."

Through the open gate now he could see the small audience walking toward them, men and women he knew, at least to say hi to, and who now no doubt wondered if he was guilty of the crimes he'd been accused of. There was Westley and Felicity James, and Westley's canine partner, a German shepherd named Dakota. Also, a red-haired search-and-rescue dog handler he vaguely recognized as Ava Esposito with her

Labrador retriever, Roscoe. And his friend Isaac God-dard, who he'd done basic training with, with his own golden retriever named Tango. Only Maisy stood alone on the porch with a plate of food in her hand, and her friends standing between them like a shield.

"Allie!" Freddy tore across the yard like an enthu-siastic missile. "Hi, Allie! I have hot dogs! You want hot dogs too?"

"Actually, we should get going," Chase said. He reached for the handle of the wagon. "I promised Allie pizza tonight. I'm sorry to interrupt you. I hope you have a wonderful evening."

"Daddy," Allie whimpered softly. "Don't want pizza. Want hot dogs with Freddy."

"Actually, Chase, can we talk? If you have a mo-ment?" Maisy called out to him. She started down the porch steps, crossed the backyard and looked around at her friends. "If it's okay with you guys, there's some-thing I need to talk to Chase about and I'd like to do it tonight, if that's possible."

In other words, she wanted to talk to him, some-where where they weren't alone and she had her trusted friends close.

Zoe and Linc exchanged a look that spoke the kind of volumes that only couples who'd been through a lot and understood each other deeply shared. Then Zoe said, "We do have plenty of food, if you'd like to stay for a hot dog."

"Absolutely." Linc stretched out his hand toward the backyard. "Freddy has been really eager to show somebody his new tent."

"Thank you," Chase said, once again finding the words inadequate for everything going through his mind. He reached his hand toward Allie to help her out of the wagon, but she was already scrambling toward Zoe's outstretched hand. Taking Allie in one hand and Freddy in the other, Zoe walked the little children over to where a long table sat overflowing with hot dogs, burgers, veggies and salad. Felicity pulled Maisy aside and the two women exchanged a quiet word. A warning, perhaps? He wouldn't blame Maisy's friends for telling her to be cautious around him. If anything, he was thankful to know she had people watching her back.

Westley stepped forward. Chase saluted. "Sergeant."

Westley returned the salute. "Good to see you and Queenie. How has training been going?"

Chase searched the master sergeant's face. The look in his eyes was cautious, much as Chase would have expected in his position, but not hostile. He appreciated that. If he were in Westley's shoes, he'd have felt the same. Just a few short weeks ago, these people had been his new colleagues in a team he'd just begun to feel like he was a part of. Now, he was just thankful they were still giving him the time of day and hadn't already decided on his guilt, like Preston had.

"Not bad," Chase said honestly. "Not as good as I'd have liked or of the level that would've been expected if I'd been able to continue training Queenie with the team. But we've been doing some basic drills at home every day."

Westley nodded. "Good to hear it. The more consistency you're able to instill, the easier time Queenie will have reintegrating with the team."

Chase could only hope that he and Queenie would

still be partners when that happened and that lingering suspicion—or, worse yet, charges being filed for crimes he'd never even dreamed of committing—wouldn't mean she was assigned to someone else.

"Why don't you unleash her and let her socialize?" Westley added. "Being around the other dogs will help with her reintegration too."

It was a good idea. He bent down and unclipped Queenie from her lead. Her nose nuzzled his hand. Her huge brown eyes looked up into his, then, tail wagging, she ran off after the other dogs. He stopped and watched as his small dog disappeared into a cluster of bigger canines, feeling oddly like a father sending his child off to play. Then his eyes ran over to where Allie and Freddy were happily piling plates with food under Zoe's watchful eye.

Had he been too hasty to pull Allie from Sunny Seeds? Would she miss the other kids? All he wanted was to protect her.

"How is she doing?" Maisy's soft voice seemed to brush over the back of his neck like a cool breeze.

He turned toward her and realized that Westley had stepped back to join Linc by the barbecue, leaving them alone.

"It hasn't been the easiest afternoon," he admitted. "But, hey, she's a strong kid. How was the rest of your day? I'm really glad to see your friends have your back."

"My afternoon was probably about as hard as one could be. Security Forces stayed at Sunny Seeds all day. Most parents came to pick up their kids early, and they all had a lot of questions about what had happened. But being out with friends tonight helps."

Maisy glanced back over her shoulder to the people now gathered around the back porch and yard, all of whom seemed to be doing an excellent job of watching them without actually letting it look like they were watching. Did any of them believe he was innocent? Did some of them think that by bringing him in closer they'd trip him up and find evidence?

"We've all become a lot closer, in a way, since Boyd broke out of jail and..." She left the sentence unfinished as a deep sadness filled the depths of her eyes. *And killed several people, including her own father.* She blinked back tears. "It brought some of us together in a tighter knit family. But all across the base I see it tearing other people and relationships apart. The fear. The suspicion. The way people have stopped saying howdy to strangers and started giving each other the stink eye. It's like Boyd doesn't have to be literally on base killing people for him to cause destruction."

Yeah, he knew what she meant. Even if he didn't know how to explain it himself.

"I don't know how to put this into words," he said. "But it's like Allie has somehow grown younger since the morning Boyd Sullivan broke onto base. She cries more. She babbles and has more tantrums, not to mention more nightmares about 'hurt man' and 'bad man.' There was a lot of mess to clean up in the house today and she was pretty agitated." He twisted Queenie's leash, wrapping it around his hand like a fighter preparing for a bout against an unknown enemy. "There are moments when she's so grown up she's like a little girl. Then other times, when she's upset, it's almost like she's still a baby."

"I know exactly what you mean," Maisy said. He

felt her hand brush his sleeve. Her bright blue eyes met his, so dark in the center and filled with far more compassion and understanding than he had any right to hope to see. "She's dealing with a lot. But she's resilient. She'll bounce back. Playing with Freddy tonight should help. We just all need to hold on until life gets back to normal." Something caught in her throat as she said the word *normal*.

Suddenly, he found himself turning toward her and taking both of her hands in his.

"Look, I'm sorry about what I said earlier," he told her. "I owe you an apology. I didn't mean to make it sound like I thought Sunny Seeds was unsafe or that Allie would be better off without you. I was frustrated. I was worried. My daughter had just been grabbed and almost abducted. I saw the Security Forces surrounding Sunny Seeds, and I was worried that I was bringing danger into your life. But I know there's no place better for Allie than Sunny Seeds, and nobody better for her to be spending time with than you. I just don't know who I can trust anymore."

"You can trust Justin Blackwood." Her hands squeezed his tightly. "My father liked him, a lot."

He wanted to believe his investigation was in the hands of someone trustworthy and honest, who'd follow the evidence all the way to the end and until it cleared his name. "But how well do you know him?"

"Better than I know you."

She watched as he rocked back on his heels. What had he expected? That she was on his side? That she would somehow be his ally? No, she was on the side of the truth. She wanted her father's killer to be stopped. She just wanted justice to be done.

Chase still hadn't spoken. She felt her mind fill with the memory of Preston leaning over her shoulder as she sat at her desk at Sunny Seeds and pulled up the security footage.

"The so-called kidnapper was probably a girlfriend or his ex-wife," Preston had said. "A man like Chase uses women. Just like he used you today."

"Hey, Maisy! We've got Frank! He's live!" At the sound of Ava's voice calling from the patio, she turned. Ava, Isaac, Linc, Zoe, Westley and Felicity were all gathered around a laptop set up on the middle of the picnic table. Ava waved her over.

Maisy turned back to Chase. "I'm sorry, one of our friends serving in Afghanistan has a birthday today. So we thought we'd set up a group call."

"Frank Golosky?" he asked. A slight and tired smile crossed his lips.

"Yes," she said. "Do you know him?"

"We were in the same Bible study when I served overseas. He's a really great guy. One of the best."

Chase was right. Frank was a really good man. More important, he was someone whose opinion Maisy trusted. What was Frank's opinion of Chase? she wondered.

"He's great," she said. "We were hoping his brother, Drew, would join us tonight. But apparently he's on leave for a few days and didn't return Zoe's calls. He's not exactly that reliable."

Linc was holding the laptop up high as if trying to find a spot where everyone could see Frank's laid-back grin and he could see everyone. She scanned the yard.

Allie and Freddy were sitting in the pop-up tent, eating hot dogs and potato chips.

"Why don't you come say hi to him?" she suggested. "I'm sure he'd be happy to see you." And she'd get to see what Frank thought of Chase.

She turned and walked over to the group, tugging on his arm slightly to get Chase to follow her. Happy small talk surrounded the group, although she got the impression that Frank was somewhere between amused and frustrated that his brother, Drew, hadn't shown. Then Frank's eyes met hers through the screen. "Hey, Maisy! Glad to see you made this shindig too. How's life been treating you?"

There was a softness in Frank's voice when he asked the question, and it was a tone she was so used to. Some days it felt like everyone had collectively decided that from now on she'd be treated like she was fragile and delicate. People rarely came out and openly asked about her actual grief. No, that was a hidden thing, like the bloody cross under the floorboards of Chase's home that nobody dared pry out. Instead, they tap danced above her pain, in a kind, gentle and loving way, as if they were afraid of hurting her.

Except Chase. He didn't talk to her like a victim. He actually told her what he thought. Maybe because he knew what it was like to be on the outside too.

"I'm good," she told Frank. "There's someone else here who says he knows you."

She waved Chase forward. Frank's wide beaming smile told her everything she'd wanted to know.

"Well, my man McLear! How are you, buddy?" Frank chuckled, leaning forward.

Chase set Queenie's leash down on the porch railing

and raised a hand in greeting. "Hey, Golosky! Happy birthday! It's good to see you."

"It's good to see you too!" Frank leaned back, crossed his arms and nodded to the other people around her. "This guy here led the best Bible studies. Bar none. He'd spend hours researching and planning them. Whenever I showed up and he was in charge, I knew we'd be in for some heavy-duty thinking. How's it going, man?"

An awkward pause spread through the group gathered in the backyard, as if everyone was collectively holding their breath to see what he'd say.

"Not great, to be honest," Chase said. "Though it could always be worse. I can fill you in more another time, on a private chat. But quickly, have you seen Ajay Joseph recently? It would really help if I could talk to him."

Frank's smile dimmed. "Nah, I haven't. Sorry, man. I heard his father was sick, so he went home to his village to be with his family."

Chase blew out a long breath. "That's what I heard too."

A happy bark sounded through the video call.

"Beacon!" Isaac leaned forward, a smile exploding across his face as a beautiful gold-and-black German shepherd leaped into view.

"Yeah." Frank ran his hand over the dog's shaggy fur. "I figured you'd want to see him."

Conversation around the patio shifted to talk about how the dog was doing. Beacon had been partnered with a close friend of Isaac's who'd died in a plane crash in Afghanistan and had recently been lured back to base by one of his former unit members. From what Maisy could gather the dog's retraining wasn't going well. Chase stepped back down the porch steps and disappeared into the darkness behind her. She couldn't tell if it was because he was disappointed about not being able to reach his buddy Ajay or if something about hearing the other K-9 officers talk about Beacon's retraining bothered him. Either way, she felt herself turning and following him down the porch steps, as if joined by an invisible thread.

She trailed him down the yard, away from her friends and the safety of the porch light, past the tent, where Chase popped his head in quickly to wave at Allie, and then through the happy mass of barking dogs and wagging tails, where Maisy lowered her hands to feel the soft noses greet her as she went. Finally, he reached a thick log at the very end of the yard, against the backyard fence, its wood worn as if people had been using it to sit and think for ages.

Chase settled down onto the log, propped his elbows up on his long legs and dropped his head into his hands. His shoulders rolled forward, as if his back was on the verge of collapsing under an invisible weight, and something about it wrenched at her heart in a way that she didn't know how to put into words. Then he looked up. His eyes met hers. The gentle yellow glow of a streetlight on the sidewalk behind the fence fell over the strong lines of his jaw. Sadness washed over his features. She sat down beside him and suddenly she found herself blurting out the one thing she'd wanted to tell someone but hadn't known how.

"I'm tired of people asking me if I'm okay," she said. "I'm not okay. I haven't been okay in a long time. I don't know when I'm ever going to feel okay again.

My father is dead, Chase. Some horrible person murdered him."

And you're accused of helping him...

He ran his hand over his head.

"I'm sorry," he said. "I shouldn't have interrupted your party. I don't belong here."

"I asked you to join us," she pointed out. "Because we need to talk."

About so many different things, she didn't know where to start. She hated how they'd left things at Sunny Seeds. She wanted to tell him about what she'd seen on the security footage. She wanted to yell at him about how he could possibly be so clueless about how her father's cross had ended up in his home, and admit that she didn't know whether or not to believe him. She also wanted to hug him, even though she wasn't sure why and was pretty sure she shouldn't.

"I know you deserve an explanation," he said. Raw emotion pushed through his voice. "For all of this. But I don't have one."

"I saw the security footage, Chase," she said. "It was too grainy to make out the face of Allie's kidnapper. But they were definitely after her. They lurked there for a while, as other kids came by the fence. There were easier targets. But they waited to grab her."

He ran his hand over his face as if trying to wipe the image from his mind. "They wanted my child. Specifically, my child."

Preston's warning that Chase knew Allie's abductor clattered in her mind.

"Preston Flannigan told me that statistically you knew whoever kidnapped Allie," she said. "That it was likely her mother or someone you're in a romantic relationship with—"

"Her mother gave up the rights to her the day the DNA test proved she was my child!" Chase's jaw tightened. "I don't have any romantic relationships. And I don't much care what Preston Flannigan thinks of me."

Something dark flashed in his eyes, warning her to drop it. But how could she?

"Who's Ajay Joseph?" she pressed. "Why is it so important you talk to him?"

"He's my alibi for the morning Boyd Sullivan broke out of jail and sneaked onto base," Chase said. "He's an Afghan local who was working as a contractor over there. He was a middleman between the United States Air Force and a group of locals on the ground who we were helping supply weapons and aid to. We were friends. We studied the Bible together and he was very new in his Christian faith. We'd talk sometimes after I moved back, and he'd call for advice. He called for advice shortly after four in the morning on April 1 because—and I need you to keep this between you and me—he'd noticed a few things missing from a warehouse manifest and suspected one of the locals might be selling things on the black market. We talked until I got the call that the Red Rose Killer was on base, that people had been killed and dogs were loose. It was pandemonium."

She felt her face pale. Yes, she remembered.

"We hadn't heard about your father at that point," he said. "But it was all hands on deck. I got off the phone and found my daughter was already up, and Ajay had ended the call. I'm guessing the sound of the dogs barking, the phone call and the chaos on base woke her up. I strapped her into a backpack carrier, put the leash on Queenie and we went out and helped round up dogs. Later, I emailed to apologize for cutting him off so suddenly and he emailed some encrypted files I promised to look at. He didn't want to wreck some guy's life without proof. The next email I got from him told me that he was going to visit his family in the mountains for a while. I figured he wanted a break away from base to think and pray."

"But you still have his files and a video log of the call," she said.

"My laptop was stolen from my truck shortly afterward," he said. "Whoever did it also got my gym bag full of dirty clothes and my toolbox—so everything needed to frame me of a crime."

But it still didn't explain her father's cross. She didn't answer and he didn't say anything more. Instead, they just sat there, side by side, their shoulders barely an inch away from touching, and their breaths rising and falling in rhythm together. He turned to her and she felt her breath tighten in her chest under the weight of the unspoken words in his eyes.

What was wrong with her? How could she be so attracted to a man who'd been accused of something so terrible? How could she crave the safety of being inside the strong arms of a man who, if not guilty, was at least being targeted by criminals? Yvette, the base nutritionist, had told her once that there was an eighty-to-twenty ratio of men to women on the base.

Why was this one man the only one to ever tug at her heartstrings this way?

Crush was such a silly, childish word to describe a full-grown and independent woman's feelings for a man. Yet, as she felt the heaviness of the emotions she'd never act on weighing down on her heart and suffocating her breath from her chest, she couldn't think of a better word for it.

"Maisy?" Chase said softly. His fingers brushed the back of her hand, like he wanted to take it but wasn't about to let himself do it. "I'm sorry for all of this. You deserve so much better than what I'm putting you through right now, and I wish…" His voice suddenly faded, leaving the thought unfinished. He swallowed hard. Then he sat back. "Never mind."

She grabbed his hand and squeezed it, even as he tried to pull it away. "Tell me. Please, Chase. What do you wish?"

The electronic chime of a cell phone alert sounded so close behind them it was like it was coming from the fence itself. Chase dropped her hand. They jumped to their feet, coming eye to eye with a dark figure in a hoodie and bandanna on the other side of the fence.

"Stop!" Chase said. "Right there!"

The figure turned and fled.

SIX

"Stay here!" Chase ordered. "Get Allie inside. Keep her safe!"

Then he ran down the yard, back toward the gate. He whistled sharply. Within a second, the small beagle was by his side. Man and dog burst through the gate. It clattered behind them.

Maisy turned, a prayer on her lips, and ran back to the house. She'd barely taken five steps before Ava, Westley, Linc and Isaac rushed up to her. Felicity was standing on the porch. She didn't see Zoe or the children.

"Maisy!" Linc said. "What happened?"

"Someone was spying on us over the back fence. Chase went after them. Where's Allie?"

"In the house with Zoe and Freddy," Linc said. "Description of the suspect?"

"Slender. Black hoodie. Black hat. Bandanna over the lower half of their face. Taller than me, but shorter than Chase. Like I said, Chase and Queenie ran after them."

"And you saw this person yourself?" Ava pressed. "Firsthand?"

"Absolutely."

The airmen exchanged a quick and pointed look. Then they gathered their dogs, with a series of whistles and calls, like a quickly mobilized team. Linc called to Felicity to brief Zoe. Westley scooped Queenie's leash up from the porch, held it under Dakota's nose and told her to track. The German shepherd barked, ran down to the end of the yard, then back through the gate, with the other dogs and trainers steps behind. Maisy stood there a moment and watched the empty space where they'd been. Then she turned back to the porch where Felicity still stood. Maisy walked toward her.

"You're sure Allie's in the house?" Maisy asked. "I promised Chase I'd make sure she was okay."

"They're in the kitchen washing their hands," Felicity said. There was an odd look on her face. It was like there was a wild coyote standing behind Maisy and she didn't know how to warn her without spooking it. "They're decorating cupcakes. Freddy's really happy to have a friend over and I think Zoe's happy to be able to reach out and be there for Allie. She, better than anyone, knows what it's like to live under a veil of suspicion."

Her tone implied that she wasn't so sure the rest of their friends had been as happy to have Chase around.

Maisy looked in the window. Zoe was standing at the kitchen table now. Maisy watched as Zoe helped each child in turn climb up onto a chair and then spread brightly colored candies, tubes of icing and sprinkles in front of them. Maisy reached for the back door, but before her fingers could brush the handle Felicity pointed to a chair. "Sit. Please. We need to talk."

Felicity sat down. Maisy turned her eyes away from

the happy domestic scene inside the kitchen and sat beside her.

"About what?" Maisy asked. She could hear barking and yelling in the distance, and prayed they'd catch the prowler.

"About the handsome man you've been making eyes at tonight," Felicity said.

Maisy felt heat rise to her face.

"Allie is one of my students," she said. "She's like this bright little light in my day and I care about what happens to her."

"And her father, Chase?" Felicity asked.

Maisy looked down at the wooden porch slats beneath her feet and shrugged. "I honestly don't know what to say."

"But you like him," her friend said gently.

"I do." Maisy nodded, miserably. "I think I have for a long time. But it was just an innocent crush, you know? It's not like I thought anything was ever going to happen between us. I just enjoyed seeing him for that few moments a day, when he dropped Allie off or picked her up. I liked that little bit of a lift, a happy little jolt, it gave to my day. It sounds foolish."

"Not foolish. Human," Felicity said softly. "It took me a while to warm up to Westley because I wasn't sure he liked me. I had no idea at the time he was fighting feelings for me. But he was my commanding officer, so he couldn't act on those feelings. Once he became my protector and I finally let my guard down…my heart took over."

Maisy watched as she spun her new wedding band around on her finger.

"All I'm saying is I care about you, you're my friend and I want you to be careful," Felicity added. "Everyone on base is under a lot of stress and it's making everything seem more important and urgent. Just look at Westley and me, or Zoe and Linc. You've never served in the military or been deployed, but there are moments in this career where it's like everything's sped up and we've all stepped on a moving sidewalk without realizing it. It's scary, and exciting, but it also leads to people making bad decisions."

"I'm not making any decisions," Maisy said. "All I did was agree to watch Allie for a bit this morning and have a conversation with Chase about the case."

"I know," Felicity said. If possible, her voice was even more gentle than it had been before. "And I'm not saying you did anything wrong. But I've seen the way you look at him and Chase isn't just the father of one of your students. He's been accused of killing your father."

"And you think I don't know that?" Maisy's eyes rose to meet Felicity's. Then her head shook. "I'm sorry. I just can't bring myself to think he's guilty."

Felicity nodded, like she was hearing something much deeper than what Maisy was saying. "And maybe he's not. I'm keeping an open mind about him and I don't know what Westley thinks. But whatever this thing is that's drawing you to him, I think it's a lot deeper than you want to admit. Just promise me you're going to keep yourself safe."

Maisy pressed her lips together and nodded. She didn't know what to say. Felicity had gotten her dead to rights. She liked Chase, in a very simple, real and honest way. There was just something about him and little Allie that got to her, no matter how much she knew that the smartest and safest thing for her to do was steer clear.

* * *

Chase stopped in his tracks and looked around in all directions. The night was still around him. The base's perimeter fence spread out ahead of him. The figure he'd been chasing was gone. He felt Queenie by his side. "I don't know what happened, Pup. They were here just a minute ago."

Help me, Lord, what do I do now?

The night had set in deeper and darker while he'd been talking with Maisy. Now, black Texas skies spread dark above his head, filled with the kind of huge bright stars he'd grown up believing a man couldn't find anywhere else.

He looked down, his eyes adjusting to the dim light, and saw the dog's attentive face turned to toward his, ready to search if only he said the word.

But track what? She wasn't trained to track people, only electronic devices. Would that work? He was pretty sure the figure had been carrying a cell phone, judging by the phone alert sound he'd heard. Normally, he'd never think to give Queenie the command to go search out in the world without knowing exactly what she was looking for.

But desperate times...

He turned to her and instantly felt his small partner snap to attention. "Queenie, go search!"

Instantly, her nose went to the ground. He watched for a second as she sniffed, back and forth, methodically. Then she howled and disappeared from view. Okay, so where had his dog gone? He'd trained her not to run away and to stay within his line of sight. He kicked himself for having not gone back for his leash before running after the hooded figure, but it hadn't felt like

there was time. He grabbed his phone from his pocket
and scanned the fence. Then he saw it, a gap barely more
than a few inches under the fence, leading out into the
thick woods behind the base. He bent down and shone
his light through the chain-link. Sure enough, there was
Queenie, sitting on the other side, with her head cocked
as if she was wondering what was taking him so long.

All right, then. He ducked low and realized the only
way he was getting through the fence was on his stomach in a combat crawl. He crawled through and came
out in the thick ravine surrounding the base. Queenie
ran up to him and then away again a few steps with
another little howl.

"I'm coming!" he said. Queenie tilted her head to
the side. "Go search!"

She took off running, her little body moving easily
through the deep scrub and underbrush. He ran after
her. For a moment, nothing filled his ears but the rustling sound of Queenie crashing through the trees,
his own footsteps pelting after her and the panting of
their breaths.

Then he heard voices yelling behind him, the sound
of dogs barking, and realized he was being pursued.
Someone was chasing after him. Just like that, he'd
gone from the hunter to the hunted, running like a
fugitive in the night. Too late, he remembered Captain Justin Blackwood's warning not to leave the base
without informing his office. He stopped and turned
around. His hands raised instinctively. Light flashed
in his face, blinding his view, just in time to see the
German shepherd barreling toward him. Its teeth were
bared. Its powerful lungs barked and a chorus of dogs
joined in behind it.

"Dakota, heel!" Westley's authoritative voice sounded in the darkness. Instantly, the dog stopped, turned and trotted back to his partner. Chase raised his hand to his eyes and shielded his face from the light as slowly the group came into view.

Westley, Linc, Isaac, Ava and their canines were striding through the woods toward him, with a purpose and strength that reminded him of the Air Force K-9 poster that had hung over his too-short bed as a child.

"Airman Chase McLear?" Westley called.

"Sergeant!" Instinctively, Chase felt himself salute. The lights dropped from his face. The cops exchanged a look. "There was a figure in a hoodie and bandanna spying on the house. Queenie and I ran after them and chased them into the woods."

Despite the fact that he and these cops had been standing around casually in a backyard less than an hour ago, he was now standing up at full attention. He was a suspect—he could see it in Westley's eyes—and he would never have their trust until his name was cleared.

If it was cleared.

Linc crossed his arms. "Outside the base perimeter?"

"We were following the suspect and they slid under the fence."

"You saw them go through a hole in the perimeter fence?" Ava asked, probing deeper.

Chase planted his heels beneath him and reminded himself their questions weren't personal. They'd been searching for Boyd Sullivan for months. The existence of a hole in the perimeter big enough that he could squeeze through no doubt rattled them.

"Queenie found the hole in the fence, actually," he admitted. "I didn't see it. When I lost sight of the suspect, I remembered I'd heard what I thought was a cell phone message alert. So I told Queenie to track the cell phone."

He felt the familiar press of warmth against his calf. He looked down. Queenie was back by his side. Had she given up because he was no longer following? Had she lost the scent? Or had she returned because he was in trouble? She was such a good dog. His heart ached to know her K-9 training was on hold because of him.

A pause spread through the group, as if each of them was weighing internally what to say.

Then Westley turned to the others. "My suggestion would be that Linc gets back to the house, checks in on his family and the others and calls it in if they haven't already. Make sure Security Forces know about the hole in the fence. Ava, can you and Roscoe search the woods and see if you can come up with any trail of the person that Chase saw?"

"Absolutely." She nodded.

"I'll go with her," Isaac said quickly. "No one should be roaming around out here alone in the dark."

Ava smiled, grateful.

"Agreed." Westley said. "I'll stay out here and talk with Chase for a bit."

Linc and Star disappeared through the night in one direction, while Ava and Roscoe, and Isaac and Tango disappeared in the other. Westley nodded to Queenie. "I take it she lost the scent?"

Chase nodded. "I'm guessing so."

"You left this behind at the party." Westley reached out and handed Chase Queenie's leash. He guessed that's what Dakota had used to track him. "It's ill-advised to have a dog tracking without her leash on in an unknown outdoor setting. It's different when it's a contained or known environment, and I know as an electronic-sniffing dog, the vast majority of the searches she's done have been indoors. But, generally speaking, unless you've got an attack dog chasing down a suspect, when you're in the ravine, we keep leashes on. Now, let's see if she can still track that cell phone."

Westley had been the lead K-9 trainer on base, until recently when Master Sergeant Caleb Streeter had taken over day-to-day operations due to the Red Rose Killer's threats on Felicity's life. Chase knew the man had the experience and the skill to direct this search.

Chase took the leash and clipped it onto Queenie's harness and told her to search. This time she trotted into the woods, leading Chase at a brisk pace. He followed, feeling Westley and Dakota one step behind him. Queenie reached a pond, dark and gloomy in the night. She whined and sat down. Had the figure tossed their phone in the pond or swum through it to hide their scent? Either way, the scent was gone. Chase leaned down and ran his hand over the dog's head.

"It's okay, girl," he said, softly. "You did a really great job."

He reached into his pocket, pulled out a piece of dried sweet potato and gave it to her.

When he turned back, Westley was watching him with a curious look on his face. "What did you just give her?"

"Sweet potato," Chase said. He watched as Queenie chewed her treat, then handed one to Westley. "I did some research about her breed. Beagles aren't picky eaters but they are prone to weight gain if they eat too much, and I can't always keep track of everything Allie drops on the floor, so I switched to dried fruit and vegetables as her main treat."

Westley rocked back on his heels, looked at Chase for a long moment and then nodded slowly as if answering a question in his own mind. Then he handed the treat to Dakota, who took it eagerly from his hand. They turned and started walking back toward the fence.

"Isaac got a bit of bad news when he was talking to Frank," Westley said. "As I'm sure you know, Isaac's best friend, Jake Burke, died in a plane crash in Afghanistan that almost took Isaac's life as well. Beacon was Jake's K-9 partner. The way Isaac tells it, Beacon and Isaac helped keep each other alive until rescue came. But according to Frank, Beacon is responding badly to his new trainer. He's aggressive. He's paranoid. If the situation doesn't change, Beacon might have to retire."

He blew out a long breath, and Chase could see just how heavily the situation was weighing on him. They kept walking.

"I've got to tell you," Westley said, after a long moment, "it can be very hard on a dog to change partners. Sometimes they get aggressive. Sometimes they get confused. Some dogs are flexible and are able to adapt easier than others. But some dogs are simply untrainable when they lose their human partners."

They reached the fence and walked along it until they found a checkpoint gate. They showed their identifications and walked through. Chase made a mental note to call Justin Blackwood's office later and report what had happened, before he was questioned yet again on how his identification had been used to sign into the base when he hadn't signed out. They walked for a few more minutes until they reached the soft yellow illumination of Canyon's residential street-lights. Chase could also feel Westley's eyes on the sweet, gentle, attentive and intelligent dog now trotting by his side. It felt like he was getting an unexpected evaluation in his and Queenie's training. A huge and unspoken question seemed to move through the night between them, and Chase was thankful when Westley came out and addressed it.

"How long has it been since you were put on sus-pension and Queenie stopped formal training with the K-9 team?" Westley asked.

"Three weeks and four days," Chase said. He took a deep breath. "Do people on the K-9 team really think I had anything to do with the Red Rose Killer's escape, the lost and injured dogs and the murders on base?"

"I couldn't tell you what people think—"

"What do you think?"

Westley stopped and turned toward him. His eyes met Chase's unflinching and guileless gaze. "I'm doing my best to keep an open mind."

Chase guessed that was all he could ask for. They turned to start walking again. But there was one more question Chase had inside him, one that he wasn't sure he had the courage to ask.

"If this investigation into these false accusations against me continues to drag on, how long do you think I'll be allowed to stay inside the K-9 training pro-gram before they reassign Queenie to a new partner?"

"I don't honestly know," Westley said. "That's no

longer my call. Sergeant Streeter is now in command and running the K-9 training center on a day-to-day basis. I'm checking in regularly as needed, but I wasn't in on his decision to allow you to continue training Queenie at home when you were suspended. Although the fact that he did makes me think he didn't expect the investigation into you to last this long."

Well, that's something at least, Chase thought.

They turned onto Linc and Zoe's street.

"I won't sugarcoat it," Westley added. "Like I said, it can be very hard on a dog to change trainers, and Queenie has been out of training much longer than I would've liked. My guess is that Caleb definitely won't let the situation go past the end of July and into August."

Chase blew out a hard breath. So twelve days, then.

"But honestly?" Westley stopped outside Linc and Zoe's front gate. "If it were up to me, I wouldn't let it go on that long. This situation has stretched out much further than it should've. I'll be filling him in on what happened tonight and telling him that in my opinion, if you're not cleared and reinstated back on active duty by the end of the week, Queenie should be reassigned to a new partner and trainer."

SEVEN

Allie's small head of blond curls snuggled tightly into Maisy's side as they curled up beside each other on Zoe's couch. In front of them, little Freddy lay on his stomach on the brightly colored carpet, watching one of his favorite DVDs of Sunday school songs and bedtime stories flicker on the television screen. He had one arm thrown around his father's massive rottweiler partner, Star. There was something about seeing the huge dog cuddled up beside the small boy that filled her heart with both a surge of happiness for Zoe and Freddy having found Linc and a longing to one day feel that safe and protected.

Behind her, in the other room, she could hear Felicity, Zoe and Linc talking in hushed tones, outside of Freddy's earshot. She wasn't sure what to think of the fact that Linc and Star had come back alone, or that Linc had asked if she'd mind watching the children while the three of them talked. Which was okay by her. After all, the three of them were members of the United States Air Force who had signed up to serve their country and were part of the Red Rose Killer investigation. All the adults who'd been at the barbecue tonight had been, and while her friends had always done their best to include her in conversations about their hunt for the Red Rose Killer, as much as they were able to tell her, it didn't change the fact that she would always be a civilian and a preschool teacher.

Being left to watch the children had never been a role that bothered Maisy. It was something she'd always gravitated to. Growing up, she'd gone to so many military get-togethers and parties, and watched the men and women in uniform stand around talking about important issues. They all seemed so strong and confident, statuesque and bold, the best that the country had to offer, standing there holding plates of food and having dizzyingly complex conversations that made her head spin. She'd watch how other young people her age—most of whom were already in the Civil Air Patrol cadet program—would stand around the edges of adult conversations, joining in and listening keenly, and it was as if she could see their minds growing into the men and women they'd be one day.

But that wasn't who she was. That just wasn't her world. Sure, she'd stood by her father's side for a while, but then she'd invariably found herself slipping off to the room where the little children and babies were. She'd played with the infants and started little games for the toddlers and preschoolers, making them smile and laugh and freeing up their tired parents to go socialize with the other adults. She'd liked it there. She fit there and felt like she belonged.

Just like she seemed to fit here, comfortably on the couch with Allie McLear snuggled into her side and Freddy lying happily at their feet. Allie's eyes closed. Then the little girl drifted off into a comfortable sleep.

Maisy sighed. There was something about just having the little girl near that filled her heart with joy. Allie was like a little bundle of…well, of everything. She was so full of energy, happiness, curiosity and joy.

If what Chase said was true, first her own mother had abandoned her and then her father had been accused of being the accomplice of a serial killer. Maisy's heart ached. That was far more than any child should have to bear. How much more would she have to go through? Maisy cradled her closer into her side. She prayed that whatever came next, Allie wouldn't have to face it alone.

She heard voices rise in the kitchen, as if the volume of the conversation had been turned up a notch by the arrival of someone else, not that she could make out the words. Then she felt fingers brush her shoulder and heard the sound of the deep and strong voice she'd have known anywhere. "Maisy?"

She turned her head, careful not to jostle a sleeping Allie. Chase was standing behind her. His hand pressed gently on her shoulder, as if silently nudging her to stay seated.

"I'm going to try to let her sleep," he said softly. "She hasn't slept through the night in ages and she's always overtired. If I'm careful, I might be able to carry her home and put her back to bed without her waking up."

She nodded. Freddy turned his curious little face up toward them, quizzically looking up at them over Star's back. She raised a finger to her lips and hushed him softly. "Allie's asleep."

He nodded and turned the television volume down three notches. She smiled. He was such a good kid, and she was both happy and thankful to see how well the little boy had adjusted to having Linc in his life. She gently nudged the sleeping girl deeper into her arms, then stood, feeling Allie's head fall against her chest. It was only then that she realized Chase's shirt and jeans were streaked with dirt, like he'd been crawling across the ground.

"You might want to clean yourself up a bit," she said.

"It's okay. I brought a blanket from her wagon." He draped the soft pink-and-purple blanket over his shoulder and chest. She walked around the couch to him and gently slid Allie into his arms. Her hands brushed against his forearms as she did so, and for one fleeting moment, she felt the strength of his biceps beneath her fingertips. She stepped back and watched as a sleeping Allie snuggled happily against her father. An odd and almost unnameable longing surged inside her chest, to know what it was like to feel that safe. But she didn't know if it was that she wished she'd known growing up what it was like for her own dad to care for her that way, or if she longed to know what it was like as a woman to be held safely by such a man.

"What happened?" She kept her voice low, hoping the sound of the television would still protect Freddy's young ears. "Did you find them?"

But she knew from the look in his eyes, even before he shook his head, that the answer was no.

"They got away," he said. "Queenie tracked them to a hole in the perimeter fence and we followed the scent out into the woods. Ava and her dog, Roscoe, are still searching the ravine. Isaac and Tango went with them."

Yeah, no one should be alone in the woods right now. The fact that they'd found another hole in the fence filled her with dread. That Boyd Sullivan was able to sneak onto the base was a horrible, daily, pressing reminder that even inside a guarded perimeter, no one was ever truly safe.

"We have Security Forces patrolling the perimeter," he said, as if reading her thoughts. "The hole will be fixed tonight."

But what about the next hole and the next? How had this horror, this fear, this tragedy continued on so long, with no end in sight?

"Well, I reckon I should be saying good-night," Chase said.

She nodded. "Yeah, you should probably get Allie home to bed before she wakes."

But still, he didn't move and neither did she. They just stood there, with their eyes locked on each other, and Allie sleeping softly on her father's chest.

"Goodbye, Maisy," Chase said.

She bit her lip. "Good night, Chase."

He turned and walked toward the kitchen, passing through quickly and professionally, with a quick word to the others, a nod of his head and Queenie by his side.

She waited five minutes after he'd left and then walked into the kitchen and joined the others. Their serious conversation had changed to small talk by the time she made it in there. On purpose or by design, she wasn't sure. But she was thankful for it. She hung around just long enough for Ava, Isaac and their dogs to return, sadly with no trace of the person that she and Chase had seen.

Her goodbyes were quick despite the fact that all of her friends had collectively decided to walk her to her car. There were kind smiles and deep hugs, along with the promises that people would be praying for each other and the reassurances that Boyd Sullivan would be caught soon. They were the kind of comfortable words that she'd gotten so used to both hearing and saying that they'd become part of the regular patter around the base. And while they meant a lot, something in her heart longed for the day conversations like these would be a distant memory.

She dreamed of her father that night. It wasn't the first time he'd walked into her dreams since his death, leaving her with disjointed thoughts she wasn't sure what to make of or how to understand. In this dream, he'd been promoted to General Lockwood and was in full dress uniform, white and gleaming with dark shoes of shining polished leather. She was a teenager in the dream, barely more than sixteen, she guessed. They were walking through a lavish fruit market filled with exotic fruits of all shapes and colors that she was sure didn't exist in the reality of the waking world. She'd asked her father if she was allowed to go out on a date with Chase, who somehow she knew was a teenager himself.

Every good tree bears good fruit, her father told her in the dream. *Chase isn't bearing good fruit. Trees that don't produce good fruit should be cut down and burned in the fire. Jesus said that.*

She'd argued back with him that Jesus had also said that trees should be given an opportunity to grow first. Jesus had specifically said that a tree should be tended, cared for and loved for a while before the farmer would truly know if it was ever going to bear fruit.

Then she'd woken up before her father could answer. She sat up and blinked, her eyes still swimming from sleep. The clock read seven in the morning. It wasn't possible. How had she slept through her alarm? For the first time since her father's death, she'd missed her morning run, and now she had less than an hour to shower, dress, eat and make it to Sunny Seeds to open the door.

It was only then she realized her cell phone was ringing and wondered if that was what had woken her. She swung her legs over the side of the bed, grabbed her phone off the bedside table and stood. It was Oliver Davison, the highly focused FBI agent who was off the base chasing down leads on the Boyd Sullivan investigation. Why was he calling her? Fear stabbed her heart so quickly that her fingers fumbled, dropping her phone on the soft white carpet before quickly snatching it up again.

"Hi," she said, feeling her breath catch in her throat. "It's Maisy."

"Good morning, Maisy," Oliver said, his voice held both dedication and sadness, along with a weariness that hinted of a long career filled with such calls. "I'm calling as a courtesy to let you know that while Security Forces were searching the forest and ravine around the Canyon Air Force Base perimeter, the body of a man was found. We've identified him as Airman Drew Golosky—"

Her intake of breath was so sharp he paused.

"Do you know him?" he asked.

"I know his brother, Frank," she said. She sat down

on the edge of her bed, grabbed a handful of blankets and squeezed tightly. "Last night I was with a group of people who placed a video call to Frank in Afghanistan yesterday. Drew was invited to the barbecue, but we hadn't thought anything of the fact that he wasn't there because he was on leave."

She'd never imagined he was dead.

"A red rose and a note were found under his arm," Oliver continued. "We believe it was the work of the Red Rose Killer. His uniform was missing, and his identification was used to enter the base within the past few days…"

Her head swam, and for a moment, the FBI agent's words seemed to distort and blur into white noise. Boyd Sullivan had been on the base in the past few days? He'd just strolled right through the gate with a stolen uniform and ID? If Boyd Sullivan was the "bad man" Allie was frightened of, did that make Drew Golosky the "hurt man"? But how would little Allie have seen them? Besides, Chase had said Allie had been yelling about a "bad man" for months, not that she had any proof of that.

Oh, Lord, please save us from this nightmare.

Dread washed through her veins, the feeling both sickening and familiar. How many more of these phone calls would there be? How many more people would die?

"Who else was in attendance at the barbecue yesterday?" Oliver asked.

She ran through the names, realizing as she did so that it was very unlikely she was the FBI agent's first call to someone who'd been at the barbecue, and so she might be telling him information he already knew.

She wondered how many identical conversations he'd been through so far today and how many more he had to go. Her eyes closed.

Oh, Lord, I feel trapped inside a nightmare with no sign day is ever going to break again. How many voices have called out to You to guide investigators to find and capture Boyd and his accomplice? Please, may Your answer come soon.

She hoped that when that day came, Chase and little Allie wouldn't be caught in the trap.

"I want to assure you that we're doing everything in our power to catch your father's killer and make sure he's brought to justice," Oliver said. "We will catch him, Maisy. I give you my word. In the meantime, please don't let your guard down."

At least the Security Forces had the courtesy to knock on his door this time, instead of breaking it down and throwing a warrant in his face, Chase thought, as he stood there in his PT uniform and looked through the front door of his bungalow at the two investigators standing on his front step. After he'd made the impulse decision to follow Queenie through the hole in the fence after the hooded figure, he shouldn't have been surprised to have Captain Justin Blackwood and Lieutenant Preston Flannigan appearing at his door. Allie was still asleep, and when he'd lost track of Queenie in the few minutes between feeding her breakfast and making coffee, he'd figured that she'd sneaked into the little girl's room. But before he could even open his mouth, Queenie had run to his side.

He saluted. "Good morning, sirs."

The officers returned the salute.

"At ease," Justin said. "May we come in?"

Well, that was definitely a change from door breaching. Not that he was about to let his guard down. Last night's barbecue had been an all too painful reminder that he was a suspect and would always be a suspect no matter how nicely or politely people treated him.

Chase's eyes rose to the clock. It was ten after seven.

"Absolutely," Chase said. "But if we can keep the volume down, I would appreciate it. My daughter is still asleep. She normally wakes up around now for preschool, but I decided to let her sleep in this morning. She's been sleeping really badly."

After last night, he was feeling even more conflicted about his decision to keep her home from Sunny Seeds. Had he made the right call? Would Allie be better off with life being as normal as possible and spending time with other kids? How much of his decision-making process was being influenced by his own conflicted feelings about Maisy? Something about seeing her last night and that moment they'd shared on the bench had shaken the fragments of his broken heart. And that same feeling had been there just as strong after he'd gone chasing after the fugitive and come back to pick up Allie.

He let the police into his living room, where they stood around his battered wood dining room table, stained from endless painting, coloring and crafting he'd done there with his daughter. "Would you like to sit down?"

"Thank you," Justin said, and Chase couldn't help but notice that this time the captain was doing the talking, while Preston stood silent one step behind him. The men sat, with Chase and Justin opposite each other and Preston at the end of the table. Justin pulled an envelope from a folder under his arm and even before reaching inside, Chase knew without a doubt that it contained the picture of another body. "We regret to inform you that another body has been found. The remains of Airman Drew Golosky were found in the ravine by search teams in the early hours of the morning. We believe he is one of Boyd Sullivan's victims."

The picture lay on the table in front of him. The tall, strong airman had been stripped of his uniform. The remains of a rose were displayed on the body along with a note. Poor Frank. Chase's head dropped into his hands as a heavy weight sank like a stone to the bottom of his stomach. The fact that his friend's brother had died hit him far deeper than the fact that these men were no doubt here to question him as a suspect.

God, please be with Frank right now and his entire family. Comfort them. Surround them with Your mercy. Uphold them with Your mighty arms.

Queenie's head fell on the top of his foot as she lay down beside him. He reached down and brushed his fingers over the top of her head.

Justin pulled a notepad from his pocket and flipped to a new page.

"We believe Airman Golosky has been dead for seven days," Justin said. "His identification and uniform were used by Boyd Sullivan to get onto base twice during this time." Which lined up perfectly with when someone had reported seeing him at Chase's house. "I need to ask you if you can account for your whereabouts on Thursday, July 12, Friday, July 13 and Monday, July 16."

Chase paused for a long moment before answering,

as he searched his brain for anything abnormal about his regular schedule on those days.

"Each day followed the same routine," he said finally. "I took Allie to Sunny Seeds at oh eight hundred. Then I came home and trained Queenie around the house until sixteen hundred. I then took Queenie to pick Allie up from preschool and we spent the rest of the afternoon and evening together."

Justin jotted down a few notes. Chase noticed he kept the book shielded, so neither he nor Preston could read it. "Any witnesses to corroborate your story?"

"No, sir," Chase said. "Just my daughter."

Who was hardly a reliable witness. How had he never noticed just how small and lonely his life had become? That there'd be no friends or colleagues there for him, showing up with meals or inviting him for dinner to help him through these difficult and trying days. Was Liz right? Did he push people away?

Just like he'd pushed away Maisy.

"How well did you know Airman Drew Golosky?" Justin asked.

"Well enough to say hello," Chase said. "I couldn't say the last time I'd seen him or we'd spoken. His brother, Frank, and I served together in Afghanistan and I consider him a friend."

"And when was the last time you spoke to Frank Golosky?" Justin asked.

"Last night," Chase said. "I was at a barbecue at the home of Sergeants Linc and Zoe Colson. It was Frank's birthday."

Justin's composure flickered slightly, but it was only a moment before his features returned to their neutral position. "Are there any witnesses to your conversation with Frank Golosky last night?"

"Absolutely," Chase said. He listed every name, rank and title of the people who had been at the barbecue, taking note of how Preston's nostrils flared when he mentioned Maisy's name.

"And what did you discuss?" Justin asked.

"We exchanged pleasantries and I asked him if he'd seen Ajay Joseph recently," Chase said. "He had not."

"Could you please give an account of your entire evening last night? From the beginning."

He did so, starting with being spotted by Linc outside the fence and then moving back to the video call with Frank. "Then I had a brief conversation with Maisy Lockwood—"

"What was the nature of the conversation?" Preston interjected. It was the first question he'd asked and he did so with such force that Chase was surprised he didn't actually bang his fist on the table.

"We discussed the kidnap attempt on my daughter at Sunny Seeds," he said. "She asked why I'd been looking to speak to Ajay Joseph, and I told her that he was my alibi for the morning of Sunday, April 1. I also assured her I had nothing to do with Boyd Sullivan's crimes and her father's death." But there'd been more to the conversation than that. Something deeper. Something he'd felt when her hands had brushed against his. "Then we heard what sounded like a cell phone alert and turned to see a figure in a hoodie and baseball cap on the other side of the fence, with a bandanna covering the lower half of their face—a figure who I must stress matched the description of the person who tried to abduct my daughter yesterday and was also seen lurking outside my home. Queenie and I gave chase."

He then explained in detail everything that had happened next, from reaching the fence, to making the call to go through, to being joined by the other K-9 officers and dogs, to Queenie losing the scent. He would go over it all, every word, in slow, laborious detail, leaving nothing out. It was the only way he'd clear his name, by cooperating and behaving like a man who had nothing to hide.

Preston sat silently through the rest of the talk as Justin went over every single question and detail that the lieutenant had drilled him on in their last interrogation, including new ones about what had happened the day before. But while Preston had questioned him like an angry dog trying to chase a rat into a corner, Justin's questioning was calmer, quieter and more methodical. Instead, it was like Chase's entire life was a tower of wooden blocks, and Justin was slowly poking and pulling each one, trying to see if he could pry it loose and make Chase's whole world crumble and fall. Preston's aggressive assault Chase could stand against. Justin's slow dismantling of his life shook him far more.

Allie cried out softly in her sleep and he could tell without even glancing down under the table that Queenie had gone from lying down to sitting up in response. His little girl wasn't fully awake yet, but she wouldn't sleep much longer.

"I have something to show you," Justin said. He pulled a folded piece of paper from his pocket. "I received an emailed response from Captain Teddy Dennis serving in Afghanistan. I had reached out to him in regards to your communication with Ajay Joseph. He mentioned that your former supervisor, Captain Reardon, had reached out to him as well."

He breathed a sigh of thanks that Captain Reardon had done as she'd said and that Teddy had responded.

"What did he say?" Chase asked, forcing himself not to ask all the other questions tumbling through his mind. Had he been able to reach Ajay? Had Ajay confirmed his alibi? If so, why was he still being questioned?

"You can read it for yourself." Justin slid the paper across the table with a grim look that made any hope Chase might've been tempted to feel dissipate before it could even form. He stared at the paper for a moment. Then he unfolded it and read.

It was an email sent from the official address of Captain Teddy Dennis, three lines long, blunt and to the point. Yes, he could confirm that somebody by the name of Ajay Joseph had been the liaison between the United States Air Force and an independent Afghan contractor and had coordinated with Chase McLear personally. The email went on to say that Mr. Joseph had gone home to visit his family in the mountains in early April, had resigned from his role in late May and that Teddy was unaware of whether he was returning to work or how to contact him. The captain closed the letter by saying that Captain Blackwood shouldn't hesitate to contact him again if he could be of any more assistance.

"Disappointing," Chase said. He looked down at the letter for a long moment. Then he refolded it and slid it back across the table. "But Captain Reardon did say she'd look into whether the records of my video calls with Ajay could be recovered. Maybe she'll turn something up."

"What did you discuss during your last conversation with Ajay Joseph?" Justin asked. His eyes rose to meet Chase's and there was a new look in there that Chase couldn't decipher. It was piercing.

"No, sir." Chase folded his arms on the table. "I'm sorry, but I promised to keep everything he said in strictest confidence."

If he had been able to receive, decrypt and read the files Ajay had sent, he could've had actionable data to report. Ajay had known that Chase wouldn't have been able to keep silent if he'd seen actual evidence of theft or fraud. But as it was, all he had were rumors, ones that could ruin innocent people's lives.

"What was the nature of the conversation?" Justin pressed.

"Again, it was personal, sir," he said. "And nothing that has any bearing on this discussion."

"Don't you think that's for me to judge?" Justin demanded. "Do you understand what's happening here, Airman? You've been accused of being an accomplice to multiple crimes, including murder. You've been accused of aiding and abetting a serial killer. Your career is hanging by a very thin thread, and you're dangerously close to being in handcuffs. To be very blunt, the only thing I care about is the truth. If the truth is that you're innocent, then I want that sorted out and settled as quickly as possible so that I stop wasting my time and start chasing other leads. If you're guilty, and your silence allows Boyd Sullivan to hurt a single other human being, then you should have no doubt that you will be caught and punished to the full extent of the law. So the quicker you stop being coy and start getting real with me, the faster a killer will be off the streets and the easier life will be for your daughter."

Chase sat back in his chair. It was the longest string of words he'd ever heard come out of Justin's mouth and he could tell by the way the usual smirk had faded from Preston's face that it surprised him too.

"So, I will ask you again, Airman, what was the nature of your conversation with Ajay Joseph? Why did he call you that morning? What did you discuss?" Justin asked.

Chase felt his shoulders straighten. "With all due respect, I'm not trying to obstruct justice, sir. I simply believe what I discussed with him is irrelevant."

Justin leaned forward. His eyes narrowed like a searchlight, locking Chase in their focus. "Even if it gets people killed, lands you in jail and destroys your daughter's life? Are you really that heartless?"

EIGHT

Heartless? The single word smacked Chase with a ferocity that stole the breath from his lungs and made a fire flare inside his veins and threaten to consume him. He hadn't wanted to tell them that Ajay had called about suspected theft in his team, because Ajay's last email had told him it'd been nothing but an accounting error and Chase wasn't about to blurt out that a friend had suspected one of his men of stealing from the United States Air Force. Trust was everything in a war zone. Even the suspicion of theft could cost countless impoverished Afghan locals their livelihoods. He'd seen independent local contractors fired for less. And Justin thought that meant he didn't care about his daughter? That he didn't care that Boyd Sullivan was out in the world murdering good men, like his friend's brother?

The captain had no idea how hard Chase fought day after day to withstand the barrage of questions, accusations, suspicion and dirty looks, or how much inner strength it took him not to stand up, flip the table over and shout his innocence at the top of his lungs.

"I don't want to hurt Ajay!" Chase felt his voice rise.

"He's my friend. He's new in his faith. He's dealing with a family crisis. I'm not about to throw anybody under the bus to save my own life."

Preston groaned. Yeah, he didn't expect Preston to get it. But was he mistaken, or had something actually softened behind Justin's eyes?

Chase took a breath. He would tell them the truth. But nothing specific that could damage Ajay or the men who'd worked for him.

"My grandfather was Senior Master Sergeant Donald McLear," Chase went on. His voice dropped. "He told me a good man never repeated slander and that even when there was proof, a wise man knew when to hold his tongue. Ajay was concerned that someone he knew might've committed a nonviolent crime. It turned out the allegations were false and I'm certainly not going to repeat them. He asked me for my advice on the matter and I agreed to look at his evidence. But his evidence was on my missing laptop and I never had the opportunity to look at it. Ajay later emailed that he'd been wrong, no crime had occurred and it had all been a mistake. All I know is that my friend Ajay was doing his best in a difficult situation and I have no desire to make his life more complicated or ruin a potentially innocent stranger's life, just to save my own skin." He crossed his arms and leaned back. "I know all too well how being stitched up feels."

He realized as he'd said the words that he could've probably said that much earlier and found himself wondering, for the first time, if his reluctance to trust other people was making his life even more difficult than it needed to be. But opening up and trusting people had never come easily to him. He felt protective of Ajay, who'd confided in him. The last thing he wanted was to find out Captain Dennis was breathing down the local contractors' necks because of him.

His grandfather always warned him that any word he spoke and any weakness he showed could be weaponized against him. Surely, it was best to stay a closed book. Life was safest if he didn't let anyone in.

Silence fell around the table. Justin leaned back and let out a long breath. "And you're sure that's the only person you're protecting?"

"Bad man hurt man! No!" A plaintive cry came down the hall, shattering the moment of tension and stealing any answer Chase might've given. Allie's gentle whimpering turned into a full on cry. Instantly, Chase pushed his chair back and stood, forgetting for a moment where he was and who he was with.

Justin and Preston stood too.

"I think we're good for now," Justin said. "Don't leave the base without going through a main checkpoint again and informing my office, under any circumstances, or I will be forced to reexamine whether further restrictions should be placed on your movement. If you can think of anything that could be helpful, don't hesitate to give me a call." He laid his business card down on the table. Allie's cries grew louder. "We can see ourselves out. Go tend to your daughter."

"Thank you, sir." Chase saluted and the two men returned the salute.

He left the men in his living room and half strode, half jogged down the hallway to Allie's room. She was sitting up in bed, damp blond curls plastered against her sweaty face. She reached for him.

"Bad man hurt man, Daddy," she said.

"I know, Sweet Pea," he said. *Not that I know what you mean by that.* He swept her up into his arms and held her tightly. His fingertips gently brushed her hair back from her face. "Daddy's here now. You're safe."

A gentle tongue licked his arm tentatively. He glanced down. Queenie had jumped up on Allie's bed and was standing there, her tail wagging gently, as if she knew something was wrong and wanted to help. Chase closed his eyes and hugged his daughter closer, feeling her tiny fists tighten around the fabric of his T-shirt.

Please, help me, Father God. I love Allie so much. She's my whole world. Save me from the snare I'm in, for her sake. I don't want to even let myself think of what will happen to her if I don't get out of this mess.

"Put me down, Daddy," Allie said, after a long moment. "I need to go to school now."

He opened his eyes and eased her back to arm's length. Her chin still quivered, but her eyes blazed with a stubborn determination that he knew meant that she was done crying for now. He hoped that she never lost her fortitude and resilience.

"What would you think of staying home from Sunny Seeds with me and Queenie today?" he asked.

The jut of her lower lip told him the answer even before her words did.

"No, Daddy. I need to go to school. I need to go see Maisy."

Of course she did. He set her down and she wriggled from his grasp.

"I dress myself." Her little chin rose and she pointed

to the door. He almost smiled. Seemed she was feeling independent today. Hopefully that was a good sign.

"All right, then, I'll go get your breakfast ready." He stepped back. It had been two months since she'd decided she needed to get dressed all by herself. After watching her futilely but stubbornly wrestle with the wooden dresser drawers, refusing to accept his help, he'd put all of Allie's favorite clothes in a special set of pink and purple plastic drawers at toddler height on a shelf by the wall. "I'll be right outside if you need me, okay?"

Or if she tried to put her red knit Christmas dress on again in the middle of a hot Texas summer.

"Bye-bye now, Daddy!" She waved, with that determined gesture that meant she expected him to leave. Her face was so serious he had to battle the urge to laugh. That old cliché that she'd grow up fast had seemed so far away when she was a tiny baby, crying in the night for her missing mother. Now he felt like he was realizing for the first time just how true it was. He stepped back into the hallway and waited a second to see if Queenie would be ordered out along with him. Then he closed the door three quarters of the way when he realized that apparently the dog was allowed to stay.

His heart ached to think of what would happen the day he'd have to tell Allie that Queenie was leaving. The deadline Westley had given him nipped like a wolf at his heels.

Lord, please. Help me. Rescue me from that day.

He turned and only then realized that Preston was still standing in his living room. Chase's shoulders set.

He turned and strode back into the room. "Can I help you with something?"

The smirk was back on Preston's face, with the same unpleasant curl as the day before, only tighter and with an added malice, and Chase couldn't help but wonder what he'd done to make Preston hate him so much. Then he glanced past the lieutenant and realized Justin was now standing just outside his door, talking on his phone. It seemed the captain had gotten a call and Preston had decided to linger inside long enough to give Justin a moment of privacy. But for the first time, the suspicion brushed the back of Chase's spine that the very thorough and detailed captain who'd questioned him earlier wouldn't do anything without a reason.

His feet planted on the living room floor and his hands clasped behind his back, Chase faced Preston. "Again, can I help you with something? Shouldn't you be taking your son to school?"

"He's with his mother this week." Preston's eyes darted up and down as if he disliked the reminder of his failed marriage.

"Do we have a problem?" Chase asked.

"Apparently, we do." Preston's arms crossed, and for the first time Chase noticed the phone clutched tightly in his hand. "I asked you to stay away from Maisy Lockwood."

Not asked. Told. And it's not like Preston had any right to make that demand of him, let alone issue that order.

"Yes." Chase spoke through gritted teeth. "And I explained very thoroughly already this morning she happened to be at a barbecue I was invited to attend last night."

Preston snorted. "Then do you care to clarify what you were doing holding her hand?"

Chase blinked as the words hit him so hard he rocked back on his heels. "How on earth could you possibly know that?"

"The whole base knows it!" Preston stuck his phone out, and Chase looked down in shock and horror as the base's anonymous blogger's page filled the screen.

Front and center on the page was a picture of him and Maisy sitting alone on the log. His back was to the camera, but Maisy's face was crystal clear, as were their hands clasped together like two shipwrecked survivors clinging to the wreckage.

A headline ran across the screen: Red Rose Killer Accomplice Finally Found? Is Clint Lockwood's Daughter in a Secret Romantic Relationship with the Man who helped Murder her Father?

All this time the base had been looking for a scapegoat to pin their fears and anger on. Looked like the anonymous blogger had just given them one.

"Maisy! Wait! Stop!" Zoe shouted, running down the sidewalk toward her as Maisy climbed out of her hatchback. The car was bright blue with Sunny Seeds Preschool and happy fruit decals on the side, and today was the first day in memory when the school's small parking lot was so full she wasn't able to pull into her usual spot, forcing her to go around the block and park on the street. Zoe raised both hands in a stopping motion. "Stay there. Don't go anywhere."

"I'm late," Maisy said. She slammed the door and

pushed the button on her key fob to hear it lock. She couldn't believe how late. The conversation with Oliver had lasted longer than she'd expected and then it had felt like she'd caught every single red light on the way to school. "The school opens in less than ten minutes, I haven't even set up anything for today and for some reason the parking lot is jammed with cars."

The words hit her ears just as she was saying them. Why was the parking lot full? Yes, it was a small lot and the front of the school did tend to get busy when parents were dropping off children. But there weren't that many students, so the lot was never actually full, unless it was parents' night. Only then did she really look up and see for the first time the scene unfolding in front of her beloved school. People crowded the front of the building. Many were parents and caregivers dropping off students for the day. But there were also the parents of former students and people in uniform she didn't recognize. There was Lieutenant Heidi Jenks, a reporter for CAFB News, and Yvette Crenville, the base nutritionist, who lived nearby and often came by to talk to the students about healthy eating. Her own classroom assistant teacher, Esther, stood by the front door, along with Bella's classroom assistant, Vance. But through the gap in the brightly patterned curtains she could see Imogene Wilson, the preschool director, talking with Esther's grandfather, Lieutenant General Nathan Hall. Why was the base commander visiting Sunny Seeds?

That's when she noticed Felicity standing halfway down the sidewalk with little Freddy in her arms, and realized she must be holding him so that Zoe could talk to her privately.

Her phone buzzed. It was a text from Ava Esposito.

Are you all right? Praying for you! I'm here if you want to grab coffee or need anything. Hugs!

Fear crept up her spine. What had happened? Another kidnapping? Another Boyd Sullivan sighting? Another creepy rose left by the Red Rose Killer with a threat for someone at Sunny Seeds?

Please, Lord, not another death.

Instinctively, Maisy reached for Zoe's arm. "What happened?"

Sadness washed over her friend's features. "I'm guessing you don't read the Canyon Air Force Base anonymous blogger's website?"

"No, of course not!" Maisy's nose wrinkled instinctively. "Why would I read that trash?"

This was all about gossip? What could the blogger have possibly written that would cause this many people to show up at Sunny Seeds? Heidi looked ready to come her way, but Felicity raised a swift hand and Heidi held back.

Zoe held up her phone. "I'm so sorry about this."

"Just let me see it." She took the phone, glanced down at the screen and felt her heart stop like someone had squeezed it.

It was her. A picture of her sitting on the log in Zoe's backyard, holding Chase's hands.

In the photo, she looked so deeply into Chase's eyes. She looked totally crush-struck. Besotted. She looked like a woman in— No, she wouldn't let herself think that word, the *L* word, not about Chase. Not now. Not ever. Standing there, on the sidewalk, she felt like someone had ripped the door off her heart and left it hanging wide-open for all to see. She pressed her hands, still cool from the car's air-conditioning, against her flaming cheeks. Could everyone tell how she felt about Chase? Could he?

"I'm so sorry," Zoe said. "The blogger has targeted me too and I know what it's like to have the truth of your life twisted up with a whole lot of gossip and innuendo and then used against you."

Her friend's voice was soft, and yet a strength, like battle-tested steel, ran through it, and Maisy suddenly realized why Zoe had been the one of her friends delegated to give her the bad news.

Maisy blinked hard and forced herself to focus on the words written on the screen. The headline was everything she feared it would be, implying in huge bold letters that Chase was Boyd Sullivan's accomplice, and that she was disgracing her father's memory by having an inappropriate and ill-advised romance with the man accused of helping to kill him.

She gritted her teeth and continued reading down the page. The first few paragraphs outlined the case against Chase, including the fact that his name had appeared on a prison visitor log, that Security Forces had raided his home after someone had called in an anonymous report of seeing Boyd Sullivan there and that her father's gold cross had been found after the house was searched. Maisy shook her head. How did the blogger know all that?

Then the blogger had written about the incident of Allie's attempted kidnapping at the school the day before. However, the post twisted the facts around to make it sound like Maisy's class was so badly run that either Allie was a little brat who'd wandered away all on her own, or that Maisy had helped Chase stage the kidnapping in an attempt to paint himself as an innocent victim.

At best, it made Maisy look like a fool who'd been duped by a potential killer. At worse, she was another one of Boyd's accomplices.

The blog trailed on, but she couldn't read another word. Angry tears filled her eyes, briefly blocking out the sea of people surrounding the front of her school.

"It's not fair," Maisy said. "Whoever wrote this is just twisting details, making wild guesses and asking questions, leaving the reader to fill in the answers."

"It's what trolls like that do," Zoe said. "I'm so sorry."

"How did they even know this stuff?" she asked, pushing the phone back into her friend's hand. "Surely, some of these details should be confidential!"

Zoe shook her head, sadness mingled with bewilderment in her eyes.

"I don't know," Zoe admitted. "If you read down to the end of the page, the blogger claims to have a source who anonymously sent the pictures of you and Chase."

She wasn't sure who the anonymous source could possibly be. But whether or not that was true, now the whole world had someone to accuse of being Boyd Sullivan's accomplice. Was the anonymous source the same person who'd cut the screen of Allie's bedroom window and tried to kidnap her?

"So that's why Heidi Jenks is at the school," she said. She'd talked to the reporter briefly after her father had died. Heidi had written a very kind obituary. Maisy knew other people found the tenacious reporter a bit much and some even wondered if Heidi herself was the anonymous blogger. But Maisy had always viewed her as polite, considerate and respectful.

"Heidi and Felicity are neighbors," Zoe said, her lip curled only very slightly to indicate that she and Felicity might not have agreed on the reporter. "Felicity thinks it might be good if you talked to a sympathetic source."

"About what?" Maisy asked. "The fact that someone printed this trash about me? How could this possibly be news?"

"There's an open letter going around among the parents," Zoe said. "It's addressed to Imogene Wilson and the base commander. The parents of almost all the students have signed it."

Fear brushed Maisy's spine. "What kind of letter?"

"I didn't sign it," Zoe said quickly. "You have to know I love you, Freddy loves you and your friends have your back. In fact, some of us are here today as a show of support."

A Security Forces car pulled up behind her with a screech of tires and it took her a second to register Preston's uniformed presence behind the wheel.

"They're demanding armed uniformed Security Forces protection at the front doors," Zoe continued. Maisy nodded. Okay, that wasn't the first time she'd heard that and while she didn't like the idea, she wouldn't be surprised if Imogene caved and agreed to it.

"Okay, and?"

"They want all field trips cancelled, the back playground and yard closed off and children kept inside all day."

What? Something bristled at the center of her core.

Keep the children locked inside all day? Why punish them like that? The thought of their sad little faces pressed up against the window looking out at the glorious Texas sunshine was cruel.

Preston was out of his car and striding toward her now, with a look of determination and purpose she didn't much like. He looked like a rhino preparing to break down a wall.

"Is that it?" Maisy asked.

"They want Allie McLear expelled and Chase forbidden from coming anywhere near the school."

"That's ridiculous!"

"Not if they think Chase is Boyd Sullivan's accomplice and that he set up a fake kidnap attempt yesterday," Zoe said. "They say it's not fair for the school's resources to be diverted to make sure one little girl isn't being used as a pawn, when there are other students to worry about."

Zoe's shoulders rose and fell, and Maisy was reminded that some people had argued she shouldn't have allowed little Freddy in her school either because he was Boyd's nephew. What was wrong with these people? How had fear and paranoia managed to infect the base so deeply? It was like a disease, destroying good will, killing faith and rotting out everything she valued about being part of a base community.

Lord, please, release us from this fear and stop this nightmare before it tears us apart. Help me continue to be a beacon and source of hope, light and comfort to these tiny children, who I know You care for too. Help me continue to do my part to chip away at the darkness.

Zoe took a deep breath. "Sorry, honey, but they're also demanding that you be fired from Sunny Seeds."

NINE

Fired? The word clattered inside Maisy's chest so painfully that for a moment all she could do was stand there, looking in her friend's sad eyes and feeling herself gasp for breath like a fish suddenly yanked from the deep, cool comforts of her pond. Imogene would never fire her. Would she? She was excellent at her job and hadn't taken so much as a day off in years, even after her father had been killed. Surely, the worst-case scenario was that her boss would put her on leave, while they started a long procedure to investigate the complaints against her. Yet, the fact that anyone wanted her to be fired hurt so deeply that it was almost impossible for her to take any comfort in that. This school was her life. Her students were her entire world. Why would anyone try to take that away from her? How could anybody think that her students would be better off without her?

"They can't do this," she said. Her feet feebly and haltingly steered her up toward the front steps and toward the gathering of friends, parents, concerned Canyon residents and those onlookers making somebody else's problem their own. "They can't say I don't care about my students because some scandalous blog decided to write rumors and lies about me, or published a picture of me being seen to…"

Words failed her. Being seen to do what? Hold hands with a criminal suspect. Gaze up into his eyes. Look up at him like he was everything she'd ever wanted and nothing she thought she'd ever be able to have.

"Maisy, we need to talk." Preston barreled to her side. His hand brushed the back of her shoulder and his stiff form fell into step alongside her, as if he'd taken it upon himself to be her personal escort. "Somewhere private."

Nothing in his tone or body language implied it was official. Whatever Preston Flannigan wanted to talk about was way down her list of priorities, and going somewhere private with him was not about to happen.

She shrugged his hand away and kept walking straight ahead without looking at him. "I'm sorry, it'll have to wait. I don't have time right now."

"But you don't know what it's about." He reached for her arm, not exactly touching her, but somehow still uncomfortably close.

"If it's about the Red Rose Killer investigation, please get Captain Blackwood to call me," she said. "I already had a long conversation this morning with FBI Special Agent Oliver Davison."

"It's not police business—"

"Then, please, it has to wait." She raised her head high and walked through the crowd, feeling Zoe close on the other side and seeing Felicity and Heidi ahead. She could hear Preston still talking behind her. Not in coherent sentences though, but blustering and sputtering out syllables like "but," "you" and "I." She didn't turn.

Eyes averted their gaze as she passed. So this was what it was like to have the Canyon Air Force Base's finger of suspicion pointed at you. Suddenly her heart ached for what Zoe had been going through ever since her half brother Boyd had broken out of prison.

And Chase…

She stopped in front of Felicity and Heidi. Zoe reached for Freddy, and Felicity slid the little boy into his mother's arms.

Maisy nodded to Heidi and was relieved to find she still had enough composure to give the journalist a polite smile. "Hi, Heidi. I don't have a statement to make about anything at this time. Okay?"

Despite her reputation for being a ruthless and relentless reporter, Heidi gave her a sympathetic look from behind her large dark-framed glasses. She nodded. "Absolutely."

"Thank you. Are you planning on running a story about me?"

"Not specifically." Heidi's eyes met hers straight on and Maisy found herself thankful for her directness and honesty. "I'm researching a story about Airman Chase McLear. The fact that his daughter was kidnapped from this school will be part of it. But the story has not taken shape yet, so I'll call you for comment before I go to press. In the meantime, feel free to call me anytime if you want to talk, either on or off the record."

She slipped her hand into her pocket and pulled out a business card, and even though Maisy was pretty sure she already had the reporter's number in her phone, she took it and slid it into her pocket. "Thank you."

Heidi disappeared back into the crowd. As Maisy watched her walk away, she noticed Preston talking to Yvette. Whatever he was saying had the very pretty base nutritionist giggling. Looked like the lieutenant had found someone more receptive to his charm.

"Do you want us go into the school with you?" Felicity asked. "I can stick around for a while."

Maisy rolled her shoulders back. Her father's words echoed through her mind. *Strong people fought their own battles.* "No, I'm good."

They paused a moment, then nodded. Zoe shifted Freddy around in her arms.

"Okay, I'm taking Freddy to class," Zoe said. "If you need us, don't hesitate to call."

"Thank you," Maisy said, resisting for the moment the urge to just throw her arms around both friends and hug them. Instead, she stepped back and looked around the chaos on the lawn. Brouhaha or no brouhaha, she was still these children's teacher.

"Esther," she called, raising her tone with her "Miss Maisy voice," as her students called it. "We need to get people sorted through and dropping their kids off. A lot of these people need to get to work. Can you please herd all those dropping their kids into a straight line by the front door? After that, start processing them through into the classroom. As always, parents are welcome to stay with their children if they wish."

Esther nodded and Maisy couldn't help but notice how her usually confident assistant's fingers shook and her dark eyes darted from Maisy's face to the ground and back. Then the younger woman hurried to her side.

"Imogene wants to see you in her office right away," Esther said, confirming what Maisy already suspected. Then her voice dropped. "I didn't tell my grandfather anything bad about what happened yesterday. I promise I didn't, Maisy. But I live with him, while I'm saving up for a house, and he said he was getting flooded with calls and emails this morning from people on base, and around the country, demanding to know why he was letting a 'known threat' near children at the preschool. Even some major civilian news outlets called him, asking for comments about Chase McLear and saying they were sending reporters. He'll be talking to the press later and wanted to talk to you first. Some people are even saying you've been helping Chase by covering up for the fact that he's working with Boyd Sullivan. He can't ignore that."

The national press was showing up at the base to ask if one of Canyon's preschool teachers was, at best, accidentally aiding the Red Rose Killer's accomplice or, at worse, if she herself was a coconspirator to his crimes? No, she guessed the base commander couldn't just let that go.

"I'm going in the side door," Maisy said. "That will keep the front entrance clear for you to lead the kids into the classroom."

As well, it would give her a few moments alone, in peace and quiet, to pray and ask the Lord for help before stepping inside. Esther nodded. Maisy slipped past the crowd and around the side of the building. She turned the corner, walked a few steps, then stopped and pressed one hand against the wall.

What do I do, Lord? Yes, I know I can dig my heels

*in. But is that what's best for my students? How do I
protect them?*

A large hand landed on her shoulder, cutting her
prayer short. She spun back, her pulse racing and her
arm raised in self-defense as she came within a half-
inch of accidentally elbowing Preston across the face.
She jumped back. He'd followed her.

"Maisy!" He leaned in. His voice was hushed and
urgent. "Before you talk to the base commander we
need to talk."

She pressed her lips together as the line she often
said to the children crossed her mind—wanting something wasn't the same as needing it.

"So you've told me." She crossed her arms. "About
something personal, that's not official police business.
And I've told you it has to wait. So, if you're here as a
parent, then either you can accompany your son into
the classroom or you can wait for me out front."

"I'm here as a friend," he said quickly. "I'm here
because I care about you."

She shook her head. But they weren't friends and
Preston couldn't just single-handedly decide they had
a personal relationship. He might be drawn to her, in a
slightly overbearing way that, truthfully, had always
made her feel mildly uncomfortable. In fact, sometimes the teacher's gifts his son gave her at holidays
were more generous and personal than she was comfortable with. Had she done something to let him think
she was open to a deeper relationship with him? Did
she need to be bolder at putting him in his place?

But he was a member of the Security Forces, the
father of one of her students and someone investigating her father's murder.

"Now is not a good time. I will talk to you later, Preston."

She reached for the side door. He stepped in front of her. "Tell me you're not involved with Chase McLear!"

The words flew out of his mouth, more like an order than a question.

"Excuse me?" Who did this man think he was? She drew herself up to her full height, even as she knew how slight it was. "My personal life is none of your business!"

"Well, maybe it should be." He stepped closer. "There's something bad going down on base and you need someone to protect you." His hand touched her shoulder. "And it should be me."

There were too many cars and people around the front of the school, Chase thought as he pulled his truck past Sunny Seeds. His eyes scanned the road. In the back seat, Allie was chirping away to Queenie in a silly little made-up language of hers that only the dog seemed to understand. If only he understood her as well as his own canine partner did. His heart ached and he let it turn into a prayer for wisdom.

Help me. Please. I feel like I'm all alone, not knowing what I'm guarding, being attacked on all sides and not knowing what to do. Help me to remember that You are my sword and my shield of protection.

"Daddy! We go pass Sunny Seeds!" Allie's voice piped up from the back seat.

"I know, Sweet Pea," he said. He palmed the steering wheel around the corner. "We're just running a little late and I need to find a place to park."

Truth be told, he'd been hoping to keep Allie home and spare her the chaos.

Coming so close to losing her—and knowing how close he still was to losing Queenie—had made him wake up determined to hold her close to his chest and never let her go. Instead, she'd been so insistent on going to see Maisy, she'd practically dragged him out the door once he'd gotten her fed and coaxed her into wearing summer clothes.

Honestly, he couldn't blame her. Something inside of him understood the desire to be around Maisy. If he'd been a different man, in a different place in time and not facing all that he was going through, when he'd collected a sleeping Allie from her arms in the living room the night before, he'd have asked Maisy out on a first date. And when they'd been sitting all alone in the backyard, with his hands enveloping hers and her eyes looking into his, he might have even asked if he could kiss her.

Instead, the blog post Preston had angrily waved in his face had been a glaring reminder that all he could bring to Maisy's life was pain and conflict. She deserved better. She deserved better than a man like him, in a mess like his life was in, and better than the further chaos he'd bring to her life.

There were far more people around the front of the preschool than usual and his heart lurched with worry as he pondered the reason.

He eased his vehicle around the corner, looking to park on a side street. Then he heard shouting. He looked out the window and what he saw made his foot hit the break as hard as he dared without jolting Allie and Queenie. Preston, standing with his chest puffed out and hands raised, was yelling at Maisy. Chase couldn't make out his words but it didn't matter—there was no way he was going to just sit there and watch her get berated.

He opened the door and leaned out, one boot hitting the pavement the moment he cut the engine. "Hey! Leave her alone!"

Preston turned sharply. His face went red, like a cartoon steam engine barely managing to contain itself from exploding. Maisy's eyes met Chase's for one long and grateful moment, and his breath caught at the vulnerability in her face. Then she turned and disappeared through Sunny Seeds' side door.

Preston's hands balled into fists. He started across the grass toward where Chase still sat, halfway out of his truck.

Chase glanced back at Queenie. "Stay! Watch Allie!"

He stepped out of the vehicle, leaving the door open, and leaned against the back door, creating a physical barrier between Preston and his precious daughter. He slid his hand behind him through the open window and felt for Allie's tiny shoulder, so she'd know her daddy was there.

"What are you doing here?" Preston demanded, punctuating the question with a swear word that snapped from his lips so suddenly it was like a whip cracking in the air.

"Watch your language in front of my daughter," Chase said, "and lower your voice."

"You should get back in the truck and take her home." Preston scowled. Something about what Chase said must've tweaked something inside Preston's conscience because his voice lowered. "It's not right for you to be here when you're under criminal investigation. There's a letter going around from people demanding that Maisy suspend Allie from school and that you be banned from school property until your name is cleared."

He wondered if it was started by Preston. Something twisted like the tip of a knife in the pit of Chase's stomach. How dare anyone try to punish a little girl for something they imagined her father had done? But then, the lieutenant added something that made the pain cut even deeper. "They're also demanding that Maisy be fired from Sunny Seeds because they suspect she must be helping you, which would mean that either knowingly or unknowingly, she's also helping the Red Rose Killer. Not that I personally think she'd ever intentionally do anything criminal. She's too sweet and innocent to get messed up in crime on purpose. But parents are demanding the preschool director do something and the base commander has been threatened with large-scale protests in front of Canyon."

Chase felt his right hand slide over his heart. No, they couldn't threaten Maisy. Not because of him. Her job was the most important thing in the world to her and she was incredible at it. Surely, her boss knew that. That anyone would harass her, threaten her or try to take anything away from her because of him hurt him deeply. Liz had always accused him of robbing her of the life she'd really wanted and now he was going to do the same to Maisy. He slumped back against the vehicle, as if his legs no longer knew how to hold him. Then he felt Allie's hand reach up, grab his fingers and squeeze him tightly.

"I can't believe you'd do that to Maisy," Chase said. "She doesn't deserve any of this."

Preston's chest rose and his face was a mixture of both pride and absolute certainty. There was nothing worse than someone who thought he was right all the time. Chase wondered what it was like to go through life that confident. He supposed it would make life easier for him, but harder for everyone around him.

"I'm doing this for Maisy," Preston said. "I care about Maisy way more than you could ever understand. She needs me to protect her from herself."

Did she now? Chase nearly snorted. He couldn't believe it. Preston thought he cared about Maisy. He might even think he loved her. Because he was selfish enough to think the fact that he was attracted to her meant something. For a moment, the question of whether Preston's determination to find Chase guilty had something to do with Maisy hovered in Chase's mind. Except Chase and Maisy had never so much as gone out for coffee together, let alone had a personal relationship, and Preston's furious grilling of him had happened before the barbecue.

Besides, how could anyone be foolish enough to think a woman as smart, kind and beautiful as Maisy would ever be with a man like him?

Something soured in Preston's gaze, as if reading Chase's mind.

"Believe it or not," Preston said, "I'm only after the truth."

No, he didn't believe it. "I'm sure you think that's true. But I don't."

He watched as Preston's fists clenched even tighter and wondered if he was going to have to block a physical punch in front of his little girl. But then, Preston turned and stormed off with a determination and anger that left Chase with no doubt he'd be back with an even harder and more impactful blow.

Chase waited until he disappeared around the corner, then he opened the vehicle door and pulled Allie into his arms.

"He was loud, Daddy," she said.

"I know, Sweet Pea." He sighed. "I'm so sorry you had to hear him."

Her little hand brushed his cheek. "You okay, Daddy?"

"No," he said honestly. "His yelling made me sad. But you and I and Queenie are going to play together in the grass for a bit, while we wait to see if Maisy is okay."

She nodded wisely. "Maisy is im-por-tant, right, Daddy?"

He hugged her tightly. Yes, Maisy was important. She was important to him in ways he didn't know how to put into words. And what kind of person was he to bring such pain and chaos into her life? His first impulse yesterday had been right. He had to pull Allie from Maisy's school. He had to disappear from her life completely until the dust settled and stop making his problems hers. He'd wait until the crowd cleared, then he'd quietly speak to Maisy in person and tell her what he'd decided. He'd do it before she could ask. He owed her that much.

He didn't have that long to wait. He and Allie had barely started their fourth round of I Spy when the side door opened and a small blonde figure slipped through. Instinctively, he stood and his arms reached for her. "Maisy, are you okay?"

"No." Her gaze traveled past him to the horizon. "I'm on vacation. I had some time available to use up and when I realized just how challenging it would be for my students if I dug my heels in, I offered to take it. My boss agrees it's the easiest way to calm the situation down short term. She will get a really good supply teacher to come in to help Esther cover my class, and I'll come back later this evening, once the school is closed, to lay out lesson plans for the next few days."

"I'm so sorry. Is there anything I can do?"

Her eyes turned toward him and he realized she was fighting back tears.

"Yes, Chase, please take me somewhere, anywhere, far away from here."

TEN

The words hung in the air between them, her incredibly honest plea waiting to be answered.

"I'm sorry," she said. "I'm not sure where that came from. But there's still a crowd of people out front, and the base commander warned me more press might be coming…"

Her words faded on her lips as Allie ran across the lawn and threw her arms around Maisy's legs in a tackle hug.

"Don't be sad, Maisy," Allie said. "Daddy says you're im-por-tant."

"You and your daddy are important too," Maisy whispered, as she reached down and ran her hand over Allie's curls. Then she looked up. Chase was looking at her, with that same intensity that she'd seen in his eyes the night before. For a moment, they just stood there, looking at each other, as if neither of them knew what to say.

"There's a wonderful little waterfall, on a very public path, just half an hour off base," Chase said. "I was thinking of taking Allie and Queenie for a hike. Obviously, I'll call Captain Blackwood to tell him before I leave base. But it's got good trails and it's far away from anywhere investigators think Boyd Sullivan might be hiding out. We could pack a picnic. What do you say? Do you want to join us?"

She could feel the smile that spread across her face as something exploded inside her chest like a shower of sparklers on the Fourth of July. "That would be lovely. If you don't mind swinging by my house first, I have a basket we could use."

"Sounds good." Half a grin curled up at the corner of his mouth, with a look that was somewhere in between handsome and cute. Then he glanced down at Allie. "If that's okay with you, Sweet Pea?"

Allie nodded. She slipped her hand into Maisy's, and they walked back to the truck. Maisy helped Allie get settled in as Chase made a quick phone call to Justin.

"All clear," Chase said. "He agrees with my assessment that the trails by the waterfall are far too public for someone like Boyd Sullivan to be camped out near, and they've been well-monitored by police recently. We're good to go."

They took his truck and left her car parked in front of Sunny Seeds, still surrounded by people on the sidewalk, gawking, gossiping and demanding answers that neither of them had.

"I'm guessing you know about the blog?" Maisy asked after a long moment.

"I do." He nodded. "I know about the letter the parents wrote too and the calls to the base commander."

"And you know about Frank Golosky's brother, Drew?" she asked softly.

"I do." He nodded gravely. "I was questioned about it this morning."

She should've known he would be. "Is it possible he's the 'hurt man' Allie has been talking about?"

"I don't see how that could be possible. Allie's been having these nightmares for weeks," Chase said. He eased the truck to a stop at a stop sign and glanced at her. "Are you okay?"

"Not really," she said. "I just want a break from all this—from the fear, the suspicion and the panic. It's like we've been in perpetual crisis mode for months, and I just want it to stop."

"I understand," he said. He reached over and brushed her hand. "So let's give ourselves a break, just for today, and let ourselves have fun."

"I'd like that." She felt a smile cross her lips. Then she glanced up at the rearview mirror at the little girl in the back seat. "And how do you think we should have fun on our picnic, Allie?"

She listened as Allie chatted happily about all the random and interesting thoughts going through her mind. Chase drove them through the checkpoint gates and off the base. She directed them to her little bungalow and felt an odd mixture of nerves and pride as she invited them into her home, with its brightly colored walls and beautifully messy framed artwork by former students. They set up shop in her sunny yellow kitchen, where she turned on the radio to something upbeat, put a brightly handled picnic basket on the kitchen table and filled the counter with breads, cheeses, cold cuts and vegetables. She left Chase and Allie to get started making a picnic and went to get changed.

"Maisy's happy," Allie chirped as Maisy turned the corner into the hall. "I like it when Maisy is happy!"

"Me too," Chase said.

Joy swelled in Maisy's heart like an old friend that she'd thought she'd lost forever. She was truly and deeply happy in a way she never thought she'd feel again.

Lord, how can I be happy when my world is falling apart? How can I feel this happy when all our lives are in crisis and the base is under a constant shroud of fear? How can both joy and sadness—hope and fear—coexist inside my heart?

She emerged a few minutes later, in well-worn jeans, a short-sleeved blue plaid shirt and a pink bandanna holding back her hair. Her eyes ran over the mess that man and child had made of her usually pristine kitchen. Chase's mouth opened and then closed again. His hand ran over his head and his face reddened slightly.

"Are you all right?" she said. "Look, if it's about the mess, don't worry about it. It won't take us long to clean if we work together."

"It's not the kitchen," Chase said. His shoulders straightened. "You just look really good. Better than good. Beautiful."

The feelings that crowded her heart swelled so suddenly she gasped to breathe. Did he have any idea how attractive she found him? How impressive he was in her eyes? Not just the outer shell, with his broad chest and strong arms, his kind mouth and the way his green eyes dazzled like a lake in the sun. But the way he cared for his daughter. The way he held his head high and didn't let himself fall into either anger or self-pity the way so many other men would in his situation. The way he'd come to her rescue when she'd needed a hero, if even just for a day.

"You look im-por-tant," Allie added.

Maisy smiled.

"Thank you," she said, pulling her eyes away from the father and focusing on the daughter. She reached into her pocket and pulled out a second bandanna. "I was wondering if you'd like to wear one of these too. I thought we could match."

"Yes!" Allie wriggled off the chair and ran toward her. Gently, her fingers brushed Allie's curls back behind her ears, her heart suddenly aching for the toddler. They sang silly songs as they cleaned the kitchen and packed the last of the food. It was a half-hour drive to the trails and yet, there was something about being there in Chase's truck with him and Allie that seemed to make the drive fly by.

When they reached the trails and climbed out of the truck, Chase clipped the lead on Queenie's harness, slung the picnic basket over his shoulder and then, to her surprise, reached for Maisy's hand. His fingers brushed hers. Her hand slipped instinctively into his. Then Chase seemingly caught himself and pulled away. "Sorry... I wasn't... I didn't..."

"Don't worry about it," she said. "I'm a preschool teacher. Somebody's always grabbing my hand."

But even as she said the lighthearted words, her heart skipped a beat to realize just how natural the movement had been for her too.

"I like holding hands!" Allie announced, stepping in between them. She grabbed her father with one hand

and Maisy with the other, holding them tightly, like the tiny link joining them.

Maisy squeezed her hand gently. "Thank you, Allie. I like holding hands with you too."

They walked through the trees and down the wide path, exploring rocks, stumps and the streams that were all but dried up in Texas's July sun. When that sun had risen high in the sky, they reached the bottom of the waterfall, spread Chase's old military blanket and Maisy's quilt side by side under a canopy of trees and shared a happy, simple meal together.

There was a four-foot tall lean-to made of criss-crossed sticks propped up nearby that looked like it had been made by a previous family with small children. After Chase had checked it thoroughly, making sure it was well-constructed and clean of debris, he agreed to Allie's pleas to let her play house inside it. Queenie lay across the entrance, her eyes closed and ears twitching at every happy noise the child made. Maisy reached into the picnic basket and pulled out a spare set of plastic cutlery and dishes. Then she pretended to tap on the side of Allie's hut. "Knock, knock."

Allie's head popped out. "Can I help you?"

Maisy pressed her lips together to keep from laughing. "I was wondering if you'd like these."

Allie's eyes grew wide. Her arms stretched out to take all of the dishes at once. Maisy carefully helped arrange everything in her tiny hands. Allie beamed and disappeared back into her hut.

"What do you say?" Chase called.

"Thank you, Maisy!"

Maisy laughed. So did Chase. He sat down on the blanket and leaned back against a log.

"She's amazing," Maisy said. She carefully put the lids back on the plastic containers and placed them back in her basket. "I can't imagine anyone not wanting to—" Her hands rose to her lips, feeling herself catch the words before they flew out of her mouth.

I can't imagine anyone not wanting to be her mother.

"What were you going to say?" Chase asked.

"Never mind." She knelt on the blanket and closed the picnic basket. "I was going to say something that's really none of my business."

"Maybe I want you in my business." He leaned forward and grabbed her hands.

She slid her fingers from his grasp. "I will listen to anything you want to tell me, Chase. But I'm not going to pry."

"Fair enough." He sat back. "I was hoping you were going to ask me about Allie's mother. Because I've been wanting to talk to you about her, but I'm not exactly good at opening up."

She sat beside him and stretched her short legs out next to his long ones. "What happened?"

"I heard somewhere once that we only accept as much love from other people as we think we deserve," he said. "I don't know if that's true. But I think I always knew on some level that there was something wrong with my relationship with Liz. It was as if she didn't like the person I was, that if she nitpicked me enough she could turn me into the man she wanted me to be. But her criticisms made me shut down even more. Our marital problems drove me back to church, to my faith in God and to dedicating myself to being the kind of man God wanted me to be. But Liz went the other direction. We tried counseling and she very reluctantly agreed to try for a child, I think, because she was surprised to realize how strong my feelings were about being a father. She said it was the first thing she really believed I cared about."

He glanced over to where Allie was happily playing in her makeshift house.

"She got pregnant when I was home on leave," he said, "then while I was stationed back in Afghanistan, she fell in love with somebody else. The marriage was over before Allie was born and Liz hasn't ever tried to see her since then. Her new husband didn't want to help raise another man's child, so I got full custody. I can't regret my relationship with Liz, because if it weren't for her, I wouldn't have Allie. But I worry I'm not a good enough dad to her. Westley told me last night that if the mess my life is in doesn't get cleared up soon, I might lose Queenie, and as much as I love my career, the worst part about it will be telling Allie. She'll be devastated."

Maisy grabbed his hand and squeezed it so tightly he blinked.

"You're an amazing dad, Chase," she said. "You have the biggest heart when it comes to her and it shines through your eyes. I don't think love like that can be faked. I really don't."

She held his hand for one long heartbeat. Then she let go and leaned back again, her shoulder just barely brushing his.

"I don't know what your father was like growing up," Chase said. "But he reminded me a lot of my grandfather. Grandpa was former military intelligence and moved in with us when my father was stationed overseas. He was a firm believer in controlling your emotions and not letting anything get to you, ever. I broke my leg when I was four and he gave me this big stack of comics in the hospital. He told me that I was a hero like them and that heroes never cried."

"Jesus cried at Lazarus's tomb," Maisy said. "I know my father cried when my mother died. He hid it from me, but I could tell. He'd go for long runs through the ravine alone and when he came back, his eyes would be red."

"Maisy, you've got to believe me when I say I have no idea how your father's cross turned up at my house," Chase said. "I would never do anything to hurt your father. I would never knowingly hurt anyone. I wouldn't. I couldn't."

Tears pricked at the edges of her eyelids. Her heart believed him, just like her heart was convinced that he'd never do anything that would risk hurting his child. But her brain just had too many unanswered questions.

If Chase was innocent, then why hadn't Justin cleared his name? Was it possible that Boyd Sullivan was the "bad man" who haunted Allie's nightmares? If so, who was the "hurt man" and how had Allie become so frightened?

"I've never told anybody this," he added. "But when I was in junior high, I was on the school wrestling team and I accidentally broke a smaller guy's fingers. Everyone knew it was an accident. But it was a wake-up call to me that I always had to be careful, because someone my size could hurt someone smaller without meaning to. I had a hard time forgiving myself and I never let myself forget that I had a responsibility to use my strength to help, not hurt."

She nestled closer to him, until her shoulder, her arm and the back of her hand were all brushing against him. Then their fingers gently, slowly touched.

"Maisy," Chase said softly. "I promise you, I will do everything in my power to protect you and keep you from ever being hurt, by me or anyone else, ever again."

Tears welled suddenly at the edges of her eyes, spilling down her cheeks. She wasn't even sure why she was crying. All she knew was that all her life she'd waited to hear a man say something like that to her, and he was the first.

"My father was a good man," Maisy said, "and I know he must've loved me. But he was walled off too, especially after my mother died. I have no memories of him hugging me or telling me he was proud of me. I never thought he liked who I was."

Suddenly, the need for a hug was stronger than her need to hold back. Her arms slid around his neck. His arms wrapped around her back. He held her, tightly, hugging her to his chest.

"Hey, it's okay," he whispered. His cheek brushed against the top of her head. "Trust me, Maisy. Your father loved you."

"So everybody keeps telling me," she said. She let her head fall against his shoulder. The scent of him filled her senses. "How can you possibly know?"

"Because I still remember the day I first laid eyes on you," he said. He pulled back, just enough that she could look in his eyes. "I asked Frank Golosky who the beautiful blond dynamite girl was reading by the mess hall. He laughed and said you were Clint Lockwood's daughter and that guys like me shouldn't stare too long if we valued our hide, because your father would kill anyone who so much as looked at you funny. He said your father would've protected you over his own career if it came to that. So I needed to get in my head fast that the most gorgeous person I'd ever laid eyes on was off-limits to normal grunts like me."

"Really?" Her eyes grew wide. "So that's why no nice guys ever asked me out? Because they were afraid of my father?"

"Probably some of them," he admitted. His hands tightened around her. "But the smart ones had to know they weren't good enough for you. You deserve the best, Maisy. You really do. You can't imagine how many times I've looked at you and wished I could be the kind of man you deserve."

She leaned toward him. The gap between them closed. Then their lips touched, softly and gently, and she wasn't sure if he kissed her or if she kissed him. It was like they'd just been swept toward each other by the same invisible current. But here she was, feeling Chase's arms around her and his lips on hers.

His phone rang, loud and shrill in his pocket, with an urgency that demanded to be heard. They sprang apart. "Hello. McLear here."

He stood. So did she. Her eyes darted to the wooden shelter. Allie was still playing happily inside, babbling to herself.

Maisy breathed a sigh of relief. What had she been thinking? What if Allie had seen?

"Got it," Chase said. "It'll take me about an hour,

but I'll be there." He hung up and turned to Maisy. "That was Master Sergeant James. He wants me to come to the K-9 training center immediately."

The sun had started its descent in the afternoon sky as Chase pulled the truck back onto the base. Hiking back down had taken longer than he'd expected, thanks to Allie's unwillingness to leave her new "tree home." Then she'd fallen asleep in the back seat of the truck, leaving an odd, uncomfortable silence filling the front seat between him and Maisy, as if the memory of the kiss they'd shared had spread a field of invisible landmines between them.

Had that really happened? Had he really held Maisy Lockwood in his arms and kissed her? It felt like a dream, one that he was afraid to wake up from. He wondered if he should apologize, and yet she'd kissed him back. She'd clung to him just as tightly as he'd held her.

"I'll drop you off at Sunny Seeds, so you can pick up your car," he said. "Then I'll head to the training center."

"I'll watch Allie," Maisy said. "I'll take her into Sunny Seeds with me. I told Imogene I'd drop back later in the day to pick up a few personal things and make sure I left Esther and the supply teacher some notes about the class."

It was a plan that made sense and one for which he was grateful.

"Okay," he said. He had no idea what Westley wanted, but he couldn't shake the threat hanging over his head of losing Queenie. It was like the phone call had sucked all the hope from his heart and the oxygen from his lungs, leaving him with nothing but the nagging questions he didn't begin to have answers to.

How was he ever going to find Ajay Joseph, barring flying to Afghanistan personally and searching the mountains for his village? If Ajay had been so concerned about possible theft in his crew, why had he just dropped the issue? Yes, he'd emailed to say he was mistaken and no crime had been committed. Plus, there'd been a family emergency. But he'd seemed so distraught about it when they'd talked. Captain Dennis's email said that Ajay had left his job as a civilian liaison and Ajay hadn't even called Chase to explain the mix-up and follow up about the files he'd emailed. None of it squared with how dedicated he knew Ajay was to his men. The thought of putting in another call to Captain Reardon or even popping by her office niggled at the back of his mind. She and Captain Dennis had always seemed close. Perhaps she could urge him to dig deeper? Yet, her warning that anyone who came too near Chase was at risk of having his or her reputation tarred gave him pause. What Maisy was going through was all too much evidence that she'd been right.

Then there was the matter of Preston's personal vendetta against him, who the figure in the hood was who'd tried to kidnap Allie and why a respected captain like Justin Blackwood hadn't yet figured out who the person was who'd framed him. Thoughts leaped in his brain like sizzling bacon fat and he couldn't get anywhere close to finding answers without someone he cared about getting burned.

The lights were off and the parking lot was empty when he pulled up in front of Sunny Seeds. The crowd had moved on, for now.

"There's a bed in a side room just off the main office," Maisy said. "She can nap there."

He cradled his sleeping daughter to his chest, carried Allie up to the preschool and waited while Maisy unlocked the doors. She led them through the darkened and silent preschool, into the small room he guessed was an infirmary. She gestured to a child-sized bed. "You can lay her down there."

He eased his daughter from his arms, brushed a kiss on the top of her head and turned to Maisy.

"Thank you," he whispered. "I don't know what Westley wants, but I'm hoping I won't be long."

"Bad man! Hurt man! No!" Allie's panicked wail shook the silence, tearing his heart in half.

He turned back. But Maisy was one step ahead of him.

"It's okay, Allie, you're safe." Maisy dropped down to the bedside. She glanced up at Chase and waved a hand to indicate he could go. "It's okay. She's still asleep. It's just a nightmare. I've got this."

Didn't she hear his daughter's terrified wail? Didn't she see the hidden pain shaking her little body? Maisy began to sing tenderly to his daughter, a simple little song about sowing the seeds of faith. Her fingers ran gently down Allie's arms. As he watched, his little girl's cries faded and she nestled into Maisy's arms.

"It's okay, Chase," Maisy said again, her voice barely rising about a whisper. "You can go. I'll take care of her."

A lump formed in his throat as he watched Maisy cradle his daughter. It was like, for the first time, he was seeing something he'd always wanted but never thought he'd find. The longing of hundreds of lonely days and empty nights crashed over him.

He walked slowly out of the preschool, with Queenie at his heels, and drove home to get changed into his uniform. Two television news vans were parked in front of his house. He pulled into the driveway past a handful of people, who by the looks of things were both reporters and random gawkers waiting around, hoping for a show. He wondered if they'd left Sunny Seeds when they discovered Maisy had left on vacation or if they'd stuck around all day, until school ended and the last of the staff had left for the day.

He clipped Queenie's lead on her harness, got out of the truck and shut the door so hard the vehicle shook. The anonymous blogger had spilled the can of worms that up to that point hadn't spread too far beyond base gossip. After almost four months of deaths and fear, the blogger had finally given the world what it wanted—a prime suspect.

He walked through the gauntlet of people shouting questions and pointing cameras at his face, went into his home, got changed into his uniform and then repeated the same walk back to his truck, keeping his head high and his composure in place. Then he drove through the base to the K-9 training center. One of the news vans followed immediately. He wondered if the other one eventually would too or if they'd continue to stake out his house. A deep, sad sigh moved through his body.

He hated this whole mess and could only pray he'd eventually find a way out.

A dozen memories clashed inside him as he eased his truck into the familiar lot in front of the K-9 training center. He remembered what it had felt like the first time he'd driven there, for his initial interview with Westley to see about joining the team, and the hope that had filled his heart. He remembered the excitement and challenge of coming day after day for training, and those seemingly endless days after his training had been completed when he'd waited to find out if he'd been assigned a dog. Then the elating moment he'd gotten the call from Westley, telling him there was a little beagle named Queenie he wanted Chase to meet. He remembered the day he and Queenie had shown up to train, only to be sent back home again on suspension.

When the engine stopped, he rested his hands on the steering wheel and prayed, asking God for help as worries welled up inside him. Then he led Queenie across the parking lot before the reporters had made it out of their van. Queenie's ears perked. Her footsteps quickened until he could tell she was fighting the urge to tug him toward the building. She loved her K-9 training so much; it would be unfair of him to stand in her way if she was able to get another trainer.

He texted Westley. The former head trainer came and met him by the door, with Dakota by his side. The two men exchanged greetings and salutes.

"Thank you for coming," Westley said. Chase expected him to lead him into either the kennels or the offices. Instead, Westley turned and led him toward the veterinary building next door. "Who's watching your daughter?"

"Maisy," Chase said. "She and I went hiking with Allie today. I'm sorry for not being here sooner. It took me a lot longer to get back than I expected."

Westley cut him a sideways glance and his eyebrows rose. Then they walked for another long minute, as if the K-9 trainer was weighing his words.

"Two more of the lost dogs, which Boyd Sullivan let out of the kennels in April, were found late last night," he said, after a long moment. "We've suspected that the dogs that are still missing are either injured or have PTSD, because otherwise they would've returned to the base by now."

He stopped in front of a glass window and pointed. Chase looked through. There, huddled together on a soft bed of blankets were two German shepherds. The larger of the two had been shaved on one side and dark stitches showed stark against the skin. The smaller dog had a cast on her leg and was shaking so hard Chase felt sympathy ricochet through his bones.

"Julius is the big one with the black fur and Penelope is the one who's a mixture of brown and black," Westley said, and Chase was surprised that he could keep his voice so level. "They're both Afghanistan service dogs. Apparently, they stuck together. Penelope was a bomb-sniffing dog, who survived a shell attack on the field and had pretty bad PTSD as a result. Our head vet, Captain Kyle Roark, thinks she broke her leg during their escape from the kennels in April. Our best guess is that Julius looked out for her, protected her and brought her food. Not sure where he got the injuries, but they were pretty deep and seem to be from some kind of wild animal attack. Searchers found him first and he was unwilling to leave her. It was touch and go for a while if Penelope would have to lose her leg, but it looks like she came through surgery like a champ."

Chase felt his hand ball into a fist.

These dogs were United States Air Force service members. They were partners. They saved the lives of men and women in uniform.

How could anyone believe he'd have anything to do with this?

He could feel the emotional weight of it all bearing down on him. Allie was having nightmares. Maisy's life had been thrown into chaos. Queenie was missing out on her training. Reporters had shown up at his home. And now, seeing these two beautiful and majestic dogs recovering from such injuries was one thing more that he could not bear.

He closed his eyes tightly and prayed, as he fought to maintain composure.

How much longer, Lord? How long do I have to withstand this? When will this trial be over? When will my salvation come?

Westley's voice dug at him like a knife. "Did you help Boyd Sullivan do this?"

"Of course not!" Chase slapped the wall, feeling the sting of his bare hand on the plaster. Despite what his grandfather might have drilled into him as a little boy, sometimes heroes didn't maintain their composure, as Maisy had reminded him by pointing out that Jesus cried. Well, Jesus had gotten emotional and shouted too sometimes.

"I don't know if you brought me here to accuse me, trick me or try to trap me!" Chase turned and faced Westley full-on. "But I give you my word, as a man, an airman and a father, that I had absolutely nothing to do with what happened to those beautiful animals. I love and respect my country, my uniform, the men, women and canines I serve alongside, and my own daughter too much to ever do anything to help Boyd Sullivan."

"What if he threatened you?" Westley crossed his arms. "Or blackmailed you?"

Chase's chin rose. "Then I'd sooner face it head-on than do anything that made me ashamed to look my daughter in the eye."

Silence spread between the two men, long and deep, like that of two airmen, weapons at the ready in no man's land, trying to determine who was friend and who was foe.

Then Westley's shoulders relaxed.

"I'm recommending a reassessment of Queenie at the end of next week," he said. "Then we can determine if Queenie needs to restart any of her training, and if she should be reassigned. I'm hoping the matters you're dealing with will be resolved by then. It appears you and she have a solid connection and it would be good if you could stay partners."

Did this mean Westley believed he was innocent? Or that he was at least willing to give him the benefit of the doubt? Either way, it was a bigger vote of confidence than he'd felt in a while.

"Thank you," he said. "Hopefully this will all be over soon."

"Hopefully," Westley agreed. They walked back through the building, with his Queenie trotting on one side and Westley's Dakota on the other.

"One more thing," Westley said as they reached the door. "Maisy is like family to Felicity and me. There are a lot of us who would hate to see anyone hurt her."

"Yes, sir." Chase nodded. "Believe me, I would hate to see her hurt as well."

"It's good we understand each other."

Chase waited in the entranceway to the building for a long moment after Westley had walked away and braced himself, hoping he wouldn't have to face a fresh throng of reporters outside. Then he stepped outside, glanced at his truck and frowned. A second news van had joined the first one. Four reporters, two with cameras, clustered around his truck. Thankfully, they didn't seem to have noticed him yet and he didn't much feel like walking past them. Hopefully, the fact that they'd followed him here meant they were no longer staking out his house. He was only a twenty-minute walk from Sunny Seeds. If he left his truck at the training center, walked to pick up Allie and walked her home, he might be able to slip in his back door before the phalanx of reporters caught up with him again. Of course, then he'd have the problem of how to come back and pick his truck up later. But he could only handle one thing at a time and right now, something inside him was itching to just walk and clear his head.

He turned sharply and led Queenie between the K-9 training center and veterinary building, then started strolling through the quiet base backstreets. To his left lay the church where he'd sat in the back during Maisy's father's funeral in April, his heart twisting in knots as he'd seen the tears in Maisy's eyes, and the training facilities where he'd sweated through basic training many years earlier, all while those same dazzling blue eyes did a number on his heart. Just like the memory of kissing Maisy by the waterfall was making that same sorry heart beat something fierce inside his chest now.

He cut right and walked along the perimeter fence that separated the base from the woods. He'd never imagined it was even possible to miss someone who he'd spent the day with and seen just an hour ago. And yet, he missed Maisy, as if a part of his own heart was hers. Would reporters be camped outside her home too? How would she feel when she woke up in the morning and had no job to go to, and gossip reporters questioning if she'd helped her own father's killer?

Ahead loomed the large warehouse complex that housed equipment, weapons, vehicles and supplies to be shipped by truck, plane and boat to Afghanistan. He'd once had an office in the very middle of that complex before he'd started his K-9 training, when he was still responsible for ensuring the security of shipments. His former boss, Captain Jennifer Reardon, worked in there now. Would she still be in her office? Had she had any progress in accessing Ajay Joseph's files? It was a shot in the dark. But sometimes that was the only type of shot left to take.

He turned and led Queenie toward the building. They entered the comforting coolness of the warehouse. A block of offices sat deep inside the expansive building with large windows looking out into the warehouse, as if someone had plucked a single floor off a regular office building and dropped it in the middle of a sea of forklifts, equipment and loading bays. The building was mostly empty, but even as he passed, the few airmen and support staff that were still on the floor seemed to avert their gaze. What would he have seen if he'd looked in their faces? Suspicion? Doubt? Hostility? Or just confusion? Was this how it would always be? Walking through his former life like a ghost of the man he used to be?

He reached the offices. Captain Reardon's light was

still on. Through the half-pulled blinds of her huge office window, he could see two figures. Looked like she was in a meeting.

His footsteps paused a few paces from her office door. He'd wait.

A yip dragged his attention back down to his feet. Queenie tugged hard on her leash and whimpered with that little whine of impatience that told him she smelled something important and wanted to go search for it. She'd been like that when he'd first started training her. He'd had to drill into her that she only searched on command and not whenever she smelled something she thought she was supposed to find. Beagles had one of the best noses for tracking and he knew they could tracks things over long distances. But he couldn't imagine how many laptops, computers, cell phones and electronic storage devices were in these offices, not to mention the warehouse. Did this mean she was forgetting her training already? He could only hope all the progress she'd made wouldn't be lost because of him.

"Leave it," he said. "When we get home, we can train."

She tugged harder, pulling him toward Captain Reardon's office door. She looked up at him, eager and impatient. Then she howled, with a yelp that was a mixture of urgency and excitement.

The office blind moved back. The calm, calculating gaze of Captain Justin Blackwood met his through Captain Reardon's office window. So, at least one of the men investigating him was in his former boss's office. Queenie's howls grew louder and sharper, echoing through the warehouse. More faces appeared at other office windows now, making him feel like even more of a spectacle. Justin's eyebrows rose, just as heat rose to the back of Chase's neck. His cell phone began to ring, its tinny sound combining with the cacophony of his frantic dog.

He glanced at the screen. It was Maisy.

"Come on." He tugged Queenie's lead. "We'll go wait for Captain Reardon outside."

The phone stopped ringing. He suspected the call had dropped. Cell phone reception had always been lousy in the warehouse, not that Maisy would be able to hear him anyway, with Queenie kicking up a fuss. Queenie was still yipping as he firmly led her back through the warehouse toward the exit.

What had he been thinking just showing up at her office like that? He'd probably shot whatever remaining credibility he had with Captain Blackwood by showing what little control he had over his canine. He slipped back outside into the evening light and leaned against the wall. Queenie had gone quiet. He looked down. Her ears drooped.

"What was that all about?" he asked. "What did you smell that was so important?"

His phone started ringing again. He answered. "Hello?"

"Hey, Chase." Maisy's voice was faint and yet something about it sent warmth spreading through his core. "Allie's awake and I'm done here. I was wondering when you were going to be back and if you wanted me to figure out something for dinner. I could take Allie back to my place and cook us something."

Did she have any idea how much he'd have enjoyed that? He was less than a ten-minute walk from Sunny Seeds now. He could probably run it in under five.

"Thanks for the offer, but I'll be there soon to take her home," he said. "There were reporters in front of my house and the K-9 training center. So you might want to keep the curtains shut and plan to have someone accompany you home tonight."

"Okay." There was something tentative about her voice, like she was trying to hide disappointment. "I'll see you later."

"See you soon." He ended the call.

Evening breezes brushed the trees beyond the perimeter fence. The memory of the feel of Maisy in his arms quickened his pulse. He should've never let them get that close. She'd been sad, they'd both been vulnerable and something inside had drawn them together, like two survivors of the same storm. And now she was stuck to the pieces of his broken heart, and the longer it took before they yanked apart and went their separate ways, the harder it would be.

The blow came out of nowhere, striking him on the back of his skull so hard he felt his knees buckle. The ground rushed toward him. Instinctively, he dropped Queenie's leash as he fell, barely managing to curl into a protective front roll as his body tumbled over the pavement. He leaped up and spun back with his hands raised ready to fight.

A panicked yelp filled his ears and his eyes caught a figure in a dark hoodie disappear down the alley, the frightened beagle clutched to their chest.

Someone was kidnapping Queenie.

ELEVEN

The figure darted around the corner as Queenie's panicked howls filled the air.

"Hey! Stop!" Chase ran after them.

There was no way he was going to let anyone get away with hurting his canine partner. He sprinted around the corner into a side alley, just in time to hear a yelp of pain and a car door slam. A hooded figure in a baseball cap leaped in the door of a small compact car. Queenie's frantic barks sounded from inside the vehicle. The small dog clawed at the passenger window. Chase's heart pounded.

No! The single thought beat through his chest, spurring his legs to move faster. They were not going to hurt Queenie. The vehicle sped down the alley with Queenie inside, howling and yelping for his help. Whoever they were, whatever they wanted, they were not going to get his dog. She was his partner. He was going to protect her with his life. The vehicle darted right and through the empty backstreets, racing down Canyon's back road. His feet pounded down the pavement. The driver swerved wildly, fighting to keep the vehicle straight. Seemed Queenie was putting up a fight. He ran after it, pushing his body past the breaking point, even as he knew he'd never catch up with the car on foot. Where could they go? Where could they hide? The vehicle turned sharply, and suddenly he realized they were making a run for the back perimeter fence. The fastest route there mapped in his mind. The vehicle would have to slow around cement barriers and speed bumps before it reached the perimeter. If he stayed on foot, he could cut them off. He was going to save his dog. He was going to stop this vehicle. He ducked through a back alley, zigzagging through an empty cut through, then he hopped over a short wall and sprinted for the fence.

He stopped, panting and looking down the empty road ahead. The vehicle was nowhere to be seen. He'd been wrong. He'd lost the car and Queenie along with it. He groaned, agony filling his prayer. *Help me, Lord, what do I do? How do I find her?*

A vehicle shot around the corner. A dark hood masked the figure's face. Queenie howled furiously and victoriously, as if she knew Chase was ahead, waiting for her. Without any further thought to his own safety, he leaped in front of the car. The driver hit the brakes. The vehicle spun as tires screeched.

The car crashed through the perimeter fence, rolling and tumbling as it fell down the incline into the ravine forest below, landing in a pond.

Chase's feet stumbled to a stop. The empty hole of the broken fence loomed ahead of him. Justin had warned him the next time he stepped through that fence without permission it could cost him his freedom. But what mattered more? His freedom or his canine partner's life?

He leaped through the fence and scrambled down the hill toward where the vehicle was sinking into the murky water. He kicked off his boots and yanked his phone from his pocket, thankful that Captain Blackwood's number was still near the top of his recent call list.

"Good afternoon, Captain Blackwood—"

"It's Chase," he interrupted. "I'm outside the perimeter fence. Southwest side. Behind the warehouses. Saving my canine partner's life."

He dropped the phone in his boot on the shore and plunged into the pond. Queenie's panicked howls sounded over the water. She was trapped in the car. It was going under. He splashed through sharp rocks and murky weeds, then he dove under and started swimming hard for the car. Before he could reach it, the door flew open. The hooded figure dove out, their soggy form thrashing furiously against the water as they swam for the far shore. The driver's-side door hung open and water rushed through.

But Queenie didn't follow. Her frantic yelps grew desperate as the car dropped like a stone. The figure was getting away. If he didn't stop them now, he might never know why they were terrorizing him. He might never be able to clear his name or get his life back.

But if he went after them, Queenie would drown.

There was no choice. He had to save his partner. He dove under, his powerful limbs propelling him toward the car. He grabbed the doorway and pushed himself inside, even as he felt it drop deeper underwater. Queenie swam herself into his arms, her paws scrambling against his biceps. He ran his hand along her harness and realized why she couldn't swim. She'd been left there buckled into the seat belt. The injustice and cruelty of that swept through his chest like adrenaline. He fumbled for her lead, unclipped her and then pushed her past him, sending her body up toward the surface. He swam upward, as the car disappeared beneath him, and surfaced beside Queenie. The hooded figure was scrambling away deeper into the ravine, until they disappeared from view. Queenie licked his face furiously as he swam alongside her to shore.

"It's okay," he said. "You're a good dog. You're such a good dog. I've got you now."

But the criminal who'd kidnapped her and terrorized his life was getting away, and with them the last hope he had to save his life and clear his name.

"The little black cat likes milk too," Allie said, guiding the plastic animal into the blockhouse she and Maisy had built on the Sunny Seeds play table. So far, five people and sixteen animals had gathered around the sprawling meal that Allie had concocted. Maisy knelt beside her on the carpet, pulled figures and plastic food from the bins and set them on the table, as Allie seriously considered each one in turn. "White bear likes cookies. Baby wants cupcakes."

Maisy's eyes rose to the clock. It had been half an hour since she'd heard from Chase. Allie had woken up with that kind of boundless, happy energy that only little children seemed to have, and Maisy had found herself needing to fight hard to keep at bay the tears that had been pricking at her eyes. If she hadn't promised Chase that she'd meet him here, she'd have put her spare car seat in her car and taken Allie home.

She needed to get out of Sunny Seeds. She needed

to be somewhere safe, where she belonged. Every inch and corner of the preschool held another reminder of the faceless mob in the anonymous blogger's comment section, demanding she lose her job. She'd read the blog again, including all 213 comments. The level of gossip that people were willing to spread about a total stranger was so hateful and vicious it broke her heart. It wasn't just herself, but first Zoe and then Chase, who had also been tried and sentenced by social media. Knowing that made the pain in her heart burn with such a righteous anger that when he'd told her there might be reporters outside her home, she'd wanted to rush home with her head held high and confront them.

Clint Lockwood's daughter never backed down from a fight. Now, here she was feeling trapped in the one place she didn't want to be, waiting on a man. It was an uncomfortable feeling. But something about Allie's voice, happily chirping beside her as she set up her imaginary party, helped her hold it together.

"How about the airman?" Maisy asked, holding up a figure in camouflage. Normally, the military figures were the most popular toys in the classroom and she practically spent all day refereeing how they were shared. She had to admit there was something fun about having the classroom all to themselves. "Do you think he'd like to sit next to the firefighter or the bunny?"

Allie wrinkled her nose. "No! He's a bad man."

"Members of the United States military are our heroes. It's their job to protect us and keep us safe." The reassuring words flew automatically from Maisy's lips. It wasn't the first time one of her students had reacted badly to a toy or a picture of someone in uniform, just like a student occasionally was afraid of things like dogs, snakes, cars or water. Her instinct was always to defuse the moment lovingly and with logic. "Airmen look out for us and protect us. They're good men and women, like your daddy."

"No! That man is a bad man!" Allie yelled the words with such force it rocked Maisy back on her heels. Her little hand rose in the air as if trying to swat it from Maisy's fingers. "He is a very bad man! Bad man hurt man!"

Something about the toy airman clearly terrified her. Once again FBI special agent Oliver Davison's words that Boyd Sullivan had stolen Drew Golosky's uniform and identification flickered at the back of her mind, sending fresh doubts creeping up Maisy's spine. She only had Chase's word that Allie had been having nightmares about the "bad man" for months, and her terror was so strong and so visceral Maisy would've almost thought Allie had witnessed a crime with her own two eyes.

Was it possible, somehow, that Boyd Sullivan had actually been in Allie's home?

Her cell phone began to ring and Maisy quickly slid the airman figurine under the table and grabbed her phone. It was Chase on the caller ID.

"It's okay, sweetie," Maisy said gently. "We don't have to invite the airman to the party. I need to go talk on the phone for a minute. But I'll stay right in the doorway where you can see me, okay?"

"Okay." Allie's eyes met hers. She picked a small brown-and-white plastic dog up off the table. "I'm gonna play Doggy, Doggy!"

Maisy smiled. "How about you hide and I'll seek you, after I take this quick phone call?"

"Okay!" Allie smiled. She stood up. Then she waved at her with both hands. "Go! I hide with Doggy now!"

"Okay." She pretended not to notice as Allie dove under the clothing rack. Then she pushed the back door open and felt the delicious warmth of a late summer's afternoon on her limbs.

"Hey, Chase," she said as she answered the call. She braced her body against the door frame, leaving the door open, and pretending not to watch as Allie scampered from one hiding spot to another. "Your daughter just had a really bad reaction to an airman toy. She kept calling him a 'bad man.'"

Chase sighed deeply. "I wish I knew what any of that meant."

"I'm sure you'll figure it out," she said. She closed her eyes and listened to the trees dancing in the summer's breeze on one side and Allie's happy chirps on the other. "I can try to talk to her about it again. I've gotten really good at speaking kid."

"Thank you," he said. She could almost hear his weariness through the phone. "I'm only about a few minutes away right now, but I wanted to talk to you quickly before I get there. I ran into some trouble."

"What kind of trouble?" She heard sirens then, both in the phone and in the evening air around her. "What's going on? What happened?"

The sirens grew louder. She heard a rustle from behind her in the classroom and a giggle as Allie ran across the room and hid under the table.

"After I left the K-9 training center I decided to walk back to avoid the press," he said. "I stopped in at the warehouse where I used to work in the hopes of talking to my old boss. I was standing in a back alley when someone nearly knocked me down and then stole Queenie."

A gasp rose to Maisy's lips. "Oh, Chase…"

"It's okay," he said quickly. "I ran them down. They crashed through the fence and into a pond. I dove in after her. The figure got away. But Queenie's safe and squirming in my arms now."

Relief filled her chest. *Thank You, God.*

"This has to stop," Chase said. "My daughter, my canine partner, my career, my reputation, you…everything I care about has come under fire. One way or another, I have to stop this."

Two gloved hands clamped around Maisy's throat, throwing her hard against the door frame and knocking the phone from her hands as they stole the air from her lungs. A boot kicked the phone across the yard, cracking the screen and silencing Chase's voice. A hand clamped around her throat, strangling the air from her lungs.

"Get inside," a voice hissed in her ear as the hooded figure tried to shove her through the open door and into the Sunny Seeds classroom. The smell of damp fabric filled her senses. "Give me the girl and I'll let you live."

No! She would not let this criminal get anywhere near Allie.

Maisy kicked up hard, bracing one foot against the door frame as she kicked the door closed with all her might. *Please, Lord, make Chase call the police. Please keep Allie safe until they get here.* Maisy thrashed, trying to wrench herself free. Her attacker hit her, cuffing her on the side of the head. Pain shot through her skull. Bright points of light filled her view. She fell, landing on her hands and knees on the pavement. The figure stood, tall and slender in a plain black hoodie, and reached for the Sunny Seeds classroom door. One gloved hand turned the handle.

No! I can't let them hurt Allie! Please, Lord, please give me the strength I need to save her.

Desperately, Maisy lunged at the figure's knees, hoping to knock them off their feet. But her attacker spun back, shoving Maisy to the ground. She fell and tried to scream, but the figure jumped on her, choking the air from her lungs. Maisy grabbed the attacker's hands, fighting for her life against the stranglehold.

But she was too weak. Pain filled her lungs as prayers filled her mind, even as she felt the darkness sweep over and take hold.

There was nobody there. Nobody to help her. Nobody to save her.

Chase, I'm so sorry, I wasn't strong enough to protect Allie.

TWELVE

She felt her body go limp. The gloved hands fell from her throat and the attacker's weight left her body. She fell to the ground. Moments passed in a haze of darkness and pain before she heard the rattling and crash of her attacker trying to break into the classroom. How long would the door hold? How long until rescue came? Dizziness dragged her mind down into unconsciousness. She battled against it, fighting desperately to stay awake.

Then a shout filtered through the darkness in Maisy's mind. Somewhere on the edges of her unconsciousness she could hear a voice calling her name, strong and powerful, like a beacon, calling to her not to give up hope.

Chase...

A dog was howling, like the hound leading a brigade into battle. *Queenie!* She heard her attacker's footsteps scramble away and a second set of footsteps, larger, stronger and more powerful than her attacker's, pounding hard up the grassy slope and the sound of someone leaping clear over the playground fence.

Then she felt Chase by her side, cradling her,

holding her and pulling her into his arms. His hands stroked her hair. His fingers ran along the side of her face and down her bruised throat. She opened her eyes and looked into Chase's deep green gaze.

"Maisy. Baby." His voice was husky, as if he was battling a deeper emotion than his lungs and voice knew how to handle. "What happened? Are you okay? Where's Allie?"

"She's inside." She pointed weakly to the closed door. "Hiding. Safe."

Weakly, she reached past him and punched a security code into the keypad by the door. His lips brushed her forehead, as at the same time he pushed open the Sunny Seeds door. "Allie? Sweet Pea?"

"Daddy!" Allie ran toward them, the relieved smile on her lips battling the worry that filled her eyes. "I was hiding! Maisy didn't find me. Then the door closed with a really loud bang." She stopped and looked down. Her nose crinkled. She reached out and stroked Maisy's head. "You hurt, Maisy?"

"A little bit hurt, sweetie," Maisy said. She sat up. Chase took her hand and helped her to her feet. "But I'm okay."

She pulled her hand from Chase's fingers, but her legs wobbled so much she almost fell, and she felt Chase tighten his grip on her hand again. Allie grabbed her other hand and squeezed it so tightly, Maisy suspected she was holding it with all her might. Queenie pressed herself against Maisy's calf, in between her and Allie. Maisy stood there for a long moment, drinking in all their care and support, until she felt her head clear and her legs grow steady beneath her.

Then came the clatter of feet. She looked up as Security Forces charged around the corner of the school.

"Chase McLear!" Captain Blackwood called. Maisy watched as his hand twitched over the gun at his side, waiting to see if he needed to pull the trigger. "Kindly step away from the ladies. You and I need to talk."

She felt Chase's hand pull from hers and, instinctively, she swept Allie up into her arms and held her as Chase saluted. "Sir."

"You ran away from the scene of an accident, Airman," Justin said.

"Yes, sir, I did and I'm really glad you all ran after me. Maisy was in trouble. Thankfully, I was there to assist her in time."

Justin's eyes flicked to her face.

"Yes, Justin, he's telling the truth," she said, crossing her arms. "I was attacked. Someone tried to abduct Allie and when I fought them off, they almost strangled me. This is the second kidnap attempt Allie has survived—three, if you count the person we saw lurking in her bushes with a knife. She's been babbling on about a 'bad man' and a 'hurt man.' This child clearly knows something." She stepped forward. "You are my friend, Justin. I respect you deeply as a cop. I have always trusted your investigation into the Red Rose Killer without question. I always believed you would catch him in the end. But now I don't know what to think anymore."

The captain's eyes met hers, strong and unflinching, but nothing in their depths did anything to dispel the questions in her heart.

"Trust me, Maisy," Justin said. "We are pursuing every lead to the utmost of our abilities and capacities."

No, that was not the reassurance she sought. She wanted him to tell her that Chase wasn't a suspect. She wanted him to tell her what Allie was so afraid of and that nobody would hurt that precious child ever again.

"Now," Justin said, his gaze cutting to Chase's face, "I need to ask you to come with me for questioning. Do you need a few minutes to sort out what you're going to do with your daughter?"

"I'll take her to Zoe and Linc's house," Maisy said. "It's only a few blocks away. Freddy will be happy to see her, and we'll be safe there."

"Thank you," he said softly, his eyes conveying more than his words. He glanced at Justin. "Give me a moment?"

The captain nodded and took a step back. Chase slid his arm around Allie, hugging her with one arm, while the other hand brushed Maisy's shoulder. He leaned forward.

"When I'm done with Captain Blackwood, I'm taking Queenie and going back to the warehouse. I'm going to give her another opportunity to find that scent. I have a former colleague, named Captain Reardon, who knows the facilities even better than I do. I'll see if I can get her to meet me there." Then he pulled back. The look on his face felt somehow more intimate than the kiss they'd shared only a few hours before. "Be careful."

"You too."

"I will be." He took a deep breath and stepped back. "There's something else I need to tell you. I really appreciate you watching Allie tonight, but that's going to be the last time I ask you to watch her. I'm going to ask for authorization to move off base, and go home to my mother's until this investigation is done. I think it'll be better for Allie, and the cops can put me under surveillance there just as well as they can here. It'll dispel any worries that I'm helping Boyd Sullivan sneak on and off base, and it will relieve the pressure on you. No matter how this ends up, whether I'm charged, discharged or cleared, I'm going to request a transfer to another base. I just don't see a future for myself here. Not anymore. Not after this."

What was he saying? That he and the little girl she held in her arms were leaving her life forever? He kissed his daughter gently on the top of the head, turned and started across the playground toward Captain Blackwood.

Chase felt his shoulders straighten as he walked through the playground and across the parking lot, with Justin on one side and Queenie on the other. He didn't dare let himself turn back. The look in Maisy's eyes had tugged at something deep inside. He hated walking away from her. He hated losing the fledgling relationship they had just started to build. He didn't know what word to put to it. It went deeper than friendship, deeper than caring or than affection. But whatever it was clung to him, and wrapped around him like roots to a deeply planted tree. It pulled him to her and pulled her to him like an inexorable force. Whatever it was, he'd been denying the existence of it for a long, long time. In fact, he felt like he'd been denying it since the moment he'd first laid eyes on her.

And now, the only way to protect her was to snuff it out, deny it and pretend it never existed.

It wasn't until he reached Justin's vehicle that he realized the captain's eyes were on him, watching him with that familiar pensive look that Chase still didn't know what to make of.

"You really care about her, don't you?" he asked.

Was he really questioning whether or not Chase loved his daughter? No, that was one line too far. He'd had enough of this. Enough of being questioned, poked, prodded at and turned around again and again, until he didn't know which way was up.

"Sir," Chase said. "As I answer that, may I ask you a personal question?"

Justin blinked as if Chase had caught him by surprise, but he regained his composure almost immediately. "You may."

"Sir, you and I are both fathers," Chase said. His grandfather had taught him a wise man controlled his emotions and Maisy had reminded him that a good man let them flow. Well, maybe he could do both and direct the feelings filling his heart to show this captain once and for all the kind of man he was. "Yes, of course I care about my daughter. I love Allie with my life. I'm all she has after her mother left. I would never do anything to hurt her or put her in harm's way. I have been praying harder than you'll ever know that you'll realize the truth of that and turn your investigation to finding Boyd Sullivan's real accomplice. But for now, with all due respect, Captain, as a man and a father, with a daughter who you love, is there anything in the world that would tempt you to let a violent, controlling and self-entitled killer like Boyd Sullivan into her life?"

A long-drawn-out silence crackled between them. The intensity with which the captain stared at him and sized him up was so relentless Chase guessed it would make a weaker man crumble. Finally, Justin said, "No, Airman, I wouldn't let anyone or anything hurt my daughter, especially not a monster like Sullivan."

He'd hit on something that mattered to the captain and it showed.

"But I wasn't referring to your daughter," Justin added. His shoulders straightened again and the momentary blink of emotion Chase had seen disappeared from his eyes. "I was referring to Maisy Lockwood. Since we're talking personally, I've known Maisy for a very long time. I've never known her to be easily swayed or quick to give her affections away. In fact, I've often thought that she was as reserved and stubborn as her father, in her own very different way, and it would take a man quite a lot to make an impact."

Heat rose to the back of Chase's neck. "I'm sure it's just that she thinks I'm innocent and wants her father's killer caught, sir."

Justin crossed his arms. "Then you're not as smart as I thought you were, or you don't really know Maisy Lockwood."

They went to the station, with Queenie in tow, and once again, Preston was in charge of the interrogation. Justin stood impassively by the wall and watched as Preston fired questions at him, slamming the same horrible pictures down on the table, showing him the victims of Boyd Sullivan's crimes, the bodies, the blood, threatening notes and the red roses tucked under their arms. Preston delved into Chase's record as an airman, pulling at every thread of every tour of duty he'd ever been on. Then he went into Chase's personal life, tearing his most valued relationships to shreds one after another, starting with his mother, father and grandfather. He asked why Liz had left him for another man, whether Allie would be better off without him and if Chase was unfit to be anybody's husband or father.

It was the hardest and harshest of the interrogations Chase had withstood. It was like standing with his hands tied as an unrelenting boxer struck and jabbed at him, blow after blow, trying to knock him bloodied to the ground. All the while Chase sat there, head held high, his answers brief and his voice steady, praying with every breath that God would give him the power to withstand the onslaught.

Why didn't Justin step in and stop Preston? Surely, it was unprofessional for Preston to keep hammering him like that? And yet, the captain stood there in the doorway, without reaction, like a referee with his own reason not to stop the fight.

At least he'd been allowed to take Queenie with him to the interrogation room this time. Feeling his canine partner's reassuring warmth curled up by his ankle gave him a strength that he didn't know he had, encouraging him on, even as he knew his days with her were numbered.

He just prayed that when he left Canyon, Westley would help Queenie find the best possible new partner, someone who would respect, protect and value her, every bit as much as he did. She was a good dog who deserved an opportunity to train and serve her country to her highest potential. She didn't deserve to have Chase holding her back.

Finally, Preston ran out of questions and released him. This time Justin didn't bother warning him not to leave base without informing his office and Chase knew he was leaving Canyon one way or another. The investigation would follow him wherever he went. All he had to do was figure out how to say his goodbyes.

The sun had set below the skyline as he finally exited the building, and the depth of color peeking above the very edges of the horizon took his breath away, reminding him of Maisy. He checked his phone when he left the building. She'd texted him twice to say that she and Allie were happily settled at Linc and Zoe's house and had ordered pizza. A third text showed simply a picture of Allie and Freddy with Star. The desire to phone her, just to hear her voice, welled up inside him with an urgency that was almost painful.

Instead, he squared his shoulders and strode through base toward the warehouses. He dialed his former boss. She picked up on the first ring. "Captain Reardon."

"Hello, ma'am," he said. "It's Chase McLear."

She cleared her throat. "Good evening, Airman. I'm afraid it's not a good time to talk. It's been a rather tiring day."

"I know," he said, as quickly as he dared without actually cutting her off. "I dropped by the warehouse earlier, hoping I could talk to you about the email from Captain Dennis and accessing Ajay's video files, but Security Forces were in your office."

"I'm really sorry, Airman," she said. "But I can't help you. I've been questioned three times about my connection to you, as have several members of my team. Multiple reporters have called me. Our entire office and warehouse complex were searched late this afternoon by officers with K-9 dogs…"

The way Queenie had sounded the alarm when he'd been in the warehouse earlier niggled at the back of his mind. At the time, he'd assumed it was because her training was slipping. What if she'd been trying to tell him something? What if she'd actually smelled something she thought was important?

"Did they find anything?" he asked.

"No." She sounded almost startled by the question. "Of course not."

He guessed he shouldn't have been surprised by the answer. It was hard to imagine anyone stashing a body or illegal explosives in the warehouse. Then again, what if they hadn't sent an electronic-sniffer dog like Queenie?

"Anyway, Captain Dennis told me that several of his men in Afghanistan were interrogated over video call today," Captain Reardon continued, "including Airman Frank Golosky, who is currently mourning the loss of his brother." He winced, and she continued, "Both Captain Dennis and I have been warned by investigators that very serious charges are expected to be filed very shortly and that anyone associated with you could be forced to testify or even face charges themselves."

His breath caught like he'd just been punched in the chest. What charges? How soon would he be arrested? This week? Tomorrow?

Anyone associated with you could be forced to testify or even face charges themselves...

Her words echoed in his mind. Was that why Justin had questioned his feelings for Maisy? Because she would be compelled to testify? Because she was at risk of being charged as an accessory after the fact?

It was bad enough that Frank Golosky had been put through the wringer within hours of discovering his brother was dead. The idea of Maisy being hurt even further cut somewhere deeper inside him than he'd ever known was possible. He ran his hand over his head and prayed, *Oh, Lord, what have I done?*

"I'm so sorry for how you've all been impacted by this," he said, bracing himself for what he was about to ask. "But I was wondering if I could come in to talk to you in person? I don't know if you'd made any headway in accessing Ajay Joseph's video files, but maybe I could help look over the data you do have. He'd been concerned about some discrepancies in the transfer logs, and while he'd later assured me it was just a mistake on his end, maybe if I looked at those too, I might see something that would help back up my story. Also, my K-9 dog Queenie started howling when I dropped in to see you earlier. I don't know why, but maybe she smelled something..."

His words trailed off. He sounded so ridiculous. He sounded like a desperate man grasping at the flimsiest straws. But what other choice did he have?

There was a pause, much longer than he liked. He gritted his teeth and prayed.

"I'll be leaving my office in the next twenty minutes," Captain Reardon said, "and then I'll be locking the warehouses down until morning. If you're able to get here before I leave, we can talk briefly. But I can't promise you anything."

"I understand!" Fresh hope surged in his heart. "Thank you, ma'am. I'll be there soon."

Thank You, God!

"Come on, Queenie." He looked down at her hopeful and intelligent face. "We're going back to the warehouse."

He ended the call and sent Maisy a quick text, telling her that he was finished with the questioning and heading to the warehouses for a meeting with Captain Reardon. Then he broke into a jog. Man and dog ran together, past personnel and vehicles. He appreciated each breath of fresh air that filled his lungs and each step his foot made onto the pavement as if it could be his last as a free man.

Finally, he reached the warehouse. They stopped outside the cargo bay door. It was open. Queenie whined. He looked down. She sat expectantly at his feet with her head titled to the side and her intelligent brown eyes locked on his face, waiting for his command to search.

There was something in there she wanted them to find. He knew it with absolute certainty.

Captain Reardon wasn't going to be in her office waiting for him indefinitely. He was on thin ice with his former boss as it was. The logical thing to do was to ignore Queenie, go meet with Captain Reardon and then, after they spoke, ask her if it was okay to let Queenie search the expansive warehouse complex before it shut down for the day, and hope and pray she agreed.

And yet, he couldn't shake the feeling that Queenie really had smelled something on their last visit. Something Queenie had thought was urgent. But he hadn't listened to her. He'd been too quick to doubt her and blame himself for the fact that she was sounding off.

He reached down, ran his hand over her soft fur and scratched her behind the ears. She'd been such a good partner. She'd been loyal and patient, quick to listen and learn, and protective of his daughter, Allie. If this really was his last night as a free man, then maybe he should spend it listening to his partner and trying to decipher what Queenie had been trying to tell him.

"Show me, Queenie. Go search."

She howled and dove through the open doorway with that excited yelp that filled his heart with joy and let him know she was on the scent. He followed her as she weaved and darted through the vehicles, equipment and palettes, heading toward the offices. The warehouse was deserted. But a light still shone from Captain Reardon's office window. He couldn't imagine what she could possibly be thinking to hear Queenie's howls echoing through the warehouses or how it would look if she glanced out her office window to see Chase and Queenie running in circles. But if he found what Queenie smelled and if Captain Reardon could help him clear his name…

Queenie rounded a corner. He followed. Then stopped.

A figure in a dark hoodie, bandanna and baseball cap stood in front of him, a gun raised high in their gloved hands. Chase's hands rose. His feet faltered. But it was too late. The figure fired. A sharp piercing pain caught him in the throat. It was a dart.

"Queenie!" His voice choked. "Run! Hide!"

The last thing he remembered before the tranquilizer swept over his body, engulfing him and pulling him down into unconsciousness, was the sound of his partner's frantic barking.

THIRTEEN

Allie and Freddy knew they were up past their bedtime. Maisy could tell by the little grins they shared back and forth, as they sat on the floor and played with Freddy blocks, figures and vehicles. They had an entire town of characters spread out over the carpet. She didn't know how late Chase would be. He wasn't answering his phone and Zoe had agreed one late night wouldn't hurt the kids too much.

So instead, she sat in an armchair, her feet curled up beside her and a cup of hot cocoa with marshmallows in her hand, and watched them play. Zoe was on the other side of the room, half lying on the couch, reading something on her laptop. A comfortable quiet spread between them, the kind that said conversation was always available but not needed. Maisy deeply appreciated it.

Her phone buzzed. Her heart leaped and she snapped it to her ear, thankful it still worked even though the screen was so cracked she could barely see who was calling. "Hello? Chase?"

"It's Preston," the caller said stiffly. "I was calling to ask if you could meet me at the Winged Java for a late coffee tonight. I have some news I want to share with you in person."

A late-night coffee date with Preston? She was sure that Zoe would be more than happy to watch Allie for a little bit if she asked, and with Linc and Star home too she had no doubt Allie would be safe. But did she really want to meet Preston for a late-night anything? She took a deep breath. "No, Preston. I won't meet up with you outside of work or professional duties. If there's anything you need to tell me, it can wait until morning."

"I'm calling to inform you that a warrant is being issued as we speak for Chase McLear's arrest," he blurted so quickly his voice was almost petulant. "It's the end of the line for him. He's going to be kicked out of the canine program—which is about time, considering some of us have been waiting a whole lot longer than he did to get partnered with a dog. He's going to spend the rest of his life in jail."

"A warrant? For what?" She stood. Zoe's eyes met hers. Maisy mouthed the word *Preston*. Then she stepped across the room to the window. "What are you talking about?"

"New irrefutable evidence has come to light that proves Chase McLear has been helping Boyd Sullivan," Preston said. "Photos turned up on a security camera that showed him talking with Boyd Sullivan and Drew Golosky at a gas station near the ravine. What's worse is his daughter was in the back of his truck, watching the whole thing."

"That can't be possible," she said. Yet, it fit all the facts of the case as she knew it, from why Allie was babbling about a "bad man," to why someone had reported seeing Boyd Sullivan at Chase's home, to why Boyd, or another accomplice, might try to kidnap Allie.

But it didn't match the heart of the man she saw in Chase's eyes.

"Well, it's true," Preston said. He sounded disappointed. Sulky, even. Like a child who was watching his balloon float away or who had dropped his ice-cream cone on the ground. No, more like a preschool child who'd suddenly decided he wanted the toy some other child was playing with to be his. "I thought you'd be happy that I caught Boyd Sullivan's accomplice! I did it! Me! Because I knew he was guilty all along. I knew it when he was chosen to work with that electronic-sniffing dog over me. I knew it when I asked Yvette if you were seeing anyone, weeks ago, and she told me she thought you had a crush on him. You never saw him for what he was. Nobody did anything to stop him. Nobody tried to protect you from him. So I stepped up and made it happen."

"Made it happen?" she said. "How? That's not how this works, Preston. You don't suspect someone's guilty and prove it. You follow the evidence."

"Trust me. The evidence will prove he's guilty!"

Foreboding filled her heart. What had Preston done?

"Bad man!" Allie yelped, pushing away the toy that Freddy was trying to put in his small parade of figures. "Bad man, no!"

What did that mean? Why did it matter so much to Allie that her chin was quivering?

"No!" Freddy said. "He's good man! Like my new daddy, Linc!"

"I'm sorry, Preston," Maisy said. "I don't want to talk to you any further about this. I'll get my updates on the case from Captain Blackwood. I've got to go."

He was still sputtering as she hung up. She dropped down on her knees beside the children on the carpet and gently pulled the toy airman from where it was trapped between Allie's and Freddy's hands.

"Why is this a bad man, Allie?" Maisy asked gently.

Allie's eyes welled with tears.

Help me, Lord. I can't save Chase. I can't find Boyd Sullivan, the lost dogs or stop false charges from being laid. But with Your help, maybe I can break through to this frightened little girl's heart.

"Let's tell a story about the bad man, okay, Allie?" she asked, keeping her voice cheerful and upbeat, in her usual teacher storytelling voice. "We can work together to tell the story about the bad man, okay? It'll be safe, because we'll be in charge of how the story goes, okay?"

Allie paused for a long moment. Maisy's heart ached and prayed. Then Allie nodded. "Bad man hurt man."

Oh, honey, I know that means so very much to you. Help me understand and why it makes you shake and cry.

"Well, then," Maisy said, "we need to find somebody to play the hurt man." She picked another airman from the pile of toys. "How about him? Can he be the hurt man?"

Allie shook her head. "No."

"Okay, how about the pilot?"

"No." Her tiny forehead wrinkled and then she turned and searched through the toys with the kind of meticulous care that took forever. Finally, she pulled out a bearded shepherd that Maisy guessed was from a nativity set.

"This!" she said proudly. "This is hurt man!"

Allie took the "bad man" from Maisy's hand, looked around for a moment and then ran over to Zoe's laptop. She made the tiny figure of the "hurt man" jump up and down in front of Zoe's laptop screen. Then bringing her small hands together quickly, the "bad man" hit the "hurt man" with a force so loudly the sound of plastic against plastic seemed to shake the room. The "hurt man" fell onto the floor.

Zoe's eyes met Maisy's, filled with worry.

"Is this something you saw on the television?" Zoe asked softly.

Allie shook her head. "On Daddy's computer."

"Was your daddy there when you watched it?" Maisy asked.

Allie shook her head. "Hurt man said, 'Hi, I'm Daddy's friend. Who are you?' And I said, 'Allie.' And he said, 'I'm...'"

Her forehead crinkled. Maisy's heart shuddered.

"Was it Drew?" Zoe asked. Allie shook her head. "Was it Boyd?" Allie shook her head again.

Maisy took in a breath and guessed. "Was it Ajay?"

Tears filled Allie's eyes. Maisy clutched her to her chest and held her tightly.

"You did a very good job telling your story, Allie. You're a very brave girl." She looked up and met Zoe's gaze over Allie's head. "Ajay is an Afghan local and Chase's alibi for the morning that Boyd broke onto base. I need to talk to Chase. He's been trying to reach him for weeks. And if Allie's story is true..."

Her voice trailed off. Zoe nodded slowly. She knew without Maisy saying the words. Then Chase's alibi had been dead for months and Allie had witnessed the murder.

"I think it's time to make s'mores," Zoe said brightly. "I think Linc would like to help us make a fire. Would you like that, Allie?"

"S'mores!" Freddy jumped to his feet.

Allie nodded. "I like marshmallows."

"So do I," Zoe said. She set her laptop down and reached for Allie with one hand and Freddy with another. Then she glanced at Maisy. "I'll be in either the kitchen or the backyard if you need me."

Zoe led the two children into the kitchen. Maisy dialed Chase's number. It rang. What did it mean that the man who Chase considered his alibi had been killed? Would it make any difference to the fact that Chase was going to be arrested tonight?

The phone call went through to his voice mail. She tried again and got voice mail a second time. Did that mean he'd already been arrested? Or did he have his phone off while he was meeting with Captain Reardon?

Help me, Lord, what do I do? If Preston's right, Chase is going to be arrested tonight. But if this is one piece of evidence that could help him or save him in any way...

She opened her eyes, grabbed her purse and her keys. The warehouse complex was less than a ten-minute drive away. She could get there, tell Chase and be back before the s'mores were even finished. If all went well, she'd catch him before he was arrested.

"I'll be back soon," she called. "I'm just going to go talk to Chase."

She ran for the door. Nine minutes later, she'd reached the warehouse. The door was open. The warehouse was dark. She pulled her phone out and turned on the flashlight.

"Chase?" She stepped in. Darkness and shadows of vehicles and palettes of equipment loomed around her. Her footsteps echoed in the darkness. "Chase? Are you in here?"

Nothing but silence filled her ears.

Where had he gone? Was she too late?

Then she heard a faint sound of whimpering. She ran toward it. "Queenie!"

The whimpering turned into a howl, then she felt a small furry body launch itself against her. Maisy dropped to her knees, brushed her hand over the small dog's soft fur and felt the gentle tip of Queenie's tongue touch her fingers. "Queenie, where's Chase? Find Chase."

Darkness filled Chase's gaze. He tried to move, but he seemed to be wedged sideways in something very dark with his long limbs cramped around him. He groaned. Cloth filled his mouth. He'd been gagged, his hands were tied behind his back and his legs were bent beneath him at an odd angle. The tranquilizer was wearing off slowly, leaving behind a horrible grogginess that filled his mouth with a vile taste and made his limbs feel like wet cement. He tried to sit up and smacked his head on something metal.

He was in the trunk of a car, a small one by the feel of it. He felt around. No tools. No latch he could easily access, either. But at least the vehicle didn't seem to be moving. Not for now, anyway.

He closed his eyes and prayed. *God, I need Your help.* All this time he'd felt like he was just one step ahead of the people who wanted to lock him away. Now he was well and truly trapped.

The idea of Allie growing up without him hurt so deeply he couldn't breathe. Then Maisy's face filled his mind. Why hadn't he told her how he felt? Even if she'd rejected him, she still deserved to know that in his eyes she was extraordinary and that if he could, he'd spend every last day of this life letting her know how special she was.

Then he heard a stubborn and determined howl and it filled his chest with hope. Queenie had found him.

"This way? Is this where he is? Chase? Chase can you hear me?" Then he heard a voice that made his heart beat even faster. The one voice his poor feeble heart would know anywhere. It was Maisy and she was looking for him.

"Maisy!" he shouted as loudly as he could, forcing his voice through the gag. His strong legs kicked hard against the trunk. *"Maisy! I'm in here!"*

"Chase!" Her fists rapped against the trunk. "Hang on, Chase, I'm coming!" He heard her hands struggle with the latch. Queenie's howls rose. "It's locked. Hang on. I'm going to open it from the front seat."

She disappeared for the longest single moment he'd ever experienced in his life. Then he heard the sound of a window smashing. The latch clicked and the trunk opened. He sat up.

He was in the trunk of a small car in a different part of the same warehouse. He guessed he'd surprised whoever had attacked him and they hadn't had long to plan. The question was where they'd gone now and what they were going to do next.

"I broke the front window," Maisy said. Her face appeared around the corner, dim in the darkness and lit by her cell phone flashlight, and he knew without a doubt that she was the most beautiful person he'd ever seen in his life. "I can't tell you how amazing it is to see you!"

Her hands flew around his neck. Her fingers fumbled to loosen the gag. The fabric fell from his mouth. Her face hovered just inches from his. He leaned forward and kissed her, letting his lips brush against hers for just a moment before her hands slid down to his back and untied his hands.

"Thank you," he breathed.

"No problem," she said. "I wouldn't be much of a preschool teacher if I didn't know how to untie some pretty difficult knots."

He reached for her face. His fingers brushed her cheeks.

"Thank you for coming to find me," he said. "Thank you for believing in me and never giving up on me. I never dreamed I'd have someone as special as you in my life."

Her eyes flickered to his face. Then his lips met hers again, softly and sweetly. He kissed her for one long moment that seemed to contain a lifetime of longing. Then he pulled back, reached down, untied his feet and leaped from the trunk.

"Good dog." He reached down and brushed the top of Queenie's head. Then he grabbed Maisy's hand.

"Come on, we need to find Captain Reardon and get out of here."

Through the maze of equipment and palettes he could see a dim light still shining in her office window. It was unimaginable that she hadn't heard Queenie's howls and realized something was wrong. Had she called the police? Had she hidden? Had his attacker gotten to her too?

"Wait." Her fingers tightened in his. "I have things I have to tell you quickly. First, Preston said charges are going to be brought against you tonight. They claim to have pictures of you, Boyd Sullivan, Drew Golosky and Allie together at a gas station."

"They're fake," he said. "That never happened. I wouldn't do that."

He started to pull his hand from her grasp, but she held on to him tightly.

"I know, Chase," she said. "I believe you. I know the man you are inside. There's more. I got Allie to tell me who the 'bad man' and the 'hurt man' are. The 'hurt man' is your alibi, Ajay. The 'bad man' is someone who killed him while he was on video chat with your daughter."

His heart stopped. Ajay was dead and his own little girl had witnessed his murder? But who had killed him? And why?

"Down on the ground, both of you, or I'll shoot you."

A hooded figure in a baseball cap and bandanna stepped out of the darkness, and Chase heard for the first time the voice of the person who'd been terrorizing him and realized just who the figure behind the mask was.

FOURTEEN

"Captain Reardon," he called. "It's you, isn't it?"

Chase dropped to the ground, holding one hand above his head and keeping the other clasped tight in Maisy's hand. Now that he found her, he never wanted to let her go.

"You were behind this the whole time, weren't you?" he said. "Don't deny it. I know your voice. What's your game here? Are you working with the person who was stealing the weapons? Did you have something to do with Ajay getting murdered? Are you working with Boyd Sullivan?"

"I have nothing to do with Boyd Sullivan!" The captain tossed her head, letting the hood fall back as she pulled the bandanna from her lips. "He was a convenient way to discredit you. People on this base are all too eager to find someone to fear and hate. This is about a small scale black market weapons business that was going just peachy until Ajay Joseph decided to look too hard at the shipping manifests, and Teddy Dennis was stupid enough to kill him when he tried to video call you about it, not realizing your little brat had witnessed it."

He felt Maisy squeeze his hand. He squeezed hers back tightly.

"So you and Captain Dennis concocted a brilliant plan to steal and sell hundreds of thousands of dollars' worth of weapons from the United States Air Force and kill a good man to make that happen, and my toddler managed to ruin your plan."

Oh, his beautiful little girl was so smart and so brave. She'd been trying to tell him all along. But it took Maisy's kind and patient love to bring it out of her.

"What's your plan here, Captain Reardon?" he asked. "You tried to take my daughter, so she couldn't tell anyone what happened. You tried to take my dog, because you knew she'd tracked something. You tried to kill Maisy for protecting my daughter from you. Why take me? To kill me in some way that framed me and ended this?"

"I didn't work this hard, for this long, to skim just the right amount not to get caught, find buyers, move weapons and coordinate all that, only to have your kid, your little dog and a preschool teacher ruin it for me," Captain Reardon snarled.

A wry smile turned on Chase's lips. His kid, his little dog and a preschool teacher. He couldn't think of a team he'd rather be a part of. He eased his fingers from Maisy's, stood up slowly and took a step forward, putting himself between Captain Reardon's gun and Maisy. As far as he knew, his former captain hadn't actually murdered anyone yet. Each time she'd attacked, she'd hesitated or run. He hoped that meant he could keep her from pulling the trigger now.

"Stop! Right now, Chase! Another step and I'll shoot her through the head!"

Well, that settled it. He threw himself at Captain Reardon, catching her by the wrist, clamping his hands over hers before the gun could fire. She fell backward as he broke her grasp on the gun. Then he stood over her, aiming the weapon at her head.

"Get down! Stay down!" Chase shouted. "This ends here!"

"Yeah it does, Chase!" a man's voice echoed. "But not for her!"

Light filled his eyes. He blinked as a man in a Security Forces uniform strode toward him. It was Preston.

"Get down! On the ground! Drop your weapon!" Preston barked. "This time, I've got you dead to rights! You're going to prison for the rest of your life."

Chase tossed the gun so hard it ricocheted somewhere deep inside the warehouse and knelt. He knew how this looked. Preston had been itching for a reason to throw him in jail for days, and now he had him red-handed, with a weapon pointed at a superior officer and no proof of a reason why.

"Preston, wait!" Maisy darted in front of him, stepping between Preston and Chase. "You've got it all wrong, Preston. Listen to me, please. Captain Reardon framed Chase because one of Chase's old colleagues figured out that she and Captain Dennis were working together to steal from weapon shipments. Her accomplice in Afghanistan killed Chase's alibi, Ajay Joseph. Chase's daughter, Allie, witnessed the murder."

But still, one important question remained unanswered. What had Queenie smelled? How had Captain

Reardon possibly gotten her hands on the gold cross and planted it?

"Whatever he says, Lieutenant, don't believe him," Captain Reardon said. She got to her feet. Her eyes scanned in vain for her gun. "Neither of them can prove a word of any of that."

"No," Chase said. "We can't. But I think I know who can." He turned to his little dog, standing obediently for her partner's word, even as he was in danger. "Queenie, search."

She disappeared with a howl, charging through the warehouse with her nose on the scent. Then she barked triumphantly and stood up on her hind legs, with her paws braced against Captain Reardon's office door.

Chase leaped to run after her, but Preston's gun kept him in place.

"She's found something," Chase said. "Let me go see what it is."

"You stay there," Preston said. "I don't care what she's found. If you move, I'll shoot you."

Captain Reardon smirked. Panic beat through Chase's chest. If there was something hiding in Captain Reardon's office and Preston didn't let him search for it, she could destroy it or remove it before anyone could ever find it.

"But you wouldn't shoot me, would you, Preston?" Maisy asked.

Chase wasn't so sure. Was Preston's jealousy so twisted he'd kill Maisy for rejecting him? But Chase could only watch as Maisy broke into a sprint, running through the darkened parking lot toward the small dog.

"Stay out of my office!" Captain Reardon shouted. She ran at Maisy. But it was too late. Maisy yanked the office door open. Queenie darted through, with Maisy on her heels. She slammed the door shut behind her and turned the lock. Captain Reardon pounded her fists on her office door. She glanced at Preston. "Shoot the lock off!"

Preston hesitated. The office blind flew up.

"Chase!" Maisy shouted. Her face appeared at the office window. The glass was so flimsy she barely had to raise her voice to be heard. There was no way it was bulletproof. "Queenie's pawing the carpet!"

"Yank the carpet up and look underneath!" Chase shouted, ignoring the gun barrel aimed at his temple. If Preston flinched, even so much as an inch to turn the gun away from Chase's face and toward Maisy and the office, Chase would be able to use the distraction to catch him by the wrist and force him to the floor.

Maisy disappeared from view.

"There's a floor grate under the carpet!" she shouted. "Hang on."

Her voice disappeared. Captain Reardon's hand paused on the door as a clammy paleness spread over her face.

Then a happy laugh filled the air.

"Chase!" Maisy's face appeared at the window, holding a blue-cased laptop. "Queenie's found a computer!"

"That's mine, isn't it?" Chase asked his former boss. But even if he hadn't recognized the laptop cover, the panicked look on Captain Reardon's ashen face would've confirmed his suspicion. He glanced at Preston, meeting his eyes over the barrel of the gun. "That's the laptop I told you was stolen from my truck. It'll have proof of my conversations with Ajay, the encrypted files he sent of the weapons transfers, his murder, all of it. Even if Captain Reardon was smart enough to try to wipe it, the machine has a secret backup drive."

Maisy disappeared from the window. Preston hesitated. Fear, anger and frustration filled his eyes. Then Chase realized that Captain Reardon had stopped trying to break into her office. Instead, she stood by the office door with her arms crossed and her lips pursed, as frozen as a computer trying to process new information. He knew that look. She was calculating.

A moment later, Maisy was back at the window. "I tried to call Justin, but the office phone's dead. I can't get a signal on my cell phone, either."

Help us, Lord. You're our only hope.

"The laptop doesn't matter," Preston said. "We still have the gold cross. Nothing on that machine will clear you of the fact that Maisy's father's cross was found in your home."

"Because you planted it there, didn't you, Preston?" Maisy shouted. "Don't lie to me. I spend all day settling squabbles between little children. You think I can't tell when someone's guilty of something? You told me yourself, you wanted to solve the crime. So what happened? You found my father's cross at a crime scene and decided that rather than processing it properly you'd hold on to it?"

"Because I wanted to give it back to you myself!" Preston roared.

"Because you wanted to be a hero!" Maisy's voice rose. "When Captain Reardon decided to try to frame Chase as Boyd's accomplice, and Security Forces searched Chase's home, you saw your opportunity to kill two birds with one stone. Captain Reardon stumbled into a desperate crime to protect herself. Little did she know she was only getting away with it because you were too focused on proving that Chase was guilty to actually do your job!"

"Because I knew he was guilty!" Preston snapped. "And if I had to plant evidence to make sure he got what was coming to him and he went to prison, it was worth it."

"Enough of this!" Captain Reardon shouted. Whatever she'd been debating in her mind had apparently been decided. "Shoot out the office window. We can make it look like an accident and because it's a big target, it'll look less suspicious than if we break down my office door. I'll go in and drag her out. You take him and we'll kill them both. I'll have your back. Nobody needs to know about any of this. I'll cut you in and I'll make it worth your while. Your problems will go away and so will mine."

Fear filled Chase's veins as he watched Preston hesitate, and Chase could see without a doubt that he was considering it. Maybe he'd been right that Captain Reardon wasn't prepared to commit murder. But the fact that her accomplice, Captain Dennis, had killed Ajay meant that clearly she wasn't above getting somebody else to do her dirty work.

"Let Maisy go!" Chase stepped forward, his hands raised. "Do whatever you want to me, but don't hurt Maisy. Let her go and be there for my daughter."

"Chase, no!" His name flew from Maisy's lips like a cry.

But he raised a hand and signaled her to hold back and trust him.

"You have to kill them both," Captain Reardon said. "It's the only way. We can leave them in the ravine, with a rose and everything, and make it look like Boyd Sullivan killed them."

"Preston," Chase said firmly. "She's guilty of treason and an accomplice to murder. The only thing you're guilty of is planting evidence."

Preston raised his weapon, steadied it with his second hand, and Chase knew without a doubt in his mind that Preston wouldn't miss the shot.

"Think about it, Preston!" Captain Reardon's voice rose. "You're going to walk out of here one of two ways. Either you're going to be seen as a corrupt cop who planted evidence to frame someone. Or everyone will celebrate you as the man who brought down the Red Rose Killer's accomplice! Maisy is Clint Lockwood's daughter. Boyd Sullivan is probably going to kill her eventually, anyway."

"I'm sorry, Maisy, but she's right," Preston said. "You should've let me save you."

"Maisy!" Chase shouted. "Get back!"

Queenie howled. Chase leaped. The weapon fired. The bullet flew. The office window shattered in a spray of glass fragments. Chase threw Preston to the ground, yanking the weapon from his grasp. Preston reared back. His fists flew toward Chase's face. But it was too late. Chase caught him by the arm and flipped him, pressing him face down into the pavement.

"Maisy!" he shouted. His eyes darted toward the empty and gaping hole where the windowpane had been. *Please, Lord, let her be okay.* Preston squirmed beneath him, fighting his hold. Captain Reardon ran for the office window, braced her hand on the window frame and prepared to leap through, destroy the laptop and Maisy. "No!"

Maisy jumped up, her face flushed, her eyes determined and an office chair clutched in her hands. She swung at the captain. His former boss shouted in pain and crumpled to the floor. Emotions surged through his chest in a wave that seemed to crash over him. Relief. Thankfulness. Admiration.

Love.

Footsteps sounded in the distance, then shouting and the sound of dogs barking.

He looked up as a group of well-armed Security Forces swarmed around them, with Captain Justin Blackwood at the lead.

"Justin!" Maisy unlocked the office door, pushed through and ran toward him, clutching the laptop to her chest, with Queenie at her heels. "Stop! Chase is innocent. Preston planted the gold cross. Captain Reardon called in the fake Boyd Sullivan sighting to cover up a murder overseas. This laptop has the proof of Chase's alibi and how he was murdered."

"I heard," Justin said. His mouth set in a grim line. "We had Preston under surveillance."

What? Chase loosened his grip on Preston, but not enough that the man could actually stand.

"You can let him up," Justin said. "We'll take it from here. We had reason to suspect for some time that he'd tampered with some evidence in order to boost his own ego."

Did that mean Chase had been used as bait, in some trap, to allow them to catch Preston? That when Justin had seen how relentlessly Preston had gone after him, he'd stepped back and let Chase withstand his attacks, in order to reach the truth?

Yet, he knew, as he looked at Justin's face, that he'd never get an answer to that question.

Two officers flanked Captain Reardon, even as she groaned and stumbled to her feet.

Justin looked from Chase to Maisy and back again. "What happened to her?"

"I hit her with a chair," Maisy said.

Justin snorted. His deep laugh seemed to rumble through the warehouse. "Well, this afternoon our tech team traced the IP address of the person who'd sent Canyon's anonymous blogger those pictures and story about you to her office computer. Unfortunately, the blogger themself changed servers before we could track them down."

Chase hoped that meant they were one step closer to figuring out who was running the blog and shutting it down.

Justin straightened his uniform.

"Airman Chase McLear, you're free to go," he added. "I'll also be speaking to the K-9 unit shortly and letting them know my recommendation that you and Queenie be reinstated to the K-9 program immediately."

Gratitude bubbled like a fountain inside Chase's heart. But Maisy's arms crossed against her chest.

"Not so fast, what about the pictures of Chase and Allie with Drew Golosky and Boyd Sullivan?" Maisy demanded. "They must be fakes."

"They're very well-made fakes." Justin's mouth twitched slightly and suddenly Chase had a suspicion that someone within the investigation had created them to tip Preston's hand. "But nevertheless fakes, I assure you."

A thousand questions filled Chase's mind that he suspected he'd never get answers to no matter how many times he asked. Instead, he straightened himself up to his full height and saluted. "Thank you, sir."

Justin returned his salute. "Thank you, Airman."

Chase stood back and called Queenie to his side. He watched as Preston and Captain Reardon were arrested, and an officer took the laptop from Maisy. Then he felt Maisy step to his side and her fingers brush his. He took her hand and held it tightly.

"Come on," he said. "Let's go get Allie."

They walked out, hand in hand, with Queenie. He drove back to Linc and Zoe's house in comfortable silence, with one hand on the steering wheel and the other holding Maisy's fingers gently and never wanting to let her go. They found Allie, curled up at one end of the couch, with Freddy on the other end and Star lying on the floor between them. Maisy walked over and quietly filled Zoe in on what had happened and promised to tell her more in the morning.

Chase reached for his daughter. "Hey, Sweet Pea."

"Hi, Daddy." Allie smiled sleepily, raising her hands toward him as he pulled her into his arms. She laid her head on his chest. He ran his hand over her head.

"We found out who the bad man is and how to stop him," he whispered. "We also found the bad lady who grabbed you and that loud rude man from earlier. Some very good men and women are going stop all of them and make sure they never hurt anyone ever again, thanks to you."

"That's good, Daddy." She yawned. Her eyes closed.

"Is Maisy here? I made us a new house, with blocks, for you, and me, and Queenie…" She yawned again. "And Maisy, all together."

He looked down. There on the floor was a small house made of wooden blocks. Inside, she'd propped up the figures of an airman and a blonde in a sparkling white dress. The two figures were holding hands. A little blonde girl and a tiny dog stood beside them.

He looked up over the top of his daughter's head. Maisy's beautiful eyes met his.

"Come on," he whispered. They walked outside of the house into the warm Texas night. The sky was a wash of deep blue-black above their heads, dotted with the bright light of what felt like a thousand stars. He slid Allie into her car seat. She'd already fallen back asleep by the time he'd buckled her in. He held the door long enough for Queenie to leap into the back seat after her. She lay down, her small snout resting protectively on Allie's arm.

Chase shut the door quietly. Then he turned to Maisy, reached for both of her hands and held them in his. Her eyes sparkled and the light in them was brighter and more beautiful than every star that spread above them in the sky.

"That was a very pretty house Allie built for us," he said softly. "It's a bit too small for us. But I liked her idea of us all being a family together."

She stepped toward him. "I do too."

He took both her hands in his and pulled her in closer to him.

"Captain Reardon was right about one thing. You might be a target of Boyd Sullivan's. I'd feel better knowing I was there keeping you safe. Plus, Allie loves you so much." He took a deep breath and felt the words he'd been dying to say for longer than he could remember. "And I'm in love with you, Maisy. I love your eyes and your smile. I love the way you think and the way you care for others. I love you in a way that I never knew it was possible to love. And I'm hoping very much you'll consider marrying me and becoming my wife, Allie's mother and a member of our family." The smile that lit up her eyes was all the answer he needed. But still, he couldn't wait to hear her say the words. He pulled her closer. "You're something special, Maisy. I'm sorry if this seems sudden, but I feel like I've been waiting to say these words ever since the day we met."

"I feel the same way about you," Maisy said as she ran her hands up around his neck. He slid his arms around her waist. "I love you, Chase, and yes, I would really love to marry you and be Allie's mother."

He lifted her up into his arms and his lips met hers in a kiss for one long and beautiful moment, as a greater happiness than he ever expected to feel filled his heart. Then he set her back down and held her to his chest, as he raised his eyes to the sky and whispered a prayer of thanks, under a canopy of dazzling Texas stars.

* * * * *

Willow Emery approached her brother and sister-in-law's two-story home in Brooklyn, New York, with a deep sense of foreboding. The white paint on the front door of the yellow-brick building was cracked and peeling, the windows covered with grime. She swallowed hard, hating that her three-year-old niece, Lucy, lived in such deplorable conditions.

Steeling her resolve, she straightened her shoulders. This time, she wouldn't be dissuaded so easily. Her older brother, Alex, and his wife, Debra, had to agree that Lucy deserved better.

Squeak. Squeak. The rusty gate moving in the breeze caused a chill to ripple through her. Why was it open? She hurried forward and her stomach knotted when she found the front door hanging ajar. The tiny hairs on the back of her neck lifted in alarm and a shiver ran down her spine.

Something was wrong. Very wrong.

Thunk. The loud sound startled her. Was that a door closing? Or something worse? Her heart pounded in her chest and her mouth went dry. Following her gut instincts, Willow quickly pushed the front door open and crossed the threshold. Bile rose in her throat as she strained to listen. "Alex? Lucy?"

There was no answer, only the echo of soft hiccuping sobs.

"Lucy!" Reaching the living room, she stumbled to an abrupt halt, her feet seemingly glued to the floor. Lucy was kneeling near her mother, crying. Alex and Debra were lying facedown, unmoving and not breathing, blood seeping out from beneath them.

Were those bullet holes between their shoulder blades? *No! Alex!* A wave of nausea had her placing a hand over her stomach.

Remembering the thud gave her pause. She glanced furtively over her shoulder toward the single bedroom on the main floor. The door was closed. What if the gunman was still here? Waiting? Hiding?

Don't miss
Copycat Killer *by Laura Scott,*
available April 2020 wherever
Love Inspired Suspense *books and ebooks are sold.*

LoveInspired.com

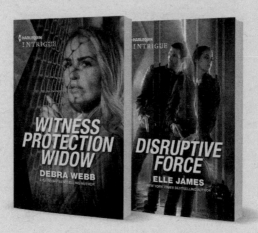